I0764363

LIFEMAGE DAWNING

A BOOK OF UNDERREALM

GARRETT ROBINSON

LIFEMAGE DAWNING

Garrett Robinson

The author greatly appreciates you taking the time to read his work. Please leave a review wherever you bought the book or on Goodreads.com.

Interior Design: Legacy Books, Inc.
Publisher: Legacy Books, Inc.
Editors: Karen Conlin, Cassie Dean
Cover Artist: Sutthiwat Dechakamphu

1. Fantasy - Epic 2. Fantasy - Dark 3. Fantasy - General

First Edition

Published by Legacy Books

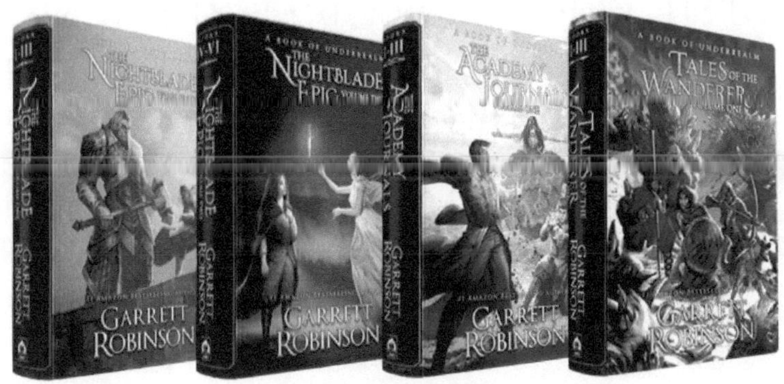

GET MORE

Legacy Books is home to the very best that fantasy has to offer.

Join our email alerts list, and we'll send word whenever we release a new book. You'll receive exclusive updates and see behind the scenes as we create them.

(You'll also learn the secret that makes great fantasy books, *great.*)

Interested? Visit this link:

Underrealm.net/Join

THE BOOKS OF UNDERREALM

THE NIGHTBLADE EPIC
NIGHTBLADE
MYSTIC
DARKFIRE
SHADEBORN
WEREMAGE
YERRIN

THE ACADEMY JOURNALS
THE ALCHEMIST'S TOUCH
THE MINDMAGE'S WRATH
THE FIREMAGE'S VENGEANCE

THE TALES OF THE WANDERER
BLOOD LUST
STONE HEART
HELL SKIN

THE RESURRECTION CYCLE
LIFEMAGE DAWNING

RISE OF THE NECROMANCER
QUEST

THE TENTH KINGDOM
A CLOAK OF RED

THE CHRONICLES OF UNDERREALM
COLLECTION ONE

THE BOOKS OF UNDERREALM

CHRONOLOGICAL ORDER

NIGHTBLADE
MYSTIC
DARKFIRE
SHADEBORN
BLOOD LUST
THE ALCHEMIST'S TOUCH
WEREMAGE
THE MINDMAGE'S WRATH
STONE HEART
THE FIREMAGE'S VENGEANCE
HELL SKIN
YERRIN
LIFEMAGE DAWNING
QUEST
A CLOAK OF RED
THE CHRONICLES OF UNDERREALM

CONTENTS

This book is dedicated to a seventeen-year-old boy who was at his lowest point, and who wrote himself a mad promise on a scrap of paper to get through it.

You lost that paper, but you kept your promise.

THE GREAT BAY
THE HIGH KING'S SEAT
THE BIRCHWOOD
WADELAND
SELVAN
DORSEA
SEMILLA VALLEY
Sidwan
The Fanrong
Berram
Bluewater
Lan Shui
Blackwind
Shades
Northwood
Lukou
GREATROCK MOUNTAINS
Mountain Pass
Westerly Road
Zimio Lake
The Melnar
Giant's Crown
Garsec
Kendal
Malo
Marol
Great Bear Pass
Telupe
Churucon
Lake Triumph
Mula
Valshaw River
Cabrus
Blofel
Lora River
THE KING'S ROAD
Varuna
LADODELL MOUNTAINS
Cordwood
The Clamour Run
Lake Sarsen
Cantal
Vianya Lake
The Langmoat
Leodrid
SHUNAN WOOD
Ur-Gat
Tentown
Yunis Lake
Kusu River
Fushan
Strapa
Wellmont
Redbrook
Dragon's Tail River
Nampo
Tora
Cava
Brillig
THE BREEZEBOUGHS
Baraka
Shinhan Forest
Kentama
Sunsong Plains
Perrin's Stand
The Rustening Verge
Ur-Yama
Renna's Reach
Rochain Lake
The Triwyrm
Deral
THE KING'S ROAD
Thaidion
Gangsu River
THE GLEANWELD
Huzhen
Capaloch
Dracmund
THE KING'S ROAD
Cormon River
Kanlena
Tumala
Leagues
0 5 10 15 20
N
W
E
S

LIFEMAGE DAWNING

A BOOK OF UNDERREALM

GARRETT ROBINSON

"Sky save me. Sky above save me."

"Sky's not going to answer. Here now, eyes on me. I said pressure."

"I don't want to die."

"You won't. You don't get to."

"There's more coming."

"Eyes on me. Pressure, dark take you. I need more bandages."

"No. No, it's all right. There's more coming. You go. No use both of us—"

"One more word like that and I'll gut you myself. Do you hear me? I'll flay you, you steer, you damned coward. You won't get any quiet death, no gentle fading. I'll make it hurt, I'll make you scream, I swear by the sky. You fight. You don't get to give up. You don't get to leave me. Pressure. Now."

"They're almost here."

"They don't get to take you, either."

CHAPTER I
THE LORD'S ATTENDANT

THE ATTENDANT WENT TO SPEAK WITH THE LORD, BUT NO ONE SAW HIM arrive. Without footfall or the scuff of boot on stone, he passed through the halls of the keep. Mayhap a curious ear turned his way or some servant thought they half glimpsed a passing figure. But when they turned, they found nothing.

He passed through the door into the lord's personal chamber and gave a weary sigh.

The windows were fitted with thick shutters of iron, but these were now open, as were the heavy curtains. Thus the sun was free to spill across the lord's desk, illuminating the map upon which he gazed. Through the open window poured a thousand fresh scents of the countryside, turned leaves and mulch on forest floors and ever-chilling breezes carrying the scent of hearthfires far away. The walls of the room were mostly covered up by shelves of books. Mighty tomes bound in leather bore the scuffs and stains of history, but with no speck of dust to be found on their well-used covers. The floor was laid with thick rugs of fine make, which helped to retain the heat of the large hearth on the southern wall. But autumn was not yet well advanced, and the hearth was empty now, for only at night were its light and warmth required. Cold, too, were the candles upon the lord's desk, though the attendant knew they would be lit that evening, there to burn until long after the midnight hour had passed. The lord did not have to sleep if he did not wish to, and he rarely wished to.

The lord glanced up and noticed his attendant at last. His full lips split in a smile that shone through his beard, which was black but greying heavily.

"I am glad you have come," he said. Thick and warm was his voice, full of power but gentle.

The attendant fell to one knee. "Of course, Lord," he said. "I shall always come when you require me. It is only my duty."

"And the fulfillment of one's duty is worthy of the highest praise," said the lord. His children heard this from him often. "You never lack for obedience, though I know the journey taxes you. It is only one of many reasons you deserve great favor."

The attendant bowed his head lower. "I thank you, sire."

"Come." The lord gestured at the map. "Look upon this with me."

The attendant was by the lord's side in the blink of an eye. The map displayed all the nine kingdoms of Underrealm, from Calentin in the northwest corner to Hedgemond in the frigid south. There could be seen across the parchment the remnants of many old markings in charcoal, now wiped away and replaced with others.

The lord's finger fell upon several marks in southern Dorsea. As his sleeve slid back along his forearm, it revealed a tattoo on the back of his hand. The design twisted in and around itself, a never-ending knot. But thorns sprung from it in all directions, as though the weave had been made with brambles.

The attendant's gaze followed the lord's finger. There were many marks there, and they had been recently scratched. In the city of Wellmont was drawn a large cross, with an arrow pointing east along the Dragon's Tail river. Many leagues east of Wellmont was a circle, drawn in the woods near the town of Brillig.

"She is here," said the lord.

For a moment the attendant simply stared at the map, nonplussed. "Forgive me, Lord," he said. "Who is there?"

"The one I have long sought."

It seemed as though the sunlight through the window dimmed for a moment, and a cold wind blew in. The attendant had gone Elf-white.

"That cannot be," he said quietly. "She was lost."

"I have never believed that," said the lord, his tone a gentle chide. "You alone were convinced of it. I knew she would surface."

"How do you know it is her?" said the attendant. "Forgive me, Lord, but even the sight has limits."

"The sight is not the only way secrets reach my ears," said the lord. "Messages come to me by mundane routes from every corner of every kingdom. You know of the Battle of Wellmont."

The attendant snorted. "If you wish to call it such."

"I do," said the lord. He smiled. "That is where she took her first step towards the truth. Just as you helped me to do long ago."

Again the attendant gazed at the map. Now all his focus was bent upon the name of Wellmont. "Then she must be destroyed. If she should come into her power—"

His master raised his hand, and the attendant fell silent as quickly as if he had been slapped.

"Our plans are secure," said the lord. "I am dispatching Enfil to deal with her. But even if he should fail, it changes nothing. Our every stroke in the coming war has been planned for years, while our foes do not even know the war approaches. Yet I would not have you carry on as a mere spoke in my wheel. I wished for you to learn this first among all my children."

Again the attendant fell to one knee. "I am undeserving, Lord."

The lord placed a hand upon his head, but the attendant could not feel it. "On the contrary. No one is more deserving. Now go."

The attendant left. The lord stared after him for a long while. His fingers gave a gentle *tap-tap* on the map, over and over.

Finally he shook himself and took a deep breath. His hands stilled on the desk, and he leaned back into the soft cushions of his chair. Closing his eyes, he stilled his breathing and let calm slide over him like a warm blanket.

When his eyes opened again, they were glowing white.

"Enfil. I have a task for you."

CHAPTER II
DEATH IN DAYLIGHT

In the early morning some days later, Oris sat on a log by her campfire. Her fingers toyed with the crystal amulet around her neck, as they often did when her thoughts were troubled. A few paces from the fire were two tents. One of them was hers, and between them they held three sleeping figures.

The little clearing was tucked deep into the woods close by the town of Brillig. The trees had not yet cast off their greenery, but merely traded it for red and gold. The morning's sunlight fell all in dapples across the ground, and Oris held her hand in the larger patches of it, letting the sun warm her blood. She had thrown just a bit of fresh-hewn pine into the fire, and its scent burned her nostrils in a pleasantly acrid way.

The day was warm enough that the fire was not strictly necessary. But building it had kept Oris busy, and that was much needed. These woods were quiet, but they did not lend her thoughts any peace. Nothing did, these days.

Nothing since Wellmont.

She gave a little growl. Her fingers clutched harder at the crystal amulet. It was plain enough, carved in a shape like a pyramid with small notches at the base. Around the notches had been tied a thin leather thong to hang the amulet on her neck.

And suddenly, as she clutched it ever more tightly, the crystal began to glow.

Oris froze as light swelled in the crystal. It was bright white, with just the faintest hint of blue.

The light flashed still brighter. The crystal grew suddenly as hot as a poker from the hearth. Oris hissed with pain and dropped it before pulling the thong from around her neck. And then, as quickly as it had appeared, the light vanished.

"What in the dark below?" she muttered.

Her gaze darted to the trees at the edge of the clearing. There was no sign of anyone there. Yet now she could sense something. None of the usual sounds of bird or beast came to her. The forest was too quiet.

Her blue vest lay on the ground next to her. She shrugged it over her broad shoulders before belting on her sword. Then she stole on mouse's feet to one of the tents and pulled the flap open.

There lay Flip, on his back beside a nude Cara. Under Flip's golden shirt, his thin chest rose and fell with gentle snores. Cara had curled on her side, her arms wrapped around her tender frame.

Oris leaned farther into the tent and clapped a hand over Flip's mouth.

"Mmmrf!" cried Flip, thrashing under her hand.

"Shut it," said Oris.

Flip recognized her and stilled. Oris lifted her hand.

"What's wrong, dear?" whispered the mage.

"Has your barrier broken?"

Flip frowned at her. Then his eyes drifted west. "It didn't break. But it isn't there anymore. What—"

"Trouble," said Oris. "Dress yourself, and hurry."

She withdrew from the tent and stole to the treeline, keeping watch. No danger presented itself, but the silence in the forest had deepened. Whatever was approaching, it was closer now.

Soon Flip emerged from his tent. He trotted towards her, still buckling his trousers around his waist. Oris waited until he had almost reached her. Then she leaped up, snatched the lowest branch, and hauled herself hand over hand up the tree. With a sigh and a groan, Flip muttered an incantation. Light glowed in his eyes, and wind swept him upwards. He passed Oris almost at once. When she came to a stop next to him, he had already settled into a position of rest, leaning back against the trunk.

"This is a great deal of fuss," said Flip. "What if it is only a bear?"

"A bear did not bring down your spell," said Oris. "The wood is too quiet. And . . ."

She fell silent, and Flip frowned at her. "And what?"

Oris' fingers played with the crystal amulet. It was still cold. "And nothing."

He snorted. "What about the lovers?"

"They'll be fine," said Oris. "No one touches lovers. Constables would drape their guts over six different kingdoms. Do you honestly think I'm a fool?"

Flip closed his eyes. "If I answer, darling, do you promise not to fling me from this tree?"

Oris smiled and shook her head, turning her attention back to the clearing. The tents stood alone, undisturbed. The campfire burned merrily, sending up a steady stream of thin smoke. All seemed peaceful enough.

And then three figures appeared from the trees to the north.

Oris slapped Flip's leg. He opened his eyes, scowling at her. She pointed.

The newcomers wore plain clothing, with flashes of blue and grey. *A uniform?* wondered Oris. Two of them were impressive looking enough, but their leader was a giant. His skin was pale under a tan, and his ear-length hair was shaggy and thick. Several days of unkept beard hung from his chin. Thick bands of muscle wrapped every part of him, so that he looked like he was trying to burst out of his leathers. Oris was uncommonly tall and strong, but she guessed this man was two heads taller than her and mayhap five stone heavier.

"What noble folk are we honored to entertain today, I wonder?" said Oris.

"No doubt the kindred or comrades of someone we've bedded or beheaded," said Flip.

Oris rolled her eyes.

"Don't roll your eyes at me," said Flip, shoving her shoulder. "Do *not* roll your eyes at me when you know I speak only the truth."

"Because something is true does not mean it's pleasant to hear," said Oris. "Often it's the opposite."

"Well, let's not jump to conclusions," said Flip. "We don't *know* they're after us."

All three of them drew weapons and crept quietly forwards. Each of the soldiers wielded a broad blade. Their leader gripped a massive axe.

"All right, so they're after us," said Flip.

The leader took position between both tents to prevent escape. The soldiers readied themselves to dive within.

"Oris," said Flip, "what if they do harm the lovers?"

Oris frowned. "No one's that foolish."

"Yet if they are . . ." said Flip.

"They're not," said Oris. But her grip on the tree branch tightened.

The soldiers dove into the tents and dragged Cara and Ombi into the open air. Both lovers were naked. They screamed in alarm, dragging blankets out after themselves and clutching them to their fronts. But when the soldiers saw who they were holding, they stopped. Both of them looked at their leader in confusion, and he lowered his axe slightly.

"What under the sky is this?" he said. Oris could just hear his growl from so far away.

"I thought we were supposed to find them here," said one of the soldiers, a short, thick man with skin nearly as dark as Cara's.

The commander turned, scanning the treeline. "They have slipped away."

The other soldier was a woman with short, flaming red hair and a nasty scar under her mouth. Now she hauled Ombi up by the wrist, brandishing her sword in his face. "You! Tell us where they've gone."

Oris tensed. But Ombi looked at the woman without a trace of fear. "You threaten two members of the Guild of Lovers. Unhand us at once, or the High King's justice will not be gentle in its punishment."

The soldier holding Cara's arm dropped it as if he had been scalded. But the fiery-haired woman only scowled deeper and pushed her face closer to Ombi's. "We do not serve the High King, and her laws are meaningless to us."

The commander stepped forwards. With one massive fist, he backhanded the red-haired woman. She fell as if struck with a boulder.

"The laws protecting lovers are older than Underrealm itself," he growled, "and they are just. The High King desecrates their history to claim them as her own, but that does not mean *you* are free to cast them aside." He turned to Ombi and bowed his head. "My apologies."

Ombi rubbed his wrist with his other hand and bowed his head in turn. "Your apology is accepted, and with my gratitude."

"Look for a trail," barked the commander. "This fire was recently built. Go."

The red-haired woman climbed to her feet with a sullen scowl, but she did as he had bid. She and the other soldier began to pace the edge of the clearing, searching for tracks.

Oris looked to Flip. "We can get ahead of them."

"Certainly," said Flip, nodding. "Kill the big one first?"

"If anyone's got answers, it's him," said Oris. "Kill the other two, and then find out who sent him."

Light flared in Flip's eyes again. "Fair enough." He tumbled back off the branch, air catching him as he fell. Oris climbed down after him.

Oris and Flip stalked through the forest. Their foes had no gift for stealth, and it was easy to outmaneuver them. They took position on either side of the soldiers' course and drew into the trees.

They came closer. The commander's heavy footfalls were much louder than his companions. Oris and Flip ducked out of sight as they passed, just a pace or two away.

Oris' gaze met Flip's, and they nodded to each other.

Oris darted out from behind her tree to the short man. With one brawny arm she seized his neck and snapped it. Flip lunged, sinking his long knife into the side of the woman's throat and dragging it out the front. She gurgled and thrashed weakly as her blood gushed down her chest.

Both of them fell to the ground as their commander whirled. His grip tightened on his axe, and he growled.

"Good day," said Oris cheerily. "Forgive us for surprising you."

"Though to be fair, you tried to surprise us first," said Flip.

"An excellent point, Flip," said Oris, nodding at him as though she had not thought of that. "In fact, I believe you intended to kill us."

Flip stepped slowly to the right. "Of course, it's not the first time someone's tried that."

"When *was* the first time, Flip?" said Oris. She started to pace around to the left, so that she and Flip moved to opposite sides of the man. He growled and raised his weapon higher as he tracked her motion.

"I think it was Corell, down near the Heddish border," said Flip. "That woman who got possessive of the merchant's son I had charmed away from her. When was that? 1300?"

"Are you drunk already? We hadn't even met then."

Flip snapped his fingers and shook his head. "Of course. Forgive me. 1305, it must've been. That was the Hedgemond tour."

"Ah, of course," said Oris, tilting her head back. "Fond memories. A more innocent time, for both of us. But do you know what, Flip?"

"What's that, dearest?"

"Even that fool knew better than to go after you and me with only two swords beside her."

Though the commander kept his attention on both of them, for the most part his gaze was fixed on Oris. Now he snarled, "Keep prattling if you wish. Your death nears regardless. And when you die, I shall be raised in my father's estimation forever, and secure my place in history."

A shadow passed over Oris' expression. But Flip put his fingers in his mouth and whistled, drawing the man's attention.

"I'm sorry, friend," Flip said easily. "I don't know that you fully understand your predicament. You're only alive because we want to know who sent you after us."

The brute bared his teeth in a savage grin. "Come closer, and I might tell you."

Flip looked past him. "I don't think he wants to play, Oris."

Oris' jaw clenched. "Then he dies."

Flip sighed and rolled his shoulders. "Fine. I need a piss anyway."

A glow sprang into his eyes. The stranger whirled to face him, crouching in a fighting stance. The glow in Flip's eyes swelled, his feet shifting on the forest floor. Under his breath he muttered words in a strange tongue, and flame sprang to life in his palms.

With a sweep of his arms, he sent the fire arcing forth. Its heat scorched the ground. The flames rushed to envelop the stranger—

—and then they split as though they had met an invisible wedge. In a moment they had died away, leaving the brute untouched. His bright teeth showed in a grin.

Oris frowned. "Flip? Don't play with your food."

Flip gave her a quick glance, his brow a confused twist. "I didn't . . . oh, never mind."

He widened his stance once more, and the glow returned to his eyes. This time when he put forth his hands, they crackled with pale blue lightning. It bounced and jittered around his fingers as he bent them, unleashing the lightning towards his foe.

But the bolt stopped just short. In midair it bent, slamming harmlessly into the ground.

Again the brute smiled. And then he advanced.

"Ah . . . Oris?" said Flip, his voice shaking.

Oris sprang towards them, but the brute was closer. He seized Flip's coat and slammed his forehead into the wizard's face. Flip went slack in his grip, stunned. The brute raised his axe to drag the blade across Flip's throat.

Oris reached them just in time. She pulled her dagger from her belt and plunged it into the man's side. He dropped Flip with a roar of pain before whirling on Oris.

Thrice Oris swiped at him, driving him back. The man was larger than she was, but just as fast. She could not land another blow. He had not slowed at all despite the dagger still protruding from his side.

Suddenly he launched a savage swing that nearly took Oris' arm off. With two hands she drove her sword into the axehead, knocking it away. But he came for her again, and now she was the one who had to retreat.

A slash came towards her face. Oris had to throw herself aside to dodge it. She rolled and came up with a fist-sized rock in her hand, hiding it behind her back.

They circled each other. Oris was breathing heavily, but the man did not seem winded at all. Clearly he was more than her match.

So she grinned at him.

"You're more of a challenge than your friends were," she said. "Now, before I finish you off—do you have a name?"

He gave a grunt of laughter. "I am Enfil. From this day forth, it is a name that shall be immortal."

Again a shadow seemed to pass before Oris' eyes. "Friend, I'm afraid you've come for the wrong person. My death shall earn you no glory."

Enfil's lip curled. "Are you lying or ignorant? I suppose it matters little."

Oris raised a finger from her sword hilt. "I'm neither lying nor ignorant. I'm distracting you."

Enfil's brow furrowed. Oris lunged with her sword, and he raised his axe to block it. But then she brought the large stone whipping around and smashed it into his groin.

He crumpled with a strangled cry, just as Flip stabbed him through the spine.

Enfil's back arched, a choked grunt escaping him. His axe fell from his limp fingers as he reached futilely behind him. Flip wore a grim little smile, despite the heavy bruise now darkening most of his face.

"Apologies," he said. "Your conversation had begun to bore me."

Oris drove her sword into Enfil's stomach. For a moment his plate-sized hands scrabbled for her throat. Then he slumped to the ground, eyes lifeless.

"He had some guts in him," said Flip.

"Less of them, now," said Oris, studying the corpse. "What was that business with your magic?" She knelt and drew both her weapons out of Enfil's body, wiping them clean on his jerkin. Fresh blood leaked out of him, soaking into the loamy ground.

Flip's expression dampened. "Tell the truth, I don't know. That's never happened before."

"Now, don't lie," said Oris, sheathing her weapons and walking off towards the tents. "I've heard from many lovers that you have trouble performing."

He punched her in the shoulder, which was a bit like a mouse trying to slap a horse. "Never, not once have you heard such a filthy lie. I pay them too much for them to spread that kind of slander."

Neither of them noticed the body as it began to stir behind them. But suddenly a powerful itch came across Oris' skin. She stopped, hissing through her teeth and scratching at her arms. There was a feeling like a vast hole in her stomach, a pit deeper than she could fathom, an emptiness devoid of either warmth or cold.

"Oris?" said Flip, frowning. "What is it?"

"I don't know," said Oris. "It's like a thousand little bedbug bites, all at once. And . . ."

Behind them, silent and unseen, Enfil rose to his feet.

Oris' amulet burst into a bright glow again. Flip recoiled, staring at it with wide eyes. "What in the dark below is that?"

Oris stared at the amulet. Then, too late, she tried to cry a warning.

Enfil's fist crashed into the back of Flip's head like a boulder. He fell to the ground, senseless.

Oris went for her blade, but Enfil seized her wrist in an iron grip. His other hand gripped her head to slam her face into his own. Stars exploded in her vision as she fell on her back in the dirt.

"You learned no lesson from me," rumbled Enfil. He knelt, straddling Oris, and his hands wrapped around her throat. "You let yourself get distracted. And now it is time for your end."

Oris could scarcely understand what was happening. Enfil's face and body were still covered in sticky red. The cloying scent of gore washed over her, making her gag. But his wounds were gone. There was not even a scratch where she had gutted him.

His knee pinned her right arm. With her left she tried desperately to pull his hands away. But his thumbs were pressing harder, tighter into her windpipe. Oris' vision was fading, and a darkness crept into the edges.

"H . . . how?" she managed to gasp.

Enfil grinned. Blood dripped from his lip to spatter on Oris' cheek. "My father's gifts are mighty. But that no longer matters to you. Sleep. Let life end."

Dark take me if I will, thought Oris.

With shaking fingers she drew her dagger and plunged it into Enfil's gut. The brute growled, but he held on. Oris dragged the dagger out and stuck him again, and then again. But each stab came weaker, each shallower.

I'm not dying here, Oris thought savagely. *I don't know where I'm meant to die, but it won't be some backwater forest no one's ever heard of.*

Yet the darkness grew thicker. Her thoughts swam. And Enfil's grip kept tightening.

Footsteps.

Someone running.

Through the darkness in her vision, Oris saw Enfil glance to his right. Then a heavy boot crashed into his jaw.

The brute fell back. Oris gasped as the darkness retreated from her eyes. She rolled on her side, clutching her throat once more.

Flip? But that had not been his boot. Oris looked up.

Above her stood a woman. She was short and slim, but wiry with muscle. Her plain traveling clothes looked dusty and worn from many leagues. Around her was wrapped a green half-cloak that ended at her rump, its hood thrown back to reveal golden hair, long but braided and done up. At her sides hung two short swords that looked to be of fine craft.

Wordlessly had she come, and wordlessly struck. Still, now, she said nothing as she drew her blades, swinging them in one quick circle. Their fine steel glinted in the shafts of sunlight that filtered through the trees.

Enfil looked up at her with a savage growl. Blood ran from his nose to join the red streaks of his earlier wounds.

"Who in the dark below are you?"

The woman did not answer. She stalked towards him, blades held ready.

Enfil glanced over. His axe lay a few paces away. Now he dove for it, throwing himself across the ground on hands and knees.

The woman darted for him. As he stretched for the axe, her blade came down and cut off his hand.

Enfil screamed, falling on his back and clutching the stump of his wrist. Before he could recover, the woman kicked him hard in the side of the head. Enfil rolled facedown, still clutching his arm.

The woman flipped her swords around to hold them reversed. With a savage thrust, she drove them into Enfil's back. The blades pierced through his shoulders into the ground, pinning him.

As Enfil screamed, his voice now muffled by the dirt, the woman knelt and seized his hair. Pulling it up, she revealed a tattoo on the back of his neck. Oris had never seen the design before. It was like a weaving, never-ending knot woven of thorny brambles.

The woman drew a dagger and began to cut the tattoo out of his skin.

If Enfil had cried out before, now he screamed loud enough to tear his throat. But try as he might, he could not rise, not with the blades pinning his arms to the ground and the woman kneeling between his shoulders.

In a moment, the grisly work was done. The woman tossed the tattoo aside. Then she stood and drew her blades from Enfil's back. His screams subsided, to be replaced by agonized whimpers.

"Father." It came out as a piteous moan.

The woman brought one sword back around and cut off his head.

The woods fell to utter silence. It lasted for several long moments. Oris stared at Enfil's body, half expecting him to move again, to rise and take his revenge on the woman.

But nothing happened.

Slowly, Oris levered herself up, rising to her feet.

"Have you any wine to drink?" said the strange woman, turning to her. "I do not often partake, but after a killing . . ."

"I—what?" said Oris. "Who under the sky are you?"

The woman pursed her lips. "Not very grateful. I just saved your lives. If you have no wine, I shall at least need a ready tent. But you should rouse your friend."

Oris had almost forgotten that Flip still lay unconscious on the ground. She went to him and rolled him over, slapping his cheeks gently until his eyes fluttered open.

"Whuzzat?" he grumbled, blinking up at her. "Oh. You're alive. We won, then?"

"After a fashion," said Oris. "Come. We have a new friend."

"I like new friends." Flip lifted a hand and then groaned as Oris pulled him to his feet. As he steadied himself, he looked the woman over unashamedly, brows slowly rising. "Hello, friend. Have you a name?"

"You can call me Silvin," said the woman.

"Silvin," said Flip. "Like the daughter of Renna the Sunmane."

Silvin inclined her head. "Just so."

"A princely name for a princely woman."

"Calm yourself," Oris told him.

Silvin smiled. Oris decided her brilliant hazel eyes were far too distracting when she did that. "Your tents are this way, I believe." So saying, she sheathed her swords, scooped up the flap of skin with the tattoo, and marched off towards the camp.

Oris and Flip looked at each other.

"Do you . . . ?" said Oris, waving a hand in the direction Silvin had gone.

"Never seen her before," said Flip. "At least not that I recall. But I sometimes get *quite* drunk behind the blue door."

"She isn't a lover, Flip," said Oris, rolling her eyes. "Come on. Let's get after her. It's past time we checked on Ombi and Cara, besides."

Ombi and Cara had dressed themselves, but only partially, and they were enjoying the fire. They glanced up curiously as Silvin entered the clearing. Ombi smiled.

"Good day," he said to her. "You seem friendlier than the last uninvited guests who came here."

Silvin smiled. "I can be very friendly. I am Silvin. You are lovers in the employ of these two, are you not?" She pointed back to Oris and Flip, who had just reached the clearing.

Cara glanced at Ombi. "We are."

"And what are they paying you?"

Again the lovers looked at each other. "Three silver a night," said Ombi.

"I thought the going rate was twice that," said Silvin.

"They are protecting us in these wilds," said Cara. "Their payment is the difference."

"I wish to end your service," said Silvin.

"I beg your pardon?" said Flip, his casual smirk vanishing in an instant.

Silvin ignored him. From a pouch at her belt she drew six gold weights. These she tossed to Ombi and Cara, three each, and they caught the coins deftly.

"I think you will agree three weights a night is more than generous," said Silvin. "You shall have to pay them their three silvers' difference for safe transport, but you still come out quite well."

"Indeed," said Cara, nonplussed. "But we are in no need of charity. We are happy with our service and have no wish to cease it."

"Oh," said Silvin, placing a hand to her chest. "Forgive me for not being clear. I am not paying you to stop entertaining them. I am paying you to start entertaining me instead."

The lovers' eyes widened. Flip and Oris had gone stock still.

"You can't do that!" cried Oris.

Silvin smirked at her. "Oh, come now. You must know the guild rules as well as I do, or better."

Flip's face had taken on a pained sort of twist. "She, er . . . she can, in fact, do as she says. But only if the lovers agree." He turned pleading eyes to Cara and Ombi. "Have we not been good to you, my loves? And generous?"

Cara raised the coins. "Not this generous."

"If the arrangement is satisfactory, then let us retire," said Silvin. "Comfort is especially sweet after a fight. We can use that tent."

"That's *my* tent!" said Oris.

"Oh, I am merely borrowing it," said Silvin. "My thanks." She looked so innocently grateful that Oris' next angry outburst died on her lips.

Silvin strode to the tent and threw back the flap. Ombi and Cara hurried inside. Silvin paused, giving Flip and Oris a final smile and a wave. Then she clambered in after the lovers.

Oris and Flip stood there for a long moment, rooted to the spot and looking at the tent.

"Who in the *dark* below is this sow?" cried Oris.

"Language!" came Silvin's voice, slightly muffled by the tent. The lovers giggled.

Flip shook his head ruefully. "Come, love. Let's get those bodies in the river before they start to stink."

• ○ • ○ •

As Enfil's life fled him, far away, in a forgotten castle, the glow of magic left the lord's eyes.

His fingers splayed across the desk, and he leaned back in his chair.

"Oh, Enfil," he said softly. "My poor child."

For a moment he allowed himself to bow his head and weep. But soon he forced himself to focus.

He had found her at last. But she did not show any sign of her power. And she had not recognized anything Enfil had said to her.

The lord had guessed correctly, then. She did not know the truth about herself.

That meant she was doomed.

It would have been preferable for Enfil to succeed, of course. His loss was a grievous blow, for the lord loved all his children. But destiny was more important than any one person. It was greater than any of the lord's adherents, greater even than the lord himself.

This was not a threat. It would only require a slightly different set of steps, now.

With a weary sigh, the lord bent over the map, trying to guess where she was heading. But hardly a moment had passed before there was a loud pounding at his door. The lord looked up, frowning.

"Come."

The door swung open, shuddering as it struck the wall behind. In strode a man—young, but massive, taller and wider in shoulder even than Enfil had been. His face would have been beautiful were it not so often twisted in a scowl, as it was now.

"Barrick," said the lord in mild surprise. "You are supposed to be on your way to the border of Wadeland."

Barrick's shoulders tensed. "Waiting in a cold stronghold, for who knows how long? I am not meant for such things, Father. When I learned you had found her, I had to come and see you at once." He fell to one knee, bowing his head. "Please, Father. You must recall Enfil and let me hunt her down for you."

His lord sighed, and his voice was heavy with grief. "It is too late for that, my child."

Barrick looked up, his eyes shooting wide. "Do you mean . . . is she dead?"

"No," said the lord quietly. "The mission claimed Enfil's life. An unforeseen player joined the game. She knew Enfil's gift and how to defeat him. She is one of *theirs.*" He practically spat the word.

Barrick rose, clenching his fists. "Then let me avenge him, and secure your victory at the same time. Send me, Father. None can stand against me in the training yard, not even Rogan."

The Lord's expression turned dour. "You received my gift not only because of your prowess, but also because of your loyalty to the cause. That loyalty must rule your strength. Power is one thing, but focus and cunning are needed now."

Barrick fumed for a moment, and it seemed he would argue. But at last he bowed his head. "Of course, Father," he grated. "I only ask you this: that if the chance should come for me to prove myself to you, you will grant me the opportunity."

"You have nothing to prove to me, my son," said the lord. Barrick started to speak, but the lord raised a hand to stop him. "But I will remember what you have said. If the time should come to send you on that hunt, I will. Leave me now."

At last Barrick gave a satisfied smile, and he left.

CHAPTER III
A BATH AND A BOND

Enfil's body threw up a tremendous splash of water as Oris and Flip heaved it into the river. The current dragged him downstream, floating with his back up. Oris lobbed the head after the body. They had already thrown the brute's lackeys in, and their bodies were now out of sight, carried off by the water.

Flip had taken something from Enfil's belt before they flung him in. Now he picked it up from the riverbank and turned it over in his hands, examining it. It was a long dagger, and as Flip pulled it from its sheath, Oris could see a rune carved in its blade.

"What's that?" she said.

"Something interesting," muttered Flip. "See here? This rune is one of cancellation."

"Ah," said Oris, arching a brow. "Of course."

Flip rolled his eyes and sighed. "It means it can stop spells. Some of them, anyway."

"Really?" said Oris. "So that's how he avoided your magic?"

"No, it . . . he . . ." Flip's mouth twisted in frustration, and his eyes flicked back and forth. He often struggled to explain magic to Oris. Its concepts were taught only at the Academy for Wizards, where he had trained, and Oris had picked up very little of such learning over the years they had traveled together.

"It only works on some spells," said Flip. "And it's cancellation, not nullification. Nullification is stopping a spell as it's being cast. It's immensely difficult to perform, and even harder to work into a rune. I don't even know if you could. A dagger that could do that . . . it would be priceless. It certainly wouldn't hang from the belt of a brute in this backwater wood."

"All right," said Oris slowly. "So this one . . ."

"Cancels," said Flip. "It stops a lingering spell that's been cast to stay put."

Oris understood at last. "Like your walls of air."

"You have it," said Flip. "It broke my wall without alerting me. A neat trick. I think I'll keep this." He flipped the dagger over the back of his fingers before sliding it into its sheath and looping it onto his belt.

Blood from all three corpses had gotten on Oris' hands and arms. Flip had cast off his coat to avoid staining it the same way. Now they went a little upriver where the water was calmer and, stripping down, they climbed in to bathe. Often, Oris' gaze turned southwest towards the camp.

"Staring won't make them hurry any, love," said Flip.

"What will?" growled Oris. "We need to be getting on our way."

"I do not think we should hurry her at all," said Flip. "After what she did to that brute . . . well, I, for one, have no wish to disturb her."

Oris sniffed, picking at some gore that had gotten under her fingernails. It had likely come while stabbing Enfil over and over again. The memory made her throat ache. She could feel his fingers there.

"What do you suppose this is all about?" Flip went on. His tone was light and airy, but Oris could hear the worry that underlaid it. "I don't just mean folk trying to kill us. That's not unheard of. But the way Enfil found us all the way out here in the wilds, and then Silvin almost at the same time. That's strange, isn't it?"

"It's a good question for her," said Oris. "Hence my eagerness for her to emerge."

Flip's mouth worked for a moment. "It's got something to do with Wellmont though, doesn't it?" His hand rose to rub at his bare chest. Oris' eyes went there, but then they sharply jerked away.

"No," she said. "It doesn't. It can't." Her voice held more denial than conviction, but that was all she could summon.

"Enfil said—"

"I'm clean enough," said Oris. She climbed out and threw on her clothes. Just before heading back to the camp, she met Flip's gaze. "Shed your worries. No one knows what happened at Wellmont."

She turned and walked off. Flip watched her go.

"Least of all us," he said sadly.

Oris rebuilt the campfire and sat by it. When Flip returned, he did not mention Wellmont again. They ate some food silently, both pretending they could not hear the muffled noises coming from Oris' tent, where Silvin and the lovers had retreated.

The more time that wore on, the more anxious Oris became. Who knew but that someone else like Enfil was coming? She might not be so lucky twice, to notice something was amiss before they arrived.

The thought gave her pause. In fact, she had not become aware of Enfil without help. She lifted up the amulet and looked through it, letting its shape distort her view of the surrounding woods. It had been inert since Enfil's rise, and no trace of a glow shined from it now. Yet it seemed suddenly a foreign thing. She could not look upon it the same way she always had.

Flip noticed her studying the crystal. His eyes lit with interest, and he scooted closer. "I'd almost forgotten. What was that business with the amulet earlier?"

"I don't know," said Oris. "But it happened twice. The first was just before Enfil arrived. It was what made me realize the woods had grown too quiet."

"Has it ever done that before?"

"Never."

"Might I take a look at it?" Flip extended a hand.

She hesitated. But it was Flip. So she lifted the leather thong from around her neck and pressed the crystal into his palm. He turned it over in his hands, inspecting it closely.

"There are no runes," he muttered.

"Why should there be runes?"

"I thought it might be enchanted. Like the dagger. Nothing holds magic better than crystal. But enchantment requires runes, so far as I know. Where did you get it, anyway?"

Oris felt a tightening in her chest. Before answering, she held out her hand and waited for Flip to return it to her. He did so at once, and she put it around her neck again.

"I barely remember," said Oris. "I've had it since I was a child. It was the only thing I had for my own."

"From your parents?"

Oris' jaw clenched. "I wouldn't know."

Flip nodded kindly and turned his gaze from her. She was grateful he did not press the matter. Flip knew more than anyone about her childhood, but he never asked for more than she gave him.

Before they could speak further, Silvin emerged from the tent at last. She squinted up at the sun as she shrugged into her green cloak. She had not laced up the front of her jerkin, and Oris' jaw clenched.

"Good of you to join us," said Oris. "Are you sure you've rested enough? By my reckoning, you've been in there for at least three hours."

"I know," said Silvin, who seemed not to notice Oris' needling tone. "I even slept for one of them."

"We heard," said Flip, grinning.

"I'll have a few answers from you now," said Oris.

"Will you?" said Silvin. "Very well. But I will have a bath, because if I do not, I might have to find something else to kill. The Dragon's Tail is off that way, is it not?" Without waiting for an answer, she set off to the northeast.

Oris blew a heavy, irritated breath through her nose. Flip's smile had only widened.

"Go on, then, dear, and question her," he said. "I'll stay with the lovers, just in case."

"Fine," said Oris. "But we need to leave. Would you pack my things?"

Flip glared at her. "I'm no manservant."

Oris had to smirk. "Come now. You never complain when Cara and Ombi order you around."

As if on cue, the lovers came out of the tent. Ombi came first, and then he turned to help pull Cara out. The girl was still a bit flustered, her dark cheeks darker still with a flush, and she leaned on Ombi's arm as she came to join him by the fire.

"Sky above," she said, sitting.

"And dark below," said Ombi with a grin. "That went longer than I expected."

"I as well," said Cara, giggling.

Flip folded his arms. "And do the two of you feel any shame whatsoever for abandoning the two of us so easily?"

Ombi's smile only widened. "None at all. Come, sit with us, grumpy one. I shall rub your shoulders, if that will ease your grousing."

"I can't," said Flip, giving Oris a glower. "Apparently I have to pack the tents."

Cara sighed. "Then we will help you, of course. Though in truth I only want to sleep the rest of the day away."

The two of them rose to help Flip pack, while Oris set off after Silvin.

When Oris reached the water, Silvin was already in it. Here the river dwindled, for it cut a deep trench into a rise in the land. The river's flow brought fresh, crisp air, and lilies collected in little pools on either shore to sweeten it. The banks were thick, packed dirt, with many rocks to hold their shape, providing an easy climb in and out. Many of the rocks had fallen into the river over time, so that it was all solid footing from one side to the other, and perfect for bathing. It was why Oris and Flip had chosen the spot earlier, and why Silvin had chosen it as well.

Silvin's wiry frame was even more impressive now, bare as it was, and Oris was struck still for a moment. There were some scars on her, but far fewer than Oris thought there might have been—certainly fewer than Oris herself bore. Now that her hair was undone and flowing freely, Oris could see that it was much longer than it had appeared. Though her face was hard, with an uncompromising look, it was also beautiful, and her hazel eyes were piercing and intense as a falcon's.

Those eyes suddenly focused on Oris. Silvin paused in her scrubbing for a moment. Oris realized she had been staring and cleared her throat, folding her arms and leaning against a tree. But she did not avert her gaze. Silvin did not seem embarrassed, and so there seemed little reason not to enjoy herself.

"You look cold," said Oris.

Silvin laughed. It had a strange sound to it, rough, as though she was unused to such a mood. "Did you come to talk, or to stare?"

Oris chose to ignore that. "Who are you?"

"You have my name."

"You seem a bright woman," said Oris. "You know I want more than that. Why are you here?"

Silvin pointed to the shore. Oris looked down and saw that a coin purse sat at her feet. "My master sent me to hire the two of you into his service," said Silvin. She leaned back to float face up.

Oris stooped to lift the purse. She undid the string holding it shut and looked inside. Her brows rose appreciatively, but then she looked back to Silvin.

"It's not good enough," she said.

Silvin's head came up, and she frowned. "You have not even heard the job."

"I mean your explanation. We don't know you. So how do you know us? How did you know about Enfil's tattoo? What was he, anyway?"

Silvin sighed and stood. She climbed out of the river and picked up her cloak, using it to dry off before she donned her trousers and then her jerkin. "I suppose that is safe to answer," she said, seemingly half to herself. "They are called shadeborn. Nasty brutes. Immune to magic, as you saw, and impossible to kill while that tattoo remains on them."

A pit had formed in Oris' stomach. It reminded her of the feeling she had had when Enfil rose from the dead. A voice in her mind whispered in warning, but she did not quite know the shape of the danger.

"There are more like him?"

"Many, I believe," said Silvin. Her playfulness had fallen away, and she looked deadly solemn as her fingers fiddled with the laces of her jerkin. "But I can explain little else. I was sent to retrieve, not to educate. My master will teach you more. But you should know this, Oreceot: worse folk than Enfil will come after you, and you will not know how to defeat them."

Oris' eyes widened. "Where did you learn that name?"

Silvin arched a brow. "*That* name? You mean your name?"

"I'm called Oris. Barely a handful of people know it's short for anything at all."

"A matron of lovers in Wellmont," said Silvin with a shrug. "Her name was Kenlin. Forgive her. She did not know you held it as a great secret, and so she saw no harm in telling me. It would seem you have loose lips when you are behind the blue door." She grinned. "But then, there is no better place to have them."

Oris ground her teeth, determined to ignore that last comment. "You've been following us since Wellmont?" she said. "Why? What do you want with us?"

"I told you," said Silvin. "To hire you. It is a nobler intention than Enfil had, I think you will agree."

"And who were they?" said Oris. "What do they want with us?" Her tone was defiant, but a yearning lay beneath it, a desire for something she could not name.

Silvin's fingers stilled on her jerkin strings, and she looked up at Oris in surprise. "Not 'us.' Just you. Did you not realize that?"

Oris closed her eyes and forced herself to take a long, slow breath. "I'll tell you the same thing I told Enfil. You've made a mistake. I'm no one special."

"Yes, you are, Oreceot" said Silvin. "Fate chose you long ago, though my master and other interested parties have only just learned of it. You should be grateful. It means you are capable of doing more good than most could do in their lives."

"But I don't want any part of that!" insisted Oris. "I'm perfectly happy with my life just the way it is, thank you."

"Are you really?" said Silvin, frowning.

"I am," said Oris obstinately.

Silvin slowly shook her head as she finished the knot in her jerkin string and climbed the bank. Just before the top, her foot slipped on a dislodging stone. Her hand swung up, and Oris caught it without thinking to pull her up. Silvin used the movement to draw closer, her face barely a handsbreadth from Oris'. Their eyes met, and Silvin let the silence stretch for the space of a few breaths. Oris was reminded of Enfil's face close to hers. But now the smell that flooded her nostrils was sweet, all faded wool and soft skin and wet hair.

"I am afraid the choice is out of your hands." Silvin's voice was barely above a murmur. "You were chosen, and many folk now know it. Some of them wish to kill you. Some will want to use you for their own ends. And some want to help you achieve your destiny. My master is one of the latter. If nothing else, you should at least be grateful that I am the one who found you first. Or second, I should say, but Enfil no longer counts."

The pit in Oris' stomach swelled. "Why?" she said again, and now she was pleading. "Why me?"

Silvin cocked her head. "What happened at Wellmont, Oreceot?" she asked quietly.

Oris swallowed hard. "Nothing. And stop calling me that. It's Oris."

Silvin gave a disappointed smile and marched off back towards the camp. For a little while, Oris could only stand there staring after her. At last, when Silvin was out of sight, Oris mustered herself to follow.

Flip had almost finished packing up by the time they reached the camp. The tents were laid out flat on the ground. Flip's eyes glowed and he twisted his hands. Gusts of wind caught the edges of the tents and rolled them up. The glow died, and Flip smiled with satisfaction as the lovers scooped them up and wedged them into their packs. Then he noticed Oris.

"You're back, dear," he said. "And just in time to avoid helping with the work. How very like you."

"We are ready to go, then?" said Silvin.

Flip arched a brow. "I'm afraid I don't understand. *We* are ready to go. I don't know how that concerns you."

Oris' mouth twisted, but she raised the coinpurse Silvin had given her. "She means to hire us."

Flip's brow furrowed. "Does she now." It did not quite sound like a question.

Silvin smiled. "Do not worry yourself," she said. "I am offering quite a lot of coin."

Flip looked to Oris for confirmation. Oris tossed him the purse, and when he looked inside, his eyes widened. "Well, that's . . . a gracious first gesture, to be sure. And what's the job?"

"The first task," said Silvin, "is to come with me to Redbrook and meet my master so that he can tell you the real task—which will come with its own payment."

Flip's frown returned. "All of this—" he hoisted the purse "—just to hear what he has to say?"

"He is a man of means," said Silvin, shrugging.

"I hope you're aware," said Flip, "that in our line of work we deal with all manner of characters. Some are a pleasure to work with. Some are less than savory. And one of the things we've learned is that an overabundance of generosity isn't a desirable trait in a business partner."

Silvin looked incredulous, and her gaze went back and forth from Flip to Oris. "I may not understand. Do you want me to reduce the payment?"

In an instant, Flip had pocketed the purse. "Don't be ridiculous," he said.

"What he's saying," put in Oris, "is that someone may well offer a great purse for a small task because they plan to reclaim it later. Say, from our corpses."

Silvin smiled. "Ah. I understand such caution," she said. "But I assure you, that is not my intention, nor is it my master's."

"I am, of course, glad to hear it," said Flip, still with his easygoing smile. "But just in case you're lying to us—and of course you're not, but just in case—please remember that the only reason you can hire us at all is that anyone who's ever crossed us ended up on a pyre. I don't know if you've heard of past times we were betrayed, but trust me: it was not quick, it was not quiet, and it was not soon forgotten about."

The clearing fell silent. The lovers looked rather anxiously back and forth between Flip and Silvin. But Silvin merely appraised Flip with narrow eyes, a thin smile at her lips.

"You are more than you look," she said at last. "I respect your caution, and I shall certainly remember your words."

Flip clapped his hands, and the tension in the air evaporated. "Excellent! In that case: through fire and flame, through fight and flight, our service, both in sword and in skill, are yours." He went to her and held out a hand. Silvin took his wrist and shook firmly. Flip turned from her and went to Oris, smiling. "Cheer up, you great oaf," he told her. "Work, money, and another day to live! What more could we want?"

"Many things," said Oris, still studying Silvin. "But I'll hold my peace about them, for now."

Quickly they all gathered their things. The lovers had their own packs, but because they were so much lighter than Flip's and Oris', they helped collect up anything that had not yet been stowed.

"Thank you, dear one," said Flip, as Cara tied his sack of travel dishes to his rucksack. "You do much to ease the sting of your abandoning me."

Cara and Ombi both laughed at that, and Ombi gave Flip a kiss on the cheek. "I shall never grow tired of the way you two speak. Heddish tongues are so odd."

Silvin's brows rose. "Heddish?"

Oris' cheeks flushed. But Flip gave Silvin a crafty look.

"Yes, Heddish," he said. "Can't you hear it?"

"I hear a Heddish accent," said Silvin. "But I did not think there were many Draydens living in Hedgemond."

The clearing went silent. Cara and Ombi were looking carefully back and forth between Flip and Silvin.

"How did you know he was a Drayden?" said Oris.

Silvin's eyes widened. "I . . . forgive me. I thought the lovers would have known."

"We did," said Cara simply.

Now Flip looked doubly shocked. "You did?"

"We did," said Cara. "Us, and every lover behind the blue door back in Wellmont. Forgive me, but to us, it barely seems you are trying to hide it. Your features, your manner . . . the way you spend coin, the way you talk under the accent. Any lover with some experience can read it in you."

Flip looked to Oris. "Am I that obvious?"

Oris shrugged. "How would I know? You're the only Drayden I've ever met."

Ombi stepped closer then, and he put a hand on Flip's arm. "We have known, and we have not minded," he said gently. "We came with you on this journey knowing it already. And no lover would ever spread the secret. The guild has rules."

"Besides, we all have yesteryears we would rather not talk about," said Cara. "My own cousin is a Yerrin."

Flip did not answer at once, but a weak smile of relief crept into his face. He gave Cara a nod.

"Thank you for your understanding," said Oris. She bowed.

"And for my part, I deeply regret having brought up a sensitive topic," said Silvin. "That is not how I would have wished to begin our relationship."

"One shouldn't complain of a rough road when its end is so welcoming," said Flip. "Only I'd beg you to be more careful with that knowledge in future. I was afraid Cara and Ombi would turn and march straight into the woods."

Cara and Ombi both laughed at that, and Ombi gave Flip a kiss on the cheek. "How could we dream of abandoning such interesting clients?" he said.

"Well, if that is sorted," said Silvin. "Shall we be off to Redbrook?"

Flip hesitated. "Ah, right. There's a wrinkle there. We're making for Kanlena by way of Dracmund."

Silvin frowned. "That is the opposite direction from where I wished to go."

"We know it," said Oris. "But we are contracted to take the lovers there safely."

"Contracted," said Silvin. "That *is* a wrinkle. The guild would have your heads, and other parts besides, if you broke faith."

"Well do we know it," said Flip, adjusting his stance.

Silvin's eyes lit, and she snapped her fingers. "Here, then. There is a house of lovers in Dracmund, and it is on the way. We can transfer the contract there. Then I can send word to my master, and we shall lie low while he comes to meet us. Provided everyone is in agreement?"

"That's up to the lovers," said Oris, looking at Cara and Ombi. "What say you? It's not so far from Dracmund to Kanlena."

Cara leaned close to Ombi, and they exchanged some whispered words. When they looked back to Oris, they nodded, but pouts twisted their lips.

"I suppose it will do," said Cara. "Though we shall mourn that our time with you was cut short."

Oris smiled. They were lovers' words, but she enjoyed them nonetheless. "And we have enjoyed every minute in your company. Our parting shall be bitter indeed."

"But that will only make future joinings the sweeter," said Ombi, smiling coyly at her.

Flip laughed, but then he turned to Silvin. "Smoothing that wrinkle, however, raises another. It costs money to transfer contracts."

Silvin waved a hand. "That is of no issue. The cost shall be covered."

"Shall it?" said Flip, raising his brows. "You're most generous with your coin. Who'd you say your master was?"

Silvin smiled sweetly at him. "I did not say. And the answer is to remain private for now. But he shall certainly introduce himself once we are all gathered together."

"And how long shall it take him to reach us?" said Oris.

"I am not certain," said Silvin. "It may take weeks. Mayhap as much as a month. I do not know precisely where he is at the moment. But once he finds out where you are, he shall make all possible haste there."

Ombi and Cara looked at Oris as though they were seeing her for the first time. "How impressive," said Cara. "You are favored by a wealthy patron, and one of great import, or so it seems."

"I'd give much to be free of such favor," said Oris through gritted teeth. "Let's be off, that I might rid myself of it more quickly." And so saying, she led them all marching east.

CHAPTER IV
LOVERS' QUARREL

WITH ORIS' GUIDANCE, THE PARTY MADE GOOD TIME THAT DAY. SHE was gratified to see that Silvin could keep a swift pace without a word of complaint. Ombi and Cara were no slouches on the march, either. In fact, Flip set the speed of the party, for he begged a rest often, and when he walked he always trailed at the end of the group, so that sometimes they had to slow to accommodate him.

When they stopped for the midday meal, the lovers sat with Silvin. Flip eyed the three of them. Oris could tell when he was brewing a scheme, and she only hoped he would not do anything too foolish. After they finished eating, Oris helped the lovers stand. She sent them walking with Flip while she stayed behind to hide the signs of their meal. But Silvin remained sitting, looking up at her expectantly.

"Would you get up, please?" said Oris in an even tone. "I'm trying to conceal our presence, now that we know folk are hunting us."

Silvin smirked. Rather than answer, she looked past Oris at Flip's retreating back. "I see why you two are friends. Never lovers, were you?"

"With Flip?" said Oris, aghast. "Not on your life. I know better than to entangle either my heart or my loins with someone as shrewd as he."

"I am glad to hear it," said Silvin, her smirk growing to a smile. "Well?"

Oris blinked. "Well what?"

Silvin raised her arms. "You helped the lovers up. I was waiting for the same."

Oris scowled. But then she stepped forwards and took Silvin's hand. She ignored the calluses on Silvin's palms, no doubt left there by her swords. She ignored the softer skin of Silvin's wrists, smooth and supple. She ignored the iron grip Silvin took on her wrist, the taughtening of the muscle beneath the flesh, and the little sigh as Silvin pulled up while Oris pulled down. Oris took notice of none of it, very deliberately.

"Thank you," said Silvin. Her smile was too knowing. "I had no idea you would be so strong, when I was sent to find you."

Oris ignored that too, and turned to set off after Flip and the lovers. Her cheeks were aflame.

Less than an hour before the sunlight vanished, Oris called a halt. They quickly built their tents. Oris built Flip's for him in repayment of his packing that morning, while Flip went off to set his magical barriers that would warn of anyone approaching. His fingers wove through the air as his eyes glowed. The air seemed to grow more solid, twisting around itself like the weave of a basket, before returning to normal. But Oris knew there was still something there: an invisible barrier that could be passed through easily, but not without setting off a warning in Flip's mind that would even wake him from sleep.

Silvin fetched an armful of firewood without having to be asked. She built it into a cone, and Flip lit it with a minor spell, a flash in the eyes and a bolt of flame that caught the kindling at once. They were all too tired to hunt, especially with such plentiful food in their packs, and so they ate of dried meat and bread.

Soon, Silvin stood from her place by the fire. "Well, I am off for sleep," she said. "I imagine we will set a watch tonight?"

"I put up a spell," said Flip through a mouthful of food. "No one's getting close without my knowing."

"They got past your barrier this morning," said Oris. "We should set a watch."

Silvin nodded. "Arrange it however you wish. Just wake me for my turn, one of you." Then she turned to the lovers. "If you two would join me?"

Quickly, Cara and Ombi finished their food and rose to go to her tent.

"A moment," said Flip, raising a finger to halt them. "We have entered into a deal with you, but I have another, separate proposal."

Silvin frowned. "What is it?"

Flip grinned at her. "The greater part of our enjoyment of this journey was our companionship, but you've taken that away. I wish to win it back. I'd like to duel you for them."

For a moment, Oris could only stare at him in shock. "Flip!" she barked. "What are you doing?"

But Flip ignored her. And Silvin only smiled at Oris. She did not seem angry, or even very alarmed.

"It is quite all right. This is interesting." Her attention went back to Flip. "Are you certain you want to fight me?"

"I am," said Flip. "And if I beat you, you'll release the lovers back into our service. *And* you'll continue to pay them the same rate you already offered. You've certainly got the coin for it."

The lovers looked at each other with wide eyes. Silvin smiled, and her nostrils flared slightly. "I do, at that. But you seem to have much to gain here, and I have little. What do I get if I win?"

"Of course, if you win, you get to keep the lovers," said Flip with a grin.

Silvin laughed—that same bark of harsh, unfamiliar delight. "You wager that which you do not possess. As it stands, I already have both the lovers."

Flip shrugged. "Then make a proposal."

Silvin's teeth flashed. "Here it is, then. If I win, you return the payment I already offered. This first job is free."

Oris reached up and gripped her hair as if she would pull it out. Surely Flip was not foolish enough to risk so much gold on such a bet.

But Flip only grinned wider and said, "Agreed."

"He does *not* speak for my share!" shouted Oris.

Flip shook his head. "Fine. You may keep your half, coward."

And then he sent a wave of flame rushing towards Silvin.

Oris cried out—but Silvin was no longer there. She had darted away from the roasting flames. Flip extinguished his fires before they lit the trees. But Silvin did not press an attack. She wore a savage grin.

"We did not discuss terms," she said. "I assume neither of us are allowed to kill or maim the other."

"Why would I want you dead?" said Flip. "And you could not lop my arms off if you tried."

Silvin brushed a lock of hair behind her ear. "Why would I want your hands? The lovers say they are weaker than mine."

That drew a laugh from Flip. "Then stop bouncing your jaw."

He loosed lightning upon her, but Silvin raised her swords. The bolt struck the blades, arcing into their wooden hilts and Silvin's leather gloves. Silvin's whole body spasmed, but she did not fall.

Flip barely had time to look surprised before she launched herself towards him. He yelped, and his eyes flashed with light again.

He pressed air into the ground, propelling himself over Silvin's head. She stopped on the spot and turned with a kick. It took Flip in the back, and he went sprawling on the ground.

Silvin darted for him at once. Flip saw her coming and lashed out with a narrow gust of air. It caught Silvin's ankle, and she went tumbling. Her swords skittered away.

Flip scrambled to his feet. Again his eyes lit, and wind blasted Silvin, knocking her on her back and flinging her legs into the air.

With Silvin's blades gone, she lunged and threw her fists at Flip instead. He dodged and struck her glancing blows with wind, yet still she pressed towards him. Suddenly he kicked hard at her knee. Silvin gave a heavy grunt of pain and fell facedown.

Flip dove on top of her, driving an elbow between her shoulder blades. He raised a handful of lightning to press into her body.

Silvin threw her head back, smashing Flip's nose. He flew off her with a cry of pain and a spurt of blood.

And then, suddenly, Silvin looked up at Oris, teeth bared in a secret grin. And in that instant, Oris realized the truth: Silvin was putting on a show. She was letting Flip keep up with her.

Then Silvin was on her feet again. She raised her fists as if she were in a bar fight, stalking towards Flip as he tried to find his feet.

"Come on, then," said Silvin. Her words were slurred as though she was punch-drunk. But now Oris could hear the affect Silvin was adding. "No swords for me, and no magic for you. Have you got the guts for it, wizardling?"

Flip's nose was a bloody mess. But he only grinned, teeth stained with red, and raised his own fists to meet hers. He ducked her first clumsy swing and planted a fist in her gut. All of the breath seemed to leave Silvin as she gave a great *whoof.* But she got two blows in on Flip's ribs, making him wince and withdraw into himself.

There was a moment. Oris only saw it because she was looking for it. Silvin had a clear shot at Flip's jaw. She did not take it. Her fist clenched, but it did not fly.

Then Flip struck her with an uppercut that lifted her off the ground.

Silvin fell on her back, eyes rolling. Her hands scrabbled at the dirt beneath her, but she could find no purchase to lift herself up.

Flip knelt and drew her up by the front of her leather jerkin, raising his fist. But he held it.

"Had enough?" he said, his voice thick with blood.

Silvin spat up at him. "Dark take you."

Flip punched her. Her head lolled to the side, though she was not quite out.

"Come now," he said. "No reason for you to go to bed early. Yield."

For a moment she did not answer, but only panted hard, looking up at him. Then she spit again—but to the side.

"I yield."

Flip smiled down at her. Then he stood—but he pulled her up after him. She looked unsteady on her feet, and Flip threw an arm around her shoulder.

"All right," he said. "I've decided I like you."

Silvin wiped blood from her lips. "I suppose I am honored."

Flip laughed, and his grip on her tightened. "Of course you are. Sleep well tonight, alone though you might be."

He released Silvin. She stumbled, but Oris caught her. Then the lovers came running up to Flip, clapping and laughing with delight. They tended to his nose and his other hurts, dabbing them gently with water and kissing them once they were clean. Flip's grin was as wide as Oris had ever seen it, and he turned it on her at last.

"The world has been set to rights," he proclaimed. "Now we may take our comfort as conquerors. Have you a preference for companionship?"

Oris shook her head. "I withheld my share from the wager. I'll also deny myself the reward, at least for one night. You've earned double, great fool though you might be. I'd better tend to our employer before she trips into the fire." She hoisted Silvin up a bit to strengthen the point.

Flip shrugged. "As you wish. I'll certainly not deny myself the gift." He kissed each lover on the cheek. "Come with me, my darlings. As I've heard it said recently, comfort is especially sweet after a fight."

He led them off like a conquering general, and they all retreated within his tent. The instant they were out of sight, Silvin's head stopped lolling, and she straightened—but she did not step away. Instead, she only smiled up into Oris' face.

"Thank you for keeping my secret."

Oris frowned. "I do not mind holding my tongue for an employer when there is no harm in the lie. But if you ask me to keep anything else from him, you will be disappointed."

"Yet I did not ask you to do it," said Silvin, her eyes too innocent. "It was of your own accord."

Oris turned from her. "You can take the first watch. I am going to bed. We wasted too much time this morning between the fight with Enfil and your dalliance afterwards. Be ready to march much earlier tomorrow."

"I certainly will," said Silvin. "But will you find sleep tonight, without your usual comfort to soothe you into slumber?"

Oris looked back at her, jaw clenched. "I suppose I shall have to suffer through it somehow."

Silvin licked some of the blood from her lips. "As you wish. Good night, then."

She sat with her back to both Oris and the fire, staring out into the darkness. Oris stood there, clenching and unclenching her fists, before she finally went for a restless night's sleep.

They traveled in high spirits the next day, especially Flip. As they went, sometimes Flip or Cara would tell them a story or sing them a song. Cara did not have quite so fine a singing voice as Flip, but she knew more and better stories, and so it was equally pleasant to listen to either of them.

Oris guessed they were eight days away from Dracmund, or mayhap as much as a week if they continued at their leisurely pace. But autumn was slowly claiming the land around them. It often drizzled, and sometimes the drizzle turned to rain.

The day after that, the rain swelled into a terrible storm. Fortunately, they had sheltered overnight in a shallow cave, and so Oris ordered them to remain there for the day and wait for the weather to lighten. They kept a fire going, sitting around it and talking all the while, and every so often Oris or Flip would steal away to their tent with one of the lovers. Each time, Silvin wore a faint smile as she watched them go.

"So, Silvin," said Flip near midday. "You know a great deal about us, and we're at a disadvantage. Tell us something of yourself. Whence do you hail?"

Silvin looked somewhat surprised. She considered for a moment before answering. "I have lived many places in my life, but lately I have dwelled near Garsec."

"Garsec?" Flip's brows rose. "I know it well."

Cara peered at both of them curiously. "I always wondered why someone would choose to live in Garsec instead of on the Seat. They are close enough that it seems you could choose either one, and Garsec cannot be as grand."

"The Seat may be bigger, but that's not always a blessing," said Flip. "Garsec has many benefits all its own."

"It is large enough to provide all of a city's finest delights," said Silvin with a smile and a nod. "Yet it is free from the intolerably arrogant folk who clog the Seat like flies in a sewer."

Flip laughed. "Just so. And do you have a family name? And what holds you in Garsec?"

"No family name," said Silvin, shaking her head. "And currently, nothing holds me in Garsec. That is why I am here."

Flip rolled his eyes and leaned back. But then, before he could respond, he winced and sat back up straight, placing a hand to his chest.

Oris' gaze sharpened. She scooted closer to him. "Flip?" she whispered. "Are you all right?"

"Fine," he groused, just as quietly. "It's the same. No pain."

"No better?"

"But no worse. And it could be much worse."

"What is it?" said Silvin from across the fire, frowning. "Are you hurt?"

"I'm not," said Flip shortly. "It's fine."

"He is," said Ombi with an easygoing smile. "On his chest. It must be bad—he never removes his tunic."

Silvin smirked. "Not even when—"

"Not even then," said Ombi, chuckling. "Mayhap it is not so painful, but only looks bad, and he is vain."

"I'm not!" said Flip.

"Well, you are, if we're being fair," said Oris.

But Silvin's smile had left her eyes, which had narrowed slightly. "When did you take the injury?"

"Don't concern yourself with it," said Flip.

Silvin frowned. "Philip."

"A jilted lover stabbed me," said Flip in exasperation. "That's why I sought comfort in Ombi. And don't call me Philip."

Cara laughed aloud. "What a scandalous tale!" she said. "And, of course, not true."

Flip glared at her. "What makes you so sure?"

Silvin ignored all of this so completely that she might as well not have heard it. "Were you injured in the Battle of Wellmont?"

That stopped Flip cold. Oris, too, now stared straight at Silvin with a razor-sharp focus.

"What makes you say so?" said Oris, fighting to keep her voice neutral.

"Oh, just a guess," said Silvin, tilting her head. "One hears many things."

"What things?" said Flip.

"You would know better than I," said Silvin, smiling a little. But the lovers seemed put off by Flip's suddenly sour mood.

As the day wound towards its close, they ran low on firewood. Oris and Silvin went out to gather more. The weather was not so bad under the trees, and Silvin threw back the hood of her oiled cloak, letting the weak daylight play through her hair. They pushed a little deeper between the trunks and began to pile dead branches to carry back to the others. Sometimes as she worked, Oris would steal glances at Silvin. But Silvin did not seem to notice, until finally Oris spoke.

"How's your lip?"

Silvin looked up at her in surprise. "My lip?"

"After your tussle with Flip," said Oris, tossing her head back towards the camp. "It was bleeding."

That drew a look of faint amusement. "It has healed well. Would you like to inspect it?"

Oris bent towards her task again, cheeks flaming. "I was only asking."

"And I am only answering."

"I've been working on another question," Oris said slowly. "Why did you let Flip win?"

Silvin pursed her lips. "Why do you think?"

Oris stopped and turned to her. "Just answer the question, before Flip wonders what we're doing out here and comes looking for us."

That drew a faint smile from Silvin. "You do love to draw straight to the point. It is admirable in its way, but so horribly dull. Let me at least give my answer in a more entertaining way. You say you have been meaning to ask me this question. That means you have been thinking about it. Tell me, then: why do *you* think I let him win?"

Oris ran her hand back through her hair, brushing some of the water out of it before pulling the hood of her cloak up tighter around her. "If I knew the answer, I wouldn't be asking."

"And I will give you the answer, but not for free. Entertain me with a guess or two first."

"Fine," said Oris. "I think you wanted to make him feel better after you took the lovers."

"A fair answer," said Silvin, nodding slowly. "But making him *feel* better. That is a 'what.' Why would I do it? How does that help *me?*"

Oris frowned. "You . . . you threw both of us off balance when you arrived. So you wanted to mollify him."

"You keep saying what I did, and you are correct," said Silvin. "But you do not guess at the reason, even though your question is *why.* So. *Why* did I let him win?"

Oris chewed the inside of her cheek. "Because you wanted him to trust you. No, not to trust you, because he doesn't. But to like you, I suppose. Yes, that's it. To like you. You knew you couldn't get him to trust you, not so quickly, but you could get him to like you well enough."

"And so he does, now," said Silvin, nodding. She had resumed gathering firewood, and now she dumped three more sticks on the pile. "I want you both to like me."

Oris folded her arms. "And do you think I like you?"

Silvin paused, looking over her shoulder at Oris and smiling slightly. "You tell me."

Oris could not help a chuckle as she stooped for another branch. "You have the most infuriating way of answering questions."

"That is because I do not answer them at all," said Silvin, her smile broadening. "I only keep asking more questions until you discover the answer yourself. It is a trick I learned from my master."

"Oh?" said Oris. "Will we find him just as irritating?"

"More so," said Silvin with her harsh laugh. "But he is the wisest person I know. I think you will like him when you meet him, though a long road may yet stretch between us." Her voice had turned suddenly sad. "I owe him my life, my—" But she shook her head and rolled her shoulders before stooping to reach for the wood. "We have been gone too long. Flip really will come after us."

Oris planted a foot on the pile of wood. She waited until Silvin looked up and met her gaze. "Why do you want us to like you?" she said. "We've already taken your coin. Isn't that enough? What aren't you telling me?"

Silvin gave her a sad smile. "Many things, Oris. But at least I am honest about it."

"What more *can* you tell me?" pressed Oris. "I need something."

Silvin stood straight. They were very close together. "You said yourself that coin should be enough. What more do you need from me?"

Oris could hear her own pulse in her ears. "A reason to trust you, for one thing. As well some assurance that we won't regret taking your offer."

"I cannot offer that," said Silvin, shaking her head. "Mayhap that can be your reason to trust me. You know I am hiding some truths, but I promise I will never lie to you. And so I cannot say you will be free from regret. If you come with me and meet my master, you will regret your choice many, many times. You will waver, and you may even break. But it is true, too, that you *must* come with me, for your sake and the sake of many others. If you do not, you will regret that even more. And your last thought before the enemy kills you will be a wish that you had come when I asked."

Oris' heart was racing now. "What kind of assurance is that?" she asked. "You paint a picture of two roads of darkness before me, and your only offer is that I'll regret yours a little less?"

"I wish I had more," said Silvin, shrugging. "But I promised you no lies."

"No," said Oris. "No, I won't do it. I won't be handed two awful choices and be forced to choose. I'd rather not play the game at all."

Silvin frowned, and Oris could see her fighting her own frustration.

"Refusing to choose is its own choice," she said. "I am sorry you do not think my reasons are enough. I have told you all I can. But you *can* learn the rest. Just do the one job I have hired you for. Come to Dracmund and meet my master. Then you can decide if you want to take the next step, Oreceot."

Gooseflesh rose all up Oris' arms and neck. "If you want me to like you, you should stop using my full name. I hate it."

She pushed roughly past Silvin and stalked back off towards the camp.

CHAPTER V
THE RUSTENING VERGE

THE NEXT DAY, THE STORM LESSENED. THEY PRESSED ON THROUGH A lighter rain that could not soak through their oiled cloaks.

But some hours before sunset, something else brought them to a halt.

They came suddenly upon a blasted land. There were no trees, only blackened stumps thrusting impotently out of tortured dirt. The river was visible some ways off to the north, but other than that, the land was featureless in every direction. The lovers huddled closer to Flip and Oris as though frightened.

"What happened here?" said Ombi.

"It must have been a fire," said Oris. "It looks recent."

"It wasn't recent," said Flip. "I traveled here once before, and I learned the story of this region. The folk who once lived here called it the Breezeboughs, and scholars who lived a thousand leagues away and had never seen it named it the Southern Forest of Mist. It was home to a Wizard King, one of the last. A man named Perrin. Like all his kind, he was an eater of magestones."

The others looked to him in confusion—all but Silvin, whose jaw tightened.

"Magestones?" said Cara. "What are they?"

"You might say *were,* for they're not to be found anymore," said Flip. "Or at least, they're so heavily outlawed that even talking about them can land you in prison. Remember that, please, and never speak of them in company you do not trust, for I should hate to be responsible for getting you in trouble with the King's law. They're black crystals, and any wizard who eats them gains unimaginable power. That's how the Wizard Kings ruled the nine kingdoms."

"Ruled them, and almost destroyed them," said Silvin.

Flip smirked. "Mayhap. In any case, the High King Andriana outlawed their use long ago, on pain of death. She sent her Mystics forth through Underrealm to depose any king who disobeyed her. King Perrin fought his last stand here, with many mages by his side. Magestones turned their flames black and terrible, and they scarred the land forever, as you can see. In the end it was not enough. Perrin was slain, though many of the Mystics fell before he did. It's only a pity he did not wipe them out."

A bitterness seemed to be rising in Silvin, and it filled the air with a palpable tremor, like the sky before thunder. "If Perrin had won, it would have spelled the doom of Underrealm," she said.

Flip's lip curled, and his eyes took on a dangerous light as he looked upon her. "Are you a lover of Mystics, then?"

The bitterness in Silvin's eyes flared to anger. "Hardly. But the days of the Wizard Kings were the darkest chapter in Underrealm's history. Not all folk have forgotten the evil they committed across the land, even if you have."

"I've forgotten nothing," said Flip with a razor smile. "I'm nothing but glad Perrin died, I'm only happy he took so many redbacks with him. I've never much loved the order."

"Because of your cousin," said Silvin.

Both Flip and Oris turned to her incredulously. "How in the dark below do you know that?" said Flip.

Some of Silvin's anger had faded, and now she smirked. "I told you from the start, my master knows a great many things. Do you think he would have sent me chasing you across Underrealm if he did not?"

The lovers seemed to sense the danger building. Ombi took Flip's hand. "What happened to your cousin?" he said gently.

"Ombi," warned Oris.

"No, there's no reason they shouldn't know." Flip kept his gaze on Silvin. "My cousin was leading a caravan through Selvan. He was waylaid in the night. Everyone was killed. Butchered. My family thought bandits did it, but they never found out who. So I went there myself, against my mother's wishes. I found a Mystic badge, trampled in the dirt near where the caravan had burned. The three rods, the circle, and the wings. Not enough evidence to convince the King's law, of course. But then, why would they arrest their own? The redcloaks slaughtered my cousin and all his attendants. He was barely even grown." He tilted his chin up slightly as he regarded Silvin. "Remember that when you think of the Mystics and their heroism."

Silvin had not looked at him while he told his story, but now she met his gaze. "I was only nine years old when the Mystics killed my parents."

Oris' lungs felt suddenly empty. Flip blinked twice.

"Wh—what?" he stammered.

"They came in the night," said Silvin. "They dragged my mother and father out into the street and gutted them. And then they did the same to the rest of my village. Everyone I had ever known. In the dark and in their bloodlust, they were about to kill me, too. Then one of them realized I was only a child. I do not remember much else of that night. In time it was arranged for me to be taken in by a nobleman—my master, who I have mentioned before. It was he who saw to my education and my training."

They all let the silence hang for a moment. Then Flip went to her and put a hand on her shoulder. "Dark take them," he declared. "Them, and all those of great wealth and power. They value our lives only as coins to be spent to achieve their own ends."

Silvin gave him a bitter smile that looked ready to shatter. "As you say."

Two days later, they woke to another terrible storm. But this time they had no snug cave to keep them safe from the sky's fury. So they huddled wearily into their cloaks and pressed on through the wet. They had passed through the blasted land and back into forest, but the storm was so terrible that the trees provided little protection against it. As the hours passed and the weather showed no signs of lessening, Oris grew worried. Marching through this all day could easily make one of the party ill, or even cause an injury.

Flip seemed to feel the same way. "We can't go on all day this way!" he said. "Let's build a camp and try to weather it."

"Our tents will be no proof against the rain," said Oris. "We'll only be sitting still, which will make the cold worse, and then our tents will remain soaked the rest of the trip."

"Can you do anything?" said Ombi, looking pleadingly at Flip.

"I'm not Dorren, and cannot command the sky," said Flip, scowling.

Suddenly, Silvin's eyes flashed. "Not Dorren. But mayhap there is something you could do," she said. "You are a wizard of some strength, are you not?"

Flip looked at Oris and rolled his eyes. "I am strong enough for my purposes and the purposes of some others," he said. "Why?"

"Can you build a roof of water?" she said. "Using the rain itself? I have seen it done before."

Flip frowned. "A roof? I . . . hm. If the runoff . . . and I would have to . . . one moment."

He stepped away from them all. As he muttered an incantation, his eyes filled with a bright glow. From the raindrops all around he formed a small globe, and then it grew larger and larger between his twisting hands. Soon he flattened it and lifted it so that it was over his head, and then it began to grow. Soon it was two paces wide, and the lovers dove beneath it with happy cries. A moment later, there was room enough for Oris and Silver to step out of the rain as well. When drops struck the roof, they joined it, and Flip shaped it so that there was a steady runoff at the back, splashing none of them. It was like being under an awning at the home of some wealthy noble, able to observe the weather without suffering from it. They all cast back the hoods of their cloaks and took deep breaths of relief.

"You are wonderful!" cried Ombi. He threw his arms around Flip's neck and kissed him on the cheek.

"Remarkable," said Silvin, looking appraisingly at Flip. "I have suggested this trick to others, but you are the first who could pull it off."

"Am I really?" said Flip with a grin. His eyes still glowed as he held the water's shape in his mind. "And where did you say you learned it again?"

She did not answer, but only smiled wider and looked again at the rain. "Wisdom may be found in many places, not just the Academy."

"Fine," said Flip, rolling his eyes. "But just now, I seek shelter and not wisdom. There must be somewhere more permanent we can hide from the rain and dry off, at least for a time."

A flash of lightning split the sky. They all shielded their eyes and blinked—all except Cara, who pointed instead.

"Look!" she said. "What is that?"

They all peered through the storm. There, far in the distance, there was a black shape atop a ridge. Oris could not be sure, but it looked like a building, and a large one.

"What under the sky?" muttered Flip. "There's no towns out here that I remember."

Another flash of lightning struck, and Oris saw high stone walls. "Not a town," she said. "A stronghold."

"So far from any settlements?" said Cara.

Silvin's expression had grown troubled. "We should avoid it," she said. "There are many such places in these lands, but they were abandoned long ago. Now they are dens of bandits or wild animals. Even in the best case, it will leave a trail for those who hunt us."

Privately, Oris agreed with her. But, too, she knew that secrecy would do them no good if they froze to death or perished from illness in the wilderness.

Suddenly a bolt of lightning split a nearby beech tree with a terrible explosion. The lovers jumped and screamed, and the light died in Flip's eyes. The roof of water fell on all their heads, soaking them straight to the skin.

"That settles it!" said Flip as he scrambled to rebuild the water ceiling. "You may do as you like. I am getting a stone roof over my head." He set off for the stronghold at a brisk walk, and the lovers scrambled to keep up.

"We can think up a better plan when we are there," Oris told Silvin. "But at least we shall have four walls to shelter in."

"Or perish inside," said Silvin darkly. But she followed along regardless.

It took them two hours to reach the stronghold, slipping in the mud and cursing all the while. The path up the ridge to the stronghold cut back and forth. Oris reflected that if the place were occupied, it would have been in an excellent position of defense. Every turn in the path was under the stronghold's arrow slits, glaring at them like watchful eyes. The top of the main keep had fallen partially to ruin, but there was a mighty watchtower that looked to be intact.

The front gate stood open, much to their relief. Across the bailey, the door to the main building yawned wide and dark. There might once have been a wooden door in the frame, but it had rotted away or been removed long ago. They crowded into the entry space within. The lovers went to sit against the wall, heaving great sighs of relief.

"Thank the sky," said Flip. "Now if we could only get a fire going, this place could almost be pleasant."

"But you are a firemage," said Ombi.

Flip smiled down at him. "I need fuel, my darling, for I can't burn stone, and it wearies me to burn only air for too long."

"I'll find some wood," said Oris. "There must be some old furniture we can use for the purpose."

"I will come with you," said Silvin. "This place has an evil feel, and you should not go alone."

"Let me go with her," said Flip. "She'll need my magic to light the way."

Silvin's jaw looked hard as iron. "I am not letting both of you out of my sight within this place."

Flip rolled his eyes. "Then all three of us can go."

Oris grimaced. "I don't think we should leave the lovers alone, Flip."

"Just go!" cried Cara and Ombi in unison. Both lovers made great shooing motions at the trio. "We will freeze to death here while the three of you argue," said Ombi. "Be quick about it. If you hear us screaming, you will know a bear has lumbered into the room. Come and save us quickly."

Oris had to smile at that. "Very well," she said. "We'll return as quickly as we may."

As the lovers sat resting against the stone wall, Oris, Flip, and Silvin left their packs and set off into the darkness of the stronghold.

"So what do you know of this place?" said Flip. "You seem to have some idea of its reputation."

Silvin never took her eyes off the shadows around them. "Long ago, many strongholds like this one were built in this land, which was once called Forelund. Underrealm was young, and this was its frontier. The scattered folk who dwelled here at the time were descended from Hedgemond, and though the Heddish chiefs were reluctant to face Roth upon the field, the farmers here fought like they had battalions at their backs.

"Roth's general was Silvin, daughter of Renna the Sunmane, for whom the kingdom of Selvan was named, and so was I. And she built these fortresses in this wild land to keep the south border secure. But as time went on, and Dorsea and the other kingdoms were conquered one by one, the strongholds fell into disuse. New roads built by new kings avoided them, traveling across open country to more directly join the towns and cities that were no longer in constant danger of being raided. Thus these places were abandoned and forgotten, though some old maps still contain them. I would need to look at one to be sure, but I think this stronghold was once called the Rustening Verge."

Flip looked impressed, and he made no attempt to hide it. "I am not the only one with some knowledge of history, it seems."

Silvin smiled, but it looked grim. "My master ensured I was well educated." But then her smile vanished. "Oris? What is it?"

Oris was staring at something. They had passed through two hallways into a large chamber that looked like it might once have been a dining hall. One door to the north surely led to the stronghold's bailey, and there were two hearths set in the southern wall, empty and cold. There were no old pieces of furniture to be found, but Oris had seen a crumpled bit of cloth in the corner that looked like a fallen tapestry. She had been walking towards it when she froze in place.

"It looks like a nest," said Oris.

Flip and Silvin came to her side, studying the fallen tapestry. It was crumpled up and curled in a sort of ridge around the edges, forming a soft place to lay in the center. It did indeed look just like a nest, of some beast larger than a human. But Oris knew of no beasts that size that made themselves nests like this.

"Could it be a bear?" said Flip.

"Mayhap," said Oris, though she shook her head. "But they don't often den in places like this."

"They do not," agreed Silvin, creeping closer. She knelt and then stood with something in her hand. "Look. A bone. The gore on it is still red."

"Dark," spat Oris.

"What?" said Flip. "Who cares if it's red?"

"It hasn't had enough time to dry out," said Oris. She turned and drew her sword. It glimmered in the faint grey sunlight shining through the windows of the dining hall, which were five paces above the ground. Silvin stepped up beside her, baring her own steel.

“So it’s recent,” said Flip. His eyes glowed as he muttered under his breath, and flame sprang to life in his other palm. “Something lives here.”

“Something that hunts,” said Oris.

“We should not have come,” said Silvin. “Let us get the lovers and leave as quickly as we may.”

“But what *is* it?” said Flip. “If we can kill whatever beast this is—”

“Hist!” Silvin’s whisper was so harsh that Flip listened. She cocked her head. Oris saw her arms twitch, as though she wished to move but restrained herself.

She turned to the two of them, her expression one of dread.

“Not a beast,” she said.

From the front hall where they had left the lovers, they heard a long and piercing scream.

CHAPTER VI
SHADOW IN THE TOWER

ORIS' PULSE THUNDERED IN HER EARS AS THEY SPRINTED THROUGH THE stronghold. Thoughts raced through her mind, each vanishing in an instant. It was some beast. It was a monster from campfire legend. It was more enemies like Enfil, and this time they did not care about the lovers' safety.

One thought kept repeating: *Silvin knows what it is.*

They burst into the entry hall. All three of them froze in horror.

Ombi lay on his back on the floor. His chest was torn open, and his eyes stared sightlessly at the ceiling. Something crouched over Cara. Her legs stuck out from beneath it, and they were kicking feebly.

Oris could not tell what the thing was in the darkness. There was something bearlike about its thick, shaggy fur, but the limbs were too long and gangly. And the way it had ripped Ombi apart . . . no, it was not a bear.

All this she saw in the space of half a heartbeat. Then she, Flip, and Silvin charged, screaming and brandishing weapons and flame.

The creature turned and snarled at them. Oris saw bared, yellowing fangs. Its eyes glinted unnaturally in the pale sunlight.

Then the creature snatched Cara up in one massive claw. It scuttled up the wall and out through a hole in the masonry there, disappearing outside. Cara's screams went on and on, until eventually the sound of the rain drowned them out.

"No!" cried Oris. She raced back and forth beneath the hole in the wall, trying to catch another glimpse of the thing.

"What in the *dark* below was that?" Flip's voice was high and shrill. He swung back and forth, waving his flames at the darkness.

Silvin ran to Ombi. She knelt to inspect him, but Oris could tell from even so far away: the lover was dead.

Oris fixed Silvin with a look. "You know."

Silvin's gaze leaped up to her. Her jaw clenched tighter. "I have only a guess."

"Well, guess, then!" screeched Flip.

"Its nest was almost bestial, but not quite," said Silvin. "It attacked without provocation, but otherwise it was like an animal. I think it is a fallen weremage."

That meant nothing to Oris, but Flip's face went even paler. "Dark below," he whispered.

"What?" said Oris. "What is that?"

"A weremage that—they've failed to . . ." Flip shook his head and licked his lips. "It is a long tale. But the heart of it is that all magic is dangerous. Fledglings learning its use must take every care not to harm themselves or others. In a student's later years at the Academy, half of all instruction teaches them to avoid the dangers of their own spells."

"So that you do not set yourself ablaze, or some such?" said Oris.

"Or some such," said Flip, nodding. "Though there are worse things than fire. Instructors can stop flames before they do too much damage. But not lightning. Some instructors refuse to teach it at all, because it's so quick and yet so violent. Some students harm their bodies beyond repair. The lightning twists their limbs and causes their nerves to suffer always from pain, as though the bolt is striking them over and over again, forever."

"Weremages turn into other creatures, and learning to do so can be a painful process," said Silvin. "When the pain is too great, most of the time it merely breaks the weremage's concentration, reverting them to their natural form. But sometimes, rarely, the pain is so great that it breaks a weremage's mind. Terror keeps them from dropping the form, and they lose their own consciousness in the beast's."

Oris turned to face the darkness, her grip tightening on her sword. "So it's human?"

"I would argue that it is not," said Silvin grimly. "But it is certainly dangerous."

"Fine," said Oris. "How do we hunt it?"

Silvin blinked. "We are not hunting it. We have to go."

Oris whirled on her. "We're not leaving. Cara was alive."

Flip looked at her, aghast. "When we saw her, yes. But she must be dead now."

"We're contracted to protect her," Oris told him. "We'll be in quite enough trouble for Ombi. We have to *try* to save her, at least. Silvin, how do we hunt the thing?"

"I can tell the guild you did all you could," said Silvin. "My master's influence will have some sway with them."

"You are *not* lying to the guild on our behalf," growled Oris. "And it *would* be a lie, because we haven't tried all we can to save her. Now for the last time, answer me, or I'm setting off into the stronghold alone. How do we hunt this creature?"

Silvin gave her a very odd look. Oris did not think she looked angry, exactly, but she could not read what the woman felt. Flip, on the other hand, looked suitably chastised, which pleased Oris a little.

"By your word, Oris," said Silvin. "Let us hunt, then."

They set off into the darkness together, Silvin speaking quietly to the both of them. "It is something between beast and human. We should therefore expect an animalistic instinct, but crossed with human wit and cunning. We must think not only like a hunter in the wild, but also like someone tracking down a fugitive. We found one of its nests, but it will have other places to retreat to, like a lord withdrawing to their keep when an enemy has taken the walls."

"An apt metaphor," said Flip slowly. "Yet I doubt it would be living in the keep here. You saw it when we came in. It's mostly fallen to ruin. So another high place."

Oris' brow furrowed. "A high place? Why?"

Flip shrugged. "Because it's part human. A beast might not take a high position to spy anyone approaching, but a human certainly would."

"Clever," said Silvin. "The tower should be this way. Come."

She led them down two turns to a long hallway. The right-hand wall was all solid stone, but on the left side there were several doors. Oris guessed they were walking along the stronghold's outer wall, and the doors on the left led to some of the other buildings along the edge of the main courtyard. But they had not gone very far when a powerful stench struck them all, wafting out of the darkness ahead.

"Dark below," said Oris, covering her nose. "What is that?"

Flip sent his flames a little ahead of them to light the way. "A corpse. Look."

The body lay propped against the wall, just next to a door that hung crookedly on its hinges. There was no way to tell if it had been man or woman or twixt, so much of the flesh had been eaten away. What meat remained was infested with maggots, and they crawled through the body and across the floor surrounding it.

"Dark below," said Oris again. Her gorge threatened to rise.

But Flip pulled a handkerchief out of his pocket. Holding it over his mouth, he approached the body. There he retrieved something Oris had not noticed at first—a bow and a quiver of arrows, undamaged and resting on the floor about a pace away from the corpse.

"I have my magic," he said. "But it can't hurt to have a weapon to hand other than my dagger. I'd rather not draw within arm's reach of that thing, if I can help it."

"A wise choice," said Silvin. "And the corpse tells us the creature is almost certainly this way."

"Wonderful," said Flip with all the false cheer he could muster. "I'll be behind you, then, if it's—"

The crooked door behind him burst off its hinges. It slammed into Flip, throwing him into the opposite wall. His flames guttered out, and the hallway went pitch dark.

Oris gave a battle cry and held her blade before her. But she could see nothing to attack. Silvin screamed. The beast roared.

Something heavy struck Oris' arm, jostling her to the side. She fell, and her hand came down on something. The something seemed to crumple, and Oris felt wet things moving.

The corpse. Her hand had come down on the corpse and the maggots feasting on it. She retched.

"Oris!" Flip's voice pierced the dark. Suddenly his fire surged again. Oris cried out in fear as she saw the corpse's face only a finger's breadth from her own. She scrambled away.

Flip's spell wavered, from fear or from wooziness at the blow he had taken. The light flickered on and off again. In the flashes, Oris saw the creature had borne Silvin to the ground. Its claws were wrapped around her blade, and nasty, gnashing teeth were almost upon her throat.

Now she got her first good look at the thing. It was indeed bear-sized in height and length, and its head was something like a bear's, with rounded ears and a heavy short snout. But the knees bent the wrong way. The claws were long and straight, long as knives and just as sharp. It looked like an awful hybrid of a bear and some demon of the darkness below.

With the thing visible at last, Silvin lifted a sword and plunged it deep into the creature's chest. It roared in pain. But then its eyes flared, and the wound sealed itself up.

Oris had seen that before. *A weremage's gift,* she thought. The same magic that let them alter their bodies also let them seal their own wounds.

Oris slashed it across the flank with her sword. It reared up, howling with anger again. One of its limbs smashed Oris in the temple. She fell, stunned.

With a cry, Flip threw himself onto the creature. He wrapped his arms around its neck and wrenched. It gave a choked gurgle as it fell off Silvin. But then it rolled with the motion. As it righted itself, one paw lashed out into Flip's chest. He was flung across the hallway and facedown.

His fires died again. In the darkness, Oris heard the creature screech. Then she heard Flip's scream, loud and long—and fading. Fading like Cara's scream as he grew more distant. The thing was dragging him away.

"No!" she screamed. "Flip! *Flip!*"

"Hold for a moment," growled Silvin. Her voice was somehow deeper, gravelly, probably from the exertion of holding the creature back from her throat. Oris barely saw her silhouette appear in the doorway the creature had come through, and then there was a heavy *crash* as she opened another door.

Cold air blasted through the space, bringing with it weak daylight. Now that Oris could see, she scrambled to her feet. But she was still woozy, and she almost fell over. "Come on," she told Silvin. "It took Flip. We have to—"

"Hold," said Silvin, her voice still thick and raspy. "Charging off is what got Flip snatched. Take one moment to breathe."

She took Oris' shoulder, but Oris threw off her arm. "We don't have a moment! Nor does Flip. Come on. Take your blades."

She went and scooped up Silvin's swords, which had fallen in the fight, and then two pouches that had fallen from her belt. But as she straightened, holding the pouches in her hands, she stopped.

Something had fallen from one of them. Something small and silver, attached to a chain. Oris bent again and picked it up, holding it in her hand.

It was a symbol. Oris had not seen it all that often, but she recognized it at once. Three rods bound by a ring, and wings behind them. She looked up at Silvin, fury building in her heart.

"You're a Mystic," she spat.

"Of course I am," said Silvin.

"Of course? *Of course?* You've never said a word about it."

"And would either of you have come with me if I had?"

"You know we wouldn't!"

"Well, there you have it."

Oris seized the front of Silvin's jerkin and slammed her against the wall. Silvin did not resist.

"That was a pretty lie you spun about your parents," she snarled. "I suppose you would've said anything to earn our trust."

Silvin looked up at her. She was smiling, but Oris almost felt afraid of her. "It was no lie."

That stopped Oris short. She blinked. "What?"

"The Mystics killed my parents, as I said. And everyone else I ever knew. I celebrate the day every year. The anniversary of my freedom. You cannot imagine what they did to me."

Oris felt that all the wind had gone out of her. This was all too much for her to know what to think about it. She loosened her grip on Silvin and stepped away. "Our arrangement is over. We save Flip, and then we're done. And we'll keep the gold you gave us, in payment for your lies."

"We are not done, Oris," said Silvin. "Whatever you think about my order, someone still wants you dead. We are the only help that will come to you."

"Some will want to use you for their own ends," said Oris. "That's what you told me at the river. Now I know who you meant. What is it they say? The Mystics have silver tongues, but they are forked."

"The enemy has followed you since Wellmont, as I have," said Silvin. "He will not be stopped. When he finds you, he will destroy you. And if Flip survives tonight, he will die defending you. Won't he?"

Oris took a deep breath to reply. But nothing came out. Her jaw set.

Silvin smirked. "But if you come with me, Oris, we will protect you. And we can provide more than protection. Do you not wish to know who you are?"

"I've heard enough about who I am," said Oris, shaking her head in dismissal. "Some chosen figure, selected by fate for purposes unknown."

"I do not mean that," said Silvin. "I mean who *you* are. Do you not wish to know who your parents were? Or where you were born?"

Oris' eyes flashed as she turned on Silvin. "You don't have those answers."

"But we can get them, Oris. We, and no one else."

Quickly, desperately, Oris shook her head. "Enough. Flip's running out of time, if he isn't dead already. And I don't care about any of that. I'm only a sword for hire. It's all I've ever been."

"It is not all you will ever be," said Silvin.

"Stop," said Oris. "I don't care. We have to save Flip."

"You cannot tell him," said Silvin.

"Of course I can, and I will."

"I mean it, Oris. Not until you meet my master, at least."

"Flip and I have been friends for years," said Oris. "I won't lie to him for you."

Silvin bent. She scooped up the bow Flip had dropped and walked off down the hallway. "If you want to know the truth, then you will lie to him for yourself."

Silvin seemed to know where she was going, for she trotted unerringly down the hallway, following it as it turned left and then left again. Oris followed, her thoughts a mess of agitation. But then Silvin stopped, drawing back against the right-hand wall of the hallway, staring ahead. The space lightened, and Oris could see that it also opened up into a wider area. The watchtower.

"Can you shoot?" said Silvin.

Oris blinked. "What?"

Silvin raised the bow and quiver. "Can you shoot?" she repeated.

"Passably well."

"Well, I am awful at it, so take this," said Silvin. "I think the thing is using Flip as bait to lure us into an ambush. I am going to go after it directly. You must wait for the right moment and shoot the weremage the moment you see an opportunity."

That made Oris hesitate. "But what if I hit you?"

Silvin shook her head. "You will not. I will give you a good opportunity. Your job is to take it. And as you have said, Flip is running out of time. Come, quickly!"

Without further warning, she turned and charged down the hallway towards the watchtower. She gave a battle-cry as she went and, drawing her swords, she slammed them against the stone walls.

Oris darted down the hallway to follow, awkwardly drawing an arrow. She burst into the tower only a moment after Silvin. It was fifteen paces tall and square in shape. There were arrow slits, but some of them had crumbled over time, and they let in flurries of rain.

A stone stairway ran up to the top, where there was a large platform running around the tower's ceiling. As lightning flashed and thunder crackled behind it, Oris saw movement upon the platform. When the thunder died away, she heard the sounds of scuffling leather on wood.

Flip is alive, she thought fiercely.

But then her attention went to Silvin. The Mystic was charging up the stairs, still screaming as loud as she could.

It worked. Far above, Oris saw the flash of yellow eyes. Then a shadowy form leaped down the wall towards Silvin. Oris crept up the stairs, arrow ready for an opening.

Silvin tumbled left and out of the way. The monster came to a skidding stop and spun to meet her. Silvin came at it in a whirl of blades. It batted one of them aside and sidled around her, placing itself between her and the wall.

Dark take the thing, thought Oris. *Come on. Closer to me, you steer.*

The creature swung for Silvin with its claws. She parried the first swing and sliced it across the forearm with her other sword. That made it recoil at last. It drew back, but then it attacked with renewed savagery, knocking one of Silvin's swords away to fall to the bottom of the tower.

It gripped Silvin in its claws and pressed her against the stair's stone railing. Silvin dropped her other sword, gripping the creature's wrist to keep from falling into empty space.

Through gritted teeth she cried, "Shoot it!"

Oris hesitated. Silvin still blocked half the creature's body. But finally she loosed, praying to the sky.

Silvin twisted savagely to the side, prying herself partway out of the creature's grip, its claws tearing her skin. The motion put the creature's head just in the path of Oris' arrow. The shaft pierced it in its open, roaring mouth. There came a spurt of blood as the arrowhead pierced out through the top of its skull.

For a moment more it stood frozen there. Then it collapsed forwards on top of Silvin.

Together they pitched over the railing and began to fall.

"Silvin!" cried Oris. She lunged back down the stairs, but there was no time to catch her. Seizing the railing, she leaned over, trying desperately to grasp Silvin's arm, but it was too far.

Time seemed to slow. Silvin's hair floated around her face as though she were underwater.

And then Oris realized that Silvin *had* slowed in truth. The monster had already struck the ground. Silvin's hair was being lifted and cast about by wind, not by water.

Oris looked up in astonishment. There, at the edge of the top platform, Flip's upper body jutted out into the open space. The wizard's eyes were aglow, his hand was outstretched, and his mouth fluttered with his incantations. Blood covered his face and arms, but he was alive, and it was his magic that had caught Silvin.

She struck the stone floor of the tower, but no faster than at a good run. She grunted with pain, but her body did not break. The tower fell to silence, and Flip rolled back out of sight with a groan.

Immediately Silvin forced herself to rise. She sprinted up the stairs, following Oris, who was climbing as fast as she could.

Oris reached the top. There was Flip. His purple coat was stained with the blood of many cuts, though none of them looked mortally deep.

"You're alive," she said.

"Am I?" wheezed Flip. "Wonderful."

Oris smirked. But then she saw Cara. The lover was still breathing. Both her hands were pressed to her throat and chest, and blood leaked steadily between her fingers.

"Sky save us," said Oris. She ran to the lover and fell on her knees beside her. She tore off her vest and pressed it hard to Cara's neck before gently pulling the lover's hands away from the wound. They rose to clutch Oris' shoulders and tunic instead, smearing them with red.

"How bad is it?" croaked Flip. He tried to come to them, but he could do little more than crawl.

“Here.” Silvin had reached the platform, and she went to Flip to pull him up. Quickly she ran her fingers and eyes over him, inspecting his wounds. “You’ll live.” She looked over at Cara. “Will she?”

“Yes,” said Oris through gritted teeth, pressing harder upon the vest to stop the blood.

Together they came to her, Silvin taking one of Flip’s arms to help him. Cara was barely conscious. Still she clung to Oris desperately, and Oris could feel the blood on the lover’s hands where they gripped her. Her eyes were half-lidded, and they twitched back and forth as though searching for danger.

Flip looked mournful. “Oris, can you . . . do anything for her?”

“I’m doing what I can,” snapped Oris.

“I mean anything . . . else.”

Oris looked up at him, confused. Then her expression turned to stone. Silvin looked back and forth between the two of them, clearly aware of a secret in their words.

“No,” said Oris. “What else could I do?”

Silvin gave her an appraising look. Then she put a gentle hand on Oris’ arm. “Oris . . . a word?”

“I’m holding her throat in place,” said Oris. “Whatever you have to say, I don’t think she’ll object.”

Silvin looked pained. But she leaned in with a hand on Oris’ shoulder and brought her lips close enough that her breath tickled Oris’ ear. “She is not going to survive the night.”

“She *will*, dark take her.” Oris’ voice was shaking with fury. “I can save her, and I’m going to.”

“Oris—”

Oris turned to her with burning eyes. “Get away from me, or I’ll throw you off the tower like that creature meant to.”

Silvin looked shocked. But Flip reached over and gently pulled her backwards.

“Come,” he said gently. “You aren’t convincing her otherwise. Trust me. We should fetch our packs.”

CHAPTER VII
BREAKING AND BINDING

CARA DID, IN FACT, SURVIVE THE NIGHT. NOT LONG AFTER THEY bandaged the lover's wounds, she fell into a restless sleep. Oris remained sitting by her side until dawn, occasionally checking on her bandages. Silvin and Flip laid out their bedrolls close by on the tower's platform. They made Oris promise to wake them for their watches.

Oris made the promise, and then she broke it.

The storm lessened some time before morning. The rain never completely ceased, but fell pattering on the roof close above their heads. Oris was glad it did not seem to have any leaks.

Silvin woke before Flip. When she looked up and saw pale dawn glimmering through the tower's arrow slits, she spoke no word of chastisement to Oris for letting her sleep. Instead, she rose and went silently down the tower. Oris wanted to ask where she was going, but instead she maintained an obstinate silence.

Silvin returned a short while later. In her hand she had a shock of uprooted plants ending in clusters of small white flowers. She built a fire and set some water to boil, and with the flowers she made a thick mash. At last she looked up at Oris.

"It is yarrow," she said. "It will help with her wounds."

"I know of it," said Oris.

"Then may I?"

Oris nodded. Together they removed Cara's bandages, managing not to wake her while they did it, and then Silvin applied the yarrow to her injuries. Cara stirred at that, her fingers twitching. Oris took her hands and squeezed them gently until Silvin was done, and then she helped reapply the bandages. Cara drifted back to stillness. Mayhap Oris imagined it, but her breathing seemed to be easier.

Flip woke not long after that and came to see Cara at once. He seemed mildly surprised and more than a little guilty to see her alive.

"I'm glad she made it," he said to Oris with a sidelong look. "And I'm simply miserable about Ombi. You were right about my cowardice last night. Forgive me."

"I forgave you before you asked," said Oris. And she meant it.

That day passed slowly. Oris sometimes drifted towards dozing, but she pinched her arms and slapped her cheeks to stay awake. Silvin studied her often, and Oris eyed the woman right back. Silvin must be wondering why Oris had not told Flip already.

Well, let her stew, thought Oris. But if she was honest, she herself was not sure why she held on to the secret.

They took the weremage's body outside and left it to the elements. Upon dying, the body had reverted to its original form—a small, pale woman, nude, with long and somewhat ratty hair. After Ombi and Cara, Oris could summon no pity for her. But Silvin could not stop looking at the woman, and her eyes were dark and pained.

By the time sunset came again, Oris could hardly keep her head up. Silvin came to her.

"Oris," she said. "Go to sleep. I will keep watch."

"I'm fine," snarled Oris.

"You will fall asleep overnight," said Silvin. "And then you will be angry at yourself, and you will take it out on us. It will annoy me. I promise you, I will not close my eyes for an instant until morning."

"You didn't even think she would survive," said Oris.

"I was wrong," said Silvin. "You were right."

Oris' jaw clenched over and over as she matched Silvin's stare. Flip was watching with a look of faint amusement, but he did not seem inclined to join the conversation.

"Fine," said Oris. "Wake me before dawn."

"I swear I will," said Silvin.

Oris unfurled her bedroll and laid it just next to Cara's, within arm's reach. She lay down, still looking at the lover.

She only meant to blink, but instead she fell into a deep sleep. But not a dreamless one.

● ○ ● ○ ●

It's mine. Not yours. Mine.

You are a foolish girl. And if you will not listen, we will do what we—

Threaten me all you want. But this you shall not take from me.

● ○ ● ○ ●

The dream had almost faded by the time Silvin shook Oris awake, but this memory remained.

Oris jerked up from her bedroll, her eyes going at once to Cara. The lover slept peacefully. All was silent. Even the rain had stopped. She turned to Flip. The wizard had spread his limbs in his sleep, one arm and the opposite leg jutting out from his blanket.

Finally Oris turned to Silvin. The woman—*the Mystic,* Oris reminded herself—was regarding her, and there was a strange expression in her eyes. Oris had seen it before, when she had insisted on rescuing Cara against Silvin and Flip's advice. It gave Oris a strange, disgruntled feeling.

"What?" she said, voice still thick with sleep.

"I am glad you are a good person," said Silvin.

Oris frowned. "What?" she said again, now more confused than aggressive.

"Because of my affiliations, honor would bind me to protect you no matter what you were like," said Silvin. "So it is heartening to me that you are a good person. Mayhap a better one than I am. I would hate to have to serve a raging, self-centered sow."

Oris could not suppress a snort of laughter. But her retort was acid.

"You may not have the chance," she said. "I haven't at all agreed to serve you or your Mystic kindred."

Silvin's eyes darted to Flip, but he was dead asleep. "Please, Oris," she said urgently. "Just wait until he wakes and we can speak privately. I cannot risk him overhearing."

"That's not my problem," said Oris. "In fact, I meant to tell him today." It was a lie, invented on the spot, but it felt good to say.

"Just wait," said Silvin. "As soon as he wakes and can watch Cara for us, let us go off alone, and I will tell you everything."

"Everything you *can,"* said Oris. "You have said this before."

"Everything," Silvin repeated, holding her gaze. "And when I am done, I will answer any question you have. I swear it."

Oris' breath had quickened. There were so many answers behind that promise. But then, there was Flip.

And as if prodded by her thought, Flip began to stir. He blinked hard, sitting up and brushing back his long hair with his fingers. His hand rose to rub his chest through his tunic.

"Good morn," he said. "Or a good enough one, I suppose. How is she?"

Now, thought Oris. *Now is when you should tell him. He's your best friend. Tell him.*

She sighed.

"Still alive," she said. "Silvin and I were waiting for you to wake. We both need to piss. Watch her?"

"Of course, dear," said Flip. He shrugged on his coat and came over to take his position just next to Cara, lowering a hand to stroke her forehead.

"Come on," said Oris. Silvin rose to follow her down the tower's stairs.

Outside, they were greeted by the first true dawn they had seen for days. Dark rainclouds still clustered to the south. But to the east, the sky was clear and blue, and the sun bathed their faces. They both stood there for a moment, letting it warm them within their cloaks.

Oris turned to Silvin.

"All right," she said. "I'll have my answers now."

Silvin hesitated. Her eyes swung back and forth, as if they were searching for the right place to begin.

"Here it is, then," she said at last. "You, Oris, are a wizard."

Oris blinked. "Are you mad? No I'm not."

Silvin smirked. "I understand why you would not believe it, but it is true. How much do you know about magic? Do you know the branches?"

Oris frowned. "Flip's discussed it before, but I'm not altogether familiar. There are four branches, aren't there? Firemagic—like Flip—weremagic, like the beast we defeated. And then there's alchemy and mindmagic."

"That is what everyone is taught," said Silvin, "from commoner's children to students at the Academy for wizards. But what is hidden from all of them is that there are two hidden branches. They are life magic and death magic. Though in halls of learning, they are called ceremancy and necromancy."

"Life and death? Those aren't types of magic," said Oris slowly. "They are . . . forces. You might as well say there's sky magic, or seasons magic."

Silvin shrugged. "Who knows but that there might be?"

"No, no, no," said Oris, shaking her head. "How could there be *hidden* branches? How could you hide them? If there were wizards out there commanding life and death, nothing could stop that rumor from spreading."

"That is because there are not life and death *wizards,* strictly speaking," said Silvin. "There is only one of each at a time, reborn every once in a great while. When they come, it signals a time of turmoil. They are born, they grow in power, and then they clash. The conflict is terrible. And the victor then determines humanity's course for the future, until whenever they are both reborn again. Enfil and his lackeys who tried to kill you—that was the first skirmish in the war."

Oris shook her head. "No. This is ridiculous. I cannot be . . . that person. That *kind* of person."

Silvin looked hard at her. "Word has spread of what you did at Wellmont. That is how I learned of you. And it is how the enemy learned of you, too."

"But no one was there," insisted Oris. "No one saw what happened except Flip and me, and we don't even understand it!"

"Someone saw it," said Silvin. "They did not know *what* they saw, but word spread, and some of us recognized the signs."

Oris began to pull on her braid, running her fingers around its turns, but then she stopped herself. That was an old habit from her childhood, and one she had worked hard to rid herself of. "So you . . . you want to protect me because . . . I'm some—"

"The Lifemage," finished Silvin. "Or the Ceremancer, if you wish to use academic language."

"I don't," said Oris shortly. "So I am the Lifemage, and I am supposed to battle the . . . the Deathmage?"

"The Necromancer, yes."

"And who is he?"

"We do not know," said Silvin. "I did not even know he was a man until Enfil called him 'Father.' My master had suspected that the two of you had been reborn, but we could find no clear trace of either of you before Wellmont."

"And who's your master?" said Oris. "You've mentioned him often enough."

"He is a man named Jordel of the family Adair," said Silvin. "And for as long as I have known him, he has worked tirelessly to prepare for the war we know is coming. He is a good man, Oris. You will be lucky to meet him, I assure you."

Oris folded her arms. "I'll judge that when it happens. But fine, then. Now that you've found me, what about the Necromancer?"

"Finding him shall be its own great challenge," said Silvin. "But it is urgent that we do. We hoped the enemy would have no more knowledge of his nature than you. But it is clear that he knows his destiny and has been gathering his strength, likely for some time. Enfil and his assassins were proof of that."

"And you—the Mystics—you're afraid the Necromancer means ill for Underrealm?" said Oris.

"Of course he does," said Silvin, as though it should have been obvious. "He is the servant of death, and we are pledged to his destruction. You likely think of the Mystics as servants of the High King's law. That is true, in the between times, while we wait for your resurrection. But royal service is not our only bond. When we take our badges, we pledge to serve life itself. We claim it as our highest duty. Most among our order know nothing of the great conflict, and they take the promise as a platitude. But some know. The truth is that the Mystics are the personal army of the Ceremancer, bound to obey them in their war against the Necromancer. But the Necromancer has their own warriors, called the Shades. The last Ceremancer thought the Shades were destroyed. But they have only been in hiding. Now the new Necromancer has been rallying them to his cause, growing their strength under our very noses. You need the Mystics now in order to survive, just as we need you to fulfill our purpose."

Oris shook her head. "You're making my head hurt. I told you: I don't care about your purpose, or anyone's."

"And I told *you,* Oris, that that no longer matters." Silvin's tone was not unkind, but it was implacably firm. "Your simple life is gone from you now. The Necromancer and his Shades will pursue you, and when they find you they will kill you. But the Mystics will protect you. We are the only ones who can. The enemy cannot be allowed to win. If he does, it will be the end of everything. Everyone."

Oris snorted bitterly. "You paint a pretty picture."

"I may have hidden truths from you, but I have not lied to you since we met," said Silvin. "And I am not lying to you now. We can keep you safe, and we can help you discover who you really are. I do not know who your parents are, but my order can find out. We have every resource, connections you cannot imagine. And we are honor-bound to use them in your service."

Something smoldered inside of Oris, and she was ashamed to admit, even to herself, that it was a yearning. Who could wish not to believe it, at least in part? Who would not desire the answers Silvin promised? But the Mystics had a fearsome reputation, and not only among wrongdoers and criminals in Underrealm.

"Let's say I believe you," she grated. "What would I do?"

"Nothing more than you have already agreed to," said Silvin. "Come to Dracmund. Meet my master. Let him explain everything I cannot, and let him convince Flip. He is very skilled at it, I assure you. And in the meantime, do not tell Flip who I am, to keep him from bolting."

"Why do you care if he leaves?" said Oris. "You make it sound as if you only need me."

"My mission only concerns you, it is true," said Silvin. "But if it came to it, and Flip left, I think you would go with him. And more than that, I think you need him. He is a powerful ally, and not just for his spells. You could do worse than to enter the coming war with Philip of the family Drayden at your right hand."

There was some truth to that. She wanted to throw all this at Flip's feet and beg him for help. He was the merchant's son, the one used to working with and walking beside power. She was an orphan and a sellsword, with no higher aspiration than a purse full of coin and comfort behind a blue door. Yet something within her said that Silvin was right. If Flip learned she was a Mystic, he would leave, and he would convince Oris to come with him.

And then they would die. And all without Oris ever knowing who her parents were, and how she had ended up in that orphanage. Not to mention the greater destiny with which Silvin tantalized her.

"I'll keep quiet for now," she said at last. "But we can't leave Flip entirely in the dark. We must tell him about these . . . hidden branches, or what have you."

Silvin's eyes flashed. "That may not be wise."

"It's the best you'll get from me," said Oris. "I'd be a fool to trust you, and so I need to hear from him. Let me take the lead in the conversation. I know how to steer him. But before we return, give me a moment. I wasn't lying when I said I needed a piss."

Flip accepted the story much more easily than Oris thought he would, and certainly easier than Oris herself had. He asked a few pointed questions, which Oris referred to Silvin when she did not know the answer. Of course, Oris said nothing about Silvin being a Mystic. And in the end, Flip nodded slowly, his gaze distant.

"It makes sense," he said.

"You think this makes *sense?"* said Oris. "Flip, if I were a wizard, don't you think we would have noticed by now?"

"Oris, we *did* notice," said Flip. His hand rose to his chest. "We were both at Wellmont."

Silvin's gaze went sharply to Oris. Oris ignored her.

"I mean before that," said Oris. "Wouldn't you have . . . I don't know, sensed the magic in me, or some such thing?"

"Why would I have?" said Flip. "Wizards rarely show signs of magic unless they are trained."

Oris folded her arms, trying not to appear as if she was pouting. "Well, I am glad the two of you have this so thoroughly worked out."

Flip smiled, and then he turned to Silvin. "Why did you not tell us from the beginning?"

Silvin frowned. "I did not want to tell you *now,"* she said. "But Oris has been pestering me since the day we met. This morning, before you woke, she told me she would not walk another step by my side unless I gave her more. My master will likely be furious with me."

Flip grinned at Oris. "That's uncommon wit, coming from you, dear." But then he grew solemn again. "Why have I heard nothing before of these clashes between Ceremancer and Necromancer? I learned history at the Academy, and I think I should've heard of something like these great wars you mention."

Silvin nodded. "This is one of the . . . stranger aspects of the situation. In the last resurrection cycle, the Lifemage won. But the war was so devastating that they wished to prevent it from ever happening again. They exterminated every trace of the Necromancer's forces they could find across the nine kingdoms, but then they went further. They wiped all mention of the Necromancer from history, from every tome in Underrealm. Only some of their chosen followers were given the knowledge, to pass it down through the generations for when they returned. The High Kings have always known, and they pass the knowledge from one to the next. Some other great figures, like my master, learn it as well, even if by accident. The Lifemage's hope was that in this way, the Necromancer would have no support when next they rose, and be easily defeated."

Flip's face twisted. "That's the most foolish thing I've ever heard."

"Flip," said Oris. "I believe her."

"Oh, I don't mean to cast doubt on her story," said Flip. "I mean to say that the Lifemage's decision was impossibly stupid. For one thing, we can see it didn't work. The Necromancer is here, and he's got followers aplenty—some of them tried to kill us just a few days ago. But more importantly, if no one knows he's coming, how are they supposed to prepare for his return?"

To Oris' great surprise, Silvin nodded. "In fact, I agree completely. I would have told everyone I possibly could. Even now, I want to tell everyone in the nine kingdoms, and I would, if my master had not forbidden it."

"Wise of you, and foolish of him," said Flip. "But so be it. This explains why some nobleman would wish to keep Oris alive. And it's not the most outlandish tale I've ever heard."

"What tale could you *possibly* have heard that's more outlandish?" said Oris.

Flip ignored that, fixing Silvin with a piercing look. Oris grew nervous. "Tell me honestly. Do you serve the High King?"

Silvin grew suddenly tense. The question was dangerously close to the truth. But she met his gaze. "I do, after a fashion. But not directly. It was not she who sent me after you, if that is what you were asking."

Flip waved a hand. "Very well. Say no more, if it'll break your bonds of honor. So long as a purse of gold still awaits us at the end of the road, I see no reason to turn aside. Do you, Oris?"

"I am . . . less certain," said Oris, thinking hard. "This is more than we bargained for. I was perfectly fine with our lives the way they were."

Flip shrugged and grinned. "The world does not exist to grant our wishes, dearest one."

Oris scowled and turned away from them both.

• ○ • ○ •

Of course, because of Cara, they could not go traipsing off at once. The lover slept all through their second day in the tower. Worse, that night she began to have nightmares, twitching and crying out in her sleep. She woke up once, wild-eyed and thrashing with madness from the pain of her injuries. Oris and Silvin had to work together to hold her down and keep her from harming herself. It was a terrible sight to witness.

To their great relief, however, Cara awoke in truth the next day just before noon. Her voice rasped out in the chill air, startling all of them.

"Where," she gasped.

"Cara?" said Oris. She scrambled over to the lover, taking her hand. "I'm here."

"Where?" groaned Cara again. "Are we?"

"Safe," said Oris. "The monster who took you is slain."

Cara's eyes closed, and tears began to leak down her cheeks.

They moved her gently to the bottom of the tower where they could build a fire. Cara barely spoke at all before falling back to sleep. But that afternoon, some hours before sundown, she woke again, and the strength in her voice was remarkable. She called out, and Oris came at once.

"Water?" said Cara.

"Of course," said Oris. She lifted the skin to Cara's lips. Cara drank too greedily, and she had to cough up some of it. "I am sorry," said Oris, brushing it off her cheeks.

"No," said Cara. "Lovely. Wine?" Her smile was impish, if weak.

"I think that would be unwise," said Oris, restraining a grin.

Cara gave a whispery little laugh. Her hand rose to clutch Oris'. "Thank you," she said.

"You're doing wonderfully well," said Flip with a smile. "Soon we'll be on the road again, the lot of us."

Cara smiled at him, but then she fixed Oris with a solemn look. "Ombi?"

Oris' heart dropped into her boots. She shook her head.

Cara closed her eyes in grief. But a moment later, she opened them and looked from Flip to Silvin. "I want Oris. Alone."

Flip and Silvin looked at each other with concern. Oris shook her head. "You shouldn't use your strength trying to speak," she insisted.

"I am fine," said Cara. And sky bless her, Oris found she believed it. Flip and Silvin exchanged another glance, and then they drew back and out of the tower.

"What is it?" said Oris, once they were alone.

Cara fixed her with a curiously knowing expression. "You all talked much," she said. "I heard . . . most of it."

Oris frowned. "You did?" she said. "We thought you were asleep."

"It came like a dream," said Cara. "But I woke and knew it was real." She gave a cough, followed by a wince. But then she focused again. "This . . . life magic. Did you use it? On me?"

Oris went stone still. Her thoughts returned to Flip, and to Wellmont.

"No," she said at last. "No, I don't think I did."

Cara nodded slightly, though it caused another wince. "Thank you for saving me anyway. It was all a fog when you came. But I remember what you said. And what they said."

Oris swallowed hard. She cast a furtive glance back over her shoulder where Flip and Silvin had gone. "Try not to blame them for that. You were badly hurt, and they were only—"

Cara lifted a hand, and Oris fell silent. "No blame. I would not have stayed for them. I would not have tried to save them. I would have fled. And I would never have regretted it."

Her hand rose and took Oris' vest. She pulled. Oris leaned down, confused. Cara could scarcely lift her head, so she had to pull Oris all the way down until their lips met, a kiss that was sweeter than it was passionate.

"You dove into darkness. For me. I will not forget it."

Again Oris gulped, and she felt her cheeks burning. "Well. We're contracted to protect you, after all."

Cara gave her a knowing smile. But then it faded. "Would you . . . lay with me? Just to hold me? I keep thinking of . . . that thing. It wakes me. The fear is terrible. It is so hard to sleep."

"Of course I will," said Oris. "Of course."

She laid beside Cara, wrapping the smaller woman up in her thick arms. Slowly she felt the lover relax, and when she looked again, she was asleep. Oris wanted to move, but she was too afraid of disturbing Cara's rest.

And so they remained that way when Flip and Silvin finally returned to them. Oris, too, had fallen asleep by then.

It did not entirely stop Cara's nightmares. But it was better, nonetheless.

CHAPTER VIII
WANDERING ENDS

THEY REMAINED AT THE VERGE FOR SOME DAYS WHILE THEY WAITED for Cara to be fit enough to travel. In pairs they hunted to keep their food supply up, and they discovered that game in the area was good. It seemed the weremage had kept the area free of humans, but she had not hunted the nearby prey down to nothing.

On their third day at the stronghold, Flip proposed that they ransack the place for valuables. Any treasures from the stronghold's occupation seemed to have been looted long ago. But there were several other corpses like the first one they had found, and some of them bore purses full of coin.

All told, they assembled more than thirty gold weights. Flip and Oris insisted on giving the money to Cara, to which Silvin easily assented. Cara demurely refused—but only once, and when they urged her again, she took the coins.

On a day free from rain, they tended to a more somber affair: the burning of Ombi's body on a pyre.

Oris, Flip, and Silvin all cut wood for the bier. When it was done and Flip had wrapped Ombi in cloth gathered from the stronghold, Oris brought Cara outside for the lighting. They put flame to the wood, and there they waited until everything had burned down to embers. Oris tried not to stare at the others; grief was a private thing if one was not invited to join in it. But she could not miss the shaking of Cara's shoulders as she wept.

As the days went by, Cara grew stronger and became more active. The other three fretted over her, trying to convince her to rest. But Cara would not heed them. Soon she was up and puttering about their makeshift camp at the base of the tower. She cleaned the place as best she could, and she insisted on taking her turn cooking at least once a day.

When a week had passed, Cara told them she was ready to travel. In fact, she all but demanded that they leave at once. Oris and Flip worried she was not yet strong enough for the road, but Cara gave them a steely look.

"I mean to leave this place," she said. Her voice had steadily been improving, though it held a rasp that Oris doubted would ever leave it. "I wish to put it behind me and never think about it again."

In the end, they were only able to convince her to stay one more day. The next morning, she was up before the rest of them, stowing her belongings in her pack.

"You can't imagine we're going to let you carry that," said Flip indignantly.

Cara raised her brows at him. "I am not so frail as you seem to imagine. Nor has my pack ever been as heavy as yours."

Silvin gave Oris a secret smile and then spoke. "I believe Flip feels it necessary to make amends," said Silvin. "If we had been more vigilant, no evil might have befallen you. It would ease his conscience, I think, if you were to let him carry your things for you."

Cara could hardly object to that, and so Flip and Oris divided her possessions between their packs. It gave Oris a new appreciation for how crafty Silvin could be, soothing tempers and gently guiding others to behave as she wished. It was both alluring and concerning, for she could imagine Silvin turning such tricks on her.

They set out before midday. To no one's great surprise, Cara wearied before a full day's travel, and they made camp early that afternoon. But the next day, they pushed a little farther, and a little farther still the day after that. Sometimes Oris grew concerned that the pace would be too much for Cara. But whenever she glanced at the lover, she saw her mouth set in a grim line, her eyes fixed determinedly on the horizon ahead.

Thus, in three days they spied the walls of Dracmund far ahead. Cara seemed ready to collapse with relief when she saw them, but she soldiered on and even increased her pace a bit.

The city was built near the mouth of the Dragon's Tail. About a league away, they could just see the river churning as it spilled out into the Wyrmgraf Sea, the southernmost ocean that touched the lands of Underrealm. The city's walls were tall and thick and built of stone. There were no watergates, as there were in many cities farther up the river—including in Wellmont, where Flip and Oris' journey had begun. The water here was simply too wide. There was no bridge to span it. Instead, a thriving system of ferries and barges conducted trade and passengers across the wide water. From midday on, the river became utterly clogged with watercraft scuttling between and around the larger ships sailing upriver from the Wyrmgraf, or down to the sea.

Dracmund swore fealty to the king of Selvan, but its western end was firmly planted on the river's Dorsean shore. Despite this somewhat tenuous position, it suffered no Dorsean raids. A confluence of interests protected it. Dracmund was the only place to cross the Dragon's Tail river for many leagues, and powerful merchants exerted their influence to keep it safe for caravans. And while the High King Enalyn could not entirely stymie Dorsea's custom of raiding their neighboring kingdoms for glory and wealth, she could, by inference and hints, let it be known that certain places were of special interest to her, and thus spare them from such aggression. Dracmund had enjoyed this protection almost from the moment Enalyn had taken the throne years ago.

The guards at the wall hardly gave them a second glance as they passed inside. After everything they had learned in the past two weeks, Oris had a fleeting thought that the city should be drawn up against invasion. But no one here had ever heard of the Necromancer. Oris was fighting a secret war that few knew about.

She wondered how long that ignorance would last.

The first thing they did within the city was find the local Guild of Lovers to transfer Cara's contract. Dracmund was a larger city than

Wellmont had been, and its house of lovers was appropriately grand. It had the customary blue door, but this one was ornamented with gold, and gold was its sensuously curved handle. Brilliant silver sconces hung to either side, and the candles in them shone light upon a bronze plaque overhead that bore an inscription:

If troubles bring you strife and pain
Now lay them here to be reclaimed
For when our skillful work has finished
Once-troubling thoughts shall be diminished

"Pithy," said Flip, smiling up at it.

"We're here on a serious matter," said Oris.

Flip's smile died, and he sighed as he looked at Cara. Her face was stony as she stared at the blue door. "I know. Forgive me."

The patron of the house, a man named Lolin, studied Oris and Flip with deep disapproval as they recounted the tale of the Rustening Verge and the fallen weremage who had killed Ombi. But his face softened when Cara lent her testimony in support.

"I witnessed their heroism firsthand, patron," she told him. "Ombi and I were freezing nearly to death, and we urged them to fetch wood for a fire. They could have done nothing to save Ombi, but they went far beyond their vow to save me." Oris' cheeks flushed as Cara's gaze fell upon her. "I owe them my life, and I will forever remember them with kindness and love."

In the end, the patron agreed not to blame Flip and Oris for Ombi's death. But still he demanded a ransom of loss, a payment of fifty weights for the death of a lover they had sworn to protect. Again Cara objected, offering some of the coin they had given her at the Verge. But this time Silvin spoke over her.

"I will pay the ransom without hesitation," she said, silencing Cara with a look. "Ombi was of especial skill in his craft, and his life was cut short too soon. The guild is poorer for his absence, and the least I can do is compensate such loss with a meager payment of coin."

She did not carry so much money on her person, but she delivered a note of obligation to Lolin. His brows raised ever so slightly, and he looked from the note to Silvin with fresh intensity. She gave him the slightest of nods. Oris doubted that Flip had noticed the exchange, but she knew that Silvin must have given Lolin a notice to recover the payment from the Mystic order in the city.

Before they left, Cara took Oris aside for a final farewell.

"You must send a letter every once in a while," she said. "I am most intrigued to hear of your adventures."

"I promise that I will," said Oris. "As often as I remember."

"More often than that, I hope," said Cara with a smirk. "I would not be an afterthought in your saga. I will ask Silvin to remind you every so often. I suspect she has a better memory for such things than you."

Oris glanced over her shoulder to where Silvin and Flip were waiting for her by the blue door. "I don't know if I'll be by her side for too very much longer."

"Somehow I think you shall," said Cara. "In any case, I hope you will visit again while you remain in Dracmund. I promise you shall never drop a single coin in this place."

Oris smiled gently and ran a hand along Cara's arm. "I'd never presume to take for free any craft so skillful as yours."

Cara smiled and then pulled her down for a parting kiss. It was the first time since they had met that Oris felt more passion than performance on Cara's part.

"Do not forget me," said Cara. "I know that I shall never forget you."

CHAPTER IX
DRACMUND

Silvin took them to an inn called The Jagged Jay towards the southern end of the city. It was clear she had visited before. The innkeeper, a thin reed of a twixt named Ashe, greeted her by name, and they rented her a room without commenting on her companions. Oris noticed with some curiosity that Ashe did not say anything about Silvin being a Mystic. She wondered if they knew not to mention it when she was not wearing her red cloak, or if they, like Flip, were not aware of the truth.

Silvin got them a modest room with two beds in it. "We should remain wary while we are in the city," she explained, when Flip and Oris looked at her askance. "That means maintaining a watch. Only two of us will sleep at any one time."

Flip groaned. "I thought I might finally get to catch up on all the rest I missed on the road."

"You still can," said Silvin, giving him a wry look. "We will not be exploring the city or seeing the sights. We shall remain in this room as much as possible. Sleep as much as you want during the day, as long as one person is awake. That should give you ample opportunity to recover before my master reaches us."

"Is it truly wise to remain here, if we're so fearful of discovery?" said Oris. "Shouldn't we go to your master instead? Journeying to a halfway point between us would speed our meeting considerably."

"It would," said Silvin. "I have been thinking much the same thing. But I do not know precisely where my master is or where he is traveling to. And moving openly across the land in search of him would only put you in greater danger. Enfil proved that. No, I think that our best course now is to remain here and wait for word to reach him."

"Fair enough," said Flip. He threw himself down on the bed, running his hands appreciatively over the bedclothes. "So long as you're footing the bill—or your master is, I suppose—I have no complaints."

"I am glad to hear it," said Silvin with a smirk. "And now, if you will excuse me, I must go and send a letter to him, or we will wait in Dracmund a long time indeed."

It was not long before the waiting became interminably dreary to all of them. Silvin was stringent about her precautions. She did not let any of them wander the city. When they left for some necessity—at Flip's insistence, "necessity" included visits to the Guild of Lovers—they had to bundle up tight and wear masks along with their hoods. Oris, in particular, was never permitted to leave the Jay without Silvin sticking close to her side.

Their little room was uncomfortably intimate. They got themselves a deck of cards with which to play moons. When each of them stood their night watches, there was little else to do. But as Oris sat there flipping cards back and forth across the wooden planks of the floor, she found herself getting distracted often. She would sometimes realize that she had been studying Silvin's face for a while. Unlike Flip, who twitched and shifted through the night, the Mystic woman slept like the dead. Whenever Oris caught herself staring, she scowled and turned away from the beds, trying to focus on the game.

In time, she noticed them all falling into behavior that was more familiar than might be wise. They would bathe at the Jay or at the Guild of Lovers, and at first Oris was somewhat self-conscious. But Silvin cared no more for modesty than she had in the river, what felt like a lifetime ago. And as days became weeks, Oris' awkwardness melted away, until she hardly even thought of it.

Then, too, when they ate—always taking their meals in their rooms—Silvin would sometimes sit on the floor, but sometimes she would sit on the bed by Oris, as though either place was equally agreeable. Their knees might bump each other, or Silvin's hand brush Oris as she reached for her pack. Oris' breath would hitch each time. But Silvin did not seem to notice anything at all unusual. When Oris was on watch, and she had to wake Silvin, she would often pause, standing silently by the side of the bed, her hand hovering over the woman's arm. Then she would shake her head, as if casting off a dream, and wake Silvin at last, telling her gruffly that it was her turn to stand watch.

You are being a fool, she told herself savagely. And each time, as she fell asleep, she tried to ignore Silvin's lingering scent on the blanket and silence her thoughts long enough for sleep to claim her.

But that did not stop her eyes or her attention from wandering where they would, and lingering where they wished.

● ○ ● ○ ●

"I am going to go and see if any reply has come," said Silvin. It was the morning of their fifteenth day in the city. "If we are very lucky, and the letter reached my master as quickly as possible, we might already have an answer. I assume I can trust you to remain here?"

"Flip will, certainly," said Oris, her mouth twisting as she regarded the wizard. He had held the last watch overnight, and now he was collapsed facedown on one of the beds, gentle snores wheezing from his mouth. "And I don't plan to go anywhere."

"Good," said Silvin with a smile. "I shall see you again soon."

Oris' jaw clenched, and she nodded. Silvin kept her expression carefully neutral until she was out of the room, but when the door closed behind her, she winced.

I shall see you again soon? she chastised herself. *You sound like a moonstruck youth.*

She forced her mind away from Oris—something that was becoming increasingly difficult as days went by. It was almost a relief to be out of the room. Away from the warmth, the scent, the *closeness,* the sheer proximity that threatened to overwhelm her.

As if that were possible, she thought savagely. *As if you deserve it.*

And just like that, her thoughts had wandered again. This time she wrenched them back, digging her own nails into her palms to force herself to focus. She pulled her hood farther down. If the enemy had been preparing for this war, they would know of her master, Jordel. If they knew Jordel, they might know of her. She had no wish to be recognized by someone who could follow her back to Oris.

She had chosen the Jagged Jay for a few reasons. First, Ashe was a good sort and more trustworthy than most when it came to keeping secrets about their visitors. But mayhap more importantly, the Jagged Jay was in the city's southwestern quarter, as far as possible from the city's Mystic stronghold. The last thing she needed was to have someone in her order accidentally reveal her to Flip. As a consequence, it took her almost an hour to reach the stronghold, the journey made even longer by the fact that she avoided busy streets wherever possible and stuck to secluded alleys and the passages between buildings. At least it was early enough that the river was not too busy. She secured herself a small ferry—little more than a rowboat—and sat huddled against the railing, her arms wrapped around herself while the ferrier rowed her across.

Stillness made her thoughts wander, and it also gave her an excuse to let them.

Oris had taken the first watch last night, and Silvin had taken the second. When Oris had come to wake her, she had first sat on the bed, and that had woken Silvin. But she kept her eyes closed and controlled her breathing so that Oris would think she was still asleep. For a long while, Oris had not moved. Silvin wondered why. What was she looking at? What was she thinking of? Was it possible that she was studying Silvin in slumber, as Silvin sometimes caught herself doing to Oris when she was on watch?

Why do you torture yourself? she thought. *Even if it were true, it could never lead anywhere. You could never let it.*

With a gentle *thud,* the boat struck the dock on the eastern shore. Silvin blinked twice as her thoughts returned to the present. She set off into the streets, once more forcing herself to think only of the here and now, watching carefully for anyone who took undue notice of her. But no curious eyes shadowed her steps.

In a short while, she came upon the Mystic stronghold. It was an impressive structure, built on a sizable hillock from which one could see the entire city laid out like a blanket of lumps and lights. The keep was a good deal larger than even the mayor's manor. The redcloaks who dwelled within it were another reason Dracmund did not face any Dorsean aggression. Dorsea's King Jun was a warmonger, but he was no fool, and he had no wish to anger the Mystics by endangering any of their soldiers.

The guard at the gate was new, or at least new to Silvin. She showed her badge. The guard spoke in sign, asking Silvin to pull down her mask to get a good look at her face.

"Who are you here to see?" signed the guard.

"Elbert, the master of letters," signed Silvin.

"I shall have to send word."

"Of course."

"You may wait inside the gatehouse."

Silvin accepted the offer gratefully. Winter continued to advance, and the air had grown bitterly cold. Soon a messenger returned from the keep, and the guard waved Silvin inside.

The stronghold was a bustle of activity. Messengers ran back and forth, popping in and out of doors like bees in a hive. Soldiers drilled in the bailey, some of them obviously fresh recruits. There was no conflict now that required the Mystics to commit their own soldiers, but the order prided itself on always being ready. *Only in Watchfulness Lies Safety.* Those were the Mystics' words, and Jordel repeated them to Silvin often.

But he had also taught her that there was a difference between being ready to fight and being clever enough to stave a fight off before it began. He believed that the latter was the better choice, and he had instilled the same belief in Silvin—hence their mission to find the Lifemage and protect her, even when most in their order knew little about it and cared less.

Silvin remembered the way to Elbert's office from when she had been here on the first day, and she wasted no time in reaching him. Her brisk knock was answered by his deep voice rumbling, "Come!" from inside. She entered and closed the door behind her before casting back her hood and pulling down her mask.

"Captain," she said, saluting with her hand over her heart.

"Sister Silvin," said Elbert. He was a portly man, an unusual trait among the redcloaks. But then, most of them did not spend their days at a desk, managing and speeding the flow of information from all nine kingdoms. The top of his head was bald, but his fringe was all lustrous black curls, which he kept neatly trimmed along with his impressive beard. "I hardly thought it would take so long to see you again. I hope you have remained safe here in the city?"

"I have."

His eyes narrowed. "I hope also that you have stayed out of trouble."

A slight smirk twisted her lips on instinct. But then she thought of Oris, and the smirk vanished. "Of course."

"Hmph," he said, his eyes returning to the papers on his desk. He lifted one, and Silvin's heart leaped, thinking it was what she sought. But he only turned it over and began to scrawl on the back. "Well, of what service may I be?"

"I came to see if any word had arrived for me."

He looked up at her from under his brows, his beard twisting as he frowned. "Word from whom?"

Her temper flared along with her nostrils, and she fought to quell her anger. *Control,* she thought. *Two deep breaths. One. Two.* "From Captain Jordel of the family Adair."

Elbert dropped his quill and clasped his hands together on the desk. "And why in the dark below would you think I would have word from him?"

"Because," said Silvin, trying hard not to sound condescending, "I sent a message *for* him a week and a half ago. Through you."

The captain tilted his head slightly, his eyes growing hard. "Let us be clear in our terms, ser. You did not send word to Jordel of the family Adair. You sent letters to our kindred in Wellmont, in Redbrook, in Cabrus, and in Garsec. And that is because, as I told you last time, Jordel has been banished from the Mystic order, and he is currently a fugitive from the King's justice."

Silvin's pulse was racing now. *Control yourself,* she thought. *He would be disgusted to see you so close to losing your head.*

"And I told you then, *captain—*" She forced herself to stop and swallow her anger. "I apologize. But as I assured you, Jordel's banishment was a mistake. It will be sorted out, and soon."

"Will it really?" said Elbert, his bushy brows shooting high. "I fail to see how. New word has reached us since last you were here. Our brethren tried to arrest Jordel north of Wellmont. He killed two Mystics with his own blade."

For a moment, all Silvin could do was stare at him. Her throat was dry, and her limbs did not seem to want to answer her will. *North of Wellmont? When? I was so close . . . could I have joined him?*

But no. She had to think of Oris now, not her regrets.

"He . . . the captain would have had good reason," she said at last. "He must have."

"Careful," growled Elbert. "That sort of talk draws dangerously close to treason. I had heard good things about Jordel, and I understand the loyalty of a knight for her captain. But with those two added to the tally, he is now responsible for the deaths of seven of our own. If you are wise, you will return to wherever you were stationed before you came here and seek new orders from whoever is next in your chain of command."

"That is Chancellor Kal, and I am still acting on his orders," said Silvin, lifting her chin slightly. "I gave you his writ last time. But your concern is noted, and I suppose I ought to be grateful for it."

"And yet you still do not wish to send a letter to the chancellor?" said Elbert.

"That is correct."

"You might understand why that would confuse me."

"I suppose I must understand it," snapped Silvin, "for in your case, I am sure confusion is easily accomplished."

She whirled on her heel and stormed out of the room, leaving the door open behind her and ignoring Elbert's angry cry. Several Mystics gave her curious looks as she stalked through their midst and back out into the city streets, but she refused to meet their eyes.

Jordel will sort it out, she thought. *He will. I only have to wait.*

But such was her agitation that she forgot to raise her hood or don her mask. Were she less distracted by thoughts of her master, she might have noticed a constable who suddenly seemed to take great interest in her, and who began to tail her through the city. He followed her all the way back to the southwest quarter and watched as she stepped within the Jagged Jay.

• ○ • ○ •

When Silvin left the Jay, Oris sat on her bed and watched Flip snore. Her fingers kept playing with the amulet, no matter how she tried to stop them. After Silvin had been gone a while, Oris stretched her leg across the space between the beds and kicked Flip gently.

"Wake up," she said.

"Whuzz," he complained. His eyes opened slowly, and he blinked. "What do you want?"

"To talk," said Oris. "It's rare we get a chance to speak alone anymore."

Flip smacked his lips as he sat up and ran his fingers through his hair. "You exaggerate," he said. "Silvin is asleep whenever we trade watches. You could talk to me then, rather than waking me up now."

"That's hardly the right time or place for secrets. The way she sleeps, she could be faking it and we'd never be able to tell."

Flip frowned at her. "What secrets do you have to discuss?"

Oris sighed, leaning forwards and clasping her fingers under her chin. "Nothing nefarious. It's not some hidden knowledge I wish to keep from her. But . . . but I want to talk about all this without her leaning over my shoulder."

"Talk away," said Flip. "But I doubt I have any answers to ease your mind, so you might just as well have talked to me while I was asleep."

"Behold the jester," said Oris, glaring at him. "How easily the jokes come to one who's not at the center of all this."

"Where else would jokes come from? There's a reason kings keep jesters instead of trying to entertain themselves." Flip leaned back on the bed and put his hands behind his head. "You need me to stop your mouth from going too sour, or you'll soon be too puckered to eat."

Oris sighed and shook her head. "I don't know about any of this, Flip," she said. "Something about it is off. We've been here too long. When Silvin first met us, she acted like her mission was more urgent than anything. Now we just . . . hang about. I'm half afraid that I've forgotten how to use my sword."

"I imagine you'll remember quickly when someone's trying to take your head off," Flip said mildly.

"But why aren't we doing anything?" said Oris. "What if this is all some . . . some trick, or some scheme? To trap us? What if nothing Silvin said was true?"

Flip's hand rose to absently rub his chest through his golden tunic. "Silvin might be lying about some of it," he said quietly. "But it's not all a trick, Oris. We know that because of Wellmont."

That silenced her for a moment. Oris watched dust motes play in the shaft of light coming through the curtains over the window.

"I always wanted to know more about myself," Oris said, nearly whispering. "I didn't think the answer would be that I was meant to save the world."

Flip spread his hands in a helpless gesture. "It's as I told you, dear. You can't change what is, nor how everyone else feels about it, nor how they react to it. You can only decide what *you'll* do. And if I were you, I'd sail upon that wind for all it's worth."

Oris frowned. "What do you mean?"

Flip looked at her, smiling slightly. "What do you mean, what do I mean? Oris, according to some very powerful and very wealthy people, you've become the most important person in the world. You could hardly ask for a better position of strength. You can have status, money—just about anything you want."

"I don't want any of those things," said Oris.

"Then give them to me."

Oris scowled. "I only want answers. And who are you to give me such advice? Your family could give you all those things, yet you spurn them."

Flip's light mood evaporated. "I've told you of my family. It wouldn't be worth the price they'd extract from me." His frown eased slightly. "But you don't face the same burden. You're privileged by birth, like me, but without any of the dark legacy to stain you. Sky above, I wouldn't be surprised if you end up meeting the High King."

Oris shook her head like she was warding off a fly. She stood from the bed. "I'm going to get some food and the strongest drink they've got."

"Your bodyguard will be cross with you for leaving the room unattended," said Flip in a sing-song voice.

"She can tell me that herself," said Oris gruffly.

She remained in the common room for some time. She chose a table in the back corner of the room, out of sight of the front door, and she pulled her hood up despite the heat of the bright hearth. Ashe brought her some food and a bottle of strong mead they said they had been saving for the right customer. Oris made her way happily through it.

A while later, Silvin entered and almost walked straight by. At the last moment she stopped beside the table, looking at Oris with wide eyes. Oris looked up at her from under her hood and arched a brow.

"I suppose you wish to tell me that I'm a fool for sitting out here," she said, her words slurring only slightly.

Silvin heaved a deep breath. "It is all right," she said.

"It is?" said Oris incredulously.

"Well, no," said Silvin. "We should not make a habit of it. But you cannot imagine you are the only one bored to death of that room." To Oris' surprise, she pulled up a chair and dragged the platter towards her. It still held a good portion of a roast chicken that Ashe had brought, and now Silvin tore into it.

Oris studied her in silence for a moment. "Silvin, are you all right?" she said.

"Of course," said Silvin, not meeting her gaze. "Why would I not be?"

CHAPTER X
BLADES AT THE JAGGED JAY

WHEN THE NEWS CAME, THE LORD WAS IN HIS STUDY, CONFERRING with the attendant. They were staring together at the lord's map, discussing where Oris could have gone.

"Would it not at least be wise, my lord, to send some agents into the lands beside the river to seek them out?" said the attendant. "They may have tried to fade into the wood, rather than making for a settlement."

"They may have," said the lord. "But we do not have enough forces to search all the wilderness. Besides, they can do nothing of value there. Only when this Mystic woman tries to unite the Lifemage with the rest of the redcloaks will she—"

Suddenly he stopped, looking off in another direction as though distracted. The attendant studied him closely. Several long moments of silence passed.

When the lord turned back to the attendant, he was wearing a small smile. "Dracmund. She is in Dracmund. One of our agents there recognized the Mystic woman."

"Dracmund?" said the attendant. "How long ago was she seen there?"

"Two days ago," said the lord. "They are at an inn called the Jagged Jay. It seems they have been there for some time. It may be imagined they will remain there for some time longer, but we cannot be certain. We must act quickly."

"Of course, lord" said the attendant. "Which of our agents is nearest the place?" But almost before he had finished speaking, his expression soured.

The lord chuckled. "Yes, my son. Of my favored children, Barrick is closest to the city."

"I suppose you had better send him, then."

"Oh, come now," the lord chided. "He is more than capable."

"Of course he is," said the attendant, bowing his head. "You may send whoever you wish, lord. I shall now withdraw, so that you may confer with him in private."

In a blink, the attendant was gone. The lord bowed his head, and his eyes began to glow.

"My son."

Barrick's head snapped up. He saw the lord as if he were standing right there in Barrick's chamber instead of many leagues away. A surge of anger rose in Barrick's breast, but he quelled it.

"Father." Barrick got out of his chair to fall to one knee and bow his head. "Why do you honor me by visiting?"

"Because, my son," said the lord. "Your great desire is at hand. I am granting the request you made of me."

Barrick's head snapped up. His body had gone rigid, and he could feel tiny quivers deep in each limb. "The Lifemage?"

"Yes," said the lord. "We have found her. She is still a good march away, but no one else is closer than you."

Barrick gave a conniving smile. "You knew, Father, did you not? Is that why you sent me here? To be ready?"

The lord's beatific expression dampened. "I did not, my son. We thought she would travel west, or north. But fortune smiled on you, it seemed."

Barrick's smile did not waver. "If you say so, Father. Tell me where she is, and she is as good as dead. I will slaughter her and send you her head to celebrate our victory."

"Patience," said the lord. "You will find her in Dracmund, at an inn called the Jagged Jay. But you must be careful, my son. Enfil was incautious, and it took his life. The Mystic woman surprised him, for she knew of my gift, and how to remove it. You must guard yourself against her. And above all, you must *not* go alone. Bring as many of your siblings as you have with you, and any others you can summon quickly."

"But Father," growled Barrick, "that will take time. We cannot let her slip away."

"It is worth it to ensure your success," said the lord. "This is my command."

Barrick hesitated only a moment. But then he bowed his head. "Very well, Father. I will not fail you."

"I believe you, my son. Make me proud."

The lord vanished. Barrick leaped to his feet and stormed out of the room to begin his preparations.

● ○ ● ○ ●

Four weeks had passed, or forty days, and Oris had grown so bored that she was ready to burn the Jagged Jay to the ground just for a bit of excitement. Silvin went into the city seeking her master's reply once every few days, leaving Oris and Flip alone. But no word came, and Silvin grew more and more agitated.

Flip still insisted on occasional visits to the blue door. Oris accompanied him on most of his trips, but she went for the change of scenery as much as for the company. Silvin would come along, shadowing Oris like a bodyguard. She never took a lover herself, but always waited in the front room until Oris was done (a reasonable time) and Flip as well (much longer).

On the first day of the fifth week, they were waiting for Flip once again. Oris had ordered a bottle of wine, which an attendant had swiftly fetched for her. Now they sat in the front room, trying not to become too distracted by the parade of beauty all around them. As was her wont, Silvin did not partake of the drink.

"Do you think your master has received your messages?" said Oris, leaning close to speak quietly.

Silvin leaned in closer as well. Oris' pulse quickened. "I cannot know," said Silvin. "But if he has not already, it is only a matter of time. The Mystics will reach him whenever he next joins their company."

"How long do you mean to wait?" said Oris. "Isn't there *anything* we could be doing? I am ready to throw myself in the river from all this inaction. Can we not turn to any of the other Mystics here in the city? Or even in another city, so long as we *know* where they are and can go to them?"

"We cannot, for two reasons," said Silvin. She stopped for a moment as a pair of young men walked over with inviting smiles. She gave them a polite shake of her head, and they bowed as they retreated. "For two reasons," she repeated. "First, as soon as Flip sees a red cloak or a badge, we will have precisely one chance to convince him to stay. I know of no one but Jordel who could make the case and manage to convince him."

"That doesn't make you sound very sure of your own argument," said Oris with a scowl.

"Say not that I doubt the importance of our mission," said Silvin, "but rather that I know the depth of Flip's hatred of my order."

"Fine," said Oris. "But you said there were two reasons. What is the other?"

Silvin glanced over her shoulder. "I am not entirely certain who among my fellows I can trust."

Oris' eyes shot wide. "What do you mean? I thought you—" She stopped herself just in time and lowered her voice. "I thought you redcloaks were supposed to be my *personal army,* or what have you." Her expression curdled.

"Yes," said Silvin. "But most of our order is ignorant of that fact. They will only be told once the lord chancellor of our order has confirmed to his satisfaction that you are who you are. Then the truth shall be revealed, but not before. And in the meantime, we must tread with all possible caution—even an excess of caution. If the enemy has been preparing for this conflict for years, or even decades, as it seems he has been, then his smartest move would be clear: to infiltrate the Mystics with as many of his agents as he can. I know no one in this city. I do not know who I can and cannot trust. But Jordel has been gathering his strength for many years, and gathering as well a list of those he can rely upon. What is more, he will know how to train you—to help you unlock the magic that makes you who you are, so that you may face the Necromancer on even footing."

Oris looked at her incredulously. "How does he know such things?"

"He seems to know most things," quipped Silvin. "It has been his life's work. He commanded me to secrecy, and because of his great wisdom, I continue to obey that command. He does not even wish to reveal you to the High King until you have come into your power."

Oris sighed and leaned back, cracking her shoulders as she stretched her arms across the soft couch she was on. "Fine," she said. "So long as he doesn't take too much longer. Once we leave, I mean never to visit Dracmund again if I can help it."

Just then, a curtain of beads drew back, and Cara stepped into the lobby. Oris rose to her feet at once, and Silvin did the same a moment later. Cara came traipsing lightly over to them, flashing bright teeth in a delighted smile. Oris' eyes ran over her body. Though the scars at her chest and neck stood out pink against her dark skin, she moved easily and without any sign of pain. A wonderful bodice wrapped around her neck and covered most of the scarring, wrapping down her front and around her waist, sheer enough to tantalize. Below it she wore a sarong tied loosely at the side of her waist, the slit revealing the length of her supple leg. Her feet had only thin, dainty sandals, easily discarded.

"You are back," she said.

"And you look sky-kissed," said Oris.

Cara gave a throaty laugh and stood on tiptoe to cover Oris' lips with her own. "Then now we both are. What are the two of you doing out here in the front room?"

"I'll give you three guesses, and the first two don't count," said Oris.

"Waiting for dear Flip?" said Cara. "You know he hardly avails himself of his lovers' services while he is here. Mostly he lounges about drinking and chatting with them for hours."

"It is good to know I am paying so highly for such a thing," said Silvin wryly. "I shall have to have a talk with him."

Cara laughed again. Then she placed a hand on Oris' arm. "If you really are just sitting here waiting for him, I could think of better ways to spend your time."

A grin crept along Oris' lips before she could stop it. "Are you not still healing?"

Cara ran her fingers lightly to Oris' elbow and back up again. "The healers call me tender, but I think I am stronger than they guess. May-hap you could help me prove it."

Oris stuck her tongue in her cheek. But then she grew thoughtful. She looked to Silvin. "I suppose you would rather I stay?"

Silvin was silent a moment, and then she shrugged. "Why would I? You know Flip. We will be here a while. And I do not think you are in any danger behind the blue door."

"Then I shall take her up on her offer."

Silvin gave a smile, but Oris thought there was a bitter undercurrent to it. "Fine. But when Flip is done, we are leaving, and I will drag you back out here if I must."

Oris returned before too long. A considerable amount of time later, Flip joined them, and they set out into the city once more. As she usually did, Silvin insisted they pull up their hoods and mask themselves.

"Must we?" complained Flip. "It draws more stares than if we simply walk openly."

"More folk might notice us," said Silvin. "But if we are masked, even if an observer thinks we look strange, still they do not know who is behind the cloth."

Flip grumbled and did as she said.

Despite her boredom with the place, Oris had to admit that Dracmund was beautiful in the golden hours of dawn and sunset. Now, with the sun sinking close to the horizon, everything had begun to take on a soft, golden glow. There was nearly always a fine mist from the river. It made dark colors darker and bright colors glisten. The air was always crisp and clean, with just a hint of salt from the Wyrmgraf not far away.

Dracmund was in some ways the most unique city she had ever visited, and she might not have despised it so if she was not always trapped at the inn. It lay on the border of Selvan and Dorsea, and it was also quite close to both Wadeland to the east and Hedgemond to the south, only a few days' travel in either direction by the King's road. Because of this, other intelligent creatures than humans could be found in the city, folk who Flip said were called the "Awakened Folk" in academic circles. She had seen some centaurs walking the streets, shorter than most humans, their lower bodies like the hindquarters of a very large goat. Some moved purposefully and were clearly familiar with the city. Others seemed to be visitors, and they looked at the buildings and wagons in astonishment—particularly any carts drawn by horses or mules.

Some Heddish merchants rode with hobs beside them on the driver's bench. The little creatures were so gnarled and rough that they looked like children's dolls stitched together from aged, stained leather. Their large eyes were squinted, bright, and glistening, and they peered suspiciously at anyone who drew near their humans' wagon or wares. Also accompanying some of the Heddans were creatures that Silvin said were called rockies. These were something like the trolls of the north, but more leathery like the hobs. Though they were uniformly hunched in their posture, still they loomed three paces tall. Oris thought that if they straightened, they might rise to four paces or higher.

Even more than the pleasures of the lovers, these walks through the city were the main reason she always came with Flip. She longed to be on the road again, wandering and walking and *seeing*, not spending week after week cooped up in a cramped bedroom. Silvin was more than generous with her coin, but that only made Oris feel like a prisoner in a golden cell.

"Silvin, I have been thinking," she said. "We must be able to go *somewhere* that we can be reasonably certain is closer to your master. Do you not even know a general direction?"

"But Dracmund is so welcoming," said Flip. His mask obscured his frown, but Oris could hear it in his voice. "Why would you wish to abandon its hospitality?"

"I want more freedom than the walls of the Jay," said Oris.

"That freedom would bring danger with it," said Silvin. "The enemy will not send only a few fighters after us next time, and in the wilderness they will be harder to avoid."

"It will be no easier to survive them here," said Oris. "Imagine if they all burst in the door of our room. We won't be able to cut our way out."

"Then I'll simply throw myself through the window," said Flip. "Oh, don't scowl at me so, Oris. Of course I'd pull you out with me. Silvin can stay behind for a desperate last stand, giving us time to escape."

Oris and Silvin had to laugh at that. And as they laughed, they turned to look at each other, and gradually they both fell silent. They were walking close, close enough that sometimes their arms brushed each other as they swung back and forth. Each time Oris felt the thrill of it even through the cloth of her cloak and Silvin's sleeve. Oris found herself wondering at the bitterness she had seen in Silvin earlier. There was no sign of it now, only Silvin's shining eyes above the mask, glowing as if with an inner light, like Flip when he cast his spells.

And then Oris realized that Silvin's eyes *were* glowing. Or rather, they were reflecting a glow from Oris' chest. Her amulet was alight.

"Dark below!" cursed Oris, as the crystal grew burning hot. She lifted it away from her on the leather thong.

"Oris?" cried Silvin in alarm. "What is that?"

Flip was staring at her wide-eyed. "Oris . . ." he said. "Does that mean—"

Oris scarcely heard them. A feeling overwhelmed her, an utter emptiness, a void deep within her that gave her vertigo.

She closed her eyes and pressed the heels of her hands into them, trying to dispel the sensation. But it would not go away. She opened her eyes and looked to Silvin.

"Silvin," she said. "My amulet had never done this before in my life—never, until that day in the Breezeboughs when Enfil and his lackeys found me."

Silvin's eyes widened. Then she seized Oris' arm and hauled her into a run. "Get to the Jay," she said. "We get our packs and we leave, at once. Damn me twice for not getting us horses!"

Luckily they were only a few streets away now. They sprinted the whole way there, Flip lagging slightly behind. They burst in through the front door and ran for their room, ignoring Ashe's startled cry.

"West gate?" gasped Flip between heavy breaths as he collected his belongings into his pack.

"I do not know," said Silvin. "They could be watching it."

"They may be watching any of the gates!" said Flip.

"Silvin," said Oris. "If you had to guess where your master was, where would it be? That's where we should go."

Silvin nodded slowly, her eyes wide but not looking at Oris. "Yes. Yes, I think you are right. North, then. That means we shall have to cross the river."

"It took a while for Enfil to reach us in the Breezeboughs," said Oris. "We may have time."

But that hope died the moment they burst back out the front door of the Jagged Jay.

There on the street before them were arrayed a squadron of foes. They wore plain clothing, but just as last time, Oris spotted flashes of blue and light grey among them. There were at least a dozen of them. Slowly they circled to surround the door of the Jay.

At their head was a man who dwarfed everyone else there, wrapped so thick with muscle and armored so heavily that he was like a walking tree shrouded in iron. He was young, Oris was surprised to see. She would have guessed he had not yet reached his twentieth year. But his eyes were filled with the malice and scorn of a much older man. In his fist was a blade that would have been a greatsword in Flip's hands, but which he wielded in one. On his arm was a tower shield that was nearly as tall as Silvin. He wore a half-helm that left his face exposed, and Oris saw a small skirt of chain on the back of it, protecting his neck.

A tattoo, she realized. *Like Enfil.*

The yawning pit in her stomach seemed to swell in size and then deepen.

"There she is!" cried the leader. "Kill her companions. The Lifemage is mine!"

"Oris, go!" cried Silvin, leaping in front of her and Flip.

The leader turned his vicious sneer on Silvin. "Your sacrifice will mean nothing when I—"

Oris threw her dagger. It plunged into the man's neck up to the hilt. His eyes widened. He choked, blood pouring from his lips. With a great crash, he sank to his knees.

"Commander Barrick!" cried one of the Shades.

Barrick, thought Oris. *At least we have a name.*

But then . . . then Oris *sensed* something. A wretched and evil glow seemed to swell around the man. It was centered on his neck. Barrick reached up to drag Oris' dagger from his throat. Immediately the flesh there began to stitch itself together.

The other Shades had stood staring in horror when Oris' dagger struck their leader. Now Flip took advantage of their distraction to loose a bolt of flame straight for Barrick's face. But the fire wisped to nothing a handsbreadth away from him.

"Dark take it," said Flip. "Mayhap the rest of you—"

A bolt of lightning shot from him, arcing for the other Shades.

But one of them raised her hands. She was a wide woman of middle height, her hair long but shorn along the sides. Her eyes glowed, and Flip's bolt fizzled and died in midair. The woman swung her hands in a spell of her own. Oris saw nothing, but Flip folded his hands, and the light died in the woman's eyes.

"A mindmage," said Flip, gritting his teeth as his magic battled with hers.

"We have to run," said Oris.

"You go," said Silvin. "I will do what I can to hold them off."

Oris gave an exasperated snort. "Dark take you for a fool," she said out of the side of her mouth. "You can't sacrifice yourself. We need you. We don't know where to go or even who your master is. If you die, we won't even be a day behind you."

"You shall be fine," said Silvin. "You can—"

Oris seized Silvin's arm and yanked her towards one end of the half-circle of enemies. The Shade who stood there was not expecting the charge, and he fumbled with his sword as Oris rushed him, screaming at the top of her lungs. Her sword leaped up to slice his throat open, and he fell to the ground gushing blood.

They fled between the members of the rapidly-dispersing crowd that was now trying to flee the fighting. Oris was grateful that Silvin did not try to remain, but ran along with the two of them.

Flip kept having to spin around and slap down the spells of the pursuing wizard. "She's not as strong as me, but she doesn't need to be," he said as he ran by Oris' side. "She just needs to distract me so one of her friends can gut me again."

Silvin looked at him sharply. "Again?"

Flip glared at her. "I mean gut me. Dark take you, woman, I'm fighting for our lives."

Risking a glance over her shoulder, Oris saw that Barrick had recovered. The other Shades had a head start on him, but he was terrifyingly fast, and he was beginning to pass the stragglers at the back of the group.

They reached the river. For one moment Oris hesitated. But Silvin turned a hard right and kept running along the docks. Flip and Oris followed her. The water was clogged with ships, all muddling about and trying not to crash into each other.

"We have to get across!" cried Silvin.

"We have no time to hire a ferry," said Flip.

"Stall them or lose them!" said Oris.

"How do you propose I—" said Flip.

"That will do!" cried Silvin.

Silvin stopped just next to a small herd of centaurs. Six of the creatures were wandering along the dock and looking avidly at all the sights.

Silvin drew her blades. For a horrible moment, Oris thought she would attack the creatures. Instead she merely clanged the steel together and gave a great cry. Flip took his cue from her and sent a small flame bolt to explode a pace behind them.

The centaurs reared, screaming. When they came down, they galloped away down the dock. They careened headlong into the Shades, who either threw themselves out of the way or were swiftly bowled over. A few of them leaped or were knocked into the river, where they vanished beneath the water with panicked cries.

Flip and Silvin did not stay to observe their handiwork, but merely kept running.

"Not nearly enough of them," said Flip.

"At least it gives us a moment to think," said Silvin.

"A moment is all you have," said Oris. She had looked behind them to see Barrick had now outpaced all his fellows, and he was quickly closing the gap between them.

Flip was wheezing hard now. Oris was worried his pace might begin to flag. "We may have to go west," he gasped. "A ferry will be our doom."

"West is useless," growled Silvin. "But you may be right. The river is so packed we would be easy targets."

Flip skidded to a stop on the dock. Oris and Silvin did the same a moment later, looking at him like he had gone mad. Mayhap they were right, for Flip wore a terrifying grin.

"The river *is* packed," he said, laughing.

Oris' eyes widened. "You mad fool."

"What in the *dark* are you two—*oof!*"

Silvin's cry cut off as Oris scooped her up around the waist and leaped off the dock beside Flip. They landed on the deck of a ferry tied to a piling. On the other side of the craft, the captain gave a shout as the deck suddenly rocked beneath her feet.

"The rope!" cried Flip, running to the bow.

"I have it!" said Oris. She drew her sword and cut the line holding the raft to the piling.

"Here now!" cried the captain. "Who in the blazes—"

"Hold on!" cried Flip, ignoring her. His eyes flared with light.

A powerful swell of water seized the ferry and propelled it out into the river. Oris and Flip gripped the gunwale.

But Oris heard heavy thuds behind them, and her heart sank as she whirled. Barrick and three of the Shades had leaped off the dock and onto the ferry's deck just before it had fired away. They swayed heavily, but they did not fall.

"Flip!" cried Oris. She ran for the bow, still holding Silvin, who struggled and cursed mightily.

"I see them," said Flip.

"Put me down!" snarled Silvin.

"In just a moment," said Oris. "There!"

Flip nodded. His tongue stuck out a bit in concentration as light swelled in his eyes again.

"Oris!" cried Silvin.

"I said I'll drop you in one moment."

"No, look!"

Oris turned. The Shades were coming closer, stumbling with the shifting ferry deck.

"Flip!"

"Now!" he said.

Oris did not hesitate. She ran to the bow and threw Silvin off it. The Mystic screamed—and then she landed on another boat. Flip had used a massive gust of wind to blow it down the river just in time. Flip and Oris leaped, crossing the narrow gap between the vessels and landing heavily on the other ferry.

The wind pushed their ferry farther downriver away from the Shades. They made a desperate final rush and a leap, Barrick at their head.

The Shades missed, and they fell screaming into the water. But Barrick's mighty jump carried him just far enough. His hand seized the gunwale, and he held grimly on as the ferry kept rocketing through the water.

Oris ran up to him, her sword held high. As she stood over him, the shadeborn looked up at her with hate in his eyes.

"You cannot run from me," he said.

"Oh, but I very much can," said Oris. And she brought her sword down on his gauntleted hand.

Barrick roared and let go, falling away from the ferry and swiftly receding in the water.

Flip stepped up beside Oris.

"Do you know what's dangerous about water?" he said.

"What's that?" said Oris.

"You don't want to be swimming in it when lightning strikes."

Flip raised his hand, and a great bolt of lightning arced into the river, bringing with it a deafening peal of thunder. The lightning jolted through the water, and Oris saw the Shades seize up and then sink beneath the surface.

But the lightning spun and turned around Barrick, leaving him untouched. He had to struggle mightily to keep his armored frame on the surface, but with his massive arms he managed it. He stared hatefully after them as they sped away down the river.

"I despise that man," declared Flip. "What good is being a wizard if some folk just don't care about my magic?"

They turned, and Flip let his wind die away. Silvin was standing there with her fists at her waist, glaring at them—especially Oris.

"I suppose you think that was terribly funny," she said.

"Don't you?" said Oris. "It's hardly my fault that you're too tiny to keep me from throwing you around like a rag doll."

Silvin was silent a moment, though Oris was gratified to see a flush creeping up her neck. At last she turned and strode away to the stern of the boat. There the ferry captain was huddled in the back corner, her tiller abandoned. She was a gangly woman and looked hard-bitten enough, but she clearly had not been prepared for the calamity that had befallen her.

"Good captain," said Silvin. "You have our deepest apologies for boarding your boat without permission. But now we need you to take us to the eastern shore as quickly as possible. I have payment enough to compensate you for the service and for the disturbance. Please be quick about it—it is a matter of the King's justice."

Oris' throat went dry at that. But beside her, Flip only smirked. "That's a nice touch," he muttered. "Nothing gets these folk to jump like the threat of angering a redback."

Suddenly he sagged and put a hand on Oris' arm, his other hand rising to cover his eyes.

"Flip?" said Oris. "Are you all right?"

"Fine," he said. "Only a little weary. I haven't had cause to unleash that much power at once since . . . well. Since Wellmont." He rubbed his chest. "Let's hope this day goes better than that one did."

Oris' mouth became a grim line.

The captain turned her tiller to guide the boat east and harangued her rowers to go as fast as they could. Silvin rejoined them as they watched the eastern docks come steadily closer.

Once they reached the shore, Silvin hurried them through the city's northeastern quarter. More than a few curious looks followed them from the docks, but soon they had faded into the crowd. Not too much longer after that, they were beyond the city walls and into open country. The King's road ran east from Dracmund, and they walked along it for a few spans before stepping off to the north to discuss their plans.

"Damn me thrice for not getting us horses," said Silvin. "If I was not terrified of any delay, I would do it now. But that would require calling in favors and collecting coin, and I do not think it will be long before that shadeborn collects his fellows and renews his pursuit."

"So we're walking," said Flip. "That's little trouble. We walked from Wellmont to Dracmund. We can walk from Dracmund to . . . where are we going?"

Silvin frowned as she thought about it. "We could go to Redbrook. That was where I meant to take you in the first place. But if I was worried about discovery here, I am doubly worried about Redbrook. It is as leaky as the boats that ply their trade there."

"The Seat," said Oris suddenly. "We have to go to the High King's Seat."

Flip and Silvin both turned on her. "The Seat?" said Flip incredulously. "If we're trying to avoid attention, that's the worst possible choice. It's right in the middle of . . . well, of everything. It's the center of Underrealm itself."

"And that's just the point," said Oris. "The Shades are enemies of the High King. Whatever they've done to gather their strength, they must be terrified of her discovering them. What place would they fear more than the Seat? Their greatest places of power, the places they've assembled the most spies and the most fighters, will all be as far from the Seat as possible. If we have to wait in one place until Silvin's master reaches us, I can't think of a safer place to stay."

Flip's mouth twisted as he pondered that. He turned to look at Silvin. She was regarding Oris silently, and in her eyes was the same strange look Oris had seen before: a curious appraisal she could not quite put her finger on.

"What?" said Oris. "Am I wrong? Besides, you said your master knows how to teach me to do . . . whatever it is I'm supposed to do. And then I'm supposed to meet the High King, as hard as that is for me to believe. Why not be close to her when the time comes?"

"Very prudent," said Silvin. "And I can think of no reason to gainsay such a plan. Very well. We shall find our safety on the Seat."

Oris nodded. Then she noticed that Flip was grinning at her. "What?" she said, frowning. "Why are you smiling like a fool?"

"My dear, precious Oris," said Flip. "Are you actually starting to believe in all this madness?"

Oris scowled. "It doesn't matter if *I* believe it. Our enemies believe it, and as long as they do, they'll keep hunting me. Us. If someone forces you to play a game, you'd better at least follow the same rules they do. So wipe that grin from your lips before I do it for you."

"Of course," said Flip, his smile growing. Oris turned from him in disgust.

From the corner of her eye, she thought she saw Silvin grinning at her as well. But Oris was trying doubly hard not to look at her at all.

CHAPTER XI
WARTIME KING

Eamin of the family Lemstad, Lord Prince of Underrealm and son of the High King, was in his chamber. It was a fine room, and large, though it felt smaller thanks to the work table he had constructed for himself. There he had many small blocks of wood and a collection of carving knives, and there were usually some scraps of wood shavings dusting the place, though he cleaned them often. Too, he had some small brushes and a collection of fine paints gathered from all corners of the nine kingdoms. When his hours were free from duties of state—which was less often than most, but more often than most would think—he would while away the hours at his little desk, carving soldiers or knights, or sometimes other figures, first whittling their shapes from the wood before painting them in bright and vibrant colors.

It was the only time and place in the palace, and indeed in all the world, where he was able to be entirely alone. At least until a knock came at his door, as it did now.

Eamin lifted his head and frowned. But his voice when he spoke was pleasant. "Come in."

The door opened. One of his guards poked her head in. Her name was Hodari, Eamin recalled, and she had only recently been assigned to him. She had a dazzling smile, and he wished she would show it more often.

"Your Excellency," said Hodari. "Idulen of the family Steth is here to see you."

"Why, send him in at once," said Eamin. He put down his carving knife and hurried to sweep away the wood shavings that littered the table. He had not quite finished when Idulen entered, and Eamin went to embrace him.

"Good day, friend," said Eamin. "I hope business has not brought you here and we can have a drink. Though I suspect that is not the case."

"Your Excellency," said Idulen, grinning. "You are astute as always. I bring a summons from the High King. She requests your presence."

"A summons?" said Eamin. "Surely she could have sent one of her own messengers."

Idulen bowed his head. "She happened to see me standing near. And it is hardly a dishonor to bring word to the Lord Prince himself."

Eamin smiled and clapped him on the shoulder. "Humility is a hard cloak to pull off, but you wear it well. Stay near, will you? I should like that drink regardless, and who knows but that I may need your help with whatever my mother wishes to speak with me about."

"Of course, Your Excellency," said Idulen, bowing his head again.

"Then excuse me." Eamin gave Idulen's shoulder a last squeeze before striding out of the room and towards his mother's throne room.

He swept through the halls, his half-cape swirling behind him, exchanging pleasant smiles and greetings with the guards and servants who scurried about seeing to the business of the palace. Not for the first time, he bemoaned the way most of them reacted to him; too deferent, too overawed. Only those who had known him most of his life treated him as a real person. But he shed such thoughts as he approached the throne room, and the guards there swung the door open before him.

"Her Majesty is in her private quarters, Your Excellency," said Olov, even as they bowed.

Eamin thanked them and strode through the empty throne room. Two attendants were cleaning it, though Eamin had never seen a speck of dirt within. They fell to one knee and bowed their heads. Eamin gave them a nod and a smile, but they did not see it, and again he wilted a little inside.

His mood darkened further the moment he saw his mother.

Enalyn sat at a small side table, where she often dictated her letters and read reports from kings and other nobles across the nine kingdoms. But there were no papers there now, and the quill lay dry. She had leaned back in her chair, legs apart, one elbow on the chair's arm and her chin burrowing into her fist. She looked . . . crushed, as though a great and invisible weight drove her towards the floor. Her eyes were distant, and she did not seem to notice as Eamin came to a stop in her doorway.

Eamin shook off a sense of foreboding. "Your Majesty?" he said tentatively.

Enalyn blinked and looked up. "Eamin," she said. She got to her feet. Almost she began to speak, but then she darted a look around at the three guards stationed in her room. "Give us a moment alone."

The guards filed out quickly and silently. Eamin kept his eyes on his mother. She looked as worried as he had ever seen her, and she seemed to be avoiding his gaze. He could think of no business that would have produced such an effect on her, no rumblings among the politicking that always plagued the palace. After the last guard left, Enalyn went to another side table and poured a glass of wine. She looked back at him and held the decanter over a second glass.

"Yes, please," said Eamin. "But Your Majesty, what is wrong?"

"Mother now, if you would," said Enalyn as she poured his wine. She went and sat at her table again. Eamin pulled a chair over from the corner and sat near her, taking his glass and then placing one of his hands over hers.

"Mother," he said. "Please, speak to me. You almost have me frightened."

Enalyn's mouth worked. "I have just received a messenger. A small party of messengers, in fact. They once traveled with Jordel of the family Adair."

Enalyn finally looked up and met his gaze.

"Jordel has died."

For a long moment, Eamin was still. Only his hand moved, sliding over to grip the arm of his chair as if for support.

"How?" he said, surprised at the quietness of his own voice.

"He died in the Greatrock Mountains, west of northern Selvan."

"But *how?*" repeated Eamin. "What was he doing there? Was it an accident?"

"No," said Enalyn. "He died in battle." She took a deep pull of her wine and then set it on the desk before leaning forwards, elbows on her knees as she rubbed her hands slowly before her eyes. "I have told you several things over the years, Eamin. Some of them were things I mayhap should not have told you, strictly speaking. Do you remember what I have said of the Ceremancer and the Necromancer?"

Eamin scoffed. "How could one forget such a thing?" But then his grim smile vanished, and he froze, staring at her.

"Yes," said Enalyn quietly. "They have been reborn. Jordel found the Necromancer's forces in the Greatrocks. He died to save others who traveled with him so that they might deliver message of this coming doom to me. So that we might prepare for war."

Eamin realized his mouth was open, and he closed it. His words seemed to come with great effort, as though each one was a boulder he had strained to push up and out of his chest. "But Your Majesty—Mother. You said they would not be reborn in your lifetime."

"I never said that," said Enalyn. "I said I *hoped* they would not be reborn in my lifetime. But that hope has failed. There is no question of it. The Necromancer has brought back his dark arts, and his favored servants now walk Underrealm again. They are those who death will not touch. The shadeborn. Worse, it seems he has amassed great strength to himself, a greater strength of soldiers and arms than should have been possible, with no one detecting it until now. The messengers spoke of a stronghold of enemies in the mountains, but the Necromancer himself was not there. That tells us he must have other points of strength throughout Underrealm, and the one we have discovered is likely not even the greatest of them."

Eamin stood, pacing back and forth. Though his mother's chamber was even grander than his own, it now felt impossibly small and closing in by the moment. "Do we know where he is? And what of the Lifemage? They must be out there. Always they are born together." He stopped and turned to her. "In fact, do we know it is a man?"

"That we know, from what his soldiers said in the Greatrocks," said Enalyn. "But as for your other questions, no. We have no idea where he might be, nor the Lifemage. In fact, I have now told you the extent of what we do know."

"Very well," said Eamin. "These are dark tidings, but now it is time for action. What can we do to prepare?"

"I must think on that and take counsel, including with the Mystics," said Enalyn. "I will require your presence at my table, of course. I hope you did not have other plans for the next few days."

"How much time do you think we can waste, sitting idly and planning?" said Eamin. "We have to make a decision, we must send all our forces to this stronghold and—"

But he stopped short as he looked back at his mother. She was not quite slumped, but she was bowed in her chair, still looking as though she was crushed by a weight he could not see. Eamin's expression softened. He went and knelt before her chair, taking one of her hands in both of his own.

"Mother," he said quietly. "It will be all right."

She was not looking at him. "All my life I have worked to maintain order and peace in the nine kingdoms. Even before I took this throne." Now her gaze slid to him. "This threatens all of it. This *destroys* all of it. There is no chance of peace, no tamping down this spark before it becomes a flame. There is every chance this war will outlast me, or even claim my life. I never wanted to be a wartime king. It will be my legacy, for good or for ill."

"That *will* not happen," said Eamin. "Not while I am alive to prevent it. We shall weather this storm and bring it swiftly to its close. Whatever skills I have that might aid in that, I pledge them to you, and all my tireless effort. Nothing else shall consume my thoughts or plans."

She gave a quiet, sad smile. "Thank you, my son." Her hands rose to cup his face. "It is for the lesser kings to decide whether you take the throne when I am gone. I shall have no say in it. But you deserve the throne. Your desire for action is no fault. It comes from your desire to make things better for our subjects, and I cherish you for that reason among many others."

Eamin gave her a worried smile. "There is no higher praise, nor anyone I would rather hear it from. Together we can withstand this storm. I swear it."

"I will endeavor to believe you."

CHAPTER XII
FLIGHT'S END

THE ORPHANAGE WAS SILENT AS ORIS STOLE DOWN THE HALL.

Though the stairs were often creaky, now they lay silent beneath her feet. She had memorized every firm spot and now stepped only upon them. The upper hall was just as quiet as the lower, but here there were lanterns on side tables. The hall was not wide enough to make hiding in the shadows worth anything, and so she merely ran down the hall as quickly as she could. Her feet, too large for her young body, yet gave only slight whispers against the wood.

Just ahead, the door to the faculty room stood ajar.

Oris gave a quick glance behind her and then to the left. No one else seemed to be up. One or another of the attendants would be walking the halls, but they must all be downstairs. That would not last long.

She took a deep breath. She had never used this door. Its hinge might be rusted and squeaky, and she whispered a brief prayer to the sky that it would not be.

Her hand fell upon the latch, and she pushed. The door swung open silently.

Oris released her breath, which seemed to hiss impossibly loud in the stillness.

There, on the other side of the room, was the cabinet. It was where the Matron stored anything she had confiscated from the children.

Oris' hand rose by instinct to clutch her amulet. But it was not there.

She scowled and stole forwards.

The cabinet was unlocked. Oris was surprised at how few items lay inside. She scanned the shelves quickly.

There it was. Crystal shaped like an arrowhead, and a leather thong tied around the grooves.

Oris scooped it up and ran her fingers over its edges. They were untouched. No harm had come to it. She loosed a long, quiet sigh.

"Oreceot."

She whirled. There in the door of the office stood Matron Fleda. The old woman was wizened and short, but not yet bent with age. Her dress was plain in cut and a lovely dark green in color, but her eyes were sharp and missed nothing, and they were trained on Oris now.

"You could not have thought I would miss its absence. Did you think this would lessen your penalty?"

"I do not care what penalty you lay upon me," said Oris. "It is mine. I will have it back."

Matron Fleda sighed and folded her arms across her chest. "Oreceot, you must be aware that it is exactly this attitude that lost you the amulet in the first place."

"There are rules," said Oris. "Your own rules. I am allowed to keep one thing. This is mine."

"Then what will make you listen?" said Fleda. "You never attend, you will not obey—"

"Your own rules," said Oris, in a voice very like a snarl. "I will not be parted from it. I will . . . I will leave if you take it again. I will run away. It is *mine*. This you shall not take from me."

For a long moment, Matron Fleda did not respond. They only stared at each other in the dim light of the lantern silhouetting her from behind. Then, at last, the old woman sighed and unfolded her arms.

"Go to bed at once," she said sharply. "I am changing your chores to chamber pots for the rest of the month of Septis, and Octis as well."

Oris could scarcely believe it. For a moment she only kept staring with wide eyes. Then she bowed her head. "Yes, Matron."

"We are not your enemies."

Oris looked back up at her in confusion. "What?"

"I and the other faculty. You always view us as foes to defeat, and nothing convinces you otherwise. You are determined to be right, regardless of what *is* right. One day I hope you learn that the world does not always bow to your will."

Again Oris ducked her head. *I know that,* she thought. *If the sky granted wishes, I would never have come here.*

But she did not say the words out loud. She had what she had come for. As Matron Fleda stepped aside, Oris stole down the hallway and crept back to bed.

● ○ ● ○ ●

Oris awoke. Her hand went to the amulet. Still there. She sighed with relief and sat up.

Flip had taken the second watch from her, and now he slept. But Silvin was awake, and Oris was only half-surprised to see the Mystic staring at her. As Oris blinked the last sleep from her eyes, Silvin gave her a nod of greeting. Above them the sky was grey with the coming dawn. A morning chill was in the air, and Oris pulled her blanket up around her shoulders.

"You were moving in your sleep," said Silvin. "Did you dream?"

"No," lied Oris. "Do you know the lands between here and the Seat?"

Silvin cocked her head. "Well enough."

"How fast can we reach it?"

"A week and a half, with luck," said Silvin, looking away to the north.

"What under the sky makes you think we'll have any luck?"

Silvin smiled without looking back. "We have evaded the enemy twice now. We will keep doing it as long as we have to. And once Jordel joins us, everything will be all right."

"Everything?" snorted Oris. "Pardon me if I doubt."

"It is quite understandable," said Silvin. She glanced to Flip and then back again. "I had a question, now that we have a moment alone. What is that amulet you wear?"

Oris sighed and lifted it out from under her shirt, twiddling it in her fingers. "I know little more than you do. I have had it my whole life. When I was a child, it was the only thing I owned all of my own. In the orphanage, there were rules. Every child was allowed to have one inviolate possession. The amulet was mine."

"But you do not remember where it came from?" said Silvin.

Oris grimaced. "I have . . . something. There was a man. I was a child, a very young one. I can see him giving me the amulet, and I remember the sound of his voice telling me to keep it always. So I have."

"Was he your father?" said Silvin.

Oris shook her head at once. "No. I know that much. There's a . . . a feeling to the memory. And besides, the man was far too old. Likely he was only a kindly old man who saw a bedraggled orphan and wished to give her a present. I doubt he knew there was anything special about it."

Silvin's mouth twisted. "I have little trust in coincidence, and especially when it comes to your life. Someone just so happened to give the Lifemage a gift that warns her of the Necromancer's servants? The chance that was an accident is so slim as to be impossible."

Oris shrugged. "Then you know more of it than I do, it seems."

Soon they woke Flip and set off north again. Their aim was to travel almost to the Great Bay. Just before they reached it, they would turn west and make for Garsec, Selvan's capital, from where they could take passage on a ship to bring them to the Seat itself.

All the first day they looked often behind them, fearful of seeing figures pursuing them across the wilderness. But there was no sign, and by the second day they grew more hopeful that they had outpaced their pursuers at last. The sky above them was grey and cloudy, a melancholy blanket thrown over the sky and dampening their mood.

"This is a good sign," said Silvin. "My heart misses the sun, but we will be harder to spot. It is a boon so long as the sky does not turn to rain."

At the end of the first day, they crossed the Carmon river, twisting and bending in upon itself on its way to join the Dragon's Tail. They kept going until they were out of sight of the Carmon's banks, and then they made their camp. But they were moving again before first light.

The land was flat and featureless at first, but then it began to break up. Hills and small ridges thrust up all around them, like rumpled skirts of the Wadish mountains far to the east. Oris and Silvin did their best to navigate around the rougher terrain, and whenever they came to a high place that let them survey the lands around, they would pause and rest for a while as they determined how best to avoid any sudden obstacles. This was the southern end of the Semilla Valley, and they knew the terrain would only get rougher the further north they went.

On the third day, the clouds parted and the sun came out. It made for a nerve-wracking day of their journey. But towards evening they breathed a sigh of relief, for they passed into a wide forest—the same great wood, in fact, that stretched far to the west and into Dorsea, the Breezeboughs where they had walked along the Dragon's Tail and Ombi had met his doom. But this was its eastern edge, and it was not so thick. That night they camped under its southern boughs, and the next night in its heart, and the next midday they emerged again into open country. It was a wide grassland, criss-crossed with small ponds and streams running between them. The twisted and spun, but all of them went northeast in the end, towards Vianya Lake far away.

"We shall not be so lucky again," said Silvin, placing a gentle hand on the trunk of the last tree. "This is the Langmoat, and it hides little. After that, it is open land between us and the Great Bay. If our pursuers should draw within a league of us, they will have little difficulty spotting us as we flee across the landscape. Now I *do* hope for rain. It will slow us, but it will hide us as well."

The world might not have been built to grant wishes, but the sky seemed to grant Silvin's now. In just a few hours, the sky grew darker, and then the sky unleashed lightning and rain upon the land. They drew their oiled cloaks tighter about themselves and pressed on through it. Each night it was a struggle to find a dry place to shelter for the night, and they lit no fires. Life became a dreary trudge, and their moods sunk to meet it. They spoke little and sang not at all.

The storm worsened as they passed out of the Langmoat and into the hilly country between the Marol river to the east and the Clamour Run to the west. But here there were some roads and local footpaths that made their way easier, though they avoided any causeway that drew too near to a settlement.

On the eighth day, Silvin started to look almost hopeful. "We are almost to the coast!" she said, shouting to be heard over the storm. "We shall have to find a place to shelter from the rain overnight, but we are almost done bedding down in the wild. Tomorrow, the coastal road should let us reach Garsec, and then the Seat."

"Thank the sky," said Flip. "Dracmund made me lazy, and I liked it. I hope your master's coin is still able to secure us some nice, soft beds."

Silvin smiled despite herself. "It shall be my pleasure."

They reached the coastal road soon after. It ran west a ways before diving into hilly country again, close to the towns of Kendal and Malo. The broken land pressed close on all sides of the road, and they could never see farther than the next bend or two. Oris got the feeling that the hills were looking down on them, looming like soldiers with weapons at their belts.

"Silvin," said Oris. "What if the Shades reached the coast before us? It would be easy for them to watch the road and prepare for our coming."

"They could hardly have traveled faster than we did," said Silvin.

"Even with that brute Barrick whipping them on?" said Flip.

Silvin frowned and did not answer.

The day was wearing on, and Oris began to think they should find a place to shelter for the night. They came upon a stone bridge that spanned a narrow cut, through which ran a river two paces below them, running north towards the Great Bay.

"We might camp under the bridge," said Oris. "It'll stave off the rain, and we aren't likely to find better shelter before it gets dark."

"Darker, you mean," said Flip, glaring at the stormy sky.

"I would rather press on," said Silvin, though Oris could see the doubt in her eyes. "The farther we go today, the earlier we reach the Seat. It could make the difference between reaching it during the day or after nightfall."

"Do you mean to keep running through the night, then?" said Oris.

"Please tell her you don't," moaned Flip. "I may want a proper bed, but just now I could die happy in my bedroll."

Silvin paused for a moment in doubt. But then her eyes shot wide with fear. "Oris," she said, pointing.

Oris looked down. Her amulet was glowing again. "Dark!" she spat, pulling it out before it grew hot to the touch.

Flip whirled, flames springing to life in his palms. Raindrops hissed and steamed as they struck it. "Bloody inconvenient. Where are they? Behind, or ahead?"

"It's not a compass," growled Oris.

"To be fair, you don't quite know what it is," said Flip.

"We cannot stand and fight," said Silvin. "We have to run."

"Either way we run could lead us straight to them," said Oris. "Do you wish to toss that coin, or do you have another plan?"

"I do," said Silvin. "This."

She seized Oris' and Flip's arms in a grip like iron manacles. With a heave and a leap, she threw all three of them off the bridge.

Sky above, she's strong. The thought whipped through Oris' mind and was gone.

Oris did not even have time to yelp in surprise before plunging into the water. Thankfully it was much warmer here than the Dragon's Tail in the south, and Oris fought her way back to the surface at once.

"Dark take you, woman!" sputtered Flip as he scrambled for the bank. "You did not think for a moment that we could have climbed down?"

"This was faster," said Silvin, stroking calmly through the water. "And we would have gone in the river regardless. Don't climb out. Swim with the current for a moment."

"Mayhap next time you could ask before heaving us off a bridge," said Oris.

"Mayhap next time you could ask before hoisting me over your shoulder," said Silvin.

"As though you didn't enjoy that," muttered Flip. "Why must I be the one to suffer the consequences of you two posturing at each other?"

Silvin ignored him. "Stop here a moment."

They reached the bank just around the next turn in the river. Looking back, Oris saw they were about a span away from the road.

Dark figures appeared upon the bridge, little more than shadowy shapes in the rain. Several figures came from the west, but then a few came from the east. One among the eastern group stood head and shoulders taller than the rest. Oris shuddered as she recognized Barrick's silhouette.

"I am glad we did not flip the coin," she said. "It looks like both sides were stamped with moons instead of heads."

"Indeed," said Silvin. "Come. We should swim on a little ways farther before coming out of the water to walk again. They may guess we have gone this way."

They followed the river for two long hours until it finally spilled into the Great Bay. The rain kept up the whole time, though it did soften before they reached the river mouth.

There they found a small fishing village. Silvin stopped them a span away from the cluster of homes, with candlelight glistening merrily from their windows.

"Stay here," she said. "I am going to get us a boat to sail a while before we sleep."

"Why not stay in the village?" said Flip. "We must be able to find a barn or some other place we can hide from this damnable rain."

"That would endanger these people," said Silvin. "Barrick and the Shades will be searching this area. If they find our trail, and it leads them here . . ."

"Fine, fine," growled Flip. "But if I catch my death of cold out here, I hope you'll feel very guilty."

"I shall be despondent," said Silvin, arching an eyebrow. "Now wait here, and stay hidden."

In half an hour she returned and led them to the shore, where they found a little boat waiting for them. Oris suspected Silvin had flashed her Mystic badge to secure it. They climbed in the boat and Oris took the oars, rowing them into open water. Then Silvin unfurled the sails and took the tiller, steering them northwest. Oris and Flip did not have much experience with sailing, but they could follow instructions, and they did as Silvin bid them to keep the boat moving.

When the last of the thin grey light was fading from the sky, they saw a spur of land protruding out from in front of them. Some spans off down its shore were the glimmering lights of a village Silvin told them was named Kendal. They landed the boat, hauled it up on the shore, and turned it on its side, providing some shelter against the droning rain.

"We should get what rest we can," said Silvin. "I shall watch tonight."

"We should trade," said Oris. "You'll be little good to us tomorrow if you're half-dead from weariness."

Silvin smirked. "This will not be my first sleepless night. You and Flip can take shelter."

"At last you speak sense," said Flip. "And I'll offer no arguments."

Soon it was done. Flip climbed in first, and Oris followed him. Their bedrolls were soaked through from the river, but they laid them out anyway to keep the sand from getting into their every nook and cranny. Oris thought that nerves might keep her awake, but she was so weary that she soon drifted off. The last thing she saw before sleep took her was Silvin sitting alone on the shore, and behind her, the Great Bay, where Oris imagined she might have been able to see the Seat if not for the rain that hid it from view.

The day dawned bright and peaceful, and curiously quiet. The rain had died in the night. But Oris groaned as she sat up, feeling a deep soreness in her arms from rowing the night before. At least she was not freezing cold—the air was decently warm, and the heat of her and Flip's bodies had made the space under the boat quite tolerable. Out on the shore, Silvin's eyes looked somewhat hollow. But there was no trace of weariness in her body as she rose and helped Oris climb out from under the boat.

"Good morn," she said. "Take heart despite your aching limbs, for our road is almost at its end. By sundown, we shall be safe on the Seat."

"Safe," snorted Oris. "Marginally safer, you mean, as I'm sure Flip will remind us when he rises."

Silvin smiled.

Silvin stopped into Kendal briefly. There she left word to be relayed to the fisher who had rented them the boat, that it could be collected from the nearby shore. The little fishing vessel was ill suited to carry them the rest of the way, and the last of their journey would be completed on foot. Oris and Flip awaited Silvin's return impatiently, and once she returned, they all set off together at a hard pace.

A well-kept stone road ran along the coast from Kendal all the way to Garsec, and it was a joy to travel on firm ground again after the slog north. It also afforded excellent vision both behind and ahead, so that they no longer journeyed under the constant fear of Barrick and the Shades appearing close by. Their steps came lively now, and their moods lightened.

Oris turned to look northwest where the Seat lay, wondering if she really could see it as she had imagined the night before. But the Great Bay was shrouded almost entirely by fog. "A misty morning," she said.

"It is not unheard of on the Bay, though it is a tad unseasonable," said Silvin. "But no matter. We shall see the Seat clearly enough when we step upon its docks. Let us get moving."

• ○ • ○ •

High King Enalyn sat upon her throne, listening to a report being read off to her by an attendant. Her mind was elsewhere, but she was reasonably certain she was being informed about tax complaints in Idris. She stared at the courtier, a tall, thin man with intense eyes and a bulging way of speaking, and let her thoughts drift away west, to a stronghold in the Greatrocks and the city of Wellmont.

A wartime king, she thought. Eamin's constant assurances were ash in her mouth. This would be her legacy, had already become her legacy. In the weeks since learning of the Shades, she had mustered every soldier she could and sent them marching west in two forces. A smaller force would investigate the Shade stronghold where Jordel had died. The larger force would proceed to Wellmont, still under siege from the city of Dorsea. Her advisors suspected the Shades played some part in fomenting the battle there.

The lack could be felt across the Seat. Even in her own throne room, there were only half as many guards as normal. A skeleton garrison guarded the city, their numbers stretched thin.

It occurred to her that she had entirely lost the thread of what the courtier was saying. She raised a hand. He stopped speaking at once and bowed his head.

"I have lost you somewhere," declared Enalyn. "I suspect it is because you are throwing so many figures at me—figures I might better understand if they were written down, rather than read off to me in a manner that keeps me from relating them to each other. Is there anything in your report you would wish to obfuscate?"

The man's cheeks flamed as he raised his head to look at her. "Of course not, Your Majesty," he said.

"Then submit to me a document of what you are trying to tell me, as well as your proposed solution," said Enalyn. "If I require your further counsel afterwards, then I shall summon you."

The man's jaw clenched, but he nodded. "Of course, Your Majesty," he said. "Shall it suffice for me to submit a copy of the last report I sent you, and to which I am still waiting to hear a reply, or would you prefer I update the figures and send a new one?"

Enalyn could not quite suppress a small smile. "You can hide a barb, I will give you that. I did not know such a report had already been submitted. I shall have my assistants locate it and—"

From outside the palace, horns began to blare. Enalyn shot to her feet. Everyone else in the room fell to one knee, but she ignored them as the horns droned on and on.

A wartime king.

• ○ • ○ •

Oris, Flip and Silvin had taken the fishing boat to avoid leaving tracks, but it was not as fast as walking. Since they had already left signs of their encampment and did not wish to take the time to hide them, Silvin decided they would travel on foot the rest of the way to the Seat. They followed the shore for a time, but eventually it began to wind enough that they decided to risk returning to the road.

Oris' hackles rose as they navigated through the hills again. But there was no sign of the enemy.

"They might still be searching to the east," said Oris.

"Or the rain could have washed away their tracks," said Silvin. "We must still be as cautious as ever."

But despite her words, they began to push west faster and faster. Soon they were half jogging, and not even Flip spoke a word of complaint at the pace. Each of them could feel eyes at their backs. There was a frightening sense that they were too exposed, as though an arrow might come flying at any moment. Could Barrick be lying in wait behind that hill? Or in that ditch?

Yet Garsec was only a few hours away. If they could just reach it, if they could just reach the Seat, everything would be all right. That was what Oris kept telling herself.

The morning wore on. The thick mist on the air slowly dissipated. The air remained cool, yet they were working up a heavy sweat, which the sun whisked pleasantly away from their skin.

"Almost there," said Silvin, panting. "Do you see that next ridge? From atop it, we can see the Seat."

"Never my favorite place," gasped Flip, "but just now it shall seem a paradise."

They began to climb. The land sloped steeply upwards, and the road cut back and forth across it. Oris' legs were burning now, but she pushed on. Nothing mattered except seeing the Seat, seeing safety.

And then an instant before she crested the ridge, in the back of her mind there came a thought.

That smell on the air . . . is that smoke?

She reached the top of the ridge and stopped. Silvin froze beside her. Flip had lagged a few paces behind, but a moment later he came stumbling and wheezing to stand beside them. He, too, froze in his tracks, and his heaving breaths slowly quieted.

The Seat lay burning before them.

CHAPTER XIII
LOSS AND FINDINGS

In more than one sense, the High King's Seat was the crown jewel of Underrealm. The city had long ago been built on the largest island in the Great Bay, a stretch of land so wide that it took most of a day to cross it the long way. At first it had only been a small settlement, a foothold and a spearhead for the armies of Roth, the first High King, as he had directed his war of conquest from the island of Southbreak, far to the northeast at the entrance of the Great Bay. It had remained a city of the kingdom of Selvan for centuries, and was soon overshadowed by Garsec, the capital, which was built on the coast nearby to the west.

Then, nearly six hundreds of years ago, the High King Andara had commanded that Underrealm's capital be moved from Southbreak, where Roth had reigned, to the island, and it was she who renamed it the High King's Seat. She declared that though the Seat was of Underrealm, it should be the property of none of the nine kingdoms, but her own personal holding, beholden to no rule but hers.

Slowly the city had grown. Where before it had covered only a quarter of the island, and the rest given to farmland that fed it, now that was no longer necessary. Food was brought by ship from the coastal lands all around, who could make the journey in only a few hours. Thus the city grew and grew, and its walls were expanded so that they circled the island's very rim. Docks covered the island's western and eastern shores. Some of the wealthiest merchants and nobility upon the island maintained gardens, and High Kings through the centuries had built various parks for the Seat's citizens. But aside from that, from one end of the island to the other there was only city.

Now a great portion of that city was aflame. A monstrous column of black smoke roiled into the air, so thick and so intense that it burned Oris' nose even from so far away.

Silvin's expression was one of stony rage. She seemed to be trying to maintain an outward calm. But fury burned in her eyes, and her fingers twitched as though they longed to draw her swords. She took two long, slow breaths. Even Flip was dour. Oris knew he had no particular love of royalty or nobility. But the Seat was different. The High King was by all accounts a fair and just woman, and the nine kingdoms prospered under her rule. To see this attack against the heart of Underrealm itself . . . Oris found herself wishing to take up her blade in the Seat's defense, though of course she could not possibly reach the city before the fighting would be over.

"Is this him?" said Oris. "Is this the Necromancer?"

Silvin pointed. "Those are Dulmish ships. They attacked from the east."

"It's rebellion, then," said Flip. "Against the High King herself."

"Yet there are other ships on the western docks, and they bear no flags," said Oris. "Dulmun isn't acting alone."

"That does not mean they are Shades," said Silvin.

Oris gave her a dubious look. "You yourself said you don't trust in coincidence. And we know the Necromancer has gathered more strength than you thought possible. This can't be unrelated."

Silvin's expression grew pained. "No. I suppose it cannot. And if that is the case, then . . . then yes. This is likely the first great stroke in the war. Let us pray to the sky he has not slain the High King, as is surely his aim."

Suddenly she turned to them, and the fury in her eyes burned brighter. "We have to get there. We have to help."

"Help what?" said Flip. "The city's already burning. We can't get there in time."

"We can be there for the aftermath." Silvin pointed to the Bay itself. West of the Seat, a small fleet of boats were making their way across the water towards Selvan's capital of Garsec, which shone like a jewel on the shore, free of flame or smoke. But these were no warships. They were fishing boats, small pleasure craft, and merchant ships. "The folk of the Seat are fleeing the attackers. The High King may be among them. They will need defense if Dulmun decides to press their attack. Come!"

She turned and ran back down the ridge towards the road. Oris followed her without a word, and Flip came a moment later, grumbling under his breath.

Garsec was still some leagues away, and it was hours before they reached the city's south wall. Oris expected to be challenged at the gate. But it stood closed, and no guards looked down on them from atop it. Silvin glared up at the gatehouse.

"That is not a good sign," she said.

"Every guard in the city has likely been drawn to the eastern docks to help the coming refugees," said Flip. "Or mayhap they are mounting a counterattack. King Anwar has always been a loyal servant of the High King."

"Regardless, we have to get in," said Oris. "Flip, could you get over and open the gate?"

Flip's mouth soured. "If someone sees me coming in, they may think I am some wizard of the enemy. I have no desire to be shot down in mid-flight."

"Send me instead," said Silvin. "I will get the gate open for the two of you to follow."

"Fair enough," said Flip. "Oris, get her as high as you can, and I will carry her the rest of the way."

Oris raised an eyebrow at Silvin. "Is that all right? After Dracmund, I won't hoist you up again if you don't wish it."

Silvin gave her a grim smile. "It was my idea. Give me a boost. I thank you for asking, this time at least."

Oris interlaced her fingers, and Silvin placed a boot within them. But when Oris heaved her up, Silvin's sword belt swung around, and one scabbard slammed into Oris' forehead. She grunted and reeled back with stars exploding in her eyes.

"Hold still!" growled Silvin, who teetered dangerously with her hands on the city wall.

"I'm trying," said Oris. "One. Two. Three. Four!"

She flung Silvin up as hard as she could. The smaller woman flailed in the air as she rose up a pace—and then she kept rising, but slower. Flip's eyes glowed as he guided currents of air around her, sending her careful braids up and spinning around her face. His jaw clenched, his lips a thin line as he tried to hold her steady, but Silvin spun slightly despite his efforts.

"I'm used to carrying myself, not others," Flip told Oris irritably. "Her swords are heavier than I thought."

Silvin made a desperate grab and seized the top of the wall. With her hands securing her hold, Flip gave a final burst of wind. Silvin flipped out of sight beyond the wall, landing with a crash on the ramparts.

"Silvin!" cried Oris. "Are you all right?"

"Fine," came Silvin's voice. "Be ready."

Soon Oris heard the clanking of chains and turning gears, and the gate swung open before them. They ran inside and rejoined Silvin, who immediately led them north and east through the city streets.

Like the walls, the streets were abandoned. Most people had gone to the docks to help those fleeing the Seat's destruction. Anyone who had remained here seemed wise enough to wait inside their homes rather than loiter about outside. No one impeded their progress through the city, though Oris saw some folk watching them, hastily hiding behind curtains and shutters as they passed by. The murmur of voices sounded ahead of them as they neared the docks at last. Finally other people started to appear in the streets, and slowly the crowds grew.

"Almost there," said Silvin, who was leading them as they jogged on. "Be ready in case it comes to a fight—Dulmun or the Shades may try to take the docks to prevent the refugees from reaching safety."

Oris nodded and placed a hand on her sword hilt as she ran, while Flip flexed his hands. Oris almost wished it *would* come to a fight, just so she could have something to hit after watching the Seat burn.

But a few streets away from the city's docks, they pulled up short as a line of red-cloaked figures blocked the way ahead of them. Oris' heart skipped a beat. *Mystics,* she thought.

"Halt!" cried one of them. Oris recognized the emblem on her shoulder that proclaimed her a captain. "No one is permitted to approach the docks."

"We are here to help," said Silvin. "Folk are fleeing the Seat."

"And we are here to receive them," said the captain. "If you want to help, go to the constabulary. They can tell you how to be of service to the refugees."

"What of the High King?" said Silvin. "Is she alive?"

The captain glowered at her. "I have no answers for you. If you want to help, go to the constabulary."

"We've come to aid you, you ass," snapped Flip. "You've got three pairs of strong and willing arms, and you won't use them?"

The captain's dark brown cheeks grew darker in a flush, and a scar showed on her chin as she clenched it. "You are unknown to me. And I am not letting you get near the docks."

"As if you could stop us," said Flip.

The Mystics tensed. But Oris snatched Flip's arm and drew him back.

"Flip," she said in a low voice. "The Seat was just attacked by former allies. They don't know who they can trust. If the High King did survive, and she's landed here, the most foolish thing they could do would be to let strangers near her."

Flip glared at her for a moment. But at last he nodded and placed his hand over hers where it held his arm, letting Oris lead him away from the docks.

Behind them, Oris heard Silvin say quietly to the Mystic captain, "Forgive our friend. Seeing the Seat burn has raised his blood."

"It has raised everyone's," replied the Mystic. "See it does not lead him to do something foolish."

Silvin jogged to catch up with Oris and Flip. Oris turned to her as they kept walking.

"What shall we do, then?" she said. "To the constabulary?"

But Silvin was looking at the streets around them, and her expression had grown anxious. "I do not think so. You raised a good point. No one knows where the attack came from—us least of all. I would not parade you about the streets of the city any more than we already have. Come. I know a place we can stay."

Flip smiled, though it seemed forced. "I hope it is near to a house of lovers again."

Silvin rolled her eyes and could not help a little smirk. "I am sure you shall find some kind of satisfaction. Now follow me."

• ○ • ○ •

Some leagues to the south, Barrick led his Shades as they trudged along the coast of the Great Bay. To the north of them, the black column of smoke continued to rise from the Seat into the sky. It filled Barrick's heart with a fierce joy, though it was unexpected. The plan had been to capture the Seat, not burn it to the ground. But as Father had often reminded them, even a plan that is perfect in the mind must yet bend to the waking world.

Barrick had grown increasingly frustrated through the night, never letting his party sleep or even stop to take a rest. Their steps flagged as they stumped along behind him. Barrick ignored them. He could keep walking for days, even weeks. And he would, if it would put the Lifemage within his grasp once again. His fists tightened at the thought.

"Step faster," he barked. The Shades around him jumped, their postures straightening slightly. "We must find her."

The others hurried their pace. Barrick knew most of them did not think they *would* find the Lifemage, but he did not care. He would find her. He had to.

"Barrick."

He stopped dead in his tracks, his eyes shooting wide. The voice in his mind made him think at once of his father. But when he turned, the man standing there was not the Lord.

Barrick turned to the rest of the Shades. "Halt. Wait here. Eat what food you have and rest, but not too well. We will search on in a moment."

He turned and stalked away without waiting for a reply, while the Shades behind him settled upon the ground with heavy sighs of relief. Barrick strode off until they were out of sight, and then he rounded on the vision, folding his arms.

"Where is Father?"

The attendant's jaw clenched at that. "Where do you think he is, Barrick? He is busy with the Seat. And it is because his attention has been drawn there that he knows the Lifemage reached Garsec. She has evaded you."

Barrick loosed a roar of wordless fury. A small sapling stood nearby. He drew his massive sword and cut it in half.

"Dark take her!" said Barrick. "I will go to Garsec, then, and I will hunt her down. I will burn the city to the ground if it means her corpse lies in the ashes."

"You will do no such thing," said the attendant. To Barrick's mounting fury, he sounded darkly amused. "Father requires something else of you."

“Then Father can come and tell me that himself,” snarled Barrick.

Suddenly the vision of the attendant seemed to swell. He rose into a dark and terrible figure, eyes filled with shadow and fury. For all his mighty size, Barrick felt diminutive before him.

“Our father is the Lord, and the savior of these nine wretched kingdoms.” Like thunder the attendant’s voice shattered the air, and Barrick flinched. “His wisdom is greater than kings and wizards, and his desires pure. He has more important duties than serving as a messenger boy merely to save the pride of selfish children.”

Barrick’s pulse thundered in his ears. Had the attendant stood before him in truth, the words might have brought him to violence. But he could do nothing to the man now.

And deep in his heart, he realized that the attendant was right. There were too many pieces, too many moving parts, for Father to deliver every message personally.

But he might have spoken, at least, to one of his favored sons, thought Barrick.

He straightened his posture and lifted his chin. “Very well,” he said. “What does Father require of me?”

The attendant’s fury diminished, and the size of the vision shrank with it. In a moment he was but a simple man again, and when he spoke, it was as though the rage of a moment ago had never been. “Rogan leads the retreat of his forces into the Birchwood. You will join him there, to participate in the scouring of the woods alongside him. Then you will help him disperse the Shades throughout Selvan and Dorsea. Further instructions will come as soon as Father has them.”

“Very well,” said Barrick. “Is there anything else?”

The attendant sighed. “There is. Father wished for me to tell you that he loves you. And he asks that you not blame yourself for the Lifemage reaching Garsec. The skeins of fate are many, and none can see the whole pattern. He loves you for your service and your devotion.”

Barrick felt a stinging behind his eyes and turned away. “I do not require your platitudes.”

“They are his words, not the ones I would have spoken.”

When Barrick looked again, the attendant was gone.

He headed back to where the Shades were waiting for him. It did not matter what the attendant said, or even what Father said. Barrick would be the one to bring the Lifemage to her end.

• ○ • ○ •

Silvin took them to the Dancing Fish. It was one of the seedier inns she frequented, a dilapidated, ramshackle building squatting in an alley removed from any main streets. Though she had not been here in well over a year, the innkeep Camil recognized her and took her silver without a word. They took food and drink, and then they retired to their room, where all three of them slept like the dead. Silvin did not even order them to set a watch, for the inn's locks were very strong.

She rose earlier than the others, a little while before dawn, and went to break her fast in the common room. Camil greeted her at the bar with a weary expression. There were bags under the innkeep's eyes, and Silvin doubted she had slept.

"What news in the night?" said Silvin.

"The High King survived the attack," said Camil. She yawned. "Thank the sky."

"Thank the sky," said Silvin fervently. "Where is she?"

Camil looked amused. "You think your redcloaks would tell me?"

Silvin smiled, but then she glanced over her shoulder. "No mention of that when my friends are around, if it please you."

Camil nodded. "Of course. Let me get you fed."

But hardly had Silvin sat down with her meal before Oris appeared in the common room as well. It was a cramped space. The table Silvin had chosen only had chairs against the wall, and not enough room to place them on the other side. Silvin was about to rise and find another table where they could sit across from each other. But Oris came over without comment and slumped down on the bench right next to her. Their arms brushed as she settled, and the hairs on Silvin's arms rose. Oris reached over to take a slice of bacon from her plate.

Stop it, Silvin told herself. *As though she would ever feel the same. As though she would even be in the same room with you if she truly knew you.*

"What's our plan?" said Oris in a low voice. The room was empty except for Camil, who was busy clinking dishes behind the bar and too far away to hear.

"I must seek information," said Silvin. "The High King's forces will retake the Seat, and then we can travel there. But for now I must see if anyone in the order knows aught of Jordel. With luck, he might have been here to help in the capital's defense. That is our best hope right now."

"Sensible enough," said Oris. "Be careful out there. It's clear our enemies have agents in more places than you thought. If they found us in Dracmund, they can find us here."

"Well do I know it," said Silvin. "I will use every caution. You should return to the room and remain with Flip. I would not have you be alone if it can possibly be helped."

They finished eating, and then Oris did as Silvin had bid and returned to the room. Silvin set out into Garsec's streets, drawing up her hood.

Refugees now clogged the city. Silvin did not see anyone wounded, or at least not seriously. She guessed, or hoped, that anyone badly hurt had been moved to safer and warmer places for healing. But anyone who could walk seemed to have simply collapsed upon the cobblestones, finding any place they could rest. Some of them had risen now and were puttering about. There was a deadness in their eyes that Silvin knew well: the shock of sudden calamity, a shifting in the world so profound that the ordinary mind simply could not withstand it. Only time would heal it, for most of them. But Silvin pushed such thoughts away, determined now to remain focused. Their long while spent in Dracmund had made her slip up, letting the enemy discover Oris. She would not make such a mistake again.

Silvin had visited the Mystic garrison in Garsec many times. Never had she seen its gate closed. The city was the capital of the centermost kingdom of Underrealm, and no one in centuries had dreamed it might be in danger. But now the stronghold was drawn up as if against an invading army, and Mystics glared suspiciously down at her as she approached. She raised a hand in greeting as she reached the gate, but no one atop the wall hailed her. Instead, a small hatch slid open in the iron door on the ground. Through the gap appeared the reedy face of a man with a thin wisp of mustache.

"We have no room for refugees," he said. "The mayor and his constables will see to your needs."

"I am no refugee." Silvin drew her badge from its pouch at her belt and proffered it. "I have come to report information and to seek it as well."

The man barely glanced at the badge before meeting her gaze again. "I do not know you."

Silvin frowned. "I do not know you, either. Now are you going to let me in?"

"I am not," said the man. "As I said, I do not know you."

Silvin glanced over her shoulder, but no passersby were close enough to hear. Still, she stepped a bit closer. "Can you not see my badge? Open the door. Who cares if you know my face?"

"The chancellor issued new orders," said the man. "Anyone unknown must be verified by an officer who has been stationed at the garrison for no less than one year. Or have you missed that Underrealm is now at war due to traitors the High King once trusted?"

Silvin's fingers tightened on her sword hilts. She was sick nearly to death of everyone in her order, everyone who was supposed to be an ally and battle-kindred, showing her nothing but suspicion and scorn. It was just this sort of thing that led her to work only with Jordel unless she had no other choice. She had no time for the politicking and bureaucracy of the redcloaks, and Jordel often navigated those treacherous waters so that she did not have to.

Control, she told herself. *Two deep breaths. One, two.* But they came shaky despite her best efforts.

The sound of many tramping feet approached her from behind. Silvin turned quickly, her pulse skipping. Yet it was only a party of red-cloaked Mystics returning to the garrison. And as she peered at them from beneath her hood, one of them gave a great cry and leaped forwards. Silvin caught only a flash of red hair, trimmed close on the sides and flopping rakishly forwards on top, before the Mystic threw her arms around Silvin in a warm embrace.

"Weath," said Silvin, holding the woman tight against her. She buried her face in Weath's neck and only with difficulty stopped from crushing her. Weath, for her part, ran her hands up and down Silvin's back and covered the top of her head with kisses, as though she could not believe her own eyes and was afraid Silvin would vanish like a dream.

"Silvin, dearest," said Weath. "I have not seen you since Brillig. What under the sky are you doing here? I thought you were still in Dorsea."

"I was, and then I was no longer," said Silvin with a smile. She drew back, and Weath immediately cupped her cheeks, staring at her with shining eyes. "It is a relief beyond measure to see you safe. Do they know you here? I cannot get in the gate."

"They do, they do," said Weath. She turned to the other Mystics behind her, who stood nonplussed as they watched the women greeting each other. "Captain, this is Silvin, a sister of our order. She requires entry to the stronghold. I can vouch for her."

The captain was a massively-muscled woman with a plain, sleeveless tunic under a leather vest with a collar that rose to cover her neck. She folded her thick arms and gave Silvin a dour look. "Are you absolutely sure it is her?"

Weath blinked. "Oh, I see what you mean." She turned back to Silvin. "You do not mind if—"

"Not at all," said Silvin, shaking her head.

Weath smiled and placed her hands on the sides of Silvin's neck. Suddenly her eyes began to glow. Silvin felt an itching along her skin where Weath's hands touched her, but she remained still.

After a moment, it was done. Weath turned back to her captain. "She is no weremage in disguise, Captain. We may trust her."

"Very well," said the captain with a sigh. She looked past them both at the guard through the slot in the iron door, who had been watching all this display with increasing irritation. "I can verify this one," she said. "The rest of us are here to report to the chancellor."

"Very well," said the man snippily. "One moment."

The hatch screeched shut, and Silvin heard large latches being turned within. After a moment the door shuddered and then swung inwards. Weath put her arm around Silvin's shoulders and walked beside her, and Silvin took one of the woman's hands in hers.

Inside, the bailey was a tumult of activity. Mystics in full uniform strode back and forth alone, in pairs, or in squadrons. Some were at drill, even this early in the morning, though Silvin was certain they would be of more use out in the streets helping the Seat's citizens. But Weath stopped her with a gentle hand on the shoulder and turned back to the others they had entered with.

"Captain, might we have a moment to speak alone?"

The captain cocked an eyebrow. "A moment, or a quarter-hour?"

Silvin's jaw clenched, but Weath only smiled. "A moment, no more. She has journeyed far to be here, and—" Suddenly Weath froze, and she looked at Silvin with wide, fearful eyes.

Silvin frowned. "What is it?"

Weath did not answer. She turned back to her captain. "We have things to discuss. Of a private matter."

A quivering sensation crept through Silvin's gut, different and worse somehow than the anger that always lurked close to the surface. She could not read this sudden change in Weath's demeanor.

But the captain did not seem to notice. She only nodded. "Meet us in the dining hall. The chancellor shall fetch us from there for our next assignment. A moment only."

"I swear it, Captain," said Weath.

The captain nodded, and the Mystics left. Silvin turned to Weath, suppressing a frown.

"Weath?" she said. "What is it?"

"Not here," said Weath. "Come. We can be alone in the stables."

"I thought you promised your captain you would not be gone too long." Silvin tried to make it a quip, but nerves turned the words lifeless.

Weath only licked her lips and shook her head. No trace of amusement shone in her eyes. Silvin followed her silently into the stables. The din from the bailey died away as Weath took her towards the back, where there were some chairs for the stablehands. The place was empty now. Weath drew Silvin into a chair before taking another for herself.

"Well, what road brought you here?" said Silvin. "The last I heard, you were stationed at Ammon."

Weath gave a smile, but it was a limp thing. "Chancellor Kal brought us south. Jormund is here as well."

Silvin's focus grew razor sharp. "The chancellor is here?"

"No. He returned to Ammon."

"You must not tell him you saw me."

Weath frowned in alarm. "Whyever not?"

Silvin leaned forwards and took her hands. "Please. I beg you to trust me."

"Of course I trust you," said Weath. "But can I trust *him?* What do you fear in him?"

"No treachery to the high crown, at least," said Silvin bitterly. "But if he learned I am here, he would command me to join him in Ammon. That I could not stomach, especially not with . . ." She stopped short and shook her head. "I cannot say everything I wish. Only please promise me you will not tell him."

"I swear it, then," said Weath. "Of course I swear it, darling."

"Thank you." Silvin realized her grip on Weath's hands had grown too tight, and she loosened it. Weath gave a weak smile of relief. "All right. I came to ask the local chancellor this, but you are even better. I have come seeking news of Jordel. Have you heard anything of him? Has he been pardoned yet? The last I heard, he . . ."

Her words died slowly, just as Weath's faint smile did. The quiet of the stable around them seemed to become total silence, until Silvin heard a faint ringing in her ears.

"Weath."

The woman slid out of her chair and knelt, gently taking Silvin's face. "My dear, I am so sorry. Jordel . . . Jordel has fallen." Her voice seemed to be coming through dark water, reaching Silvin weakly in the depths.

Nothing. Then, "On the Seat?"

"No, not in the battle. It was . . ." She paused for a moment, thinking. "It would have been more than two months ago now. He died in the Greatrocks. Word reached us not long ago, and from here it has been spreading."

"No."

Weath's eyes filled with tears. "I am sorry. I know you . . . I wish . . ."

She reached up to embrace Silvin, but Silvin caught her wrists and held them away—not harshly, but irresistibly.

"No," she said again.

I have to get away. I cannot be here. I cannot be near her, or any of them, not in this place, I have to go.

She rose from her chair and strode towards the door.

"Silvin," said Weath, following after her. "Darling, please, stay here at least a moment."

"No."

Away. As far away as I can.

"Silvin, please!" cried Weath. "You should not be alone. Do not . . . do not *do* anything."

"I have to go." But she did stop, just for a moment. She looked back at Weath. "I have to go. But I swear this: you need not fear for me."

Not for me.

Weath stopped. She looked terrified and hesitant, but she gave a slow nod.

Silvin whirled and stalked away.

The world around her came in flashes. There was the rage, red bloody fingers pushing into her eyes, stinging them like acid, burning, turning to fire in her chest, stoking the flame higher. There was the grief, the stranger, the unwelcome guest in the home of her mind, the hollow pit more frightening than hate.

There was Oris. There was Weath's soft neck.

She was in the city street.

Not far enough.

How had she left the stronghold? Did they open the door for her or did she push past them?

Closest wall was north.

Not far enough. Not here, not in this place.

The city gate stood ahead, and it was closed. And then she was outside it. Did she show them her badge?

Don't look back. Farther. Not far enough.

Was anyone else on the road close by? She could not see them, could not see through the red.

The woods. The trees of the Birchwood standing around. How far from the city?

Not far enough. Nowhere is far enough.

But it would have to do.

He would want you to control yourself. He would want you to be calm. Do not let go. Do not lose control.

Red turned to white, turned to black, to darkness that sank famished teeth into her.

Control. He gave you control.

"And he is gone!" she screamed into the uncaring wood.

He left you this gift. Control. Two deep breaths. One—

The breath came out in a scream that tore her throat.

Red to white to black to nothing.

She was kneeling. Her head hung low. Spittle dribbled from her lips and she tasted blood in it. Every careful braid undone, blonde hair spilling into the spit, soaking with dirt and the filth. Hands clutched to her chest.

Hands?

She lifted and looked at them. The gloves were shreds. Her knuckles lay open and bleeding. Three nails had ripped out.

Slowly, head shaking with the effort, she looked up and around. Splintered wood. Four trees ripped and broken on the ground, torn until no piece left was large enough to bother with. One of her swords lying on the ground two paces away, the other buried in the trunk of a fifth tree a little farther off.

Still the rage. But the familiar red, no white and no black.

And now the shame. Endless, fathomless, like the very dark below. Vast enough to lose herself in a thousand times over.

The shame. What would he think if he could see her?

But he could not. And he would not.

Never again.

Shakily she got to her feet. At first she failed, slipping on the muddy ground. Her face came up caked with it, and she gasped at the cold, at the feeling of the dirt in the battered wreck of her knuckles. At last she rose quivering to her feet. It felt with every step as though her legs would send her crashing down again.

She retrieved her swords and turned to the south. But then she thought better of it. She needed to clean herself up before she returned. And she would need to clean the dirt out of her wounds. The shore of the Great Bay was close to the east. And she remembered a stream nearby to the west.

She turned east. The salt water would hurt more.

• ○ • ○ •

Oris waited in their room at the Dancing Fish after Silvin had left. After a little while, Flip awoke and together they went into the common room. They ate and then they waited, all the while in silence. There was a pressure upon them both, a weariness and a weight, and Oris suspected that Flip's thoughts were much like her own: reliving the sight of the Seat burning, and the terror in the city.

When two hours passed and Silvin had not yet returned, Oris began to grow worried. She had been gone for long periods before in Dracmund, but the danger now was more present and much more clear. She began to grow nervous as she realized she was sitting here exposed to anyone who happened to come by—something she had never worried about in Dracmund.

A thought struck her. What would she do if Silvin did not return? She did not know what her next step should be. She did not know what to do about any of the madness that had overtaken her life. It was a frightening thought. She could hardly go about proclaiming herself to be the Lifemage and asking people to help her.

But just as this trail of thoughts was beginning to spin back in on itself,

Silvin arrived at last. Oris watched her come through the door with a sigh of relief—which cut off the moment she saw Silvin's face. She looked haggard, as worn as if she had gone a week without rest. As she pushed through the common room towards them, Oris noticed her hands: they were badly bandaged with white cloth already showing bloodstains beneath.

"Silvin?" Oris did not remember rising to her feet or clenching her fists. "What happened? Who did this to you?"

She went and wrapped an arm around Silvin's shoulders, gently guiding her to the table with Flip. The wizard was staring at Silvin in stark astonishment—and, to Oris' surprise, not a little concern. He slid over to make room for her at the table, and as Silvin stumbled half-senseless into a chair, he leaned forwards on his elbows to peer at her.

And then, as they both watched her, Silvin almost seemed to transform before them. Slowly her hunched shoulders straightened, and she sat upright. Her bandaged hands fumbled only slightly as she reached up and tied back her hair—not the intricate braids Oris had grown accustomed to, but a single tail. She then lay her hands flat on the table and met their eyes.

"My master is dead."

A long moment passed. Then Flip stood from his chair. Oris frowned up at him, but Flip ignored her. He went across the room to the bar where the innkeep, Camil, was trying very hard to clean her cups without looking the least bit interested in whatever was going on. Flip leaned over the bar towards her, and Camil glanced up as if she had just noticed him.

"I don't want there to be less than two full bottles of wine on our table at any time, for the rest of the day. Understood?" He reached into his pocket and scattered what had to be half a dozen gold weights on the bar in front of her.

Camil gave him a wide-eyed nod. Flip returned to Oris and Silvin, and Camil was only two steps behind him, three bottles in her arms. She jogged back to the bar and soon returned with cups.

But Oris had turned her attention back to Silvin. The Mystic's gaze had drifted away again, staring at nothing. Oris lifted a hand and almost put it on Silvin's hand, but placed it on her forearm instead. Silvin did not seem to notice. She looked still as a stone. But Oris could feel her twitching, the muscles jumping around underneath her skin, as though she was aching to fight anything she could get her hands on.

"I'm sorry, Silvin," she whispered. "I wish there was anything I could do."

"We both do," said Flip. He lifted one of the bottles and filled all three cups before pushing one towards her.

Silvin glanced down at it. "I . . . I do not usually drink."

Flip whisked it away at once. "Foolish of me. I should've asked first."

"No," said Silvin. "Please. Today, I want to."

She held out her hand. Flip returned her cup, though there was an uncomfortable look in his eye. "Is that . . . please understand, but . . . is that wise?"

Incredibly, Silvin gave a small smile. "Thank you. But yes. Just . . . please, if it seems like I am having too much, only . . . only stop filling my cup. I will not argue if you do."

"Of course," said Oris. "We're here. We'll watch out for you." Her hand tightened slightly on Silvin's arm. Then she told the hand to let go, and it obeyed her in its own time.

Silvin lifted the cup. But Flip raised a hand to stop her.

"To your master," he said, raising his wine in toast. "And other beloved in the darkness below."

Oris quickly took her cup and lifted it. "To Ombi."

Silvin's mouth twisted. "To my parents."

Oris' heart quailed at that. But she quickly joined in as Silvin drank deep. Her eyes closed, and Oris watched the curve of her throat shifting as the wine slid down it. When she lowered the cup again, it was empty. She blinked twice and licked her lips. When she pushed the cup forwards, Flip refilled it.

"I suppose . . ." said Silvin slowly. "I suppose the two of you should find your own way from here."

"What?" said Oris. "Why?"

"I have failed," said Silvin. "I brought you all this way, and it was all for nothing."

Flip gave an amused snort. "Hardly for nothing. For one thing, we're alive because of you. That's not nothing, at least not from my view."

Silvin gave a little shrug. "That may only have delayed the end. Now we are nowhere. I have no plan and no idea where to find one. And the person who did know, who had a plan, he—"

"He left us a way forwards," said Oris.

Silvin looked at her. "What? What way?"

Oris met her gaze. "He left us you."

Silvin stared at her without a trace of recognition.

"I trust you," said Oris. "Just like he trusted you. You can't tell me he was going to do everything himself, teach me all on his own. He had to have others he could rely on. You have folk you can rely on, too. Here's two of them." She pointed at herself and then at Flip. "Who else? Who could teach me what I need to do?"

Slowly Silvin's gaze drifted away from her. "I suppose . . . there are some I could ask. One or two, who may still be on the Seat. If they survived the attack."

"Then let's find them," said Oris. "If there's only one thing I know for certain by now, it's that I'll die if I'm out there on my own. And I don't know who I can trust besides the two of you. So I'd be a fool to leave you now. You're fully half the folk whose hands I can place my life in." She smiled fiercely at Silvin. "Besides, I know you want to make someone hurt for what happened to your master. So do it. Turn me into what I'm supposed to be."

Silvin's eyes began to dart back and forth, as though she were watching flitting birds that Oris could not see. "All right, then. Who knows if we shall succeed, but I will not stop trying. Here we will rest until folk begin to return to the Seat. When they do, we shall return with them. And we shall find a way to help you become the Lifemage and fulfill your destiny. I swear it."

"Excellent," said Flip, reaching for the wine bottle again. "And now, to drink too much."

CHAPTER XIV
THE HIGH KING'S SEAT

The three of them spent four more days waiting in Garsec. Silvin gathered reports each day of the goings-on beyond the city walls. The High King's fleets scoured the Bay all around the island, watchful for the return of the Dulmish fleet. Meanwhile, more troops gathered to Garsec from the lands all around, and word came that the High King's armies were returning from Wellmont and northwestern Selvan.

But the Dulmish ships continued on their voyage home, showing no signs of returning. And so, on the fifth day, people began to return to the Seat, sailing back across the narrow waters on whatever craft they could get. Silvin paid their way on a fishing boat; the captain told them it was now more worth his while to serve as a transport than to ply his normal trade, for the coin was more plentiful.

Silvin took them to an inn called the Crescent Bulwark, which lay near the southern end of the city. When Oris heard that it cost two gold weights a night for room and board, her eyes bulged. Flip gave her a rueful smile.

"Welcome to the High King's Seat, dear," he said as they lugged their packs towards their spacious room. "Everything costs more coin, and yet the inhabitants act as though you should be grateful to pay it."

"One reason I was happier to be stationed in Garsec," said Silvin. "One gets most of the luxury without nearly so many noses turned up at you."

The next day, Silvin led them out of the Bulwark and into the city. The whole island buzzed like an anthill. Crafters and artisans of all stripes trucked their tools along the streets in carts or on muleback, or else they were already at work. The air rang with hammers and saws, and the occasional sharp rumble of a building being pulled down, damaged too badly for anything but reconstruction.

Silvin took them north until they neared the city's center, and then she hooked west. There was a main boulevard that ran along the center of the island with few curves, but Silvin avoided it. There were too many watching eyes, she said. Instead they followed its course, but on smaller side streets where everyone seemed too preoccupied with their own work to notice three strangers passing by.

Soon a great building loomed up ahead of them. Oris had noted it when they had entered the city yesterday, but it was too far away for her to get a good look at it. Now it grew and grew before them, and she realized just how massive it was. Its stones were laid in a granite so dark it was almost black, its trimmings all in silver. Near its northeastern corner was a high bell tower, from each side of which hung the same banner: a white cross in nested orbs on a field of black. To the south was a large wing with a great glass dome, and high walls surrounded the whole structure.

Flip looked at Silvin askance. "Silvin, if I didn't know better, I'd say we were heading for the Academy."

"What makes you think you know any better?" said Silvin.

"The Academy?" said Flip with a groan. "What are we doing *there?*"

"Oris needs to learn to use her magic," said Silvin. "I know of no better place to seek such knowledge."

Oris looked to Flip in wonder. "The Academy for wizards? This is where you trained, isn't it?"

"It is," said Flip. "Many and more a year ago, now. And I did not wish to return."

Soon they stood on the street before the entrance. There, the high walls joined the front of the building, and there was no gate, but only a massive black iron door. Looking closer, Oris could see that it was inscribed with many small symbols etched into the metal. Studying them made her eyes hurt.

Silvin looked to Flip. "As a former student, you shall have to be the one to request an audience."

"Ugh," said Flip, scowling. "And whose attention am I seeking?"

"Dasko."

Flip's brows shot for the sky. "Dasko? Is he still here?"

"I desperately hope so."

It seemed to Oris that Flip was suddenly much less reluctant. He stepped briskly up to the door and used the great iron knocker that hung there.

Almost at once, a small hatch slid open at chest height. It was so cleverly hidden that Oris had not noticed it until it opened. A wizened old face peered out at them through it, squinting heavily at the sunlight outside. The milky eyes focused on Flip and narrowed until they looked like raisins plunged into dough.

"You," growled the old woman.

"Mellie, dearest!" said Flip with a grin. "How long has it been?"

"Eleven years, one hundred and eleven days," said Mellie. "Near enough to eleven hours as well, since you left just as curfew started. And not nearly long enough, if you ask me."

Flip blinked. "May we all be blessed with a mind as sharp as yours in our dotage. As with your gnarled old fingers, it's like a bear trap, with no hint of rust."

"Cease your flattery," said Mellie. "What do you want?"

"Why, I'm a returning alumnus," said Flip, "and I desire nothing more than what I've earned by that right. I'd like an audience with Instructor Dasko."

Mellie's eyes flitted to Silvin and then to Oris. When the old woman's gaze fell upon her, Oris felt a creeping sensation along her skin, as though she was being poked and prodded like a horse. "And these with you?"

"Friends and companions whose advice I rely upon," said Flip. "They shall be my wards while we are here."

"Hmph," said Mellie.

The hatch slammed shut.

"You're popular," said Oris.

"Always was," said Flip.

Silvin smiled.

There was a sharp screech of metal as a latch turned. But when the door began to swing inwards, it was nearly silent, with only a faint hum through the thick metal. Flip stepped through the door without hesitation, Oris and Silvin following a little more slowly. But once they stood in the wide entrance hall, Flip came to a stop. Oris halted as well, overawed by the sight of the place. She had never been in a chamber so large. A great stairway led up to a landing in the center of the far wall and then ascended again to two hallways leading off. The walls on the ground floor had many doors, and two hallways just under the ones on the second level. The place was lit by great chandeliers hanging from a ceiling ten paces high, but also by sunlight filtered through stained glass windows depicting many figures who bore coronas of light around their bodies.

"Magnificent," whispered Oris.

"Hm?" said Flip, shaking himself as he looked at her. "Oh, yes. A fine enough place to call home, if you like everything it comes with." He turned to Mellie, who now stood just beside the door, her arms folded and her beady eyes glaring. "Is Dasko's office still where I remember?"

"I can make no claims as to your memory," growled Mellie.

Flip's smile only broadened. "I'll say that's a yes. Come along, you two. Don't get lost."

He set off down the hallway to the right. Oris let Silvin go first so that she could bring up the rear. It let her take a bit more time staring around, pausing to look at the fine tapestries and immaculately polished doors they passed.

Flip took a couple of turns that immediately had Oris lost within the long passages. But soon enough, he stopped at a door of plain brown wood, though it was finely crafted and well polished. He gave two sharp raps at the door.

A pause. Then a bemused voice spoke in what was almost a question. "Come?"

Flip opened the door and stepped through. Inside was a study, simple in nature, five paces wide and a little longer than that, with tall windows against the back wall. Behind a desk in the corner sat a man of middle years, with dark shaggy hair streaked with grey, especially at the temples and in the beard. His face was not particularly lined, but it was somewhat haggard and careworn. Oris guessed that this must be Instructor Dasko.

As Flip entered the room, Dasko looked up at him blankly for a moment. But then his eyes narrowed, and his shoulders dipped slightly. It seemed he barely repressed a sigh.

"Philip of the family Drayden," he said. "It has been some time."

"Instructor Dasko," said Flip, smile still wide. "Don't look quite so pleased to see me. My friends shall grow jealous."

Now Dasko could no longer hold back his sigh. But at Flip's words, he glanced at Oris, and then Silvin. And as Silvin lowered her hood, Dasko's eyes shot wide. He leaped out of his chair and came towards them.

"Silvin!" he cried. "What under the sky are you doing here with . . . that is, what are you doing here?"

Silvin accepted his embrace with a smile. "Hello, Instructor," she said. "It warms my heart to see you after so long."

"Too long," agreed Dasko. He pushed her back at arm's length to look at her. "I cannot imagine you just happen to be accompanying young Philip here on an errand."

"No indeed," said Silvin. "We are here on my errand, in truth."

"Why did you not send for me yourself?" said Dasko. "I could have met you outside of the Academy."

Silvin's smile dampened. "In fact, it is quite preferable that we speak here. A moment."

She turned and closed the study door. Then she went to Oris and placed one hand on her back, gesturing at her with the other. "It is my pleasure to introduce Oris."

"Hello," said Oris awkwardly. Between Mellie at the door and now Dasko, she was feeling more and more like a prize being shown off.

"My pleasure," said Dasko, and they took each other's wrists. His grip was firm but not harsh. "A friend of Silvin's is welcome here." His eyes flicked to Flip, but he did not speak further.

"May we sit?" said Silvin.

"Of course," said Dasko, waving them to the chairs before his desk. But there were only two of them, and Oris hesitated.

"Sit, sit," said Flip. "I'll wander about and amuse myself. This is your conspiracy." He went to Dasko's bookshelf and began to peruse the titles, drumming his fingers lightly against each spine in turn.

"Conspiracy?" said Dasko, arching a brow as he took his seat. "May I take this for Philip's . . . unique sense of humor?"

"Only partially," said Silvin, settling into her chair. She leaned forwards and pressed her hands together in front of her. "Instructor, we need your help. Or at least, we need help, and you are the only person I could think of who might be able to provide it, though I fear even that hope may fail."

"I may be unequal to the task," said Dasko. "But if I can serve you without dishonor, I shall. What troubles you?"

"Before I speak on that," said Silvin, "I must ask you a favor. When you hear what I have come to ask, you may be able to help, or you may not. Or you may refuse me. But no matter your answer, you must promise absolute discretion. What we are about to tell you can never leave this room."

"Fair enough," said Dasko. "Yours will hardly be the first secret I have kept."

"Yet this secret is not like any other," said Silvin. "And it shall require more from you. I must ask you to forego all other bonds and pledges of honor. If the Dean should come and demand you tell him what was discussed here, you must refuse. If the High King herself should command you, you must deny her. I know that is a great deal to ask. But believe me when I tell you it is important enough to warrant such a request."

Dasko was silent. He leaned back in his chair, his fingers picking at the upholstery on the arms, and his eyes were cool as they studied Silvin. Oris' throat felt dry.

"That is no light request," said Dasko finally. "And I will not make that pledge lightly. Can you, in turn, pledge that this will not be an evil conversation? Can you tell me that it will do no harm to the Academy or the High King?"

"Not in any way I can foresee," said Silvin. "In fact, the very reason I have come to you is to protect them both from a coming calamity."

Dasko snorted. "Coming? Calamity is already here. But very well. This is a time for great deeds. I suppose some of them will have to be secretive. And I trust you more than most. If your promise has been given honestly, then I can give mine in turn. No word spoken here shall leave this room. Now, what sort of trouble are you in?"

Silvin gave a deep sigh of relief. "Thank you, Instructor. In that case . . . do you remember my particular field of interest? The one I have been pursuing for a number of years now?"

"You and your master both," said Dasko quietly. "I heard of his passing. I am sorry."

Silvin's jaw clenched hard. "Many folk are."

"In any case, yes," said Dasko. "I remember what you have long sought. Do they know of it?" He tilted his head towards Flip and Oris.

"They do," said Silvin. "In fact, they are directly involved. I have found what I was looking for."

There was no trace of recognition in Dasko's eyes. "You . . . what do you mean you *found—*"

Suddenly he went still. His gaze shifted from Silvin to Oris, and Oris found it hard to meet his gaze. Now that she thought on it, he was only the second person she had met who knew what she was—aside from those who were actively trying to kill her, of course. And as long as Silvin had been with them, she had been concealing much of her own knowledge of Oris. This was the first time Oris had been able to see the realization come upon someone even as it happened.

It was not a particularly pleasant experience.

Dasko stood and walked to the front of his desk, sitting against its edge. Though they had already shook, he offered his hand to Oris. "Dasko of the family Gelram," he said.

Oris took his wrist. "Oris. Just Oris."

Dasko held on to her for a moment longer, slowly shaking his head. "My honor. Remarkable. Absolutely remarkable. Where are you from?"

"Nowhere special," said Oris. "An orphanage in Cabrus."

"Cabrus?" said Dasko. "Where did you pick up your Heddish accent?"

"On campaign in Hedgemond," said Oris, dropping it. "Flip and I enjoyed it so much, we claimed it for ourselves."

Dasko's gaze darted to Flip, and he gave a little grimace. "I thought he sounded odd. You say you grew up in an orphanage. Did your parents . . . that is—"

"I could write a history book for you, if you like," said Oris, her cheeks flaming. "Though I'm a bit short on the details. My parents are likely dead."

"My apologies," said Dasko, bowing his head. "That was insensitive. You are not a tome to be pored through."

"I'm certainly not," said Oris, though her irritation subsided at how genuinely remorseful he looked.

"If you do not mind my asking," he went on, "how long have you . . . that is, when did you realize who you were?"

Oris looked to Silvin, but Silvin only gave her an encouraging nod.

"Something . . . happened at the Battle of Wellmont," said Oris slowly. "I didn't know what it was at the time. But word of it spread. That's how Silvin found us."

"Wellmont," said Dasko. "Interesting. Many things were set in motion there, it seems."

Oris frowned. "What do you mean?"

"Rumors have swirled ever since the battle," said Dasko. "The High King sent a great force there to quell Dorsea's invasion. That was a mystery to many of us. But if she heard rumors of . . . of whatever it is that happened, then that explains much." Suddenly he paused, looking to Silvin again. "At the start, you asked me to keep this council secret, even from the High King herself. Why? Why not go to her? Surely she would help you."

"I do not because Jordel would not," said Silvin. "He always counseled secrecy, and with good reason. We have seen that the High King's palace is no impregnable place, and secrets leak from there like a sieve. Oris' existence—or at least her location—is a secret now. Once that secret is out, it can never be taken back. I would not reveal her until I am absolutely certain it is the right thing to do."

"I see," said Dasko slowly. He turned to Oris. "And you agree with this course?"

Oris' jaw clenched, and she saw a surprised look come to Silvin's face. But she only said, "I've known the truth about myself for two months, and I've still got much to learn. Silvin and her master have been studying and searching for me for years. I think my wisest course now is to trust her."

"Hm," said Dasko. "If that is your decision. And so now we come to it. You asked for my help. What, exactly, do you hope I can do for you?"

"Oris needs to learn her power," said Silvin. "Jordel had a plan to teach her, but I never learned it. I hoped you might know something that could help us."

Dasko frowned. "That is a tall order indeed. Almost no one in Underrealm even knows of the Lifemage and the Necromancer. Even here at the Academy, I think I am the only one who knows of them."

"But you teach magic, don't you?" said Oris. "So teach me magic."

To her irritation, Silvin and Dasko both rolled their eyes, though Dasko at least tried to hide it. Over at the bookshelf, Flip gave a brief chuckle that he quickly suppressed.

"Magic does not quite work that way," said Dasko gently. "I am a therianthrope. I teach therianthropy."

"What?" said Oris, looking from him to Silvin.

"Weremagic," said Silvin. "Its academic name is therianthropy."

"My apologies," said Dasko. "I often bemoan the use of language that excludes the common folk, and yet sometimes even I find myself slipping into it. The Academy has its rules. But yes, I teach weremagic. I could not teach firemagic to someone like Philip, or any other branch of magic, for that matter."

"But isn't it all magic?" said Oris.

"Aren't all weapons weapons?" said Flip. "You're more skilled with your sword than most. Couldn't you teach someone Calentin archery?"

"An apt analogy," said Dasko, "and a revelation that Philip likely paid more attention in his classes than he let on. But even then, it is inadequate. You know the essentials of how a bow and arrow work, and you can find a Calentin archer easily enough to see how they draw. Even without knowing the craft, you could fumble around imitating them until you learned the skill. But here, you have no references to draw from. There is no other Lifemage to observe, to see how they use their magic in their own unique way."

"Fine," said Oris, frowning. "I'll take your word for all that, since it's your specialty and not mine. But then, what do we do? You heard Silvin. We lost the only plan we had. What's our new plan?"

Dasko sighed. "Well, there are two answers to that. The first is that you *can* just fumble around. You used your powers once, or Silvin would not know who you are. And there are some commonalities between different branches of magic—not many, but some, and I can teach them to you."

"And the second answer?" said Oris.

"Education at the Academy is in two parts," said Dasko. "First is the direct teaching of magic. The second is teaching in general. The library here contains tomes of history and the arcane stretching back to the time before time. I know of nothing about the Lifemage in any of them."

"You would not," said Silvin. "Not after the purge enacted by the last Lifemage."

"Just so," said Dasko with a nod. "Yet a general study of magic may be helpful. Or it is possible, through diligent work, that you may be able to find something about the Lifemage that was not caught in the purge."

Flip suddenly groaned, so loudly that the other three turned to him in alarm. "The library?" he said. "I was ready to live the rest of my life without ever visiting that prison again."

"I believe you," said Dasko, chewing his cheek. "Yet Oris may need its knowledge if she hopes to get anywhere. And to study there, she will have to accompany you and be in your charge. You are the former student, not she."

"Ugh," said Flip. "I will get you in the door, but dark take me if I will spend all day sneezing my way through dusty old tomes."

"It is something of a plan, at least," said Silvin. "When can we begin?"

Dasko's mouth twisted. "You can begin right away. But that raises the question of secrecy. The students have not yet returned to the Academy after the attack, but it is intended that they shall do so in four days. When that happens, I do not think it would be wise for you to study here during the daylight hours. I think you would do better to come at night. I can make special arrangements with Mellie at the door."

"That sounds perfect for our purposes," said Silvin. "We should begin at once, then."

"Then it is settled." Dasko clapped his hands. "Let me get you situated, and then I really must return to my duties."

"Of course," said Silvin. She stood from her chair. Oris took the cue and stood as well. "I cannot tell you how grateful we are for your help."

"It is my honor," said Dasko, inclining his head towards Oris. "But if you would, I desire to speak alone with Philip for a moment."

Flip froze in the middle of poring through a green tome he had pulled from Dasko's shelf. "Me?" he said. "Why?"

Dasko looked to Silvin and Oris, waving a hand towards the door. "If you would?"

Oris looked to Flip. He shook his head slowly, but he said only, "It's all right."

Oris and Silvin filed into the hall. But by unspoken agreement, they clustered together right next to the door, which they had left slightly ajar. Oris became suddenly aware that they were leaning against each other, arms pressed together, and it raised gooseflesh on her skin.

Dasko wasted no time getting to the point. "There is a new Drayden at the Academy."

"Is there?" said Flip, in a too-indifferent voice. "My family must be thrilled. Is Cyrus fawning over them like a favored child? Or is he jealous of another wizard in the clan?"

"While you are within these walls, I must insist that you follow at least some standard of courtesy," said Dasko. "But as to your question . . . *Dean* Cyrus has been missing since the attack."

"Missing?" said Flip. Oris could hear the frown in his voice. "Missing how? Where?"

"The nature of the word *missing* rather implies that I would not know," said Dasko wryly. "Some think he perished in the fighting, but if he did, no one saw it. Others have . . . less noble suspicions."

"When it comes to him, that's always a safe bet," said Flip. "In any case, I have little interest in either him or whichever new whelp my kin have sent here. I have nothing to do with them, and it's my eternal, earnest wish that they have nothing to do with me."

"It is Momen's little brother."

The office fell to silence for a long moment. Oris and Silvin looked at each other, and it seemed to Oris that both of them were holding their breath. She could read nothing in the silence, neither joy nor grief nor danger, and the longer it stretched, the more she feared whatever would break it. *Momen* . . . the name meant nothing to her, but she remembered the story of Flip's cousin.

"Ebon?" said Flip at last. "Little Ebon?" His voice was so small, Oris hardly recognized it. He sounded troubled, not with anger or bitterness, but with a sort of longing, the pleasure of a painful memory stripped away. His Heddish accent had vanished.

"Not so little anymore," said Dasko. "He is a man now, or near enough. And he is . . . you would be surprised how like Momen he is, and not just in looks."

"I do not think I would be surprised," said Flip, sounding curiously absent. "He worshipped Momen, too."

"He . . . struggles," said Dasko. "I know little of his standing with the family, but what I have heard is not good. It might help him to have someone to rely on, someone who understands—"

"No," said Flip sharply, and it was as if his momentary confusion had never been. "If he needs guidance, then be his guide. I will not return to them. Not to any of them."

"Would I ask you to?" said Dasko. "I do not say you should speak with any of the rest of them, but Ebon—"

"No," said Flip again. "You do not know them like I do."

A moment's pause. Then, "Would not Momen want you to?"

"Oh, he likely would," said Flip viciously. His Heddish accent had returned. "He spent his life walking a razor line, trying to do the right thing while still being a Drayden. And the razor cut him down, like it always does. It's a clean break or nothing. If you want to help Ebon, teach him that."

"Philip—"

"That's all, Instructor. Will you accompany us to the library?"

Dasko sighed. "I shall."

Oris and Silvin stepped quickly away from the door. When Flip came out, he was wearing only a cheery smile. But Dasko frowned as he led them away.

Oris followed the rest of them through the Academy's halls, where soon they came to a great set of double doors made from dark wood. When Dasko pushed them open and led them inside, Oris once again halted, struck silent by the sight before her.

Three stories high the library of the Academy stood, and it stretched for a span from end to end. Shelves ran along all the walls, with many more standing shelves in the center, and all of them crammed full of books. Tables and chairs were laid out for sitting and reading, and most of them were stacked with books as well. Covered lanterns hung plentifully along the walls and the shelves, though all were unlit now, for the library had better illumination. Now Oris recognized the golden glass dome she had seen from the outside. It formed the roof, and it cast the sun's gentle rays down upon them, painting the whole scene in a brilliant soft glow that warmed her the instant she set foot into the room.

"Who wrote them all?" she breathed. "There are so many."

"Countless folk throughout history," said Dasko, who wore a quiet smile. "Most of them have gone to the darkness below, of course. But here, they live on."

It was a fascinating thought. Thousands and thousands of authors, scribbling away at their pages. And most of them gone now, leaving only the legacy of their words. Come to think of it, if most of these books were decades or centuries old . . . that meant that most people who had read most of these books would have died by now as well. It struck Oris as a peculiar window through which to view the world: whispers of a past long gone, which she could never truly know, but only hear echoes of in the words of those who had come before.

Dasko let them take it all in for a moment. Or rather, he let Oris take it in. Silvin was studying Oris more closely than the library, while Flip seemed merely bored. But then Dasko cleared his throat gently, and Oris mustered her thoughts.

"History might be the best place to start," said Dasko. "The information you seek will likely be found in its own absence, holes in our knowledge of the past where your predecessor had records expunged."

"But I need to learn to use magic," said Oris. "You said there were tomes of the arcane here as well, did you not?"

Dasko pursed his lips. "Yes, and more in the classrooms, which I am sure Philip will happily fetch for you. I warn you again that you have little hope of learning much from the study of other branches of magic than your own. But who knows? In this search we are all of us unknowing, and my counsel may be of little value."

Flip sighed. "Very well. If we're doing this, then let's get started."

Silvin looked around, appearing suddenly uneasy. "I would rather we did not study out here in the open. We will be coming at night, but some students or faculty have to come by on occasion, do they not? No one should see us at all, if we can help it."

"Then I suggest you move to the upper levels," said Dasko. "If anyone does come here in the night, they are likely to remain on the ground floor."

"Is there seating on the third floor?" said Silvin, turning to Flip.

"Most likely," he said, shrugging. "I think I remember some."

"There is indeed," said Dasko, hiding a smile. "But now I will leave you to your own devices. There is much to be done before the students return to the Academy."

"Thank you again," said Oris, giving him a half-bow.

"The honor is entirely mine," said Dasko.

He left them, and they made their way up one of the winding iron staircases to the third floor. There, Oris was surprised to see that the library seemed to extend back in a northern direction into the Academy itself, so that the third floor was in fact larger than the first. In that portion, the light of the domed roof did not reach so easily, and so there were many more lanterns to aid in reading, some of which they lit.

"That might be a good place," said Oris, pointing. There was a small nook tucked into the back corner of the building, up against the farthest wall. In the nook were three soft armchairs, with several wide tables around to hold extra books.

"Perfect," said Silvin. "It is partially hidden from view as well."

"All right," said Flip with a resigned sigh. "Let us begin our slog in the bookshelves."

CHAPTER XV
JOURNEYS INTO HISTORY

THEY SPENT ALL THAT DAY GATHERING A LIST OF BOOKS TO BEGIN THEIR search and locating what they could among the shelves. The library's organization was somewhat arcane, and they were helped not at all when they realized Flip knew nothing about it. But Silvin and Oris managed to puzzle it out, and Oris learned it with surprising speed and skill. Then, when at last they found their first books and began to read, Silvin and Flip were surprised again when Oris closed her tome an hour before the end of the day.

"Giving up?" said Flip.

"What?" said Oris, frowning. "Of course not. I'm finished."

"Finished?" said Silvin. "With what?"

"With this book." Oris held it up with a confused look.

Flip looked down at his own book. It was only slightly thicker than Oris', yet he had not quite reached the halfway mark in it. Silvin had read about the same. "How much of it did you read?" he asked.

Oris scowled at him and came over to grind her knuckles in his hair. "All of it, you great ass. Mayhap you have little wish to be here, but

I'm searching for knowledge that could save my life. I think you could give the search at least *most* of your attention."

"I'm studying the very hardest I can," said Flip, swatting her hands away, "and certainly more than I ever intended to do again in my life, particularly in this place. How was I to know that an oaf with arms like ale barrels would also have a scholar's mind?"

"Hardly," said Oris. "Though you shouldn't be surprised that the orphanage at least taught me to read."

The day ended with no great revelations. When they left through the front door, Mellie gave Oris and Silvin a deep bow and Flip a horrible grimace.

"I adore that woman," said Flip with a grin as they stepped out into the early twilight.

"We shall return tomorrow," said Silvin. "And I think we should come later in the day. The students will soon return, and it will serve us well to get used to staying up all night."

"This idea sounds worse and worse by the moment," said Flip.

"And do you have a better one?" said Oris. "By all means, let's have it."

Flip scowled. "Not yet. But trust me, I'm thinking on it."

They stayed up late that night, Oris and Flip deep in their cups and all of them discussing their plans for how they would pursue the knowledge they sought. The next day they returned to the Academy just after sundown. This time Mellie did not even glare at them through the hatch before letting them in, though she still eyed Flip with deep misgiving plain in her eyes.

This quickly became their routine. They would study until the glass roof began to lighten with dawn, and then they would retreat from the Academy, only to return after nightfall and resume their studies. After a few days, the students returned to the Academy, just as Dasko had said they would. But it hardly mattered. The students were still asleep when Oris, Flip, and Silvin left each morning, and they had mostly retreated to their dormitories before the three arrived each night. Flip always took them through the passages where he said they would encounter as few other people as possible. And even when they chanced upon a member of the faculty, Flip explained who he was and dropped Dasko's name, and they were allowed to pass unhindered. It seemed an alumnus returning to use the library was not so rare as all that.

Though the nighttime schedule did wear upon them all over time, they also found themselves growing more and more comfortable in their little nook on the third floor. The three of them would sprawl on their armchairs in all manner of strange positions, shifting any time they grew uncomfortable, until the chairs were more like bunks in a barracks than places for proper sitting.

Though they had at first thought they would need Flip's help to understand the library, Silvin and Oris' knowledge of it soon eclipsed his. He became something of a spectator to the research. Oris was surprised to find that while Flip had a good memory for a book once he had finished it, he had a tendency to get his words mixed up, as if they were turning around themselves in his mind. When she and Silvin realized this, they would relieve him of any tome that was particularly wordy or difficult, dividing the work to give him materials he could more easily absorb. Soon he began to tear through them at a rapid pace, and he no longer complained about their studies so loudly as he once had.

But despite the long hours they put in each night, Silvin soon began to grow agitated at their lack of progress. They could find not even an oblique mention of the last Lifemage or Necromancer, no matter how deeply they delved. Nor could they seem to find any of the "holes" in history that Dasko had advised them to search for. It seemed that the last Lifemage's purge was more effective than they had hoped.

Oris had to admit to herself that she was not as great a help in the search as she might have been. It surprised her that she was the fastest reader of the three. But she was also prone to losing herself in the books she tore through, pausing to linger on one passage or another, wondering at this or that thread of branching lore that seemed to hang from their edges. Sometimes she would pursue a line of research from one book to the next to the next, until a small tower of books stood on the table beside her, haphazard and leaning somewhat dangerously. But when she at last exhausted the search, she looked back only to realize that she had almost forgotten about finding the last Lifemage, and had been drawn off in some other direction entirely, such as the burial practices of ancient Idris, or the casualty reports from battles in Roth's conquest of the nine kingdoms.

If anyone were to find what they were looking for, it seemed it would be Silvin. She did not read quite so fast as Oris, but she kept a razor-sharp focus and would quickly abandon threads of lore that did not seem to be leading in the right direction. No tome was thick, wordy, or incomprehensible enough to daunt her. When she was deep in her research, she would sometimes shoot up in her seat, lay her book down, and stalk off towards the shelves.

"Oris, come along," she would say.

After the first couple of times, Oris obeyed without a second thought. Silvin would go dragging her fingers along the shelves until she found what she was looking for. If she could reach the book when she found it, she would pull it down and walk briskly back towards the little nook, mumbling "Never mind," and Oris would smile behind her back as she followed. But if the book was on one of the upper shelves, Silvin would snap her fingers at it and say, "That one." Then Oris would step in close and reach up, or grab a stool if it was too high even for her, and pull it down for Silvin, who would barely mutter a "My thanks" before walking back towards the nook, already tearing through the pages in her search.

Sometimes Silvin would stab her finger into a page and look up. "Oris, come look at this." Oris, usually after shaking herself out of whatever passage she was reading, would rise and come over. As she leaned over Silvin's shoulder, Silvin would read the passage out in her clear voice, emphasizing whatever she wanted Oris to notice—usually some reference to a historical figure who seemed important, but who saw little mention in other texts, which were the leads Silvin sought for the most.

If the passages were very long, or if Oris' and Silvin's discussion went on for more than a moment, Oris would, quite without realizing it, sometimes find herself sitting on the arm of Silvin's chair, leaning in close, sometimes tracing another passage of the book with her own finger. Then mayhap Silvin would fall silent, or Oris would lean closer still and catch a brief breath of the smell of her hair, and suddenly she would jerk upright, inventing an excuse to return to her own book, to which Silvin hastily agreed.

It did not improve Oris' mood that, every time such a thing happened, she could reliably glance over to find Flip grinning. But he never looked up at them.

Knowledge came slowly, but it did come. Between Silvin's focused interrogations, Oris' general studies, and the anecdotes and tidbits Flip gleaned from the journals and summary texts he preferred, they began to piece together a cohesive picture for what might have happened the last time the Lifemage and the Necromancer lived.

"Three hundred and twenty-seven years ago," muttered Silvin, flipping through a sheaf of the notes they had taken. "At least, that is when their clash would have ended. Or mayhap that is when the Lifemage died at last."

"And it seems the fighting took place in Selvan," said Oris. "It's the place written of least in that time, when it comes to politicking. Yet it's long been the centermost kingdom of Underrealm."

"And while there are few tomes of courts and kings, there are many of metallurgy and weapons," said Flip. "You can see the diagrams and sketches smiths were drawing, and how they made great leaps and advancements in the course of just a decade."

"Signs of a war that no one wrote any details about," said Oris. "All right. We're agreed on the when and where. And that leaves us . . ."

"Precisely nowhere," said Silvin, slumping back in her chair with a dejected sigh. "It's *too* well hidden. With nothing written of the Lifemage, I would not know where to begin studying how they learned to use their power."

"Quite some weeks we've spent coming to such an answer," said Flip, dropping his book down on the side table with a loud *slap*.

"It's only the first step," said Oris. "There's more to learn. You don't think your master learned it all in less than a month, do you?"

"He had more time than we do," said Silvin, pinching the bridge of her nose. "Or he thought he did. We have no idea when the Necromancer's next stroke could fall. And the High King could declare open war any day. In fact, I cannot imagine why she has not."

"Even the strongest crown quails at making war in winter," said Flip, shrugging. "The sleet, the cold, and the storms she'll face on the Great Bay make any such attempt less enticing than normal, and I am sure it was never an enticing thought to begin with."

"We'll find it," said Oris. "We have to."

But she, too, was beginning to feel a sense of growing danger, as though sand was slipping ever faster through an hourglass.

Yearsend came, and as it was a leap year, it was four days long. The holiday, normally a happy affair, was relatively cheerless for Oris. She and the others were deep in their discouragement, and feeling no closer to teaching Oris what she needed to know.

And then Flip surprised them. "I'm taking us out for a Yearsend feast," he declared.

It was evening, and they had just woken after sleeping all day. Through long inactivity, or mayhap laziness, they had stopped setting a watch while they slept. Oris and Silvin, who were still pulling on their boots, looked up at Flip in surprise.

"A feast?" said Silvin. "That is hardly a good way to remain hidden."

"We won't hold the feast in the High King's palace," said Flip with a smirk. "I'm taking you to a place called the Silver Stag, where I've secured a private room."

Silvin licked her lips, seemingly despite herself. "I know the Stag. There's no better supper served on the Seat. But there are few places more frequented by the wealthy and powerful."

"We've worked ourselves nearly to death the past few weeks," said Flip. "I don't know about you, but I'm nearly mad after being cooped up day after day. The pages of books spin in my dreams each night. We need to relax."

"The way you two celebrate, we can hardly expect to have a productive night in the library afterwards," said Silvin doubtfully.

"Good," said Flip. "Then let's spend the evening behind the blue door, or simply come back here and sleep. You may have been built to work tirelessly forever without rest, but I, for one, am not. And I think Oris has been feeling the same weariness."

"When did you arrange this?" said Oris.

"This morning, via our own innkeeper," said Flip with a smile. "And you're welcome."

Soon he had hurried them out of the Crescent Bulwark and into the city. Silvin kept telling them to pull their hoods down lower to hide their faces, and Oris and Flip obeyed as best they could. Though she had her own misgivings about losing a day of study, Oris could not deny the relief she felt at taking a night off.

When Flip ushered them in the front door of the Silver Stag, Oris could only stare. The craftsmanship involved in every square pace of the place rivaled the grandeur of the Academy itself, or what she imagined royal dwellings must look like. The walls were painted with mysterious creatures of legend, as well as many people in scenes of rest and comfort. A quartet of fiddlers in the corner gave a lovely but gentle accompaniment to the evening. And the smells . . . dishes Oris could not identify cast their tantalizing fingers of scent through the air, ensnaring her and luring her deeper in. Her mouth became a river, and her belly gave an angry rumble.

"Sky above," she breathed. "What are they serving here?"

Flip smirked at her, and even Silvin was smiling. "What do you want them to serve?" replied Flip. "Odds are, they've got it."

The Stag's master was a woman named Canda, who Oris swiftly decided was one of the more charming people she had ever met. Flip, true to his word, had secured them a private room. The round table was set against the back wall, into which a round alcove had been built to accommodate it, with a single round, cushioned bench that let them lounge while they ate, as if they were in their alcove in the library.

Every dish brought to them tasted better than the last. There was lamb and a fine roast and chicken, all of them of the highest quality. But the sauces and the spices set everything apart, so that Oris felt as if she were tasting entirely new meats she had never heard of before. Flip sat in the middle, and he insisted on Oris and Silvin trying everything, even feeding them tiny morsels so that they would not have to reach across the table. Oris and Silvin also offered each other selections they particularly enjoyed. But they did not feed each other, and there was a curious tightness in Oris' chest when she saw Flip pushing food between Silvin's lips. She might have imagined it, but Silvin seemed to be studying her very closely whenever Flip did the same for her.

The wine, too, was exquisite, and the Stag seemed to have anything else to drink that they could possibly wish. Flip ordered a bottle of his favorite brandy, and he scowled jealously when Oris asked to try it. But in fact it turned out that he had ordered three glasses to go with the bottle, and he poured it generously with a laugh when it came. Silvin sipped gingerly at her wine and had none of the brandy, but Flip and Oris caroused just about as hard as they ever had before. Soon the three of them were giggling, Flip and Oris leaning on each others' shoulders as they recounted tale after tale of their adventures before meeting Silvin.

But with the situation hanging over their heads, it was only a matter of time before things became somber once again. It happened when Flip was telling a story—one of many—of Oris preventing him from making a fool of himself.

"I am eternally ashamed," said Flip, burying his face in his hands. "She was tall and had a sharp look to her. The greenest eyes you've ever seen. But Oris told me afterwards that she was barely more than a girl, and looked upon me with nothing but slightly horrified amusement. I don't even remember what I said."

"You mustn't be too hard on yourself," said Oris, chuckling. "I've rarely seen you drink so much. And even drunk as you were, you didn't push past good sense when I told you to lay off."

"It's not often I let wine get the better of me," said Flip, shaking his head ruefully. "But it's simply embarrassing when someone who's not a professional—or Oris—sees it happen."

Silvin gave her harsh laugh. "When was this?" she said.

Flip's expression fell. "It was, in fact, during the Battle of Wellmont," he said quietly. "It was . . . I believe it would have been on the eighth day, the night of the third Dorsean attack."

"I see," murmured Silvin. "If I have my days right, that would have been the day before—"

"Yes," said Oris. "It was."

The room fell silent. Though the space had seemed more than large enough for their little party, Oris now felt that the walls pressed a bit closer than they had before.

"What if this doesn't work?" said Flip.

"What doesn't work?" said Oris.

Flip waved vaguely. "All of it. Our plan." He turned to Silvin. "I make light of things often. I see it as my job, or one of them. But I'm not unaware of the peril of our situation. Is it time to think of an alternative? In case we can't find the answers Oris needs?"

"I am always thinking of alternatives," said Silvin. "I have some in my cloak pocket, as it were, in case our situation should grow more dire. But all of them involve informing others of not only Oris' existence, but also her location. That is something I still wish to avoid. And as for me personally, I know no one else who would have a better way to help us than Dasko."

"But you *do* know others?" Oris pressed. "Other friends of your master, mayhap?"

Silvin suddenly glowered. "One in particular. But I would not bring you to him unless I had no other choice."

"Who is he?" said Flip.

"He was . . . well, it is not quite so simple, but you might say he was my master's master. He taught Jordel of the Lifemage in the first place."

Flip and Oris looked at each other incredulously. "You mean there's someone else out there who knew what your master knew?" said Flip. "Why in the dark below haven't we gone to him at once?"

"He knew very little compared to Jordel," said Silvin. "Though he often pretended at greater wisdom than he had."

"But he knows *something,* " said Oris. "That's more than we've got."

"You say that easily, yet you do not know him," spat Silvin. "I can think of few people in Underrealm who I despise more. He shrouds himself in a cloak of righteousness, and then he uses that cloak to smother and choke the life out of any joy or enjoyment that comes into his view.

"You have both served in fighting forces. You know drill sergeants, and you will have met some who were good and some who were awful. The awful ones are those who enjoy using power as a cudgel to beat their underlings into submission, all to satisfy their own arrogance. This man is among the worst of that sort. He will abuse and harangue everyone in his power endlessly, to the point where they break. Then he will offer the most halfhearted of apologies, even while he blames you for his mistakes, and tell you that he is only passionate because of the importance of his mission—because he knows that if you know the mission, you cannot deny the truth of what he says. And then, hardly before the apology is out of his mouth, he will return to his berations and his castigations, finding your every worst thought about yourself and tromping on it until you would rather throw yourself from a tower than live a moment longer with the shame *he* has made you feel. His name is Kal of the family Endil, and I would march you straight into the High King's palace before I brought you within a league of him."

Silvin looked down. Her hands had clenched into fists as she spoke, digging her nails through the wood of the table and carving furrows into it. Slowly she forced herself to relax, flexing her fingers and taking two long, deep breaths.

Oris reached across Flip and took her wrist. "I believe you," she said softly. "I believe he is what you say he is. Let us not speak of him again." Flip nodded.

Silvin gave them both a weak smile. "That I can agree to easily. And though I have no wish to end a pleasant evening on a sour note, I think it is time we left. Already we have stayed overlong."

They finished their last morsels and headed out of the Stag. The crowd in the front room had only grown with the lateness of the hour, and they had some trouble navigating their way through the press. Halfway through, a door opened and a server emerged with a tray full of food. Silvin had to swerve quickly to avoid slamming into him, but that only made her slam shoulder-first into another patron.

"My apologies," she muttered.

The man turned. "Think nothing of—Silvin?"

Oris froze. She and Flip turned. The man before them was short, mayhap a pace and two thirds. His thin hair was combed back, letting his balding pate shine through its wisps. Oris' heart sank. He wore no cloak of red, but pinned to his shoulder was a Mystic badge. Silvin's eyes were wide.

"Sky above," he said with a little gap-toothed smile. "It *is* you! What are you doing here on the Seat?"

"Nothing at all," said Silvin nastily, glaring at him. "Passing through. I will not be here more than a day or two."

To Oris' immense relief—and no doubt to Silvin's—the man's eyes flashed with recognition. "Of course. Well, do not let me interfere with your night. If you have a chance before you depart, come by for dinner, will you?"

"I will not have time," said Silvin. She hurried away, not looking at Oris or Flip. They met each others' gazes and followed more slowly, drifting slightly away from Silvin so that they did not appear to be following her out.

In the open air again, Silvin's look was one of pure anger. Flip glanced back over his shoulder and spat. "Arrogant steer. How did you know him?"

"A job I had to take, once upon a time," said Silvin. "You are more than correct. He is indeed an arrogant steer, and worse."

Flip chuckled, and in a moment they set off together towards their inn. But once he was no longer looking, Silvin's expression turned to one of deep concern. Oris saw it, and she worried for what it might mean.

• ○ • ○ •

Lord Prince Eamin entertained a guest for dinner the next day: Tamas Farco, chancellor of the Mystic Order and one of the higher ranking officers upon the Seat. Though the last day of Yearsend had been only yesterday, they wished each other happiness for the holiday, and then they began to tuck in.

"How go the order's preparations?" said Eamin, once they had eaten enough to take the edge off.

"Slower than we would like," said Tamas. He ran his hand back across his shiny, mostly bald head. "Slower, certainly, than I am sure your esteemed mother would prefer. But between coordinating our efforts to rebuild and planning for the campaign—well, there is only so much speed you can put into five thousands of soldiers at once."

"No one could blame you for that, least of all my esteemed mother." Eamin grinned. "Though she may say differently when in council with the lord chancellor."

Tamas gave a wide, gap-toothed smile. "Power demands its own employment if one wishes to keep it. The lord chancellor understands that better than most."

"Have they decided where to send the greater part of the Mystics?"

"Feldemar," said Tamas. He tilted his goblet of wine towards a large map on the north wall, depicting all the nine lands as well as some of the area around them. "A stronghold called Ammon."

Eamin frowned. "I am not sure I am familiar."

Tamas grew solemn. "It is a point of strength in the eastern part of the kingdom. It belonged to Jordel of the family Adair, who bequeathed it to the order after . . . well. After."

Eamin bowed his head, and when he raised it again he also raised his goblet. "To Jordel, and all the others taken by the darkness."

"Hear, hear," said Tamas, raising his own goblet. "Though Jordel left a greater impression on Underrealm than most. Never sat a throne, but I would have traded him for many who did—your venerable mother being an exception, of course."

Eamin chuckled. "I understand completely, and I could not agree more. The coming war will be harder without him—without his strong sword arm, and without his keen mind."

"Funnily enough," said Tamas, "I ran into one of Jordel's protégés just last night, while I was taking my holiday at the Silver Stag."

"Did you really?" said Eamin. "Though I suppose that is hardly surprising. He had so many of them."

"That he did," said Tamas, nodding firmly. "This one was a woman named Silvin. I do not know her well myself, but I know Jordel was particularly fond of her. A knight, once stationed in Garsec, I believe?

She was out of uniform—some secretive business. Had two others with her, and I suspect they did not know she was of our order. Nearly bit my head off when I spoke to her, which, well. We have all been on assignments where we had to pretend ill manners."

Eamin's expression did not change. But his eyes had fixed upon Tamas with exceptional focus.

"It is regrettable how often such subterfuge is necessary," he said. "I suppose you did not find out where she was staying, then? I should like to visit her and pay my condolences for the passing of her master."

"A noble desire," said Tamas. "I should have thought to do the same, though I suppose not if she was trying to keep her identity hidden." He chuckled. "But no, she very nearly sprinted away the moment she recognized me—or the moment I recognized her, I should say. It was almost comically abrupt. Though if she is working secretly here on the Seat, there are a few favored inns among our order for that kind of work. Though then again, if she is truly trying to be secretive, she might avoid those places like plague." He gave a faint titter. "I could make inquiries."

"Pray do not trouble yourself," said Eamin. "The coming conflict keeps us all more than busy enough."

Their conversation drifted to other things. But though Eamin never lapsed in his manners, he was less talkative than usual, and he soon brought their meal to a close.

The moment Tamas had gone, Eamin summoned Idulen of the family Steth. When Idulen came, he found the Lord Prince pacing back and forth in his chamber, and Eamin looked up with grateful relief as Idulen entered.

"Idulen," he said. "Thank the sky. I need you to do something for me."

"Of course, Your Highness," said Idulen. "You have but to name it."

"There is a Mystic woman here on the Seat. Her name is Silvin, of no family name that I know of. She is concealing her identity as a redcloak, and I have no wish for you to reveal it. But I need you to locate her at once, and bring her location to me."

"Of course," said Idulen. "Should I expect danger from her?"

"No no," said Eamin. "No force whatsoever. I only need to see her."

"Yes, Your Highness," said Idulen, bowing. "I shall see to it at once. What is this about?"

"Nothing," said Eamin. "Not yet, at any rate. Just a hunch."

• ○ • ○ •

Oris, Flip, and Silvin spent all that day in the Crescent Bulwark, Oris and Flip nursing piercing headaches after their excesses the night before. But when evening rolled around, Silvin dragged them both out of bed and got them ready for another night at the Academy.

"Tonight?" groaned Flip. "You can't be serious."

"We wasted a day already," said Silvin. "And while I appreciated the rest, now it is time to return to work."

They kept grumbling—Flip more than Oris—but they roused themselves. And their routine resumed. Night after night, as winter began to climb out of its own depths towards spring, they burned away candles and pored through stacks of books in search of answers.

On the thirteenth of Martis, they left the Crescent Bulwark as usual. But when they reached the Academy, they found Dasko pacing before its wide front door. His eyes sharpened when he saw them, and wordlessly he gestured them to follow him away from the door and around the corner of the Academy's front wall.

"Dasko?" said Silvin. "What is it? What is wrong?"

"Many things," said Dasko. "Something has been happening at the Academy. There have been attacks."

"Attacks?" said Flip, his expression suddenly grave. "By whom?"

"We do not know," said Dasko, rubbing his hand over his face. "But people have been killed. A member of the faculty, a student. We thought we had arrested the culprit. But last night, another student was killed. The Dean has ordered that the Academy be closed to all outsiders. Even the students' routines have been restricted. Alumni are prohibited from using the library except with express permission from the Dean or the High King herself."

"Could you convince the Dean to authorize us?" said Oris. "We cannot stop our search now."

"He is focused entirely on the danger to his students," said Dasko. "I could not intervene without expressly telling him *why* you need the library so badly." He paused and gave Flip a wry look. "And even then, he would be reticent to allow a Drayden into the Academy, particularly now. Though I will admit some part of me would be tremendously amused to see the two of you meet."

"You have to find another way to help us," said Silvin. "Please, Dasko. You know what is at stake."

"I do," said Dasko. "And I know the value you place on secrecy. But if I cannot tell him the truth, my hands are bound."

"If we cannot find the knowledge that Oris needs, everything is in danger," said Silvin. "That includes the Academy, and the Dean and his students."

Dasko sighed. He stepped forwards and took Silvin by the shoulders. "You know that I know that. I am sorry, Silvin, but arguing with me will accomplish nothing. Do you not believe that I would help you if I could? Do you not think I have tried to find any way I could? I can think of only one. Go to the High King. Tell her why you are here. She will grant you access to the Academy, and likely more help besides."

Silvin's arms were twitching, her fists curling and uncurling. Oris watched as she took two deep breaths, the first shaky, but the second more measured. Finally she bowed her head. "Very well. I believe you, and I am sorry for doubting you. I . . . I will consider your advice."

"Good," said Dasko. "Think hard on it, and I know you shall choose the right path."

"Thank you," said Silvin. "If ever you need to reach us, you can find us at the Crescent Bulwark. If anything here changes . . ."

"I shall summon you at once," said Dasko. "And I shall rejoice if I do, for it means the Academy is safe again." He let go her shoulders, stepped back, and gazed upon them sadly. "Fare well. You have my hopes for better days—for all of us."

Their trek back to the Bulwark was much slower than when they had left it. Oris studied Silvin from the corner of her eye. Silvin's eyes kept darting in every direction, her gaze remaining far away.

"We'll think of something," said Oris.

"Of course," murmured Silvin.

"I think Dasko's right," said Flip. "I don't even know if we have other choices, but if we do, they're swiftly running out. Why not bring ourselves to the palace?"

"I . . . we might," said Silvin. "If we have to."

Flip snorted, but he spoke no further.

The moment they entered the Crescent Bulwark, Oris could feel that something was wrong. The innkeeper, Ellden, was rigid behind his bar, and his eyes widened as he saw them. Silvin, too, seemed to notice something was wrong, and Oris felt her tense. But Ellden came scuttling out from behind the bar and stood before them, wringing his hands obsequiously.

"Some—" His voice cracked, and he cleared his throat. "Someone has come to see you."

Oris and Silvin seized their blades, and Flip raised his hands. Several people in the common room looked sharply at them. But Ellden squealed and waved his hands desperately at them to stop.

"No! No no!" he cried, seizing Silvin's wrists and then lowering his voice. "Please don't be a fool. I would never have let him remain here if he meant you harm. He . . ." His eyes darted to the corner.

A figure rose from a chair. Oris, Silvin, and Flip whirled on him as he came forwards. Oris was expecting the massive frame of Barrick, or mayhap another shadeborn. But this man was of normal size, if a bit broad in the shoulders. He was a man of square jaw, lightly dusted with stubble. He looked youthful, Oris' own age, in fact. But there was a severity to his eyes, a weight in his gaze that spoke of much wisdom or much painful experience, or mayhap both, and there were strands of grey in the fair hair she could glimpse under the hood.

Silvin's arms went entirely limp. Flip, on the other hand, went as rigid as she had been a moment before.

Oris looked between the two of them. "What?"

Flip gave a single high-pitched bark of a laugh that sounded more like a scream.

"What?" said Oris.

"Might we retire?" said the stranger. "I would guess you have no wish for prying eyes, and neither do I. Already too many people have noted this meeting."

"Of course," gasped Silvin. "Our room."

"Very good." The man turned to the innkeeper. "Thank you, Ellden. Your service has been invaluable, as always, and my gratitude only increases."

If Ellden was trying to answer, his quiet squeaking was a poor substitute. Since no one else seemed capable of movement or even further speech, Oris gave an exasperated snort and started off towards their room. Silvin and Flip stood transfixed a moment longer, until the stranger began to follow Oris, at which point they hurriedly came along behind.

Once they were in the room and the door closed behind them, Silvin went to sit in the single chair. But the moment her rear touched it, she leaped back up. "I . . . you should sit," she told the stranger. She went and sat on the bed instead, but then leaped up just as quickly, as she seemed to realize that the stranger had not yet sat down.

"Please, do not trouble yourself so," said the stranger, raising a hand to calm her.

"For the love of the sky and hate of the dark below, will someone tell me *what is going on?"* growled Oris.

The stranger cast back his hood, revealing rugged but immaculately trimmed hair and a bemused expression—but Oris thought he also looked a little sad. Flip, on the other hand, wore an entirely manic grin that could have doubled as a terrified grimace. He spread one arm wide to gesture at the man, as though presenting an actor at a theater.

"Oris, may I please introduce you to Eamin of the family Lemstad," he said, "eldest son and only child of Enalyn of the family Lemstad, High King of Underrealm, chief in Her Majesty's council, the Lord Prince of the nine kingdoms and presumptive heir to the throne."

Oris stared at Flip. And she kept staring at Flip. Because how could she look at the Lord Prince *now?* How could she ever look upon him again?

At last she blinked twice, and then she walked over to the chair. She sat. And the instant her rear touched it, she leaped up as she realized Eamin was still standing.

"Let me make a proposal," said Eamin slowly. "I am going to sit down now. And then all of you are going to sit down, and we are all going to forget about whatever it is we are thinking hardest of in this moment."

He dropped down on the floor, sitting with his back to the wall.

"Your Highness!" screeched Silvin and Flip at once.

"Your Grace!" cried Oris at the same time.

"No, you fool, it's Highness," snapped Flip. "He's not some lesser king."

Silvin ignored them both as she flapped her hands uselessly at Eamin. "Please, you cannot—the chair, or the bed, if you prefer, but I would be—"

"Sit," said Eamin. "Down."

Silvin fell back upon the bed at once. Oris looked down and found with some surprise that she had sunk into the chair, and Flip was now sitting against the opposite wall from the Lord Prince.

"Very good," said Eamin. "Now." He turned to Silvin. "You are Silvin, of the—"

"Of no family, Your Highness," said Silvin. It looked as though it pained her beyond reason to cut him off, but she did it.

Eamin's eyes flashed. "Oh," he said carefully. "My mistake. In any case . . . I had heard that your master had passed. I knew him—though not as well as some others, and certainly not as well as I would have liked. I came to pay my condolences. The nine lands have rarely seen a greater servant than he."

For the first time, Silvin's overawed look faded. "He did indeed pass," she said, somewhat stiffly. "And I thank you for your kind words. I know he would have been honored beyond measure by them."

"The honor would have been mine. In his life, he provided a greater service to Underrealm than I have been able to, restricted as I am by the politics of the court." Suddenly he leaned forwards and pressed his hands together where they hung limp off his lap. "I have come for another, secondary purpose. Jordel was working on something before he died. A task that took him all over the nine kingdoms. I wondered if you were ever included in that task."

Silvin swallowed hard. She looked to Oris, and Oris looked back.

"We lost the Academy," said Flip. "I don't know that we have any other choice."

"We might," said Silvin. "I just need more time."

"Silvin," said Oris quietly.

Silvin's gaze remained locked on hers for another long moment. Then, at last, she sighed and turned back to Eamin.

"Yes," she said. "Yes, Jordel told me of his plans. And I aided him in them. And . . . and we have succeeded. Though to my great pain, Jordel never knew it before his end."

Eamin's gaze grew razor-sharp. "You succeeded? But where . . ." He looked between Oris and Flip.

But Flip gave him a wide grin. "Oh, not me, Your Highness." He pointed to Oris.

Eamin looked at her. "You are . . ." He let the question hang.

"I have been led to believe that I am, Your Highness," said Oris.

Eamin got to his feet. But before the rest of them could rise, he went to Oris and knelt before her chair. Silvin tensed, and Flip's eyes were as wide as Oris had ever seen them. She felt more uncomfortable than she could believe as Eamin looked earnestly up into her face.

"You cannot imagine what your arrival means to me—to all of Underrealm," he said.

He now looked as awestruck by Oris as Flip and Silvin had been when first they saw him. Oris hated it. It was like . . . like he was looking at her as a thing, a strange and unknown creature of mystery and wonder, like an Elf.

"I don't mean to be rude," said Oris slowly. "But I wish I had never arrived at all. Or that someone else was this thing that everyone else expects me to be."

To her surprise, Eamin gave a sad smile. "I think I understand."

Then, suddenly, his manner grew brisk, and he rose to his feet once more. This time Oris, Flip, and Silvin did the same.

"Very well," said Eamin. "Now that we are here, we should act quickly. I shall need all of you to come with me to the palace. I will introduce you to my mother, and we can begin—"

Again, though it looked like she would rather die, Silvin interrupted. "We cannot do that, Your Highness. We have to keep Oris a secret."

Eamin frowned, deep lines forming in his face. "A secret?" he said. "Whatever for?"

"Because our enemy is too well prepared," said Silvin. "He has been planning his campaign against us for . . . well, we do not know for how long, but much longer than we have known of Oris' existence. The attack on the Seat is proof enough of that. He distracted Her Majesty in Wellmont and drew her strength there, and when she was exposed, he enlisted Dulmun's aid to depose her. Only good fortune saved Underrealm then. Who knows what other kings have heard his whispers in their ears? All of us are on the back foot. Revealing Oris would only make her a target."

"Of course the High King would understand that," said Eamin. "She would know we had to keep Oris a secret from the world at large."

"Secrets don't exist in the palace, Your Highness," said Flip. "Meaning all due respect. I'm personally of the opinion that you're right and we should tell Her Majesty, but I don't say that under any illusion that Oris will remain hidden for more than an hour once we do."

Eamin's mouth twisted. "I . . . suppose I cannot argue that point," he said. "Let us say I was to agree with you, Silvin. What, then, would be your aim?"

"We are trying to help Oris uncover her magic," said Silvin. "But we don't know how. We think Jordel had some idea, but he is gone. I had a contact at the Academy who was letting us use the library. That was of limited usefulness, but we might have been on the right trail. And yet even that resource is lost to us now."

"Because of the attacks on the students. I understand." Suddenly Eamin's eyes flashed. "I may have it. I may be able to get you what you need."

Silvin frowned. "How?"

"Few enough in Underrealm know of the Lifemage," said Eamin. "Among them, fewer still are given the knowledge of what to do when they are reborn. But the High King is chief among those few."

"Yet we do not wish to reveal her to the High King," said Silvin.

Eamin shook his head. "I will not. Yet I am inquisitive, and she knows it. Let me worry about how to get the information. What will you do with it if I find it?"

"Teach Oris," said Silvin at once. "Once she is in command of her powers, then we can reveal her to Her Majesty, and she can take her place at the head of this war."

Oris did not much like the sound of that. But Eamin nodded eagerly.

"Very well. Then I have little else to do here." He turned back to Oris and smiled at her. "Honestly, I doubt you can know how relieved I am that you are here. For the first time since messengers brought word of the Necromancer to the palace, I can allow myself to hope again."

"Your confidence is . . . overwhelming, if I am being honest," said Oris. "I do not know that I can be who you are expecting."

"I suspect you have had a life that makes you feel less than you are," said Eamin. "But when the occasion comes, you will rise to meet it. I know it."

He gave Silvin and Flip each a solemn nod. Then, raising his hood, he let himself out the door. The moment it closed behind him with a soft *click,* Silvin fell back upon the bed, staring at the ceiling.

"Sky above," she breathed. "Sky above."

"And dark below," said Flip.

"Do you really think he can keep the secret?" said Oris. "What if the High King realizes what he's doing?"

Silvin shook her head. "He is the Lord Prince. He has grown up in the court. I doubt there are any minds in the nine lands sharper than his, or more skilled at hiding things. If there was one agent to send into the palace to help us, without telling anyone else, I could not have chosen a better candidate."

Oris nodded. But she stared doubtfully at the door through which Eamin had left.

CHAPTER XVI
THE PAST RECLAIMED

Idulen was waiting for Eamin on the street outside the Crescent Bulwark. He stepped forth quickly as Eamin emerged from the inn.

"Your Highness," said Idulen. "Everything went well?"

"Not entirely," said Eamin. "But now there is much work ahead of us."

"What work?" said Idulen. "Forgive me, Your Highness, but what is this all about?"

"And you must forgive me, my friend, but I cannot tell you," said Eamin. "I have pledged my silence. But with any luck, not for long. Listen now. When we return to the palace, I need you to request an immediate audience with my mother."

Soon they reached the palace, and it was done. Idulen returned and told Eamin his mother would see him at once.

"Thank you, Idulen," said Eamin. "Ever are you faithful and diligent in your service. The rest of tonight's work is mine. Get some rest, but stay close, just in case."

Eamin quickly made his way to the High King's chambers. There was a small delay as he was inspected by Kris, the captain of the palace guard. A slender twixt with neatly trimmed short hair and only half a left arm, they could be warm, but their face was now impassive as steel. Additional security measures had been enacted since the attack on the Seat. First Kris inspected Eamin for his family mark: a small tattoo on the inside of his upper arm. It depicted a circle in two halves, one white and one black, the dividing line diagonal. When Kris was satisfied, they sent for Asbeth. He was a young dwarf, and the High King's personal weremage, and he inspected Eamin to ensure he was not another weremage in disguise. But finally, Kris was satisfied that Eamin was who he appeared to be, and they permitted him through the outer parlor and into Enalyn's study.

When at last he stood before her, Eamin found Enalyn wearing a wry look. "Good evening, Lord Prince," she said as she gestured for Eamin to take a seat with her. "I must say I admire your adherence to decorum in sending Idulen. But you *are* my son. You are allowed to come and visit me without putting it through diplomatic channels."

Eamin chuckled. "Thank you, Mother," he said. "But I would rather not put you under any obligation to take audience with me if you are already in council. And for my own sake—now and in the future—I would rather not have someone like the lord chancellor see you refuse me, and send me away like a little boy."

Enalyn's smile dampened. "That is very wise of you," she said with a sigh. "I confess that to this day I sometimes struggle to navigate our relationship. To me, you *are* still my little boy, though it is plain for anyone to see that you are your own man now, and shrewder even than I was at your age. But it grows too late to waste time on idle thoughts. What do you require?"

Eamin eyed Kris and the other two guards in the room. "It concerns that matter I spoke with you about not long ago."

"Kris," said Enalyn, lifting a hand. Kris beckoned, and the guards swiftly withdrew from the study to the parlor. When they were gone, Enalyn arched an eyebrow. "We have spoken of many things recently."

Eamin leaned forwards, rubbing his hands together. "Yet only once have we spoken of the Lifemage."

Enalyn's eyes flashed. "The Lifemage? What is it? Have you heard something?"

Inside, Eamin quailed. But he was an expert at keeping his inner thoughts hidden. Enalyn had taught him that herself. And she had also taught him to assuage his own conscience by avoiding a lie even while hiding the truth. "You are much preoccupied with the coming conflict in Dulmun," he said. "I am of limited use to you in such counsel, since I will not be joining the fight personally."

Enalyn's voice took on a note of irritation. "I cannot and will not risk your life in—"

"Mother, please," said Eamin, holding up a hand. "We have argued that point enough, and I am not trying to convince you otherwise now. But there may yet be another way I can be of use. You are spread thin, and most of your thought must be bent on the conflict of arms. Let me be your servant in this other matter. I know you have access to secret information about the Lifemage, things no one else knows. Maybe there is something that I could use to help us find them, wherever they are."

The study fell to silence. Enalyn's fingers tapped on the arm of her chair, and her gaze slid past Eamin to the far distance, as it often did when she was playing thoughts through her mind, considering possibilities. When she spoke, it was slowly.

"If you were preoccupied with such studies, it could raise awkward questions about why you are not participating in the war. I do not know how I would answer such questions without telling people things they are not meant to know. Mayhap one of your agents could pursue the matter—someone like Idulen?"

"I will use Idulen's help, certainly," said Eamin. "But I cannot tell him everything. In this conflict, there are matters that will have to be handled by those of us who are highest on the ladder."

"Hm," said Enalyn. "Very well. But I will still require your presence at every council. We cannot undermine your authority or give any appearance of my having lost confidence in you. Now least of all."

"Of course, Your Majesty."

Her mouth twisted. "Enough of that. Come with me."

She rose, and Eamin stood as well, expecting her to lead him out of the room. But instead, Enalyn simply went to the back wall, where a tapestry hung. She took the pole it hung on and swung it out, revealing a wood panel that looked blank. But Eamin knew there was a door in it, cleverly hidden and closed with a secret latch. Enalyn inserted two fingers into a crack in the wood and tripped the latch, and the door swung open. Inside there was another study, alike in appearance to the outer room, but much smaller.

Eamin balked. "It is in *here?*"

Enalyn looked back at him curiously. "Where did you think I kept it? The dungeons?"

"No, of course," said Eamin. "Only . . . only, I have known about this study since I was not yet grown. For years and years, I used to sneak in here and read for hours. I am surprised I did not stumble on the truth long ago."

"I remember those days," said Enalyn, and her voice was wistful. "But I never showed you this."

She went to one of the bookshelves in the room and placed a hand on the side of it. Then her hand slid around the back, and Eamin heard a familiar *click.* Then, slowly, as Enalyn pulled, the bookshelf began to roll away from the wall. Behind it stood another blank wall—or at least, it looked to be so.

Eamin could not help but bark a laugh. "Sky above," he said. "A secret within a secret."

"Layers and layers of protection," said Enalyn. "When the Shades ransacked our palace, they savaged everything in my private chambers. But they did not discover my secret study. Let us imagine, however, that they happened to discover the secret door. It is doubly likely they would not look further than that, thinking they had penetrated to the very core of my defenses."

"You have taught me this since I was only a child," said Eamin, shaking his head. "But I never thought of its use in this manner. You tell me often that I am uncommonly wise for my age. Yet my greatest fear is that I will always be measured against your own wit, for then I think I will always be found wanting."

Enalyn smiled. Then she turned a key in a crack in the wall, and the second secret door swung open. Inside was an even smaller study—nothing more than a chair, a table, and a single bookshelf. Above the table was a shelf built into the wall, where were laid some parchment, several quills, and a full inkwell. They did not look to have been used in some time.

"Only my most precious things are in here," said Enalyn. "The secrets it is most important for no one else to discover."

"I see," said Eamin. He chuckled. "You make me very suspicious, Mother. Even now, I find myself thinking there must be another layer of secrets behind this one."

Enalyn turned to him. There was no trace of a jest in her eyes. "There is," she said. "But you shall find out about *that* when it is your turn for the throne."

Eamin's smile died, and he bowed his head. "Of course, Your Majesty."

Again her mouth twisted. She stepped into the room. Eamin did not follow her, for the place was not big enough for more than one at a time. She gestured to the shelf with the quills, ink, and parchment. "You may use those to take notes as you study." She ran her hand along the top shelf, which held several books of different sizes, but all of them in the same sort of black leather binding. No titles were written upon them that Eamin could see. "This is where you can hope to find what you are looking for."

"Thank you, Mother," said Eamin. "I shall get to work at once."

"Do not stay up too late," said Enalyn. "Both for your own sake, and because I will require your presence at council tomorrow. But I wish you good hunting. And I ask only that you keep me appraised of anything you discover."

Again Eamin wilted inside as he thought of Oris, waiting for him in a tavern not far away. But he only nodded. "I shall certainly tell you of anything I think will help."

• ○ • ○ •

Two days passed at the Crescent Bulwark with no word from the palace. The waiting was much worse than it had been in Dracmund, what felt like a lifetime ago. Then, the prospect of the coming war and Oris' role as the Lifemage had seemed like faraway things, vague possibilities. Now they were an inevitability, and yet Oris could do nothing to prepare for them.

"Cheer up, dear," said Flip on the third day. Oris was sitting on one of the beds with her arms folded, and Flip had splayed out across it, laying his head in her lap. "You're far too eager to see the bad of our situation, when there are so many things to enjoy. Namely, free food and lodging. When have we ever wanted more?"

"I've never wanted an axe to be hanging over my neck, for one thing," said Oris.

"Ah, but with all the times we've been in danger, what's another?" said Flip.

Oris poked him in the eye. Flip howled and recoiled from her, but it did less to cheer Oris up than she had hoped it might.

Silvin, meanwhile, sat on the other bed with her legs folded, leaning back against the wall. She was studying Oris openly.

"Flip is not wrong," said Silvin now. "There are many things we cannot control. There is virtue in appreciating the things we can, when they are going well."

"I think our comforts are far outweighed by the dangers," said Oris. "I'm supposed to win a war against the very lord of death. He's been preparing for who knows how long, and even now he's carrying out plans we know nothing about. Meanwhile, I'm languishing here and trying not to drink myself to death."

"Worse ways to go," growled Flip, rubbing his eye and taking a swig from a wine bottle he had just remembered.

Silvin climbed to her feet. "All right," she said. "Come on. I am getting you out of here."

Oris frowned. "Out of here? Where are we going?"

"You complained about languishing," said Silvin. "Do you really care where I am taking you?"

"Are you certain?" said Flip, arching an eyebrow and concealing a grin. "I could go out instead and let the two of you have the room to yourselves."

"Go to the dark below, Flip," growled Oris.

"I agree with Oris," said Silvin, though she, too, was hiding a smile. "Flip, we are going beyond the city walls to the southern cliffs. If you need us, that is where you can find us."

"I know the area," said Flip, waving a hand at them. "Have fun."

Oris got herself bundled up and followed Silvin out of the Bulwark, though she grumbled and growled as she did it. They raised their hoods against the snow as they stepped into the open air. But despite the chill, Oris felt better the moment she was outside. She had not left the room for anything but the privy for days, and it felt good to get blood pumping through her legs again after so long idle.

They had left Flip behind, and so Silvin flashed her Mystic badge at the southern gate. Beyond the walls, there was a sort of narrow plain running along the edge of the island, which ended abruptly in sheer cliffs that fell half a span to the cold water of the Great Bay far below. A road ran through the gate and turned both left and right, but it was not much traveled, having been built mostly for city guards to circle the city without being slowed by the streets. Silvin took Oris west, and before too long, they passed enough turns in the walls that the gate was out of sight.

"All right," said Silvin. She stopped, turned to Oris, and reached up for the clasp of her cloak, undoing it to let it fall at her feet.

Oris hesitated, looking around. There was nothing here, only the city wall half a span away. There were no passersby, though she did spot one guard atop the wall, looking down at them with passing interest.

"All right what?" she said. "What are we doing here?"

Silvin smiled. Despite shedding her cloak, she did not look at all cold. "Sparring."

Oris stared, dumbfounded. She blinked. "Sparring?"

"We have all been cooped up," said Silvin. "It is driving us mad—you most of all, but myself as well, though I am better at hiding it. So you and I?" She pointed to Oris, and then to herself. "We are sparring."

Unbidden, a smile spread across Oris' face. "No swords."

"Agreed."

Silvin unbuckled her blades and lay them carefully atop her cloak. Oris shed her own cloak and sword belt. The biting cold struck her with a thousand tiny knives, but she did her best to hide it. If Silvin could take the cold, Oris certainly could.

"You'd better not let me win the way you did with Flip," said Oris.

Silvin gave her a savage grin. "I told you once I would never lie to you. That includes *never* letting you beat me. One rule, though. We should not hit each other in the face. We do not need to attract notice for having bruises and split lips."

Oris grinned. "Fair enough."

And she drove her fist into Silvin's gut.

Silvin's breath *whooshed* out of her as her eyes widened in shock. But she recovered quickly and struck back, jabbing Oris twice in the chest and ribs.

Oris fell back two steps and raised her fists. From the corner of her eye she noticed the guard on the wall. He was watching with much more interest now, though he seemed to recognize this was no true combat, and he made no move to raise an alarm. Oris grinned.

"Are you sure about this?" said Oris. "I've got the reach and the weight."

"An odd boast, but all right," said Silvin.

Oris came in swinging. Silvin warded off the first pair of blows. But her eyes were on Oris' arms, and so Oris brought a swift knee right under her ribs. Again Silvin's breath left her, this time with a groan. Oris brought her fists together and slammed them into Silvin's back just below the neck. The Mystic fell facedown in the snow.

"Come now," said Oris, smiling as she backed up. "You said you wouldn't hold back, but you've got to be."

Silvin's head whipped up. In her eyes was a fury that struck the smile from Oris' face.

"Now, now—" Oris began.

She could not see quite how Silvin did it. The Mystic launched herself from lying on the ground into a feral leap that covered the pace between them in a blink. Her bony shoulder crashed into Oris' stomach, making her reel away. Even as Oris winced, Silvin battered her with flat hands that felt like knives. Oris' right arm went numb.

But years as a sellsword had taught her many dirty tricks. She fell to one knee as if winded. When Silvin moved to press the attack, Oris suddenly seized her legs.

For a brief moment it struck her just how *hard* Silvin was—it was like grabbing two rods of iron. But she was still light, and Oris shot up. Silvin flipped over, landing badly on her back with a grunt.

Oris came after her warily, but not warily enough. Silvin rolled back on her shoulders and pushed off. But instead of leaping up, she brought her feet together and slammed both of them into Oris' groin. It was like being rammed by a bull. Oris wheezed and stumbled back once more. It gave Silvin the time she needed to regain her feet.

"Dark below," said Oris, trying to will the pain away. "I doubt you learned that trick as a Mystic."

"No," said Silvin. She was smiling now, but the fury still blazed in her eyes, and Oris could not look away from them. "I learned tricks like that to survive. The Mystics taught me other things—mostly how to fight wizards."

That made Oris curious despite herself. "It's not good enough just to punch them?"

Silvin's hackles seemed to come down. "Most times it is. But it helps to know how to disable their magic. Every type of wizard takes a different trick. Mindmages, for example. You hit them in the eyes. If they cannot see, they cannot cast their spells. With an alchemist, you break their hands and fingers. They have to touch things, and they have to focus while they do it. Here is how you hit a firemage."

Oris had relaxed her guard. She barely had time to think *I'm a fool* before Silvin punched her hard in the throat, and she fell back choking.

"Firemages have to speak to use their magic," said Silvin. "Weremages, on the other hand, only have to think. So you do this."

Her hands lashed out, one fist crashing into each of Oris' temples. Oris grunted and nearly fell as the world exploded into bright stars. She stumbled away, glaring.

"I thought we weren't supposed to hit each other in the face?" she choked out.

Silvin smiled, showing her teeth. "Only a child complains they are losing a fight because it is *unfair.*"

"Fine," said Oris.

She rushed in. Silvin readied to ward punches, but Oris grappled her instead. Her massive arms enclosed Silvin's, pressing them tight against her body. Silvin growled and tried to strike with her hands like knives again, but she could not swing them wide enough.

Oris drove a knee into Silvin's groin in repayment for the earlier blow, and then she did it again. Then she lifted Silvin off the ground, and as the Mystic struggled to find any purchase, Oris slammed her forehead into Silvin's nose. All the while she kept tightening her grip. She could feel ribs creaking.

"You shouldn't let someone get their hands on you when they're as big as I am," she said through gritted teeth.

Silvin only snarled in response. The rage in her was mounting, and from it she seemed to draw strength. Oris stared in disbelief as Silvin's arms began to push out, forcing Oris' grip to slacken.

That's strong, thought Oris. *Too strong.*

Then Silvin's leg came whipping around. It hit Oris' knee, and she buckled.

Oris just managed to turn as she fell. Her full weight crashed into Silvin as they hit the ground together. The smaller woman did not even blink, and she kept inexorably pushing Oris' grip farther and farther out.

Oris gave up the grapple and whipped her hand up to seize Silvin's throat, pushing herself up. Silvin gurgled, but her fists struck Oris in the ribs.

That was harder than Enfil, thought Oris, even as she wheezed.

But her hand was still on Silvin's throat, and she lifted her other fist. Twice it crashed into Silvin's temple, and Silvin's gaze started to wander. She had just enough presence of mind to drive her fingers hard under Oris' arm holding her throat.

The limb went dead. With a curse, Oris raised her other elbow and dropped it into Silvin's sternum.

"Hark!"

Oris froze. Silvin's eyes flashed, and the temper seemed to leach out of them. Together they looked up. There, about four paces away, stood Flip. The wizard had his arms folded with his hands buried beneath both coat and cloak, looking utterly miserable in the cold.

Over his shoulder, Oris saw the city guard who had been watching them before was still there. So were about half a dozen others. They were all still as statues.

"I called your names five times before you noticed. What in the dark below is wrong with you two?" Then he snorted. "As though I cannot guess. I am afraid your bout is at an end. A messenger came. We can expect our esteemed visitor again, tonight."

Oris looked down at Silvin, and Silvin looked back up at her. Slowly, the same grin spread across their faces.

"That is not a win," said Silvin.

"I suppose, then, that we'll have to try again another day," said Oris.

"I suppose so."

Oris got to her feet first, but she pulled Silvin up behind her. They went to fetch their cloaks. Both of them were breathing hard. From the wall, Oris faintly heard a chorus of groans.

Neither she nor Silvin looked at each other—not then, and not all the long walk back to the Crescent Bulwark.

• ○ • ○ •

With Eamin visiting, it seemed wise to clean themselves up. Oris and Silvin took baths—separately, by unspoken agreement. As she sat in the warm tub, scrubbing the sweat and blood off herself, Oris' mind kept wandering back to the fight. Silvin's strength seemed to exceed understanding. Oris had gotten enough opponents in her grasp over the years. Once she had them, it was rare for them to get out. Mayhap someone with a shadeborn's size could. Certainly no one as small as Silvin.

She thought again of the furor that had burned in the Mystic's eyes, from which her power had seemed to flow. Oris had heard of berserkers before, warriors who had learned to channel their rage into great feats of strength, or who could remain standing long after a normal fighter should have fallen. But so far as she knew, the Mystics did not teach the skill. If Silvin had joined the order young, just after her parents died, where did she learn it?

Oris shook her head and rose from the tub to dry off. Her life now was too many questions, and none of them with any answers.

Eamin knocked on their door an hour before sundown, and they hurried to admit him. He greeted each of them in turn, but when he looked upon Oris and Silvin, his gaze lingered a moment. Oris felt a flush creeping up her neck. Though they had bathed, both of them bore clear signs of a fight. But if they did not feel the need to explain, Eamin seemed willing to accept it, for he made no comment.

"I have spent much of the last few days studying the lore the High King possesses, and from it I have gained this." Eamin produced a scroll from within his cloak. "There is more to study, and I am not certain this will help. But I thought it best to bring it to you regardless, for I know you have been waiting with little to do."

"Thank you, Your Highness," said Silvin, taking the scroll from him. "We are even more honored that you took the time to deliver it personally."

"I would have sent it with Idulen and continued my studies," said Eamin. "But this information is not meant to be possessed by anyone except the High King. Please bear that in mind. Do not let the scroll out of your sight for even a moment."

Behind him, Flip rolled his eyes. Oris shot him a warning look, and he raised his hands as if to say *I'll leave it be.*

"Well," said Silvin. She held the scroll towards Oris. "I suppose you should read it."

Oris blinked. "I . . . I suppose I should."

She undid the tie holding the scroll shut and unfurled the parchment. It had become slightly rumpled in the Lord Prince's cloak, and she tried to smooth it out upon the bed. Eamin's handwriting was neat and methodical, small but not too small to read easily. An incredible amount of information filled the long parchment in her hands.

"I'd just as soon not sit here reading while everyone stares at me," said Oris. "We'll all three study this in time, Your Highness, but could you give us the gist?"

"I can try," said Eamin, "though magic has never been an area of particular study for me. You have learned this already: there are four branches of magic, and then two others, life and death. But ceremancy and necromancy are not simply 'hidden' branches. They are the *senior* branches. They are not separate from the others, they are above them, and it is from them that the other four branches draw their power. This is why there is only ever one Ceremancer and Necromancer. They are the source, and they are entwined with the lesser branches in equal measure."

Oris frowned as she kept scanning the scroll. This was far beyond her limited understanding. Silvin sidled over and began reading over her shoulder, but she seemed to have no greater flash of insight than Oris did. Even Flip was frowning in consternation, with no sign that this was good news, or even news he understood particularly well.

"That's interesting, Your Highness," said Oris at last. "But to me it feels like the idea of a tale, not a whole story. I don't know what you're trying to tell me."

Eamin ran a hand through his sandy hair. "I hardly understand it myself. As I said, my studies of magic are limited. There are . . . mirror branches, I believe they are called?" He looked to Flip, who nodded. "They are reflections of each other, and each can defeat the other. Ceremancy and Necromancy are something else. They behave differently. They respond to each other, waxing and waning in accordance with each other. They grow together and fade together."

"You're saying they rely on each other?" said Flip. "If that were true, how could the Necromancer have come into his power? He's never been in the presence of Oris' magic. Dark below, neither had Oris until very recently."

Eamin shook his head. "Say not that they are dependent on each other, but that each strengthens the other. They are not in contest, but in tandem."

"What is this bit here?" said Silvin, pointing to a part of the scroll. Oris had already read it, but the words had washed over her like a wave, leaving no understanding. "'The test of life and death is the echo of the lesser branches.' What does that mean?"

"I am afraid I do not know," said Eamin, shrugging. "Two different texts repeated it, and so I copied it down, but it means nothing to me."

"The test of life and death?" said Flip. "Does that have anything to do with the Academy's tests?"

Oris frowned at him. "The Academy's what?"

Both Flip and Eamin turned to her in surprise. "The Academy's tests," said Flip. "The ones to detect magical talent, that they give you when you're a child."

Still Oris stared at them blankly. Silvin gently cleared her throat. "The tests are only mandatory for nobility." She nodded to Eamin, and then to Flip. "And families with coin often pay for them to be administered to their children. Commoners are only tested if they manifest the gift naturally."

Both Flip and Eamin flushed with embarrassment. Eamin bowed his head towards Oris. "My apologies," he said. "A nobleman forgets his place more easily than a commoner, and I dishonor myself to do so."

"Please don't worry about it," said Oris, quickly turning her attention back to the scroll. "All right, well. If there's testing for the four branches, there must be testing for the two hidden ones, mustn't there? Did the books say anything about that? This is no explanation."

"Echoes," murmured Silvin, staring at the scroll.

"What?" said Oris, turning to her.

Silvin stepped in front of Oris. A curious feeling hung on the air, for Eamin and Flip were now looking hard at her. Oris hid a hard swallow as she looked down into Silvin's brilliant hazel eyes.

"Strange," said Silvin, almost whispering. Then, suddenly sharp, she said, "I did not know your eyes were blue."

A queasy feeling filled Oris' stomach. Suddenly the room around her flashed, as though a brilliant lantern had been lit and then immediately doused.

Oris frowned. "They are not. My eyes are brown."

"Sky above!" cried Flip, lunging forwards and staring at her. Beside him, Eamin had gone quite pale.

"What?" said Oris, hands balling to fists. "What under the sky are you looking at?"

"Oris." Again Silvin's voice was a whisper, and now her eyes were shining. "Oris, that was the test for weremagic. And it worked."

"What do you mean it worked?"

"Your eyes turned blue," said Silvin. "Just for a moment, but they changed."

Oris' throat was desert-dry. "So . . . so what?" she croaked. "I'm not the Lifemage? I'm a weremage?"

"No, no," said Silvin, her voice shaking. She went to a cupboard in the room, from which she produced a candle and lit it from the lamp. "Oris, look at the darkness in the center of the candle."

Oris frowned, but she reached for the candle. Silvin withdrew it slightly. "No. Just look at the darkness in the center of the flame. Ignore everything else."

"It's a flame," said Oris. "There's no darkness."

"Look, Oris," insisted Silvin.

Oris sighed in frustration, but she did it. She focused on the candle flame, dancing gently with Silvin's breath. But it was just a candle flame, like any of the countless others she had—

Wait. No. No, there *was* a darkness in the center of the flame. And as she focused on it, again there was that strange sensation, a sense that the room around her had grown lighter, just for a moment.

Oris blinked. The candle flame was out.

Flip seized his long hair and looked ready to rip it out. "No. No, that's impossible. That's *impossible."*

"Was that me?" whispered Oris.

"It was," said Silvin.

"But that cannot be," said Eamin, stepping closer. He was staring at the doused candle. "No wizard commands more than one branch."

"I doubt she *commands* them," said Silvin. She had not taken her gaze from Oris' face. "These are only echoes, as the text said. I suspect she could achieve no great strength in any of the lesser branches. But it is the threads of all four that make her who she is."

"Let's try the other two," said Flip.

"Have we not seen enough?" said Silvin, frowning. "Showing two branches is more than any wizard on record, even Dorren."

"Oh, I believe she's who we think," said Flip, breaking into a wild grin. "But come now. Don't you at least want to *see* it?"

Silvin fetched a cup of water and had Oris stir it with her finger. She told Oris to change the water, and after focusing on it for a moment, Oris felt her eyes flash. The water turned to a turbid, oily substance that made her grimace. Finally, Silvin spun a coin atop a table in the room. She sharply commanded Oris to stop the coin without touching it. Again a flash, and the coin shuddered and stopped, standing on end.

When it was done, Flip sank down to sit against the wall. His eyes were wide and staring into a far distance. Oris felt like he looked. Her mind raced, and she sat down upon the bed. But Silvin stayed on her feet beside the Lord Prince.

"So," said Flip. "That . . . that was more than I ever thought to see beneath the sky."

"More than I ever thought to do," muttered Oris.

"If there were any doubts, let them be banished," said Silvin, turning her shining eyes down upon Oris. "It is true, just as I knew it was. You are the Ceremancer."

Oris met her gaze. But then, suddenly, as she saw the look on the Mystic's face, the wonder and near-worship in her eyes, a strange feeling came over her.

Not a feeling. A sight, like a vision. Or a memory.

An old man stood before her. No, not before her. Above her. Looking down at her, much taller, for she was only a child. He was older, with grey hair that was mostly bald on top. A bristling goatee. She was in a room she half-remembered. Finery coated the walls. A tapestry, crossed axes hung over the mantel.

Beside the old man was a table scattered with some objects. They had meant little to Oris then, but she recognized them now. A coin. A cup of what had once been water. A candle.

And the old man looked down at her with wonder in his eyes.

Oris had stood without realizing it. Her hands were fists at her sides. Flip, Silvin, and the Lord Prince were looking at her in alarm.

"Oris, darling?" said Flip. "What's wrong?"

"I remember." Oris had not meant to whisper, and she spoke again, louder. "I remember. I remember being tested before. I was only a child. Very young. Before the orphanage."

The orphanage.

The same old man. Now he stood before her on a street in the city of Cabrus. There was the orphanage just behind him, a building that would one day become painfully familiar to Oris.

Oris remembered him speaking, but not what he said. But she remembered the cold feeling in her palm as he pressed something into it. She looked down just as he curled her fingers around the object.

Crystal. Shaped like a pyramid, but with notches for a leather thong. The amulet.

Keep it always. *She remembered the words, but she could not hear them in his voice.* This they shall not take from you.

"The orphanage," whispered Oris, no longer seeing Silvin or Flip before her, nor the Lord Prince in the corner. "He took me there, and he gave me the amulet."

Her vision came back into focus. She looked to Silvin, and then she locked gazes with Flip.

"He knew what I was," she said. "And he took me away from my family."

CHAPTER XVII
UNCOVERED SECRETS

Flip, Silvin, and the Lord Prince spoke then, each of them pacing in turn. They marveled at seeing Oris perform the tests, they argued what it all might mean, and they debated what they should do next. But Oris said nothing, and she heard little of it. She sat on the bed staring through them all, her hands limp in her lap.

Eventually Flip noticed her silence and her stillness. He came to sit beside her, taking one of her hands in both of his own. "Oris," he said quietly. "Are you all right?"

"How could I be?" she said. "Someone knew. A long, long time ago. Yet they never told me, or anyone, it seems."

"Do you remember his name?" said Silvin.

"No," said Oris, shaking her head. "I barely even remembered his face until this very moment. But . . . but he *tested* me. In my home, before the orphanage. That means he knows where I come from."

"What of your parents?" said Flip gently. "Do you remember them?"

Oris' jaw clenched. "No." She saw Silvin looking at her in sympathy, but she refused to meet the Mystic's gaze.

The Lord Prince leaned against the wall, bearded chin buried in his fist. "This man," he said slowly. "He must have been a servant of the enemy. Why else would he keep Oris a secret for all this time?"

"I do not think so," said Silvin, shaking her head. "If he served the Necromancer, and Oris was only a child, why would he not simply kill her? Or at the very least, deliver her to his master for some evil purpose? I think he was hiding her away."

"But why?" said Eamin. "Why hide her? That serves the cause of neither the Necromancer nor the Ceremancer. Why leave Oris to sit in obscurity—forgive me—instead of coming into her own?"

"Your Highness," said Flip suddenly. There was an edge to his voice that stopped Eamin and Silvin in their tracks. Even Oris looked at him in surprise. Flip tilted his head towards her. "Might I remind you both that you speak of a real person who's sitting here now, having to listen to the both of you argue about how she should have been murdered as a child, or how she might better have been groomed to fight in a war she wants no part of?"

Eamin's cheeks flushed, and he bowed his head. "I apologize. Again I forget myself, and this time inexcusably."

Silvin came to sit on Oris' other side upon the bed. "Flip is right, of course. Please forgive us, Oris."

"Think nothing of it," said Oris gruffly.

"What else can you tell us about him?" said Silvin. "Did he work at the orphanage?"

Oris shook her head. "No. I never saw him in all the years I lived there. Yet mayhap he lives in Cabrus. This could be what we need, the next step we've been looking for. If he knew who I was, if he knew how to test for me, he had to know more. He must know how to train me."

Silvin looked at her a little sadly. "Oris . . . how would we go about finding him? You don't know his name or where he might be found. How would we start such a search?"

Silence fell. Oris covered her eyes with a hand. "I don't know," she said.

Eamin looked upon her with pity. "I cannot imagine how hard this is," he said. "Yet you have recovered something of your past. Mayhap in the future you shall learn more, and we can pursue the matter further."

"Mayhap," said Oris. She wanted to feel hopeful about the prospect, but she could only feel tired.

Silvin went to the bedside table and lifted the scroll Eamin had brought. "I think we should return to this matter of life and death magic, and the way they strengthen each other. That could be the key we need, instead." She turned to Oris. "You have been in the presence of necromancy. Did anything happen then?"

Oris thought back. She remembered the woods when she and Flip had gutted Enfil together. He had come back from the dead. She remembered the terrible itch clawing its way through her skin, the sensation of a void in her stomach.

"There was something," she said. "A feeling . . . my skin crawled, and I felt like I was empty inside."

Flip's eyes widened, and he nodded. "I know what you're speaking of," he said. "Well, not the emptiness. But the crawling feeling in the skin. It's the way I feel when firemagic or mindmagic are used around me—my branch, and its mirror."

"I have heard of that," said the Lord Prince. "All wizards experience the same, do they not?"

"They do," said Silvin. "Oris, that was your magic responding to the necromancy."

"It didn't feel like it was strengthening me," said Oris. "It was only discomforting."

"You did not know what you were looking for," said Silvin. "Mayhap next time you can focus on that feeling. Try to draw strength from it, or the same power that you manifested at Wellmont."

Eamin's eyes flashed with interest. "What happened at Wellmont?"

Oris glared at Silvin, but she could not put much fire behind her annoyance. "It was the first time I used my power," she said. "On accident. I barely remember it."

"What did you use it to do?" said Eamin.

Oris and Flip shared a look. "Sky's truth, I don't honestly know," said Oris.

Suddenly Silvin's eyes brightened. "Wait, Oris," she said. "Your amulet. You say that old man gave you the amulet. Mayhap this passage in the scroll was part of it. The amulet was given to you to help you find agents of the enemy. And then you were supposed to find your magic in response to theirs."

Flip nodded eagerly. "This is similar to how they do things in the Academy. It's always easier for students to study magic when they're watching another perform it."

"So I could learn to use my magic by watching you?" said Oris.

"No," said Flip, shaking his head. "You have to see your branch, or its mirror. But this could still help us. We know the Necromancer has had time to learn his magic. You could do so more quickly by focusing on the magic of a shadeborn when they cheat death."

"That would be dangerous well past the point of being foolhardy," said Silvin. "The shadeborn are impossibly dangerous. There is a reason we ran from Barrick in Dracmund."

Eamin frowned. "You have fought shadeborn already?"

"Two," said Flip. He pointed at Silvin. "And she killed the first one rather easily. So I'm afraid I don't quite understand the sudden reticence to square off with another."

"I was able to surprise Enfil," said Silvin. "And he was already bleeding his guts out after Oris had stabbed him a dozen times, with his master's magic desperately trying to stitch him back together. Don't forget that if I had not arrived, you'd both be dead."

"Of course we haven't forgotten," said Flip. "And we're grateful. But we didn't know what we were up against. Now we do."

"Knowing what you face is little help if what you face is this powerful," said Silvin. "Knowing you face a storm is no protection against being struck by lightning. And forgive me for saying so, but it is laughable to hear that *you* will do better next time you fight a shadeborn. Your magic is no proof against them."

Oris shook her head slowly. "Be that as it may, I think Flip's right."

Silvin's eyes went wide. "You do?"

"The only time I've felt any sense of my magic," said Oris, "outside of what happened at Wellmont, was when I was facing a shadeborn. I wasn't able to learn anything then, but I didn't know what I was looking for. We've got no better leads, Silvin. And we've even lost the Academy. I don't know another way forwards."

Eamin raised a hand, almost like a child in lessons. "All right. This seems like a possibility, at least. And now it seems to me that it would be wisest to bring this to the High King. You need to get your hands on a shadeborn. My mother can assemble a fighting force. They will root out these traitors, and you will learn your magic from them."

"I still do not think that is wise," said Silvin. "There are traitors hiding in the wilds, but we know they are in our midst as well. The last thing I wish to do is surround Oris with hundreds of armed soldiers, any of whom could be a Shade in disguise. With Jordel dead, I trust no one but the four of us in this room."

"And the High King, I assume," said Eamin with a frown. "But I take your point."

"Pardon me, Your Highness, but that hardly matters," said Flip.

All of them looked at him in shock. "What do you mean it doesn't matter?" said Oris. "That's my neck you're talking about."

Flip gave a cold smile. "The axe hangs over us both, dear. But use your reason. Silvin doesn't want to surround you with hundreds of swords if a few of their bearers *might* want to kill you. Yet we need to find you a shadeborn. What, then? Shall the three of us march alone into an enemy army, all of whom *certainly* want to kill you?"

Silvin opened her mouth to reply. Nothing came out. Slowly her mouth closed, though her eyes were troubled.

Eamin sighed with relief. "Very well, then. Are we agreed that it is time to present this to Her Majesty?"

"I . . . suppose so," said Silvin. It sounded as though each word pained her.

"Then I shall notify her at once," said Eamin. "We shall keep things as quiet as we possibly can. I expect she shall wish to take council with us tonight. Be ready."

He gave them a final nod and turned to go. But before he stepped out the door, Flip stopped him. "No Mystics."

Eamin arched an eyebrow. "No Mystics?"

"In Her Majesty's council," said Flip. "I don't trust a single one of them with Oris' life."

Eamin glanced at Oris and then at Silvin before turning back to Flip. "I may be able to secure agreement on that point for your initial meeting," he said. "But the High King might mandate their involvement with our future plans."

Flip's smirk turned frosty. "I shall convince her otherwise."

To Oris' great surprise, Eamin actually laughed at that, though it subsided quickly. "I see. Well. I wish you the best of luck with that. Stay ready. I shall send Idulen back here to fetch you once your counsel has been requested."

He left them at last—but not before giving Silvin one final, long look. Silvin's nod was so small that Oris only saw it because she was looking for it.

• ○ • ○ •

Eamin half-ran back to the palace and requested an audience with his mother immediately. Again he was inspected by Kris and Asbeth, and then he was alone with the High King in her study. Only when he saw the keen interest in her eyes did he realize how flushed and eager he must look.

"Lord Prince," she said with a nod. "You look very nearly breathless. Have you discovered something in your studies?"

Eamin took a moment, both to consider his answer and to compose himself. To fill the time, he poured them both wine. When he brought her goblet to her, the High King leaned back in her chair and sipped at it. But Eamin remained on his feet as he drank.

"Your Majesty," he said at last. "I did find something in your tomes. But in order to fully explain it, I must confess that I withheld something from you beforehand."

A moment's silence stretched. Then, "Did you." It was not a question, and the High King's expression had drifted towards stony.

"I did," said Eamin. "I have found the Lifemage. She is on the Seat."

Enalyn shot to her feet. "She is *what?*"

"Please, Your Majesty," said Eamin, holding up a hand to forestall her. "If you must chastise or punish me, wait until I am done. If it is any comfort, I have not known this for long. The Lifemage has been here since the attack on the Seat, but I only learned of her a few days ago. It was the same day I first asked you about the book."

Enalyn's jaw was twitching as she clenched and unclenched her teeth. Her hands looked steady, but the wine in her goblet quivered slightly. "Go on," she finally said.

"She was brought here by a Mystic," said Eamin. "A knight named Silvin. She was a pupil of Jordel's. They kept her presence secret because they were afraid agents of the Necromancer would find her."

"Who is she?" said Enalyn. "The Lifemage, I mean."

Eamin shook his head. "No one, to be truthful. Oris is her name. A common woman from the city of Cabrus, an orphan in her youth and a sellsword of late."

That seemed to surprise Enalyn enough that she forgot to be angry, at least for a moment. "So she had no idea who she was?"

"Not until very recently," said Eamin. "And for the most part, she still does not. They have been trying to find a way to bring her into her full power. Apparently Jordel knew something of the process, but with his passing they were left aimless. So far in your tomes, I have found only the barest information that could help. Now we think we have a plan to learn more, and Silvin agreed that the time for secrecy is over."

"I see," said Enalyn. She slowly sat back down in her chair, resting her goblet on the table again. "How glad I am to hear you have made that decision for me."

Eamin straightened slightly and clasped his hands behind his back. "As I said, if you wish to punish or reprimand me, I accept it."

"I do not need your permission," said Enalyn. "Nor can I afford to punish you, at least not publicly. I could reprimand you, I suppose. But I think it would be more profitable for you to do that yourself."

Eamin blinked. "Forgive me, Your Majesty. I do not understand."

Enalyn lifted a finger. "Put yourself in my chair. What would my reprimand sound like, do you think?"

The Lord Prince quashed a grim smile before it could begin. "I imagine Your Majesty would tell me that I was incredibly foolish," he said. "You would remind me that the coming war, the future of Underrealm itself, depends on the Lifemage. We must control her, and we must keep her safe. Secluding her away in secret, hiding her presence from you, is one of the more recklessly dangerous games I could have played with the future of the nine kingdoms."

"I might have gone into more detail," said Enalyn. "But you have the basic idea."

"And I respectfully disagree, Your Majesty."

Enalyn's jaw clenched again. "Do you."

"I do," said Eamin, nodding. "We think of the palace as one of the most secure places in Underrealm. But just weeks ago, you and I almost died here. We know that agents and spies have infiltrated it in the past, and mayhap even lurk here now, wearing friendly guises but carrying daggers behind their backs. I thought it was worth taking at least a few days to think about it before bringing Oris here. The moment it was clear that that was the best decision, I did it. That is why I am here now."

"Some decisions are not yours to make," said Enalyn.

"And some are," said Eamin. "You tell me often that I am worthy of the throne. You say you are working to leave it to me one day. When I have it, I shall have to do what I think is best. And, just as you do now, I shall have to rely on servants who do what *they* think is best. I will have to trust them to keep things from me, if that is the wisest course. You know some of your servants do the same."

"Of course I know that," said Enalyn in a voice of steel. "I am looking at one of them now."

"You deal with many of them every day," said Eamin. "You value them because they know when a matter must be kept secret. But more importantly, they know when the time for secrets is over. The time for secrets is over. Here I am."

The study was silent for a long moment, neither of them breaking gaze with the other. Then, finally, Enalyn sighed. She lifted her empty goblet. "Please."

"Of course, Your Majesty." Eamin refilled both their glasses, and now at last he sat with her at the table.

"What, then, is next?" said Enalyn after he had settled.

"I am bringing her here," said Eamin. "She has agreed to meet with you. They will tell you everything they have learned so far."

"And then we ready for war, I imagine?" said Enalyn, raising her brows.

Eamin winced. "That . . . is not quite what they have in mind. But let them come to the palace and tell you themselves."

Enalyn's mouth twisted. "Very well. Have them come at once."

Eamin bowed his head. "Of course, Your Majesty." He stood, leaving his goblet on the table. But he paused before leaving. "One last thing."

"Of course there would be," said Enalyn under her breath.

"I told you of Silvin, the Mystic who brought Oris here. There is a third in their party. His name is Philip of the family Drayden." Enalyn's brows shot up, and Eamin went on hurriedly. "Yes. I know. But Philip is estranged from his family and utterly loyal to Oris. He also has a deep mistrust of the Mystics."

"Yet he travels with one."

Eamin's wince deepened. "Silvin has kept her affiliation secret from him. I thought it important for you to know about the secret, and how disastrous it might be to reveal it. Also, I promised Flip that there would be no Mystics present, at least for the initial council."

"You cannot be serious," said Enalyn, her voice rising. "The lord chancellor must be kept appraised of this situation. It directly concerns the entire order."

"I agree," said Eamin. "And we can tell her straight afterwards. I had to promise this much just to get them to come to the palace. After this first council, Lord Chancellor Konnel can be brought in."

"This is ridiculous, Eamin," snapped the High King. "We are meeting to discuss the saving of the nine kingdoms and everyone in it—*including* the Lifemage and this Drayden man. Self-interest alone should decree that they come here at once and do whatever in the dark below I tell them to do!"

Eamin was aware that his jaw was clenching, just as hers often did. He forced his muscles to loosen. "May I speak freely, Your Majesty?"

"Whyever would you stop now?" said Enalyn acidly.

"You would sacrifice the Lifemage to save Underrealm."

"What are you talking about?" said Enalyn with a scowl. "I would never harm the Lifemage. She is our best hope to defeat the enemy."

"Of course," said Eamin. "But if the cost of the war—if the cost of defeating the Necromancer meant sacrificing Oris in the fight, you would do it. I know it is true, because I would do the same thing in your position."

Enalyn studied him. She did not respond, but Eamin nodded as if she had.

"That is a hard decision, and you must make many of them. But please understand, Your Majesty: Underrealm is not the most important thing in Oris' life. She does not even *wish* to be the Lifemage. She wants to live alone and free. Oris and Flip—and Philip, forgive me—are only here on the Seat at all because they think it is their best chance of survival. They are not evil, but they *are* selfish. And yet they are also far more clever than I first thought them. They know, like I know, that if you had to sacrifice her to save the nine kingdoms, you would. They know it because they know you are a great ruler. And while that makes you the perfect servant of Underrealm's common good, it also makes you very dangerous to people of great importance. People like Oris and Philip. They do not fear that you would use them for evil. But they know you would sacrifice their power for the greater gain of the powerless."

The silence this time was longer. But Eamin read in her eyes that this was no quiet fury. A mourning had filled her.

"Dark below," she whispered. "What has this throne done to me? To both of us?"

"It has done what it must," said Eamin quietly. "It does what our subjects hope it will do, for their sake. And the throne would do worse, had you taken it with intentions less noble than you did. I trust you with it as much as any of them do—or better, because I know you, and I know you understand the weight on yourself. It is the only reason I desire it myself one day, really: to free you from the burden."

Enalyn lifted a hand. Eamin came to her and took it, and she pulled him to her side, cradling his fingers against her cheek. He laid his other hand in her hair, stroking it gently. A moment she allowed them, and then she mustered herself.

"Summon them," she said. The mourning was gone from her voice, but so was the fire. "The Drayden's terms for the meeting are accepted."

Eamin sighed with relief. "Thank you, Your Majesty. One last thing. I will tell your guards as well, but . . . the Mystic. Silvin. Have you heard of her?"

Enalyn looked away and sipped at her wine. "Yes. Jordel told me. Do not worry. My guards know what they need to know."

"Good."

"Eamin."

He turned at the door. "Your Majesty?"

"Do not do anything like this again."

Again he felt his jaw clench. "I will endeavor not to, Your Majesty."

"I need better than that."

"Then I will give you a better promise," said Eamin. "I promise you I will always do the right thing, as I see it, no matter the cost. That is to say, I will do as you have taught me."

And then he was gone.

• ○ • ○ •

That night, Idulen came to them at the Bulwark, bearing with him a summons from the High King. They had already prepared, and they went with him immediately.

"So," said Flip to Idulen as they walked. "What's your place in all this? Lackey of the Lord Prince? That's a lofty position. How'd you get it?"

"Flip," said Oris, glaring.

But Idulen only seemed faintly amused. "Speaking honestly, I am honored you would think of me as the Lord Prince's personal servant. But I am nowhere near of noble enough birth for such a thing. His Highness seems to enjoy my company, and so he employs my service as he sees fit—and I could ask for no higher honor."

"And what does he trust you with?" said Flip. "What do you know about all this?"

Idulen's gaze flicked to Oris. "He told me a little, though I am sure there is more to know. I know about . . . well."

Oris sighed. "You know who I am."

"Yes," said Idulen. "And though my first duty is to the Lord Prince, if there is any way I can be of aid to you without dishonor, you have only to ask."

Flip gave a chuckle. "All right. I suppose you're a fine enough sort. But pull the stick out, would you? I don't trust people drawn as tight as you seem to be."

Idulen walked them past the main entrance at the front of the palace walls and to a heavily fortified side gate. It looked like a place for servants and messengers to pass in and out. There was only a single guard there to let them in, and then Idulen brought them across a wide, empty courtyard and into the palace. The service entrance led them to a narrow hall that ran along the palace's outer edge, and then to a circular staircase which they took up for two flights. Oris expected to see servants in droves, but there was no one. If she did not know better, she would have sworn the palace was abandoned.

Then they stepped out of the servants' hallway and into a great hall. At the other end of it was a great wooden door covered with designs of gold inlay. The marble floors and lustrous tapestries took Oris' breath away, just as the Academy had done weeks ago.

Here, too, there were other people. A number of guards awaited them, their expressions stern and their weapons keen and polished. One of them, a twixt with half an arm missing, stepped forwards.

"Your weapons," they said.

Silvin pulled off her sword belt and drew out her knives without hesitation, handing them over at once. Oris did the same, a bit more slowly. Flip had only his long dagger, which he proffered with a smile.

"This is all I've got," said Flip.

One of the palace guards stepped forwards. She was a thin reed of a woman, and she carried no sword. She held up a finger blazing with fire, and her eyes glowed white. "We know that is not true. I will be watching you."

Flip stuck his tongue out at her.

A final guard came forwards, a little dwarf who looked mayhap a few years younger than Oris. His eyes glowed as he looked them over, though Oris did not know why.

Silvin leaned in close. "He is inspecting us for weremagic," she whispered. "They want to make sure we are not anyone other than who we say we are."

"Right," whispered Oris, flushing as the dwarf continued his inspection. He passed over the three of them and gave the captain of the guard a little smile and a shake of his head. But her face remained stony as she nodded and motioned him away.

"I shall bring you to Her Majesty's council room now," said the captain. "Your possessions shall be returned to you afterwards."

"Of course," said Silvin. "Thank you, captain."

The corners of Flip's mouth twitched.

Guards swung open the heavy doors at the end of the hall. Inside was the throne room. As they were led inside, Oris saw that the room was empty, but that did little to diminish its majesty. Complex patterns of gold inlay and broad diamond-shaped carvings were wider at the entrance, gradually drawing together in lines that arched over the room and converged on the wall behind the throne. It gave the impression that whoever sat that chair was at the center of the world, their presence spreading wide arms to reach over everyone else around them.

But they passed through that chamber swiftly and through a door on the left-hand wall near the back. Here was a smaller chamber, though hardly intimate. It was a council room, with a wide table in the center and chairs all around. There at the table stood the Lord Prince Eamin. And beside him, at the head of the table, stood a woman Oris knew at once must be the High King Enalyn. She was of average height, but she had the gift of presence, so that even beside the Lord Prince, one's gaze was drawn to her alone. Her dress was elegant but restrained now, and it looked as fit for battle as for courtly graces. Wisdom was on her brow, and strength was in her arm. Oris had heard that she had personally fought in the battle of the Seat, and taken many foes that day. Her eyes were sharp and searching.

Silvin took a knee at once. Oris did the same, and then Flip joined them both, though Oris thought she saw him roll his eyes.

The High King nodded solemnly at them. "Please, stand," she said.

"Thank you, Your Majesty," said Silvin.

The High King's gaze darted to her, but then they gravitated back to Oris. She stepped forwards, and Oris tensed. Calmly the High King reached out a hand for her.

"I am told your name is Oris," she said. "I welcome you into my home. To tell the truth, I hoped never to meet you in my lifetime. But it is a great honor nevertheless, and I am grateful you agreed to come."

"Of course, Your Majesty," said Oris. She took Enalyn's wrist, and they shook.

Enalyn went to Flip next. "Welcome, Philip of the family Drayden. I have heard little of you other than your loyalty to your friend. That is admirable, and it does much to raise you in my estimation."

"I imagine I started rather low in that reckoning, what with my kin," said Flip with a smirk. "I wonder how far I have risen. Nevertheless, I thank you, Your Majesty."

Oris could feel Silvin tense beside her. But to her surprise, Enalyn returned Flip's smirk. Then she went to Silvin. "I have been told I have much reason to be grateful to you, Silvin," she said. "All of Underrealm owes you a great debt for finding Oris and keeping her safe while you brought her to me."

"It is the honor of my life, Your Majesty," said Silvin. She gave a deep bow.

Enalyn gently took Silvin's shoulder and raised her to standing again, and then took her wrist to shake it. "Your service shall not be forgotten. Nor shall the service of your esteemed master. I knew Jordel very well, and I was grieved beyond reckoning to hear of his loss. I know he would be proud of how you have carried on in his stead."

Silvin's voice came suddenly thick. "I thank you, Your Majesty."

Enalyn held her gaze a moment. Then she nodded and gestured towards the table. "Come. Sit. This council has been too long delayed, and we are swiftly running out of further time to waste."

They sat, and wine was served for all of them. Then Enalyn had them tell her of their journey that had ended at the Seat. Oris noted with some curiosity that she did not have them tell the tale as it had happened. Rather she walked them back step by step, beginning with how they had met the Lord Prince just a few days ago. Then she asked them of their studies in the Academy, and then how they had come to the Seat, and then Dracmund. Oris let Silvin do much of the talking, only answering questions or prompting when a detail skipped her memory. With all of the High King's questions, the tale took long in the telling, and Oris guessed that at least two hours had passed before Silvin finally spoke of the day she had found them in the woods and saved their lives from Enfil.

"Very well," said the High King, looking back and forth between the three of them. "A startling tale by any estimation. But now tell me: why were you out in those woods, searching for Oris in the first place?"

Silvin glanced at Oris. "Because word reached me, through my master's master, of what had happened at the Battle of Wellmont. He thought he recognized the signs, and he sent me to investigate. When I reached Wellmont, I learned that his suspicions were correct."

"Wellmont," said Enalyn. She leaned back in her chair and pinched the bridge of her nose for a moment before looking back at Oris. "Much began there, it seems. We received word of the Necromancer long before we learned of you. We thought he had something to do with Dorsea's attack on Wellmont, and I sent great strength of arms there in hopes of uncovering him and ending this war swiftly. That is why the Seat was vulnerable to attack. It seems our enemy has had a great deal of time to prepare his plans, and I fear we are struggling to catch up."

Oris did not know quite what to say to that. Instead she looked upon Eamin. The Lord Prince had said almost nothing the whole time as Silvin had told her story. He had provided only a little bit of information at the beginning, filling in his part of the tale when he had gone looking through his mother's tomes, and then he had listened with rapt attention while Silvin spoke. Now he was staring at Oris, just as his mother was. As Oris looked at him now, he gave her a quiet, encouraging smile, but he held his peace.

"I . . . hope I can help, Your Majesty," said Oris at last. "But as you have no doubt gathered by this time, I am afraid I do not know how."

"Yes," said the High King. She leaned back, steepling her fingers beneath her chin, her eyes never leaving Oris. "I admit I do not envy you. This all must be terribly overwhelming. If I understand correctly, before Wellmont, you knew nothing of your . . . true nature, let us say."

Flip snorted, and Oris smiled at him. Enalyn's eyes flitted between the two of them. "Forgive me, Your Majesty," said Oris. "It is only that I still feel like I know nothing of my 'true nature,' as you put it. It is . . . frustrating, to say the least."

Enalyn leaned forwards now, one elbow resting on the table. "I can only imagine. Yet I think we have danced around the issue long enough. Everything began in that battle, for you and for many across Underrealm who heard of it. So, now, let us have it from you directly. What happened at Wellmont?"

Oris dropped her gaze to her lap. Her hands had clenched on the arms of her chair without realizing it, and she forced them to loosen. She looked up to Flip, almost pleading.

He shrugged and gave her a sad smile. "It's up to you, dear."

Oris took her empty cup and lifted it. "With your permission, Your Majesty?"

"Of course," said Enalyn, motioning for one of the guards to fetch the bottle.

"No, please," said Oris, rising from her chair. "I'd rather stand as I speak."

She went to the table at the side of the room that held the bottle, as well as several others. She poured her cup to the brim and then took a deep pull from it before returning to the table. But she did not go to the chair where she had sat before. She went to the other end of the table from the High King. There she put down her cup, and then she started to pace, back and forth, just a few steps in either direction before turning. From the corners of her eyes, she saw the High King and Lord Prince looking at each other uncertainly.

"All right, then," she said. "Here it is."

• ○ • ○ •

Flip and I were in the Hawthorne Call. They're a sellsword company out of Hedgemond. We'd not been with them long, mayhap a month, when they were called to Wellmont.

You know sellswords and how they're used. We're thrown to the front when lords don't want to risk their own troops in a risky maneuver. So the Call was sent on a sortie beyond the city walls.

The Dorseans were ready for us, and they fought hard. I remember their banners of red and gold shining in the sun. I saw the man next to me take a spear to the gut and go down right before I stuck the woman who got him.

Flip and I are smart. We know how to hold a position and keep ourselves alive, especially with Flip's magic. He likes to hide it to keep expectations off him, but if things ever get really drastic, he can always get us out. And things got drastic then. Flip and I are smart, but we can't account for officers. Our captain let us get cut off on the west end of the city, though at least she died for her mistake. But that didn't matter to us then. The Dorseans backed our squadron up until we were pressed against the river.

They had us four to one, and we couldn't hold them for long. Soon everyone was down but us. Flip did use his spells, then. Flame ripped them from their saddles. Lightning tore along their ranks.

When Flip resorts to magic, my job's to keep his flank safe from a stray knife, and I do a good job of it. I kept anyone from sweeping around him to stick him. I remember taking four of them who tried it. Our blood was up, and we fought like stories. Only a few Dorseans were left to stand against us. It should have been a good day to remember.

But then many things went wrong, one after another.

The first was when Flip used wind to sweep two arrows out of the air. One went wide completely. The other grazed my temple, and I fell.

That distracted Flip for just long enough. He went to try to help me up, and one of them rushed him. They stuck a long dagger between his ribs, tearing up his guts. Flip stayed on his feet just long enough to roast them and the two behind. That cleared the field, but Flip was bleeding to death.

I'd recovered by then. I went to him. I couldn't let him die. I'd lost friends in war before. But I wasn't going to let Flip be one of them. I *wouldn't* let him die.

He tried to tell me to go, said it was fine, and I called him a steer. He was resigned to it, but I told him that if he gave up, I was going to make it painful for him.

Then the others came. Another squad of Dorseans, sweeping in to finish off anyone their fellows had missed. And just the two of us left, alone on that bank beside the river.

● ○ ● ○ ●

The council chamber faded to silence. Oris was standing by the chair now, her knuckles white as they gripped its back. The High King and Lord Prince were studying her curiously. Silvin looked upon her with shining eyes. But Flip stood and came to her side, and he rested his forehead on her arm, his hand rubbing her back gently.

"I shouldn't have given up," he said. "I'm sorry."

Oris sniffed and blinked twice. As she raised her head, she saw the High King's eyes. They seemed to hold an understanding, as though she had finally come to realize the answer to a question that had puzzled her. But she waited patiently for Oris to collect herself.

Eamin, however, cleared his throat. "Forgive me, but . . . what happened next?"

"I don't remember," said Oris flatly. "The last thing I remember was feeling Flip in my arms. And a sensation like a hole in my chest. An emptiness. The same emptiness I felt when Enfil's body stitched back together. And I saw the dark-taken Dorseans coming for us, and I felt the emptiness engulf me. I think I remember saying *No.* And then a flash of light. Purest white, and blinding. When it was gone, everyone was dead. Everyone but Flip, who was alive, and no longer dying."

Flip put a hand on her arm. "I think I should show them."

Oris' mouth twisted. "Are you sure? You've kept it hidden well enough since then."

Silvin's eyes widened. "You never took off your shirt."

Flip smiled at her. Then he spoke to Oris again. "No better time."

"It's yours to show," said Oris with a shrug.

Flip nodded. Then he turned to the other end of the table. "Your Majesty," he said. "With your permission, I should like to show you my injury. I shall have to partly disrobe to do so."

"If it causes you no discomfort," said the High King. "I admit I am intensely curious."

Flip unbuttoned his coat, pulled it off, and draped it over one of the chairs. Then he lifted his tunic up over his head.

Enalyn, Eamin, and Silvin all gasped.

There was the wound. It was a hole about three fingers wide, placed on the center of his torso just beside the sternum. But this was no scar, nor even a sealed wound. The hole was still there. The flesh inside was still visible, though no fresh blood poured from it. Even as they watched, it pulsed with his heartbeat, quivering slightly.

Silvin's expression was full of wonder. She got up and came over to

Flip, bending slightly to look more closely at the wound. She raised a shaking hand, but then stopped, looking up at Flip.

"Oh, you can touch it," he said. "I've probed it often enough since then. I was always that child who picked at his scabs. It doesn't hurt."

Silvin touched it, gingerly at first, and then she pressed harder. Flip gave a slight grimace of discomfort, but not of pain.

The Lord Prince leaned forwards, resting his chin on his fist. "It has not healed?"

Oris shook her head. "It hasn't changed since. I didn't . . . I didn't *mean* to do it. I gave him his life back, but I didn't truly heal him. I don't know how."

"But you *did* keep me alive," said Flip. He began to pull his tunic back on over his head. "Sky above, Oris, for all we know, your magic is still the only thing holding me up. Why do you think I never let you out of my sight? And I, for one, am grateful."

Oris gave the back of his neck a squeeze before turning back to the High King. "And that's what happened, Your Majesty. We didn't know what was going on, but we knew we didn't want to be in Wellmont anymore. We acquired companionship and began to travel towards Kanlena. We didn't know that anyone had seen us. The battle was focused on the south side of the city, where they were still holding the gate, and we were a good distance to the west."

"This is where I may be able to fill in part of the gap," said Silvin. "You were right that the city's attention was focused on the south wall. But one soldier was on the western wall. Their cousin had fallen to an arrow there, and they were searching for him. But as they stood there looking around, they spied the two of you down on the field. They saw Flip take a mortal wound. And they saw the blinding flash of light, and then a field littered with enemy corpses. They were a servant of my master. A twixt named Vella of the family Persin. And we can assume that at least one agent of the enemy saw the blinding flash as well, and that is how word reached him."

The High King leaned back in her chair. "And so the whole story is told, or at least as much of it as we in this room know of. Now we return to the present. It seems the Lord Prince has been conducting research on our behalf, trying to learn how to train you in your power. What have you discovered? What is our next step?"

Eamin cleared his throat. "Your Majesty, the texts speak of ceremancy and necromancy waxing and waning in accordance with each other. When one strengthens, the other grows as well. That may give us our way forwards. Your forces are hunting the Shades in the Birchwood. We want to put Oris in the presence of a shadeborn. We could send another, smaller force into the forest, as secretly as possible, with Oris at their head. Now that she knows what she is looking for, she may be able to use the experience to gather more of her power."

"Maybe she'll learn what she needs to finish fixing me," said Flip brightly. Every eye in the room turned to him. His smile dampened, and he raised his hands. "Not that that's what's most important, of course."

Enalyn sat up. Her shoulders straightened, and her hands came to rest on the arms of her chair. Oris felt the hairs on her arms stand up.

"Thank you for your recommendation, Your Highness," she said to Eamin. "However, I cannot support this plan. It puts our greatest asset in terrible danger, against the most powerful foes our enemies command. And to gain what? A hope that you will somehow uncover power you have not felt before, despite facing the shadeborn already? There must be methods of training that do not involve pitching oneself directly into the maw of the most dangerous beast one can find. After all, it seems clear the Necromancer has taught himself how to use his magic without ever facing you."

Silvin swallowed hard before speaking up. "Yes, Your Majesty. But he has had time. Years, mayhap even decades, for we do not know how long he has known what he is. We do not have that long. We must accelerate the process."

"And so we must," said Enalyn. "But we shall do so in a sensible fashion. We shall place your education in the hands of those whose duty it is to perform it."

Silvin blanched, and Oris' hand tightened on the back of her chair. Eamin looked between the two of them nervously. But Flip stared uncomprehending at the High King.

"An army—an entire order, in fact—exists to serve you," Enalyn went on. "It is their highest purpose. Their true purpose, whatever else they declare openly. They have maintained themselves at readiness for this exact reason for hundreds of years, ever since the last Lifemage walked beneath the sky. And you have avoided them because of personal prejudice that I frankly have no more time for."

Flip glanced at Silvin, and then at Oris, and he read the fear in their expressions. He turned back to the High King. "Forgive me, Your Majesty. Everyone else seems to know what you're talking about, but I don't."

Enalyn met his gaze. "I am given to believe that you have an intense dislike of the Mystic order."

Flip's expression darkened so suddenly that Oris grew somewhat frightened. "You might say that," he said stiffly.

"You shall have to overcome that dislike, or I am afraid I will not have very much use for you," said the High King. "Whatever you think the Mystics are, you are wrong. They have one singular purpose. Their greatest purpose, in fact. They exist to serve the Lifemage, and to fight with them against the Necromancer. And in the years while they wait for the Lifemage's return, they are trained and taught to watch for them, and some among their number are given the signs of their arrival so that they know how to find them."

She nodded towards Silvin. "Just as Silvin was. And her master."

Flip went stone still in his seat. Silvin's face had gone from pale to Elf-white. Eamin's jaw spasmed, and though he held his tongue, he looked fit to burst. But Oris felt a terrible emptiness inside her, like a shadow of the sensation when she felt the Necromancer's magic. Flip was not looking at her, but she could *feel* his mind going to her, thinking, calculating, reading her reaction even without looking.

At last Flip turned to Silvin.

"You lied," he said. "All this long while. To both of us. Sky above and dark below . . . to think I almost thought you were worth liking."

Now. Now is when you should tell him. He's your best friend. Tell him.

"She didn't lie the whole time," said Oris. "At least not to both of us."

Flip's eyes widened a moment before he turned to her. Oris did not flinch.

She saw the fury leach from his gaze, to be replaced by something far worse.

He pushed his chair back, stood, and walked from the room.

"Well," said the High King. "Now everything is out in the open. And I think that should conclude our business, for tonight at the least."

"Your Majesty." Eamin spoke through gritted teeth.

The High King looked to all of them, but when she spoke, she had eyes only for Oris. "I can imagine what you all are thinking. I can read it in your faces. But I have sat my throne for many years, and no one living has had more dealings with more people with more power than I. Please believe me when I say that it is better this way. The longer a situation like yours simmers, the worse it would have been when he eventually found out, as he surely would have done."

Silvin was taking deep breaths, one after the other, and she would not look at the High King. But Oris dropped her gaze to the floor, and her cheeks burned with shame. Because of course that was the truth.

Enalyn pushed back her chair and stood. Silvin shot to her feet, while Eamin joined her a bit more slowly.

"Tomorrow I will wish to take further counsel with all of you," said the High King. "I shall bring the lord chancellor of the Mystic order to the table, whose knowledge in this matter is even greater than my own. She shall be able to provide better guidance than I can. New arrangements have been made for all of you to sleep here. You should fetch your friend, if he will deign to grace my halls."

"Your Majesty," said Silvin. Still she would not look at the High King.

She turned from the table and made for the door, motioning for Oris to follow her. But they were barely out the door before Oris heard quick footsteps behind them. Eamin followed them out without even excusing himself from the High King's company. A few paces down the hallway he turned to them, and they stopped.

"I wish that had not happened," he said in a low voice. But his eyes said more than his words. Oris could read his fury at what had just happened, even if he would not speak against his mother and liege lord.

"We wish the same," said Oris. "But I, for one, hold you blameless."

His expression softened ever so slightly, and he shook his head. "Good night. I do not blame you or Flip if you do not wish to sleep here this evening, but I hope you will."

He turned and reentered his mother's council room. Oris and Silvin set off towards the door leading to the stairway down. But when they reached it, Oris spoke to Silvin.

"I need to get him myself," she said. "Your presence won't help."

Silvin took a slow, deep breath. "Of course," she said. Oris had never heard her voice so small, save for the day she had found out Jordel had died. "I must echo the Lord Prince. I am sorry it went this way. I should likely have told the two of you who I was from the beginning."

Oris shook her head firmly. "If you had, we would not have gone with you. And I would be dead. It is . . . it is simply a bad circumstance. There is blame to be shared in every direction."

Silvin nodded. She raised a hand, paused, and then placed it on Oris' arm. A moment she held it there, and then she let go.

CHAPTER XVIII
CONSPIRACY

EAMIN TURNED AND STALKED BACK INTO HIS MOTHER'S COUNCIL ROOM. She was taking a sip of her wine when he came back in. She studied him over the rim of the glass, and then she returned it to the table.

For a long moment they remained that way, her looking up at him, and he looking down at her. Then, at last, Enalyn sighed.

"You have something to say. Say it."

Eamin's jaw clenched. "Am I speaking with my mother right now, or my liege lord?"

"I have always been both."

"Fine, then. You have divided them. You have created a rift between the Lifemage and the people she relies on most."

"I have created nothing," said Enalyn. "I merely exposed a rift which already existed, and which you were perpetuating. Do you think the secret would have kept forever? You were fostering a far greater schism than the one they face tonight. You might have sundered them forever. It was time for them to stop dancing around secrets and lies."

Eamin scoffed and walked to the other end of the table, pacing as

Oris had done a short while before. "This from the woman who only days ago told me to always keep another layer of secrets behind the ones you let your enemies discover."

"You are not nearly foolish enough to believe your own words," said Enalyn. "These folk are not our enemies. Secrecy is a tool, Eamin. The truth is also a tool. The most important knowledge you will acquire in this life is knowing when to use which tool. If you use a saw when you are supposed to use a hammer, you will be a very poor carpenter."

"A good thing I have no wish to be a carpenter, then," snapped Eamin.

Enalyn's lip curled. "Enough. You are being petulant. I expect you at council tomorrow. You are dismissed."

Eamin took a deep breath to calm himself. "Mother—"

"No. We will both be more productive after a night to rest and think. Leave me."

For a moment, Eamin did not move. Then at last he bowed to her and excused himself. Kris stood at the door, unmoving and unblinking as he walked past them. He wondered if they agreed with his mother, or if they felt a pang of sympathy they were duty-bound not to express.

Back in his chamber, Eamin paced for what felt an interminable time. He drank more wine than he should have. But both his pacing and the furiously spinning wheels of his mind were interrupted by a knock at his door. He looked up at it, frowning.

"Come."

The door opened, and Idulen let himself into the chamber, softly closing the door behind him. Eamin's expression softened at once, and he managed a smile.

"Idulen, my faithful friend. It is good to see you. But why so late? I hope you did not wait all through that council."

"I did, Your Highness," said Idulen, ducking his head. "I thought you might have need of me."

Eamin sighed. "I thank you for your diligence. But I do not know that I require any aid tonight. Or rather, I do not know if aid is possible."

Idulen's mouth soured. "Your proposal was not accepted, then?"

"It was rather roundly rejected," said Eamin. "And Her Majesty told the Drayden fellow that Silvin was a Mystic."

"Sky above," said Idulen, his eyes widening.

"Indeed," said Eamin. "It remains to be seen whether that rift can be repaired. Or what now we shall do to bring Oris into her own."

The chamber fell to silence for a moment. Then Idulen went to the bottle of wine and filled Eamin's cup before filling another for himself, which he raised.

"A toast to your health, Your Highness. Whatever darkness may come, I am confident you are fit to face it."

Eamin chuckled. "Your confidence warms my heart, even if I do not share it." But he joined Idulen in the toast.

Idulen drank and then set his cup down. "Your Highness, I think it is time for me to depart the palace. Mayhap even the Seat."

Eamin froze. His eyes were aghast as he stared at Idulen.

"You wish to *leave?"* said Eamin. "Whatever for? You are incredibly valuable here. Has your service to me proved too onerous?"

"On the contrary," said Idulen. "My service to Your Highness continues to be the greatest honor of my life."

"Then why?"

Idulen gave him a careful, piercing look. "You see, Your Highness, I wish to take a more active role in the coming conflict. Every day I hear reports of Her Majesty sending forces into the Birchwood to track down the Shades. My father . . . well, he is a lord in northern Selvan. The issue is close to home, in a very real sense. In fact, a whole company of my father's troops are stationed in Garsec right now. I led them in the march there myself. I have been thinking that I might resume my command of them and march them into the Birchwood, seeking for the enemy as the High King's other forces are doing. It might be more useful than staying here on the Seat, no matter the kindness of Your Highness' compliments."

Eamin lifted his chin as he studied Idulen. "That is . . . an interesting proposition," he said. "When would you want to go?"

"Oh, quickly," said Idulen. "Rather immediately, in fact. If I am being honest, if Your Highness gave me permission, I should like to secure passage for myself for first light, to sail with the tides. I would be gone from the Seat before anyone would know I was gone, and reach Garsec by midday. From there, I could have my forces ready to march into the Birchwood almost at once. They know of the High King's expeditions, and they have held themselves at the ready for some time. I have a vessel waiting at the docks for me, and only for me. It has plenty of bunks for other passengers, if there were any."

Eamin stepped forwards and held out his hand. When Idulen took it, Eamin pulled him in for a one-armed embrace.

"Thank you," said Eamin quietly.

"It is my privilege and my honor," said Idulen.

Eamin drew back slightly and met his gaze. "Hear me now. I think this course of action is for the best, but it is risky."

"I will accept the consequences of the High King's ire," said Idulen.

"I do not mean that," said Eamin. "She will not be able to chastise you. She shall have to claim this plan as her own, or it will make her look weak. I speak not of the political ramifications, but the course of action itself. You are bringing our most powerful ally into danger. No one in the nine kingdoms is more important than she is."

"Your Highness certainly is," protested Idulen. "Not to mention your moth—"

"I mean it, Idulen," said Eamin firmly. "Your loyalty is admirable, but it is misplaced. If it came down to my life or Oris', I would throw myself upon the blades of our enemies without a moment's hesitation. You *must* keep her safe, at any cost."

Idulen dropped his gaze. "I vow to you, here beneath the sky and in fear of the dark below, that I will let nothing happen to her."

Eamin smiled and clapped him on the shoulder. "I believe you. If we fail in this, it will not be from any failure of the stout heart of Idulen of the family Steth."

Idulen's cheeks flushed. "Thank you, Your Highness."

"You cannot tell anyone that I had anything to do with this. Though it disgusts me to say so, there are politics involved."

"I would never, Your Highness," said Idulen. "You have taught me better than that. And now I must away, if we are to succeed in our aims."

"Fare well, then," said Eamin. "May your road be one of safety, and your feet carry you like wings."

"Certainly shall I fly with all speed, Your Highness. But no safe road lies ahead of us."

It took Oris longer than she wanted to find the Crescent Bulwark. She had hardly been let out of the tavern while they stayed there, except when they traveled to the Academy, which lay in the opposite direction from the High King's palace. These streets were unfamiliar to her, and she had to ask many people for directions. She got lost more than once. But at last she spotted the familiar green-and-gold door and let herself into the common room.

There was Flip, alone at a table as if he was waiting for her. He was leaning almost all the way over, his chest resting on the wooden tabletop while he traced a circle on the wood with one finger. Two bottles of wine were on the table before him, and one was already empty. Oris sat on the bench beside him and reached for the other bottle.

"Didn't buy that for you," said Flip. His words slurred slightly.

"Dark take you, then. Weak piss, anyway." Oris flagged down a barman. "Your best brandy." He returned soon with the bottle and a glass. Oris sent the glass back and took two large swallows from the bottle before sucking a sharp breath in between her teeth.

"You think that's impressive?" said Flip. "If you weren't so oafishly huge, that would knock you on your rump, and I'd still be up."

"We're to spend the night in the High King's palace," said Oris.

"Like Elves we are. I'm fine here."

Oris shook her head. "I don't care how angry you are at me, Flip. You'll never make me believe you're not going to take advantage of royal hospitality when it's offered freely."

"Freely?" Flip sat up and stared at her wide-eyed. "Oris, you can't be that big of a fool. You just *can't.* That hospitality comes with more strings attached than any sellsword contract we've ever taken in our lives. You must know it."

"They need us," said Oris. "We've got the advantage here."

Flip shook his head. "Oris, I'm telling you. I'm used to dealing with those who wield power. Some wield it through money, and they're bad enough. They'll sell their own kin to eke out another weight's worth of profit. But those whose power *doesn't* come from coin are worse. You know there are merchant families richer than mine. But my mother . . ."

His gaze went far away, through the tavern's front door, and he wrapped his arms around himself. Oris reached out and laid a hand on his shoulder.

"I know, Flip," she said. "I do."

"You don't," said Flip. But his voice did not sound so harsh as it might have. "There are folk whose power comes from another place. It's a threat of death and the promise of your dreams, both at once. It beats everything. You have to learn to see the blade behind the coin they offer you. Threaten someone's family, and there's nothing they won't do, no matter how much someone else is paying them." He turned his dark eyes on Oris. "They'll do the same if you promise to give their family back."

Oris met his gaze. "I'm not some moonstruck child, Flip. I don't think finding my parents will fix anything."

"Then why do you care?"

"Wouldn't you?"

Flip snorted and turned away. "I know my parents, and I can tell you that I often wish I didn't."

"The stew always looks better in the next bowl," said Oris. "But Flip, before we met, I'd spent my whole life—"

"And that's just the problem," said Flip. "They know that. Silvin knows it. That's the gift she promises to give. And as long as you're focused on that, she doesn't have to brandish the threat."

Oris frowned. "What's the threat?"

Flip's gaze remained locked on the tavern door. "I suppose we'll find out if you refuse to return."

"You walked out. Silvin didn't stop you."

"She doesn't want me, darling. She wants you." A little of his smirk remained as he glanced at her. "And to hire you as well."

"Stop it," said Oris. Then for a little while she sat lost in thought. At last she shook her head slowly. "Mayhap she has no threat because she doesn't need one. The Necromancer won't stop hunting me. The High King, the Mystics, they're the only allies we've got. Where else could we go?"

Flip slumped in his chair. "There's the core of it. And you already know my answer. I don't know."

Oris took another drink of the brandy. She stared at her hands as she spoke. "I wish I hadn't found out before you did."

Flip dropped his gaze to his own bottle, scowling. "And when did you find out?"

"The Verge. The night the rogue weremage took you."

A flash of anger crossed Flip's face, quickly suppressed. He snorted. "Hmph. That's a long time, Oris. A long, long time."

"It is."

"I thought upon it the whole way back here. I should have guessed it. The way she reacted to my story about the Mystics. The endless coin she dropped on us too freely. The mysteries, the half-truths, the way she led us on. I should have seen that, guessed at least, or suspected. But I could *not* have foreseen you. No sign could have told me that you would keep a secret like that from me. Because I trusted you. And I've always been able to in the past. It's the two of us, dear. It's always been the two of us."

At last she looked up at him. "This is bigger than the two of us now.

If Silvin had been anyone else, if it had been about anything else, there's no way in the dark below I would have done what I did. Tell me you believe me."

"Oh, I believe it," said Flip, sneering. "You've always been a fool for a nice rump and golden hair."

Oris' jaw clenched. "You're insulting me so I'll pound the snot out of you. Thought you were smarter than that."

Flip waved a hand, like clearing away cobwebs. "You can do what you want." Then he reached over the table and took her brandy bottle, drinking a long swig.

Oris clasped her hands and dropped her gaze to them again. "Flip. I need you. Have you any idea how far I'm in over my head? This is . . . it's nobility and Mystics and merchants and power, and money on a scale I've never imagined. We consult with the Lord Prince now. We just took counsel with the High King. What under the sky am I supposed to do with that? How am I supposed to do it without you?"

Flip lurched forwards, seizing her wrist. His eyes burned with an intensity like magelight. "Why in the *dark* do you want to do it at all? I certainly don't. That's why I left home. That's why we met! And I liked you at once, because I thought you didn't give two pints of piss about that world either. This is the opposite of anything I've ever wanted. It's why I'll never go back to my family."

His grip on her wrist felt like a brand. Oris' pulse quickened, and her jaw clenched. She thought of the High King and the Lord Prince, the way they held their tongues and quelled their words so often, and she took a deep breath.

"Flip. If there were someone out there, some cabal . . . let's say the family Yerrin. And if the Yerrins wanted to kill you *just because* you were your mother's son, and they were hunting you across the nine kingdoms, *just because* of that, and for no other reason . . . you'd go back home."

Flip's nostrils flared. "I wouldn't."

"You would," said Oris flatly. "You'd be a fool not to. You'd return to the family you hate so much, and you'd rely on their protection. You're only so cavalier about it because no one out here gives a shit who you are. But if your mother's enemies wanted to use you to get to her, you'd take refuge with her again to keep yourself safe. And you know that's true. You walked away from the life you hated because you're lucky enough to be able to."

"Oh, certainly," spat Flip. "I'm just *so* fortunate."

"Yes, you *are,* dark take you." Oris had not meant it to come out as a snarl. "And I'm *not.* You were perfectly happy with our schemes when you thought we'd be serving only the High King. Now you learn the truth about Silvin and that you'll have to work with the redcloaks, and now it's a problem. It's the same game. You're only mad about the players. So you piss off and abandon me, if you don't want to get involved in any of this. Fine. Leave, like you left your family. But I'm not your family, which you never chose. I'm your best friend, and you picked me, and *I can't do this without you.* The people who want to kill me . . . they're never going to stop, and it doesn't matter that I don't want to be who I am. But I'm just smart enough to know that the Mystics and, dark below, the High King herself, they'll all want something from me, too. They may have better intentions for me than the Necromancer does. But they'll all be trying to use me, and who I am, for their own ends. And if you're not with me, they'll do it. I'll be their tool, a puppet dancing on their strings at the carnival. So I'm asking you to stay, because you're smarter than they are."

When had the brandy bottle emptied? And the wine? Oris did not know. But now they were staring at the bottles, because it seemed too mighty a feat to look at each other.

Oris might have imagined it, but she thought that from the corner of her eye she caught a glistening in Flip's. He scrubbed at his forehead, but he might have swiped at his eyes on the way up.

"You should have told me," whispered Flip.

"Mayhap," said Oris. "But then, mayhap you would have convinced me to leave Silvin. And then we'd both be dead. So mayhap not."

Flip stared at the empty bottles. Then he stood up, slowly.

"Come on," he said. "The High King must have better stuff than this swill."

Oris rose to her feet. The floor seemed to buckle beneath her, but only slightly. "I'm sure she does."

They made for the door. But almost at once, Flip stopped and turned to glare at her. "I'm not friends with Silvin, though. Dark take her, and dark take you for going along with her."

"Fair enough," said Oris.

Flip pursed his lips and nodded. "So long as that's clear."

The palace guards admitted Oris and Flip back within the walls. A steward waited to lead them to the chamber that had been prepared for them. It was made up of a common room with couches, chairs and a table to sit around, as well as two doors on either side leading to beds to sleep in.

In the common room was Silvin. She was lounging on a couch when Oris pushed open the door, but she shot to her feet at once.

"You are back—"

"Ah-ah," said Flip, raising a forefinger. Silvin went still. "Nothing from you now." His words came quite slurred, and he stumbled past her towards the second bedchamber on the left, closing the door heavily behind him.

Silvin turned back to Oris with wide eyes. "How was it?"

"Not as bad as it might have been," said Oris. She was somewhat surprised by how slurred her own speech was. It had not seemed so bad when she was talking to Flip, who was worse. "It'll take some time. But he's here, and that's good."

Silvin glanced towards Flip's door again. "I suppose it is."

A knock came at the room's front door. Oris and Silvin turned to look at it for a moment before giving each other a look.

"Expecting anyone?" said Oris.

"Not I," said Silvin. Her hands went to the hilts of her swords.

"Come," called Oris. Her fingers curled to fists at her side.

The door opened. There stood Idulen of the family Steth. Oris relaxed, though she noticed that Silvin remained at the ready. Idulen gave them both a quick nod before stepping inside and closing the door behind him.

"Idulen," said Oris. "What is it? Have we been summoned?"

He gave her a shrewd glance, and Oris thought he must have heard the brandy in her tone. But he said only, "I am leaving on a ship before first light. I am traveling to Garsec, where a company of my father's troops await me, there to march into the Birchwood seeking the Shades."

Silvin sighed, her mouth twisting. "Someone should have informed you of the results of our council with Her Majesty. That is no longer the plan."

"I understand it is not Her Majesty's plan," said Idulen. "It is still mine, however. And there is room on my ship for the three of you."

Oris looked at Silvin askance. "Are you suggesting—"

"I am offering. You already planned what you thought was the best course of action. His Highness agreed. I have nothing but the highest respect for Her Majesty, but I know where my deepest loyalty lies."

"And what does His Highness say to such a scheme?" said Silvin.

Idulen's mouth crept towards a smirk. "The Lord Prince could never be involved in any such matters as these," he said. "He could give neither his approval nor his blessing, nor could he be known to have known about it—no matter what he might say privately, or what secret councils may have been held behind closed doors."

"We understand," said Silvin. "But you must realize that you risk stoking the wrath of the High King herself."

Idulen sighed. "Well do I know it. And I know, too, that her judgment would not fall on you, but solely on my own head. Yet I can deal with that when it must be dealt with. For my own part, I would rather take that risk and return with you at your full strength than sit here and let the redcloaks play games with your fate." He gave a quick nod to Silvin. "I have known many noble Mystics worthy of great honor. But the order as a whole . . . well, I love them not much more than your friend Philip."

The door to Flip's room opened so suddenly that Oris jumped. Flip lumbered into the doorway, leaning heavily on the jamb.

"What's this you're saying?" said Flip. "Some scheme to make the redbacks look like fools? We're in."

"Were you listening at the door?" said Oris.

"'Course I was."

Silvin looked doubtful. "I have my reservations about going directly against the High King—to say nothing of the new lord chancellor of my order." Her gaze shifted to Oris. "But I leave the decision to the Lifemage. After all, Jordel was banished from the order before he died. I suppose I would only be following in his footsteps. And the High King herself honors his memory, so that cannot be entirely a bad thing."

"It is your choice, then, Lifemage," said Idulen. "What say you?"

Oris turned from Silvin back to him. "I say that you'd better not get in the habit of calling me that," she growled. "But I'm in. I've no wish to sit here idle when there's a chance to do what's needed."

Idulen nodded. "Very well. Then get what sleep you can. I shall send someone to fetch you when it is time to leave."

"Thank you, Idulen," said Silvin. "You do your family proud."

"Ever have I endeavored to." Idulen gave them a bow and left. Flip lurched away and vomited in his chamber pot.

• ○ • ○ •

Eamin received a summons to the High King's chamber the next morning. When he arrived, she looked quite unhappy, and she dismissed her guards at once so the two of them were alone.

"It appears the Lifemage and her friends slipped out of the palace in the night," said Enalyn without preamble. "Do you know where they have gone?"

Eamin waited a long moment while he considered his response. "Whatever else she is, Oris does not seem the duplicitous type. Therefore I can foresee no malice in her actions. Mayhap she simply decided she knew better than Your Majesty, and she is heading off to enact her original plan. Would you like me to go after her and fetch her home?"

"Of course you are not to risk yourself in that way," snapped Enalyn.

She took a piece of bacon from a plate on the table before her and chewed it. Quickly she rose from her chair and paced behind it. At last she stopped, gripping the back of the chair tightly.

"I will not ask if you knew of their plans," she said. "I have no wish for you to confess to what might be construed as treason. Nor would I force you to lie to me."

Eamin wondered what he could possibly say to that. In the end, he chose to say nothing.

"You need to take this lesson to heart," said Enalyn. "When you sit the throne, you will have more power than anyone else in the known world. But your power will be eclipsed by your responsibility."

"What do you mean?" said Eamin, frowning. "The one is dependent on the other."

"They are *not* the same thing," said Enalyn. "There will always be things you cannot control. Even a High King's power is not absolute. The Lifemage and the Necromancer, for example, are not within my control—as is *stunningly* evidenced by this latest madness.

"But though my power diminishes in this matter, my responsibility does not. If Oris should die, and our best chance at defeating the Necromancer vanishes, that is still my responsibility, though I am powerless to stop it. I will have to live with my failure for the rest of my presumably shortened life. The Lifemage's death will be part of my legacy, though I did nothing to instigate it and everything in my power to prevent it. And now it is your responsibility as well. I hope you are prepared to live with that."

"I think that I am," said Eamin.

"Do not *think.*" Enalyn's voice was acid. "You had better be sure."

A knock came at the door. They both turned to it as it opened, and Kris stuck their head in.

"The Dean of the Academy for Wizards to see you, Your Majesty," said Kris.

Enalyn sighed and sat again, covering her eyes with a hand. "I sent word for him to meet me this morning so I could tell him of Oris. Now I cannot, or you will have made me look a fool. I must invent some other reason to have brought him here."

Eamin's brows rose. "Tell him you invited him here for breakfast with both of us so that he can inform us how the Academy investigations are going."

Enalyn's scowl deepened. "I told him it was a matter of the strictest confidentiality."

Eamin could not entirely suppress a smile. "Tell him I do not want to be seen with him, or have anyone know I was in the same room as him. He might laugh."

"Get. Out."

"Your Majesty."

But Eamin did not walk straight to the door. He went to her instead, taking her hand and bending down slightly to kiss her forehead. Enalyn gave his hand the slightest squeeze before he left.

CHAPTER XIX
SKEINS CLOSING

THE SHIP REACHED GARSEC BEFORE MIDDAY, JUST AS IDULEN HAD SAID it would. A carriage brought them through the city and out beyond its walls. The fields outside of Garsec were filled with camps of soldiers, farmland now covered with rows and rows of tents. Forces from several kingdoms had gathered, as well as more than one mercenary company. Oris thought she recognized one or two of the banners. There was the green chalice of the Emerald Draught, as well as the four red slashes of Bashang's Bears. But they kept themselves hidden behind the carriage's curtain, for Idulen was adamant that no one should see the Lifemage passing by.

Idulen's force awaited them at the northern end of the fields. One hundred soldiers were gathered there. Oris, Flip, and Silvin stepped down from the carriage, and Idulen made quick introductions to the captains and officers. Oris studied all of the soldiers arrayed before her. They looked grim and battle-hardened to a one. Idulen had told her that many had fought in the battle of the Seat.

The company had received word to be at the ready, and so it was less than an hour before they marched north towards the Birchwood. There was a road at first, but it gradually faded to little more than a footpath, and the company made its slow way through bracken and underbrush. They pressed their way between the trees, and though the wintry air was bracing, darkness seemed to gather as the evergreen branches above them slowly blocked out the sun.

Days passed in the Birchwood without sign of any foe—or, for that matter, any friend. They were following in the path of previous companies sent by the High King, but there was no true trail to follow. They had only reports of others' travel here, and Idulen spent much time poring over maps of the area, trying to determine the next best course to take.

Oris and Flip fell into their old military routines rather easily. But one thing that was missing was the camaraderie with their fellow soldiers. None of Idulen's troops knew the real reason Oris was there—as far as they were concerned, they were only seeking Shades to wipe them out, just as the High King had been doing ever since the attack on the Seat.

"I apologize," Idulen told them on the first day, "but it is better if no one else knows who you are. You shall have to pretend to be my advisors."

"We don't care," said Flip with a shrug. "I'm used to playing down my own inestimable talents."

Oris rolled her eyes and shoved his shoulder, which sent him stumbling. "The only thing that matters is finding what we came here for," she told Idulen. "We'll say whatever we need to say."

They came upon several villages deep in the woods. They were all small, most of them so small that they had no names. Many were abandoned. It was a chilling thing to walk through places that so clearly had once teemed with life, but from which everyone had fled with the approach of the enemy.

Worse than the empty villages were the sites of slaughter.

The Shades had not scoured the Birchwood entirely when they had marched on the Seat, but they had stumbled upon many villages in the woods and put the inhabitants to the sword. Idulen's troops would find some buildings burned down each time, while others stood like silent monuments to the lost. Blood often stained the walls. In some of these villages, the High King's forces had come previously, and they had given the inhabitants a proper burning, so that a great communal pile of ash lay just outside the village borders. But they came upon two such places where no troops had come before, and bodies littered the ground. It had been months now, and many of the bodies were rotted, though thankfully the chilly winter air kept the stench from being too bad. Carrion birds were plentiful in these places. Some wild animals in the woods had grown more feral on a gluttonous diet of human flesh, and they had to be driven off. At each village, Idulen's company took a day or two to gather up the remaining bodies and set them to the torch.

Some villages gave them more hope. They would enter a place that seemed abandoned, the doors closed and the windows shuttered. But as they prepared to move on, or went marching by in the woods not far away, the village's inhabitants would suddenly emerge, having recognized them as soldiers of the High King. A rumor of terror had passed through the Birchwood, and it seemed that all who dwelled there knew the Shades were about, and they hid themselves as best they could. From some of these survivors they heard vague rumors of the enemy's coming. The forest folk had seen the Shades moving east through the Birchwood before the attack, and then passing west afterwards. But they knew nothing more than that.

"How far do we mean to go?" said Flip one evening, as they were building camp and setting a watch.

"What do you mean?" said Silvin.

Flip glowered at her. Tensions between them had not eased during their journey through the woods, and Oris' hackles went up whenever the two of them spoke to each other. Rather than answer Silvin directly now, Flip spoke only to Oris. "The Birchwood spans Selvan's northern border. Do we mean to cross the entire kingdom?"

"We mean to find the Shades," said Oris. "Wherever they may be."

"So have the High King's armies, ever since the attack on the Seat," said Flip. "How will our quest end any differently than theirs? Some of the troops who have been sent into the Birchwood have never returned."

"You seemed to think this plan a good one when we thought of it," said Oris.

"I was happy to get you out of the clutches of the Mystics. Or at least most of them," said Flip, glaring at Silvin again. "Now that we've accomplished that, we might think of something wiser than simply wandering lost in the woods like the sister moons."

"Then think of something wiser," snapped Oris. "And until you do, still your tongue and its biting remarks."

"What about your amulet?" said Flip.

"What about my amulet?"

Flip reached over and lifted it up, dangling it on its leather thread between his fingers. "It's meant to find the enemy, isn't it?"

Oris pulled it out of his grasp. "I know nothing more than you do about what it's *meant* for. All it's done so far is warn us. But it can offer no warning if there is no threat."

Silvin looked uneasily out into the darkness beneath the trees. "I think it is inaccurate to say there is no threat. The enemy is here somewhere. We have to find them eventually."

"We don't," said Flip. "There are a thousand and one reasons we might never find them at all. They might not even be here. They could have left the Birchwood, slipping out of it singly or in small groups, only to reconvene and strike at Underrealm again from a new and unexpected direction. You can't tell me all your redback brethren, with the wise and the great among you, haven't thought of that."

Silvin took two deep breaths. "Of course we have," she said slowly. "And we have been watchful throughout Selvan and Dorsea for just such a possibility. But there have been no signs of their egress. And you said it yourself: some of the High King's troops vanish within the forest. What happens to them, if the Shades are not here to destroy them?"

Oris tensed up as Flip opened his mouth to begin an angry retort. But just then, Idulen approached them. Oris and Silvin stood to meet him. Flip remained seated on the ground. But at least he let his argument with Silvin die for the moment.

"Good eve, Idulen," said Silvin.

"Good eve," said Idulen. "I would have your counsel. Do we have anything new?"

"You mean since the midday meal, when last we talked?" said Flip. "Surely you realize that if we had learned or seen anything new, you would know about it already."

"Flip," said Oris, giving him a sharp look. Flip rolled his eyes and subsided. Oris turned back to Idulen. "We were just discussing that, in fact. We do not have any new ideas about where to go or what to do. Can you think of any better course for us to take?"

"I have never been the cleverest of advisors," said Idulen. "But my troops and I are willing to carry on the hunt as long as we must to find what you need."

"And your diligence is appreciated," said Silvin.

Idulen gave her a smile, though it looked slightly wan. "Another night of good rest, then, and another day of searching to follow. Keep up your hope! The enemy cannot evade us forever."

• ○ • ○ •

A half-hour later, Idulen went striding to the edge of the camp. A sentry stood there just within the treeline, bow in hand and an arrow nocked, but undrawn. She turned at the sound of footsteps, and when she saw Idulen, she saluted smartly with a fist over her heart.

"Ser."

"Rest easy," said Idulen, returning the salute. "No sign of trouble?"

"No, ser," said the sentry.

"Good, good. I am off to relieve myself. You have the night's password?"

"Third tower. Give your call from a good distance, if you please, ser. I dislike the darkness beneath the trees, and I would hate to mistake you for an intruder."

"Your caution is commendable, and I will match it." Idulen gave her a final smile and set off into the trees.

When he was well out of sight of the sentry and the glow of the campfires was only a faint glimmer between the tree trunks, he had himself a piss. But no sooner had he finished than a branch cracked in the trees not far off. Hurriedly he finished putting back his belt, and then he whirled with his sword drawn.

Two figures stepped out of the woods. The moonslight now shining from above barely illuminated their grey clothes and blue cloaks.

Idulen sighed with relief and sheathed his sword. "Thank the sky. I worried you were a bear or a pack of wolves."

One of the figures stepped forwards. He threw back his hood, revealing a careworn face and a bald head, though he looked somewhat too young for either. Idulen did not recognize him. "We came as quickly as we could."

"Did you?" said Idulen in irritation. "It seems to have taken an eternity. What delayed you in finding us?"

"Messages take long to travel through the Birchwood. Those of us who remain are in hiding, only striking when it is safe."

"Well, never mind that," said Idulen. "I have her. I have her with me. She is in my camp right now, this very minute, and I have only a hundred of troops with me."

The Shades looked at each other before the man looked back to Idulen. "Your troops. Are they ours?"

"They are my father's, and more loyal to Selvan than to me alone," said Idulen, his mouth twisting. "They will not kill her simply because I tell them to. But if I give them a command to our benefit in battle, it will give them a moment of confusion. That may be all you need."

"It will be more than enough," said the Shade. "We will bring word of this to Barrick."

Idulen's eyes widened. "Barrick is here?"

"He is. You should lead your forces south and east. You will find a hill with rocks around its rim. The locals call it the Giant's Crown, and it looks the part. The attack will come there. Be ready when it does. Once we have the rest of them occupied, you should strike down the Lifemage at once."

Idulen gave a bark of laughter. "Are you mad? She has a Mystic bodyguard who watches her like a hawk, and her friend the wizard does the same. No one gets within a pace of her. Not even me. No, I will lead them to the Crown, but it will be up to you to bring down the Lifemage. I will help in the fight only if I am absolutely sure it will not cost me my own neck."

The Shade frowned. "The Lord does not love a coward. Captain Barrick loves them even less."

Idulen stepped towards him, fury curdling his face. "You call me a coward? You could never do what I have done, never perform the service I have given our father. Over a decade have I spent worming my way into the heart of that simpering princeling in the palace. I was not even a man when it started, and since then, I have lied to his face and his mother's, and they have held not a whit of suspicion. Every day I have walked through their halls, knowing a dagger is ready to plunge into my heart if they should even suspect me. Only a handful of our brethren could do what I have done, and I will not be called a coward for it, by you or anyone."

The Shade's expression remained stony. "We will see if Captain Barrick agrees with your . . . impassioned oratory. Somehow I do not think so. But we shall tell him what you have said."

"Good," snapped Idulen. "Then run along and carry my words. I must return before the guard wonders if I am pissing blood."

The Shade's mouth twisted. He pulled up his hood, and then he and his companion faded away into the woods. Idulen hurried back to the camp, slowing his pace as he approached the outer edge.

"Third tower!" he called out.

The sentry lowered her bow. "Thank you, ser. The darkness grows thicker."

"We have nothing to fear from it," said Idulen, smiling and clapping her shoulder. "Not while we have stalwart fighters like you to stand against it."

Barrick was in a foul mood, but that was not uncommon these days. For three nights he had been lurking in a dead village. The Shades had put its inhabitants to the sword months ago, when they first came east to attack the Seat. Now it was like a hollow shell, and he a crab who had taken it for his own residence, but found it too small to contain him.

It was not long after dawn when two messengers approached him from the trees. They came swiftly and, after his guards challenged them and received the password, they drew back their hoods. Barrick recognized Raloren, a young man but already balding, and his lover, Disan, a quiet lad but vicious in a fight.

"Hail, Raloren," growled Barrick. "Tell me you have brought me something interesting."

"I have, captain," said Raloren. He was out of breath, as though he had run all the way here. Barrick's pulse quickened. "She is here, in the woods, now. Less than a day's march away. Idulen of the family Steth leads the force that guards her, and he is going to guide them south to the Giant's Crown."

"She is here?" cried Barrick, his fists clenching. "Now? You are certain?"

"I could not draw close enough to see her for myself," said Raloren. "But Idulen swears it. He is a worm, but he would not lie about a matter so grave."

Barrick's breath quickened. He took Raloren's wrist in his massive hand and drew him close, cupping the back of his head with his other hand. "Well done. Well *done,* brother. Rest now, and eat well. And then be ready, for we will march upon her at once."

Raloren and Disan went to recover from their journey. Barrick dismissed his personal guards and strode off into the woods. Once out of sight of his brethren, he drew his dagger and slashed it across his forearm. His face did not even twitch as the blade laid open his flesh and the blood ran down. Soon he felt it: the connection, the magic swirling through his form through the tattoo on the back of his neck.

There stood Father. Barrick blinked hard and tried to swallow past a sudden lump at the back of his throat. Father's expression was one of deepest concern, but when he saw Barrick standing before him, his eyes faded to gentle curiosity.

"What is it, my son?" Even as the Lord spoke, his eyes glowed. Barrick felt the magic flowing through him, banishing the death and pain clustered around his wound, allowing it to seal itself shut as though it had never been harmed at all. "You were due for a report in less than two hours. What news has reached you that cannot wait so long?"

"She is here, Father," said Barrick. "Here in the Birchwood, now. Soldiers protect her, but too few. We can have her."

The Lord's brows rose. "I know."

Barrick stared at him for a long moment, feeling shock, and then wonder, and then a quiet, brimming rage. "You know?"

"I have known for days. Weeks now, if I count my days aright."

"Why have you not told me, Father?" growled Barrick. "I have been here all the while, lurking like a coward in these trees. I could have hunted her down and ended her!"

"That is not your appointed task," said the Lord. "I mean to send Rogan after her."

Barrick's breath came quick now. "Rogan is far to the north in Dorsea. I am *here,* Father. You must let me hunt her down. This war can be all but won, and it can happen today."

"There are more things at play here than you can imagine, my son," said the Lord sternly. "It is *supposed* to be Rogan who brings the Lifemage down. Not for any purpose of honor or favor that you imagine. I have foreseen it."

"You tell me—you have told me endlessly—that the future is never certain," said Barrick. "There is only what is likely, and what is less likely. Nothing is impossible. Will you tell me now, instead, that the way forwards is carved of stone? Is there no future in which I bring the Lifemage down? If even one skein leads that way, I will not fail to find my way to its end."

"I do not doubt your resolve," said the Lord. "But you are just one person, Barrick. As are all of us. Even me. Your strength will not save you if enough threads of fate pull against you."

"Then you are like the old kings," spat Barrick. "You do not offer me my freedom. You mean to dictate to me what I can and cannot do, where I can and cannot go. My own wishes are nothing. I am a tool at your belt, not a free person with my own will. I thought better of you."

It seemed like the vision of the Lord before him swelled, as the attendant had done days ago. The Lord's modest frame swelled to dwarf Barrick, and his eyes blazed with an evil fury like darkfire. Bared teeth shone like a skull's behind twisted and wrathful lips, and a growl slipped from between them of its own accord.

But now Barrick stood firm, his shoulders squared and his hands balled into fists at his side. He met his father's gaze unflinching, and his eyes blazed with a fury just as bright.

The Lord paused. And then into his eyes came a profound sadness, mingled with shame. He passed a hand over his eyes, and it was as though the wrath had never been. His form diminished.

"I am no king, Barrick," said the Lord. "Only a father worried for a beloved son. But you shame me with the truth. I will not deny you that which you believe you desire."

Barrick's eyes shot wide. "Then I may hunt her?"

"You are your own person," said the Lord. "You may do as you wish. I have advised you, but I will not forbid you. But I will give you one final warning. If you mean to take her, you must do it quickly. The Lifemage has been beyond our reach for a long while now. In that time, she has been studying her power. It is not yet entirely within her command, but she is close upon the truth. If she masters herself, you will be in grave danger."

"Danger?" said Barrick. His fists clenched tighter, and his arms seemed to swell with strength. "I have had her in my grasp before, and she had no hope but to flee. She is the only one in danger, Father."

The Lord sighed. "I hope for your sake that you are right, my son."

CHAPTER XX
BETRAYAL IN DARKNESS

"I THINK WE NEED TO BRING OUR FORCE SOUTH," SAID IDULEN.

It was an early dawn in the Birchwood. Mist drifted gently between the trees, obscuring sight more than the shadows of the boughs, at least until the rising sun burned it away. Oris, Flip, and Silvin were breaking their fast. As they sat around the small campfire eating, they were silent, staring into the flames. That had become the norm whenever they had a moment to sit and think in silence. The thrill of a new venture had long since passed, and now they were in a doldrum. But they looked up in surprise as Idulen spoke to them.

"South?" said Silvin. "Why south?"

"We are plunging through the heart of the Birchwood," said Idulen. "It is too much ground to cover. No matter how we spread ourselves, no matter how we scour the woods, we cannot hope to explore more of this place than all the forces the High King has summoned to cleanse it. Yet we may fare better on the border. The Shades must have forces arrayed along the north and south of the Birchwood, to keep watch for any of the High King's forces who may encroach upon them. We stand a better chance of discovering those sentries than we have of stumbling upon wherever the Shades are hiding."

"A fair enough point," said Flip, leaning back on his hands. "And I'll not deny I'd like to see something other than endless trees and nothing else."

"We shall need to resupply soon in any case," said Oris. "Drawing close to the border would make that easier."

"Then it seems we are decided," said Idulen. "I shall prepare the troops for the march."

For two days they made their way south through the wood towards Selvan. Now that they had a direction, all the soldiers' steps came livelier, and their speed increased considerably. It was something Oris and Flip had often seen as sellswords: any plan, no matter its quality, was better for morale than interminable wandering.

On the third day, there was a call of alarm from the force's western flank. Sentries there sent up a cry. Around Oris there came the sound of many blades unsheathing. Silvin and Oris drew their own weapons. Flip's eyes began to glow as he held a globe of fire in his palm, and he slid out his long dagger.

There was a small commotion through the trees. Oris tensed and began to move that way, Silvin and Flip at her side. But then came a cry of "Peace!" Soon two of Idulen's soldiers appeared. Between them they were escorting a woman. Both men had to help support her, for she looked thin and wasted, and her feet kept slipping out from under her. Her hair was wild and matted with dirt and sticks, and her eyes shot in every direction, searching for danger.

"Here now," said Idulen, coming forward at once. He dropped his pack and pulled a blanket from it, wrapping it around her shoulders before looking to his soldiers. "Where did she come from?"

"West, ser," said one of them. "She came running from the trees."

Idulen took the woman's hand. At first she shied away from his touch, but after a moment her eyes focused on him.

"Be at ease," said Idulen gently. "Whence have you come?"

"My village," said the woman, her voice shaking. "They . . . they came. They killed . . . they killed everyone. Everyone they could."

Idulen glanced at Silvin and Oris before returning his gaze to the woman. "Who did? Did they bear any colors?"

"Blue and . . . and grey," said the woman. Her voice began to rise, cracking every few words. "The rumor of them . . . we have heard tales. But we thought . . . we thought we were safe . . . we thought they were north . . ."

Silvin came forwards. Gently she placed a hand on the woman's shoulder, guiding her to sit upon the ground. The woman started to shake harder, the thrill of her flight slowly seeping from her, leaving behind it only weakness and terror.

"You are safe now," said Silvin. "You escaped. We are servants of the High King, here to find these traitors and end their terror. Can you tell us where your village stands?"

"It no longer stands at all," said the woman. Again her voice broke. "They burned . . . they burned our homes." Now she started to weep, and her voice became a high, keening wail. Oris looked around nervously, hoping no enemy was close enough to hear it. "They took the children. They cut . . . they cut us down while we fled. A great brute led them . . . he laughed as he did it. My wife . . . my wife . . . *sky save me."*

Her grief, long held at bay, struck her at last. She fell forwards, curling over her own lap, the blanket sliding down her back. Her hands clutched at her shoulders, and she lost herself in wailing and weeping.

Silvin put a gentle arm around her shoulders and looked up to the rest of them. Her jaw was like iron, but her eyes were as dangerous as southern ice.

"We have them," she said.

"A great brute," said Flip. "One of the shadeborn."

"So it seems," said Idulen. "But if we wish to catch them, we shall have to depart at once. There is no telling how long they will remain in the village."

"Leave someone to see to her safety," said Oris. "Better yet, leave two."

Idulen frowned, and Silvin dropped her gaze. Flip looked uncomfortable. "We don't know how many of them there are, Oris," he said at last. "We may need every blade we have."

Oris' gaze snapped to Idulen. He flinched and then sighed. "You are right, of course. We cannot leave her alone like this." He gave a sharp whistle and held up two fingers. "Enzo. Zaira. Stay with her until she is ready to move. Then bring her south with all speed, and find the nearest town you can where she will be safe."

Two of his soldiers came forth and nodded. Silvin gave the woman's shoulder one last squeeze and then stood.

"Double-march," said Silvin. Hidden in her voice was a rage that almost frightened Oris. "I want to find that village before day's end. At last we have our quarry, and I will not let us lose them."

Not long before the end of the day, they found signs of the slaughter.

The woods cleared, and in the open space there rose a great hill, towering over the trees all around. It culminated in a great wide curve, like the head of a balding man. Around the lip of it were many large, broken stones, like a crown.

There lay the bodies. Dozens of them splayed out in the snow. No one seemed to have been spared except the children the fleeing woman had spoken of. They saw folk young and hale, and old and bent, all of them twisted now in death.

"Spread out!" called Idulen. "Search for signs of our foes leaving this place, and find out where they went."

Some squadrons of his soldiers rushed to obey his command. The remainder drew together atop the hill, searching for any survivors. There were none.

"Where's the village?" said Flip.

Oris turned to him with a frown. "What village?"

"The woman who found us," said Flip. "She said her village was attacked. There's no homes here. Only bodies."

Oris' frown deepened. Silvin turned to her. "Let us join Idulen's men in searching for signs."

They ran down from the crown of the hill and circled its base in opposite directions. To the west end they met each other, and by then both of them wore troubled looks.

"Many tracks," said Silvin.

"I found the same," said Oris. "All of them heading away from the hill, only to circle back around straight towards it."

"Why were they moving in this one area so much?" said Silvin.

"There's a river to the west," said Oris. "They could have used it to hide their trail."

Silvin's eyes widened. "The blood," she said, her voice scarcely more than a whisper.

"What blood?"

Silvin seized her arm and dragged her back to the top of the hill. She fell into a crouch and began stalking around the ground, inspecting the bodies. Oris followed her, concern mounting in her breast.

"Silvin?" said Oris. "What is—"

And then she saw it.

Many bodies. All of them dead, hacked open in the most violent and terrible manner.

And no spatters of blood. No red staining the white of the snow all around. None but what had dripped from the bodies.

These people had not been killed here. Their corpses had been *brought* here.

On the heels of that thought came a flash of light. Oris looked down with a gasp. Her amulet had begun to glow.

"Dark below," growled Silvin. The air rang with the hiss of her blades as she drew them and slid to Oris' side. "A trap."

"What?" said Idulen, drawing his own blade and looking at Oris' amulet in a panic. "What does that mean?"

"Our enemies laid a ruse for us," said Oris. "The refugee who found us was one of theirs. Your soldiers we left with her are likely dead, or else she slipped away from them."

"Ser!" cried one of Idulen's soldiers to the north.

Oris turned that way. Figures began to appear from the trees. Their clothing was grey, and their cloaks were blue. There were many of them, and more still were stalking forth out of the trees.

"Dark," spat Silvin. "This is not a raiding party. It is—"

"More to the south!"

The cry drew all eyes in that direction. More Shades appeared in the woods, blades drawn and faces grim. Oris turned to the east even before the final cry of alarm went up. More Shades from that direction.

And at their head was a figure greater than all the rest, towering above his brethren with sword and shield in hand. Oris' heart skipped a beat as she recognized the massive form of Barrick, the shadeborn they had seen in Dracmund.

They were hemmed in, their back to a river that was too wide and too deep to cross before they were caught and slain.

"Blood and fire," muttered Flip. "They've got us, haven't they?"

Silvin turned to Idulen. "Oris must escape this place. Whatever else may occur, she has to get away. The rest of us might have to fight a last stand to make that happen."

"Dark take that notion," said Oris. "I'm not leaving."

"Dark take it, indeed!" said Idulen. "I am not dying for her."

There was a moment's incredulous silence. Then Flip turned to Idulen with wide eyes.

"You dark-taken piss stain," he spat. "You betrayed us."

"What?" said Idulen. "How *dare—*"

"What are you talking about, Flip?" said Oris.

Flip did not answer her, but turned on Idulen instead. His eyes glowed, and twin globes of flame sprang into his palms. Idulen yelped and fell a step back. Two of his soldiers stepped between him and Flip, their eyes grim.

"Are they deep in your counsel, or are they merely fools?" snarled Flip.

"Explain yourself, Philip," said Silvin. But her eyes never left Idulen.

"All this business of coming out into the woods," said Flip. "You orchestrated it, and then you told them where to find us. For what price? A guarantee of safety, and a place in the enemy's court? For that, you betrayed us? You betrayed the *Lord Prince?* And what of your own soldiers? You would let them die here today as well?"

The two who had stepped between Flip and Idulen lowered their blades slightly. One of them gave an uncertain glance over her shoulder at her lord.

Idulen began to sputter. "I am . . . you have no . . ." His eyes darted left and right.

Suddenly Oris saw it. She *knew.* Flip was right.

"Oh, dark take it," growled Idulen, and he plunged his sword into the back of one of his guards. While the rest of them could only stare in shock, Idulen fled, plunging towards the line of Shades to the east.

"Not today," snarled Flip.

He stretched out a hand, and lightning arced from it, lancing through the air towards Idulen.

And then the lightning stopped in midair, curving to slap impotently into the ground.

Idulen shoved his soldiers aside. Shock seemed to hold them transfixed, and he burst into the open on the other side, reaching the Shades who stood in the forest beyond.

There, where Barrick stood, a woman appeared. Her eyes still glowed, and she held a hand up in warding against Flip's spell.

"They brought their own mage," said Flip. His tone was light, airy, as though he was commenting on the dress of a courtier. "That will complicate things."

But Oris barely heard him. All her focus was trained on Barrick, as it had been since he first stepped out of the Birchwood. Her skin crawled as she beheld him, a feeling like a thousand tiny creatures crawling across her, each with a thousand legs.

And now . . . now there was something new. Now that she knew what to look for. She was aware of something surrounding him, like a sickly glow. It filled the air, burning her nostrils like a cloying, filthy smoke. It was the magic. The magic that surrounded him, that protected him, that kept him from the death his master controlled. Now that Oris knew what to look for, she could feel it like a putrid oil on her skin.

If Barrick noticed her new recognition, he did not show it. He only wore the same confident, savage grin she had seen from him when they first spied each other in Dracmund. And now, as Oris stared at him, frozen under his gaze, he raised his sword.

"Take them!" he roared. "Spare none! Hew them even as they fall! Until life ends!"

"Until life ends!" cried his soldiers in response. And they broke into a mad charge, flying up the hill.

Idulen's soldiers raised their shields and hefted their spears. But their lord had slain one of their own and then fled, and now they wavered.

Silvin shot Oris a desperate look. "Oris!" she cried. "If you would like to unleash a flash that strikes your enemies dead upon the field, now would be the time."

But still Oris could not drag her gaze from Barrick. He strode forwards, only a few paces behind his attacking soldiers. The magic that surrounded him, that Oris could now see for the first time, seemed to pierce her mind.

Look inside yourself, she thought. *Find the magic to answer him. It's what you came here to do.*

There was nothing. No magic. Only the same pit in her stomach she had felt the first time, with Enfil near Brillig, and then again in Dracmund. Only now it was no pit but a chasm, a yawning gorge of dark and nothing.

Sky above, he is going to kill me, he is going to kill us all, I am going to die, I don't want to die.

"I can't," she croaked. The weakness in her voice terrified her and filled her with shame. "I don't know how. There's nothing inside me. Only emptiness."

Silvin looked to her in shock. Then she turned to Flip. "This was a mistake. Fed by Idulen, I do not doubt. We have to get her out of here."

Flip's eyes were ablaze, as bright as Oris had ever seen them. His hands twisted, but nothing came out, and Oris knew he must be trying to hold off the efforts of the Shades' wizard.

"Love a suggestion," he said through gritted teeth. "Their warlock is keeping me from doing much."

Silvin turned, her golden braids flaring out as her head whirled back and forth. The Shades had reached Idulen's soldiers, and they were cutting their way through with practiced, terrifying ease. And still Barrick approached.

Then a light came into Silvin's eyes. Oris saw it, and it cut through the terror and the emptiness, giving her a glimmer of hope. Silvin turned to Flip. "There is a river to the west."

"I saw it," growled Flip. "It's too wide to cross before they catch us or shoot us."

"No, you fool," said Silvin. "A *roof.*"

Flip risked a glance over his shoulder, eyes still glowing. His jaw clenched with the effort of his magic, but still his lips twisted in a smile. The hope in Oris grew, swelled like a light that banished the darkness of her despair.

"Oh," said Flip, chuckling. "Oh, that's good."

"Are you strong enough?"

"Let's find out together. Oris, are you ready to run?"

"What?" said Oris, still held in the grip of Barrick's gaze.

"Run!" cried Silvin and Flip at once.

They seized Oris' arms and dragged her down the west side of the hill towards the river. Their flight shattered the last shred of morale in Idulen's troops, and the Shades surged forwards with bloodthirsty cries.

As they pulled her away from Barrick's gaze, Oris found strength in her limbs again. Together they pelted down the slope towards the water. Ice clung to its banks, and Oris could scarcely imagine the freezing cold of it.

Terror turned to giddiness, and Oris shrieked the most gleeful laugh she had let out in years. "What in the dark below are we doing?"

"Jump into the water!" screamed Flip.

I can't.

We'll die.

They won't have to shoot us. We'll just freeze.

They were a pace away from the bank. Oris closed her eyes and banished every clamoring thought.

She jumped.

She could not keep her eyes closed all the flight through the air, the flight that felt like eternity. She opened them at the last moment. It was the only reason she saw the water split before them, turning into emptiness that revealed the soft, mucky, silty bottom of the river.

The three of them landed hard, sinking halfway up their calves. It had been Silvin's idea, and of course Flip's magic, so the two of them were expecting it. They each fell to their knees. Oris fell flat on her face, mud caking her front.

Flip looked up and twisted his hands. The water shimmered and slithered overhead, joining together again to form a roof over their heads, just as he had done with the rain near the Rustening Verge.

Oris came up from the mud gasping and spitting out dirt and water. Silvin helped haul her to her feet. All three of them turned their heads towards the water above. Mercifully, there was no sound, but Oris could imagine it. The sound of blades clashing, of screams, of death.

"They're going to die," said Oris. "All of them."

"They were going to die no matter what we did," said Silvin. "At least we saved you."

Oris could not answer. She turned her face away from the thin glow of sunlight through the water.

"Come," said Flip. "I don't know how long I can hold this. We need to get as far as we can before I lose my will."

He began to run off south, and Oris and Silvin were forced to follow him. The water shifted around them, swirling and splashing, and together they sped off into the darkness far from the sky.

CHAPTER XXI
LIGHTS BURN LOW

THEY EMERGED FROM THE RIVER A LONG WHILE LATER. FLIP SPLIT THE waters above them, and they scrambled up the muddy west side. Oris' heart felt ready to give out. All three of them collapsed upon the ground dripping wet, filthy with mud, and heartsick. The river churned behind them, slithering against its banks. The forest had thinned around them, but still the trees were too close and too dense for Oris' liking. She imagined Shades behind every trunk, watching them, waiting to strike. But she was simply too tired to do anything about it.

Silvin was the first to rise. She pushed up to her knees and slammed a fist into the ground.

"That steer," she growled. "That *filthy* little steer. I should have seen it."

Oris rolled over onto her back. The cold was starting to set in, and she began to shiver. "You couldn't have known."

"I could have," snarled Silvin. "We know they have agents everywhere. The Lord Prince's closest advisor should have been top of my list."

"Oh, certainly," groaned Flip. His face was still pressed into the muddy bank. "Let's go around suspecting treason from everyone we meet. That's a way to live a life."

"Be quiet, Flip," said Oris.

She climbed shakily to her feet and went to pull him up. But Silvin turned and sat, her knees up, burying her face in her hands.

"I have ruined everything." Her voice shook—and for the first time since Oris had met her, it was with grief instead of rage. She did not weep, but her shoulders shook. That was frightening in a way Oris had not expected.

"You've ruined nothing," said Oris.

"Nothing?" said Silvin. "I am a Mystic, and I betrayed my oath to the High King. That cannot be forgiven."

"She forgave your master."

"And he is dead," said Silvin. "Leaving us to fend for ourselves, groping in the dark. I tried to be like him, and it has ended in disaster."

"It hasn't ended," said Oris. "We have to move. They've likely sent people to search for us both upriver and down. It'll only be a matter of time before they find us."

Silvin uncovered her face, but she did not look at Oris or Flip. She only stared at the icy waters racing past them. Flip was shivering in Oris' grip, and Oris felt her limbs starting to seize up with the cold, but Silvin did not seem to pay it any mind. Her eyes were unfocused, her gaze a world away.

"What in the dark below are we even doing here?" whispered Silvin. "We have to get back to the Seat. We must cast our fate in with the High King. Or with *anyone* who will not handle it as disastrously as I have."

Oris went to Silvin. She seized her shoulders and yanked her to her feet, shaking her hard for a moment.

"Stop it," she hissed. "Enough whinging. You may pity yourself when my life is no longer in your hands. Until then, come to your senses and get moving."

As Oris shook her, a flash of familiar rage came into Silvin's eyes. *That's good,* thought Oris.

Silvin took two deep breaths, her nostrils flaring. "Fine. Let us go, then. We should be able to follow this river to the Melnar, which we can follow all the way to the Great Bay."

"No," said Oris. "We're not going back to the Seat."

Silvin blinked. "What do you mean? We must. It is the safest—"

"Nowhere's safe," said Flip. "And they'll be expecting us to go back to the Seat. They'll hunt us down long before we reach it. We have to head another way, scatter the trail."

"You're right, but that's not what I mean," said Oris. "The Seat holds only Mystics and the High King herself, all trying to keep me in a golden prison where no one can hurt me—and where I can do nothing. I left the Seat to learn the truth about myself. I still aim to do so."

"What do you mean to do?" said Silvin.

Oris knelt and dragged another cloak from her pack. The oiled leather had protected its contents from the dripping water of the river's roof, and quickly she replaced her wet cloak with a dry one. She sighed with relief as it began to warm her skin.

"We're going to Cabrus," she told them. "To the orphanage where I grew up. We're going to find out who the old man was who brought me there, and anything else we can learn."

Flip's expression fell, and he looked sadly at her. "Oris . . . if they knew anything of where you came from, wouldn't they have told you growing up?"

"Why would they?" said Oris obstinately. "I hated it there. They were too busy disciplining me to volunteer answers to questions I never asked."

Silvin slowly shook her head. "Oris, it is too dangerous. Idulen was on the side of the enemy, but he can hardly be the only one. Anyone we meet on the way, or in the city itself, could be another Shade waiting to strike."

"Then you'd better fulfill your oath to keep me alive," snapped Oris. "But I'll not be denied this any longer. My *life* was taken from me before I could decide what I wanted my life to be. I have parents, or had them, and a home, and they took it. Someone knew who—*what* I was, and they kept that from me, too. No more. If we go back to the Seat, the High King will never let me out of her sight again. She certainly won't let me seek the truth. So I'll find it now, because it's *mine.* No one will keep it from me any longer. And there we'll find our answer. The man who brought me there—he'd be able to help me find my power. I know it."

She turned to Flip. "Are you with me?"

Flip was swaying on his feet. The magic he had sustained to get them this far had drained him to the point of exhaustion, and his eyelids fluttered. "Of course. We can die on the Seat, or we can die in Cabrus, or we can lie down and wait to die here. What's the difference? Though lying down sounds more appealing right now."

Oris turned him around, pulling out a dry cloak from his pack. She pulled off his coat and wrapped him in the cloak before seizing his chin in her thick fingers.

"I told you in Wellmont," she said. "Remember? You don't get to give up."

"Oris—" Silvin began.

She stopped as Oris whirled and marched up to her, stopping barely a handsbreadth away. Their breath misted out, mingling as it rose up into the forest air.

"That goes for you, too," said Oris. "Leave if you want. But if you walk beside me, you don't get to give up. Not while I'm still fighting."

Silvin met her eyes. She took two deep breaths. Oris wondered what she really wanted to say. Somehow she knew that it would not be whatever escaped her lips.

"By your word. Lifemage."

• ○ • ○ •

"No sign of them, commander. Neither to the north or south. But we still have scouts out searching. They'll uncover something."

"Fine," snarled Barrick. "Keep them at it. Give me any news."

The captain nodded and then turned to see to her troops. Barrick stalked back up to the top of the Giant's Crown. There Idulen was pacing, his fingers playing at the edges of his belt, twiddling them nervously. His eyes swept nervously over the bodies of the soldiers all around. *His soldiers,* thought Barrick. Fighters who had followed him, and believed in him, and whom he had consigned to death.

"You," snarled Barrick.

Idulen's gaze snapped to him. He saw the rage in Barrick's face and wilted. He had the good sense, at least, to keep his hands from his sword, but he backed away with wide eyes and his hands up in placation.

"I could have done nothing more," said Idulen.

"And what exactly *did* you do?" said Barrick. He did not stop his advance as Idulen retreated. The smaller man was forced to scuttle back, half-trotting. "Too cowardly to raise a blade against the Lord's greatest enemy. Too cowardly to even join us in the fight. I see no value in your actions at all, nor in your continued existence."

Idulen stumbled as he retreated, his foot catching on a stone. He sprawled in the snow, still holding one hand up. The Shades around them had stopped, watching the display. Their eyes were on Idulen, and their grim expressions were filled with a disgust to match Barrick's.

"The Mystic sow was right beside her," pleaded Idulen. "I would never have been able to strike her down, and then they would have killed me. I did not spend all those years hovering at the elbow of that simpering prince only to throw my life away needlessly."

"Yet now you will fall by my hand instead." Barrick unsheathed his blade. "So even that pathetic attempt to survive has failed."

"Wait!" screamed Idulen, even as Barrick raised the sword. "I can still serve! I can help you find her!"

Barrick paused, but the fury never left his face. "How?" he growled.

"I know where she means to go."

Barrick remained still for a moment. Then at last he lowered the sword, returning it to its scabbard. He looked past Idulen to Raloren, who was looking upon Idulen with scorn.

"Get him up," said Barrick.

Raloren seized Idulen's collar to haul him up. Sulking, Idulen dusted off the seat of his pants, clearing off the mud and snow.

"Where is she going?" said Barrick.

"Cabrus," said Idulen. "She spoke of an orphanage there. It is where she was raised. She wanted to go there in the first place, but the Mystic convinced her to come here instead. Now that this venture has failed, that is where she will go next."

"Why?" said Barrick. "The wiser course would be to go to the High King's Seat, where we cannot again strike in strength. There the Mystics and the High King would keep her safe—or so they would hope."

"Oris and Philip greatly mistrust the Mystics," said Idulen. "And neither of them wish to be under the thumb of the High King. They are headstrong beyond reckoning. It was that mistrust that made them so easy to manipulate, to draw them out here and put them at your mercy."

Barrick fumed, his chest heaving with rumbling breaths. "You are a worm and a traitor," he said. "For years you have worn a mask of deception and lies. What under the sky makes you think I would believe you now? You would say or do anything to keep yourself alive, as you have proven today."

To his shock, Idulen drew up straight and lifted his chin. "I have deceived only our enemies," he said. "I have lied only to them. Everything I have done has been in the service of the Lord. Our father has recognized me and praised me for it. You call me a coward because I will not throw myself on our enemies' blades. I wonder if you would be so brave were you not enchanted to survive such a thing."

Almost Barrick lost himself. More than anything, he wanted to ram his sword through Idulen's gut.

But he thought of Father. Barrick had promised that he would not fail. Even now, Father was likely watching him, shaking his head in disappointment.

But Barrick could fix it. If he could catch the Lifemage . . . if he could still hunt her, and bring her down . . . then he would have proven himself the greatest of Father's children. Mightier even than Rogan. And Cabrus was only a few days away at a hard march.

"Fine," said Barrick. "We will track her to Cabrus and bring all of this to an end."

"You are wise," said Idulen. "The Lord will reward you for—"

His words died with a squeak as Barrick lunged forwards and seized him by the throat. With one brawny arm, he hauled Idulen off his feet and into the air, where he squirmed, feet kicking. His breath came out in strangled gasps.

"When the fight comes, you will not withdraw again," said Barrick. "You will not shrink or hide. If you do, you will not have to worry about the Lifemage or her Mystic. I will end you first."

• ○ • ○ •

The Lord turned. His eyes grew far away, and his head cocked as though he were listening.

He was—or he appeared to be—on the outskirts of a camp in northern Dorsea. There he was conferring with Rogan, highest in favor among his most favored children. Rogan was a finger or two shorter than Barrick, though any average person would still have called him a giant. He wore an ornate set of plate in all his waking hours, which weight he carried as though it were cloth. At his side was the greataxe

Imani, its head twice as wide as a human's, and its edge shining with enchantment. But though Rogan was a terror to all his foes on the field, his eyes were soft and his demeanor kind towards his kindred. Now, as the Lord turned from him, his expression became one of concern.

"Father?" he rumbled. "What is it?"

"Barrick has failed," said the Lord.

"Failed in what?"

"Hunting the Lifemage."

Rogan started, his eyes going wide. "He was not supposed to hunt her, Father. That is to be my task, and only at the appointed time."

"Do you think I did not tell him that?" The Lord's words were chiding, but he smiled at Rogan to soften them. "He is jealous of you, my son. Nothing could restrain him from pursuing her. He thinks that if he can bring her down, he will rise in my estimation, rivaling you for my affection."

"He must know better than that," said Rogan. "You have given us both the same gift. Your children are all equal—if not in ability, then at least in your love."

"So we have tried to teach him all his life—and his second life," said the Lord. "Yet his heart hides passions and fears we cannot quell. And he insisted."

"He is dead, then?" Rogan's voice had gone husky.

The Lord sighed and bowed his head. "Not yet."

Rogan stepped forwards. "We can save him?"

"We could," said the Lord. "But only by sacrificing all our other plans. And that I will not do. I told Barrick everything. I told him I had seen his failure lying ahead. I even tried to forbid him from pursuing this course. And he told me I was like the old kings."

For the first time, Rogan's eyes flashed with anger. "He said that? How dare he call—"

The Lord lifted a hand, and Rogan fell silent. "He was right," said the Lord. "We are all of us trying to build a better world. But we still carry the vestiges of the old. I forgot myself. The High King tried to forbid Oris from her own free will, and she was wrong to do so. I tried to do the same to Barrick, and I was wrong to do that, too. I needed him to remind me of that. You and I, my son—we foresee, and we advise, and we warn. But we cannot command. We cannot forbid. We must not. Or what is the purpose of the coming war? To put ourselves on the thrones of those who have broken the world? Simply to take their place and continue the same tragedy? Never would I consign myself, or you, or any of our kindred, to so much violence and misery for so anemic a dream. I am grateful to Barrick for reminding me of that."

Now tears leaked at last from Rogan's eyes, mingling with his short, well-trimmed beard. "Then I am grateful to him as you are," he said, his voice breaking. "And I am grateful to you for giving me the wisdom to see it. I, too, wear the trappings of the old world, and I find it more difficult to cast them aside than I would wish. But must such a lesson cost us Barrick's life? We have lost so many already, Father."

"So many," agreed the Lord. "But not too many. This is the price of a free world. We could sacrifice our aims to save Barrick's life. But what would his life, or any of ours, be worth then?"

• ○ • ○ •

Oris, Silvin, and Flip ran until night shrouded the world around them. Then at last they dared to stop and rest, though they lit no campfire. Silvin took watch while Oris and Flip huddled in their blankets against the cold, and then she woke them once the moons were straight overhead. Oftentimes they would stop and look behind, or find a high vantage point to climb to survey the land. They never saw any sign of pursuit. But still the woods were dense enough to keep Oris from feeling any degree of safety.

"They may still be after us," said Silvin. "We know nothing of their force, neither how many trackers they may have in their number, nor how skilled. We must keep trying to hide our trail, and at the same time we should assume that they are following it anyway, and keep pressing ourselves hard."

Oris nodded silently, almost too tired to speak. Even Flip gave no word of complaint, and that was as worrying as anything else.

Early on the second day, they reached and then crossed the Melnar, trotting across a stone bridge that was built high above the river. Silvin allowed them a brief stop to refill their waterskins.

"The world's covered in snow," Flip pointed out. "There's fresh water everywhere."

Silvin arched a brow at him. "Oh, forgive me. Did you not want to stop for a rest?"

Flip held up a finger. "You raise an excellent point."

Beyond the bridge, the land ran flat for a long while, with thickets and brush appearing often to the east and west. They stayed out of the trees, however, for now speed was more important than remaining hidden. And the King's Road hid tracks better than the trees would, for the snow and mud were thick in the woods, leaving deep impressions of every footfall.

By the end of the second day, the land began to rise in a ridge to the east. Oris had passed this way before, and she was reasonably certain that the ridge ran south to peter out just north of Cabrus, the King's Road skirting its edge the while.

Again they stopped to make camp, and again they built no fire. They were all weary to death of dried meat and stale bread, but they forced themselves to eat it. Flip made many disgusted faces and groaned, but he was not fool enough to starve himself.

Silvin finished eating before the other two, as she usually did. She studied Flip as he continued to eat, and Oris could not place her expression. At last, when Flip was almost done with his food, Silvin finally spoke.

"I am sorry I lied to you."

Flip looked up at her in mild surprise. He chewed for a moment and then swallowed hard, forcing the last of his food down his gullet. He shrugged. "I know why you did it. Doesn't change the fact that you're a sow for it."

Silvin's jaw clenched. But she said only, "And I am sorry I told Oris before you."

"That's as much her fault as yours." Flip sniffed. "And for what it's worth . . . you seem a better sort than most. If all Mystics were more like you, I might feel differently towards them. Yet you walk by their side regardless. You can be as good as you like, but it doesn't wash their evil off your cloak."

"Flip," said Oris. "That's not fair. You can't paint her with their brush."

"Whyever not?" said Flip, waving a hand. "She wears their colors. She bears their badge. It's all well and good to say she's better than the rest of them. Yet still she marches along with them. If I'd stayed with my family, never joining in their evil deeds, but knowing of them all the same, I'd call myself no good man. It's true there's a middle ground in life, if you can't rid the world of evil folk. But it's to refuse, at least, to stand beside them."

"Yet you'd go back to your family if you had to," said Oris.

"And leave the moment I could again," said Flip. "And never let them think I honored them in the meanwhile. Yet you, Silvin, call the redbacks battle-kindred. The ones who killed my cousin. It's not your fault. But neither is it something I can forget, nor understand."

Oris gave a frustrated snort and started to speak again. But Silvin held up a hand to stop her.

"He's right."

That made Oris pause for a moment, dumbfounded. Even Flip looked entirely surprised. "I am?" he said.

"You are," said Silvin. "There is something else I have not yet told you, but which I told Oris long ago, the night she found out about me. I spoke the truth when I told you of how the Mystics killed my parents. But in that truth I hid a lie. I said it to make you think I was on your side, that I had a personal stake for hating the Mystics.

"The truth is that they saved me. Or at least my master, Jordel, saved me. My parents were . . . they . . . ." She stopped, and for a long moment their little clearing was utterly silent. Finally she went on. "You come from an evil family. I come from a worse one."

Flip scoffed. "You don't know my family."

Silvin's gaze snapped to him. "I am a Mystic spy. Of course I know your family. I know things about them you do not. So when I tell you that the worst of them pale in comparison to my parents, I speak with the knowledge and authority to say so."

For a moment, Flip only stared at her. Oris, too, felt transfixed, for she could hear the fury in Silvin's tone—and beneath it, the pain.

"And then Jordel found you," said Oris softly.

Silvin's throat seemed to tighten. She looked to Oris. "Yes," she said, the words coming thick. "When he found me, I was . . . they had . . . ." She stopped for a moment, thinking. "I knew nothing of the world. I knew nothing of his red cloak, nor the silver badge on his breast. I knew only what *they* had told me. What they had made me. A monster. Worthless. Worth less than worthless. A servant of evil, destined to follow in their footsteps when I was an adult. When it was my turn to twist and shatter the lives of others. For they were Shades."

Flip and Oris blinked. "They were what?" exclaimed Flip.

"Yes," said Silvin. "Jordel could never find hard proof of it. But he was hunting rumors of the Shades, for years and years before he finally found them in the Greatrocks. My parents were part of a small cabal.

That is how they have operated in secret for years beyond counting. Small groups of them hidden across Underrealm. I say hidden, but they are often in plain sight. It is only that everyone has forgotten what to look for. And in these little clusters, they practice their evil, preparing for their coming war. They investigate dark magics, secrets that have remained buried since the last Necromancer. And they sow discord and chaos. Little instances of evil, each one able to be quelled easily. But so numerous that they hold the attention of all the nine kings, and the High King herself, so that they cannot spare a glance for the dagger slipping from the shadows."

"And they brought you into these schemes?" said Oris.

Silvin's whole face contorted. At first it flashed with fury, and then it seemed as though she might collapse and weep. "Oh yes," she whispered. "Yes, they brought me very deep indeed."

"What did they—" Flip stopped short, closed his eyes, and shook his head. "Never mind. I believe you. I am sorry, and I believe you."

She seemed unable to speak for a moment. Then at last she nodded. "And I believe you. About your cousin. I know nothing of the matter, but if you say that is what happened, then I believe you. I know the Mystics have done evil things—that they still do evil things today. Yet I cleave to them for the same reason you would return to your family if the need arose. I have seen the coming darkness. I have seen it closer than anyone else on our side. I lived it. And I know I cannot fight it alone. But the Mystics can fight it together. After that . . . well. Who knows? I like to think Jordel would have known what to do then. I like to think he, too, remained with the order because he knew they would be necessary to defeat what is coming. It is not the answer I wish I could give you. I doubt it is an answer that will satisfy you. But it is the only answer I have. Who knows if it will even matter?"

She sniffed and rubbed at her nose with the back of her hand. Oris sighed and climbed to her feet.

"My turn to watch," she said. "Both of you settle in."

Silvin shook her head. "You need your sleep."

"You got none last night," said Oris. "You can't do that forever. Sleep."

Four days passed. Four days of running through half the night and all the next day. Four days of terror at every noise in the darkness, of looking over their shoulders, of waiting, expecting an attack at any moment. Soon Oris felt less like a person and more like a shell, a form stumbling along with no spark of life inside to illuminate it. She moved her feet, but she could hardly remember why. She felt the fear of pursuit, but she did not know whence or why it came, or would come.

And then, on the fourth day, they saw Cabrus in the distance. It was near to dusk. The moment they came around a bend and saw the stone walls, Oris stopped dead in the road. The others shuffled to a stop beside her.

"Finally." Flip's voice was a croak.

"There is nothing final about it," said Silvin, the words dry and cracking. "Let us do our business here as quickly as we can, and then move on. Our enemy could be right on our heels."

"We've kept an endless watch for them," said Flip. "If they haven't caught us by now, they're not going to."

Silvin fixed him with a look. Her eyelids fluttered, and she swayed where she stood. "Where, in all our long road together, have you found any reason for such optimism?"

Flip grinned. Oris thought his face looked like a skull.

The guards at the gate watched them warily as they approached, for the sun was now almost out of sight. But when they reached the gate, Silvin reached into a pouch and produced her Mystic badge. After the guard captain inspected it closely for a moment, he gestured for the gates to be opened.

As they passed in through the gates, Silvin gave Flip a sidelong look. "My apology stands. But I must tell you what a relief it is to show that badge openly after so long."

Flip snorted. "I don't blame you. It certainly would've made our road to the Seat much easier. Though I suppose we wouldn't have walked that road with you, if you were bandying it about so freely."

"We have to hurry," said Oris. "The orphanage will soon be closing its doors for the night. Let's find a place to drop our things."

"Do you know of such a place?" said Silvin.

Oris grimaced. "To be honest, I haven't returned here since I was a child, and I lived in the orphanage then. I know the city's streets well enough, but not its inns."

"Where is the orphanage?"

"On the eastern side of the city, just north of the Pauper's Quarter."

"Very well," said Silvin. "Follow me. I know a place."

She took them east and then hooked around south. Flip gave a longing glance to the west as they went.

"What about the Wyrmwing Inn?" he said. "I've stayed there before. There's no softer beds in the city outside the mayor's home, and if they still have that cook . . ." He swallowed hard as though trying to restrain his drool.

Silvin shook her head. "The Wyrmwing has something else we would do well to avoid: the presence of many eyes, sitting in wealthy and powerful heads. I will not have Oris noticed by someone highly placed in the Mystics, or a merchant who in fact serves the Shades."

Flip sighed. "I thought as much. But you can't blame me for trying."

Oris barely heard them. Her mind was overwhelmed, her thoughts lingering on every alleyway and every door they passed. Some of them were only vaguely familiar to her, like the face of an old friend glimpsed through mist. Some brought a flash of memory that threatened to leave her senseless. There was a launderer's door where she had skinned her elbow. There was a steep stair leading to a second story apartment, behind which she had often hidden when playing with other children. Her memory was somewhat hazy, but she felt certain she could take them to the orphanage right now. It was just a few spans away, waiting. A sudden, powerful urge to do so almost overtook her, despite her earlier words of caution. There it waited for her: its imposing front door, all of thick wood; the south wing, rising above the rest of the building; the high fence to the north, surrounding the courtyard where the children played.

She steeled herself and focused on following Silvin's hasty footsteps. And soon enough, Silvin came to a swaying stop in front of an inn. Oris looked up and read the sign: The Table Mark.

"Why is the table marked?" said Flip, the words slurring with weariness.

"A tally of those who have eaten at it before," said Silvin. "They encourage the practice, if you can believe it. Come."

Inside, they saw at once that Silvin had spoken true. It was a lively, cheery place, though the cheer was lost on the three of them, for they could barely remain upright. Oris peered at the tables and saw that they were all covered with deep tally marks. Even as she watched, someone came from a room upstairs, sat down, and pulled out a knife to scratch another tally mark into the wood of their table.

Silvin secured them a room, where they dropped their travel sacks. Flip sat down on the bed while Oris and Silvin were securing their things, but Oris hauled him up by the shoulders at once.

"No," she said. "Not a chance. If you sit down for even a moment, I doubt we'll get you up again."

"And I would be happier for it," groaned Flip. But though he scowled, he remained on his feet.

"Come now," said Oris. "We're almost at the end of this road. A little more work, and then we can sleep, finally."

"We cannot go there yet," said Silvin. "Not looking like this. We are haggard and filthy. We would frighten the children to death."

Oris smirked. "I suppose that's true enough. But we can't take the time for a real bath, and I doubt I'd remain awake through one anyway. Let's find ourselves a well."

The innkeeper, a pretty young woman named Malora, pointed them in the right direction. They drew up a bucket of water and splashed it across their faces, hissing and shivering at the icy cold of it. A few passersby gave them odd looks, but they were far too weary to care.

Flip used some of the water to slick back his greasy, tousled hair and then rubbed hard at his eyes. When he finished, he looked at the other two. He loosed a harsh bark of laughter. It sounded like Silvin's.

"This hasn't helped at all," he chuckled. "We might frighten the children to death anyways."

Oris' mouth set in a grim line. "It'll have to do. Come along. I remember the way."

CHAPTER XXII
CLOSED ROAD

Turn left here. Pass two intersections. A right. The street will loop around. This alley's a shortcut. One more left.

The instructions played through Oris' mind as she led the other two along. It was more than half a decade since she had been here last, yet she was astonished to find she remembered every turn perfectly. But then she realized it was not that strange. Yes, she had been away for several years, but she had lived here for nearly twice as long. It never seemed that way when she thought back on it. No matter the truth, she felt as though her whole life had been spent far away from this place, far away from Cabrus, and her time here as a child had passed like a blink. And yet here were these memories, this familiarity. For a disconcerting moment it reminded her of what she felt when she had confronted Barrick in the woods, that sense of strange recognition she had not at first recognized. But she shook that thought away quickly.

And then, too soon and at last, they stood in front of the orphanage.

The door had been replaced, Oris realized. She wondered why. Had it been damaged by some child's prank? Or had the wood simply worn away over time? How many people had passed through this doorway, in and out, since she had left? How many new children brought to this new home for the first time, all of them wishing they could be anywhere else?

Were any of them truly like me, I wonder? Did any of them have parents and a home they were taken from, waiting for them to return?

"Oris?"

She shook herself. There beside her was Silvin, her expression one of worry and slight impatience. But Flip only looked a little sad, though he tried to smile at her through it. He placed a gentle hand on her arm.

"We're here," he said. "Go on."

Oris swallowed and nodded. But she did not move for another long moment. Finally she stepped forth and knocked, her coarse knuckles echoing loud on the wood.

At first there was only silence. Then, from inside, the shuffling of feet. At last the door cracked open slightly, and a face peered out at them. Flaming red hair bound back in a tail, though it frizzed valiantly under the restraint, and beneath it, a young, pretty face with light brown eyes. Those eyes slowly grew wider as they took in Oris and the others. Oris was shocked to realize she did not recognize the woman, and then she wondered why she should be shocked.

"May I help you?" asked the woman. Her voice held a slight Dulmish accent that was at odds with her Heddish looks.

"We're sorry to disturb you," said Oris. "I . . . I grew up here. I am visiting for the first time since I left. It has been a very long time."

The woman blinked twice. The door opened a few fingers wider, and she smiled politely. "In that case, welcome. We will soon be putting the children to bed, but—"

"I would not take up much of your time," said Oris. "Is—" She stopped as a wave of dread struck her. She realized she had no idea what the answer to her next question would be, and it meant more to her than she had thought it would. "Is Matron Fleda here?"

The woman barely reacted at all. "She is upstairs," she said simply. If she saw the relief wash through Oris, she did not remark upon it. "I can fetch her, if it is her you would like to speak with."

"Please," said Oris, her voice weak.

"Your name, please?"

"Oris." Oris paused, closed her eyes. "Orececot is my full name."

"Of any family?"

Oris's face contorted, and she looked at the woman aghast. The girl's cheeks flamed deep crimson, and she blinked twice again.

"I only mean, were you adopted when you left here?" she squeaked.

"No," said Oris, doing nothing to restrain the bitter edge in her voice.

"Very well," said the woman. "Please, come inside to wait."

They did so, stepping off into the waiting area just to the left of the door. There were four chairs and a bench there, thinly cushioned and not very comfortable. Oris longed to sit, but she thought she might collapse into sleep straightaway.

She became gradually aware that Flip and Silvin were staring all about the place with wide eyes, peering curiously down the hallways left and right. Straight ahead was the hall leading into the dining room, and there were many tables and chairs visible from where they stood. A few children sat there, finishing what looked to be the last scraps of the evening meal before bed. One or two of them looked curiously up at the new visitors, but after a moment's study, they returned their attention to their food. Oris and her friends hardly had the look of adults come to adopt a child, and so they mattered very little to the children who lived here.

A faint smile was playing at the corners of Silvin's mouth. Flip was looking unabashed at everything, thumbs hooked in his belt as he paced around, scuffing his feet on the stone. Oris frowned. "What are the two of you looking at?"

"Oh, nothing in particular," said Flip. "So this is where it all began, is it?"

"No," growled Oris. "It began earlier, somewhere else, with a real family. But I can't remember any of that."

"It looks pleasant enough here," said Silvin.

Oris sighed. "It could be, sometimes. They had to be strict, but they were never cruel. None of us wanted to be here. Not the children, at any rate, and I doubt the faculty loved it too much more than we did. But that was because of *why* we were here, rather than anything about the place itself. They did the best they could."

"Where did you live?" asked Flip.

For some reason she could not name, Oris felt her cheeks flush, and she ducked her head. "Off this way," she said, pointing.

She led them down the right-hand hallway to the dormitories. It reached a wall and split off left and right again. In the hall were three doors, all of them now closed. To the right the hallway ended in a staircase leading up, and to the left it ended in a door leading out to the courtyard. From that direction came the sounds of children playing outside: some shouts, some peals of laughter, and many cries of instruction and argument, the sound of youth engaged in debate of the utmost importance, such as who was current king of the rock and whether her friend had, in fact, struck her down according to the rules.

"Which dormitory were you in?" said Flip, pointing to the three doors in front of them.

"They divide the children up by age, and move them along according to the room they have," said Oris. "The youngest children are in that room, closest to the stairs, for they're most likely to need the faculty's help in the night. Middle children in the middle room, and oldest to the left. So I lived in all three rooms, at one point or another. But I wasn't in the older children's room very long before I left."

"You said you were not adopted," said Silvin. Oris shook her head. "Why did you leave, then? And when?"

"Ran away," said Oris simply. "I'd only seen fourteen years, but I was already the tallest child here, and as tall as most of the faculty. And . . . well. As I said, they did their best. But as I also said, none of us wanted to be here. Mayhap I was too foolish to know how good I had it. Mayhap I was foolish enough to think I could be truly happy out there." She glanced again at the door leading to the courtyard. "They'll all be outside, fighting to stay awake until the faculty force them to go to bed. Come."

She led them into the middle dormitory, but she stopped just inside the doorway. There were three rows of beds, the feet of them all pointing towards the door. Oris frowned.

"They rearranged the beds. I liked it better before. I wonder if they found . . ."

In the back corner of the room, she knelt and probed a stone with her fingers. It shifted slightly. She tried to push her fingers around the sides of it, but they wouldn't fit. She frowned.

"My hands used to be smaller. But it looks like they never fixed this."

She pulled out a dagger and used it to pry out the stone. Beneath it was a small hole, only big enough for a fist. Inside the hole was a folded scrap of paper, and some string twisted into a strange pattern, all balled up.

"This was my hidey hole when I lived here," she said. "I never had anything exciting to hide here, just the occasional copper sliver or two. And . . . and when Matron Fleda threatened to take my amulet away, I'd hide it here. It was mine. She wasn't supposed to take it from me."

For just a moment her hand extended, fingers reaching for the paper and the string. But then she stopped. Slowly, her hand withdrew.

"Looks like it's someone else's now."

"Here." Flip stepped forth and pulled five gold weights from the purse at his belt. He dropped them into the hole with a *clink.* "Let's make the little one faint next time they come to hide something here."

Oris and Silvin both chuckled. But then there came the sound of footsteps from the hallway. For a moment, Oris again felt like a child trying not to get caught. She hastily replaced the stone and stood, placing herself between the hidey hole and the door.

The door swung open to reveal the same attendant from before. But this time, she was leading Matron Fleda. The matron looked so much older than Oris remembered her. She could not tell if she had really aged so much, or if it was only a fault of memory. Fleda leaned on a cane, and the attendant held her other arm. She moved with a pronounced limp that Oris was certain had not been there before. Her eyes looked much bigger through thick spectacles, and she blinked owlishly as she looked into the room at the three of them.

"Good evening," she said. It was a voice Oris remembered well enough. Still strong, still a bit terse, brooking no nonsense, thank you very much. The huge eyes blinked through their spectacles again as they came to rest on Oris.

Oris took a hesitant step forwards. A flush was creeping up her neck, and she did not know why. "Matron Fleda? Do . . . do you remember me?"

It seemed to be the voice that did it. A spark came into Fleda's eye. "Oh. Sky above. Oreceot. It . . . well, it has been a long time."

And once more, Oris was a child. She dropped her gaze to the stone floor and fought the urge to clasp her hands behind her back. "Yes it has, Matron Fleda."

Fleda's mouth twisted, though whether towards a smile or a grimace, Oris could not tell. "No need for that formality anymore, I suppose. Fleda will do. Or you may call me Matron, if my name is too uncomfortable for you. It is for some."

She did not speak harshly, and there was no ill mood hiding in her voice. But neither did she speak warmly. She seemed neither happy nor aggravated to see Oris again. It was as though this was simply another task, one on a long list of things duty required her to take care of today. Oris felt a flash of regret that she had come here.

"Come to the dining hall," said Fleda. "I do not like to stand for too long, these days."

They followed her as she tottered along. The young attendant held firm to Fleda's arm, but she kept stealing glances at Oris and the rest of them as they went. In particular, her eyes kept straying to Oris' sword and her brawny arms. Oris thought she saw Silvin hiding a smirk.

No children remained in the dining hall. But tall windows on the east wall let them see out into the courtyard, where all the children now seemed to be playing. They sat at a table near the entrance, Fleda sinking onto her bench more heavily than the rest of them. Oris sat across from her, facing the windows. Her gaze strayed over Fleda's shoulder to the children running about outside, and she forced herself to focus.

"Well," said Fleda. "It has been a very long time, as I said, and I doubt only pleasure or fond memories brought you back to this place. How can I be of help to you?"

Oris' jaw clenched, but she forced herself to speak. "I . . . I have some questions. About my past. About when I was brought here. I never thought to ask them while I lived here, but they have become important."

Fleda's brows shot for the ceiling. "Important? Well, then. My memory is not what it once was, but we have many records. What do you want to know?"

Oris glanced at her friends, but they only looked back at her. This was her journey. She had brought them along. It seemed the questions would have to be hers.

"I want to know how old I was when I was brought here," Oris began. "And if you have anything in your records about my amulet, I would like to know about that as well."

"Ah yes." Fleda's mouth puckered. "That amulet."

The three of them shot up straight on the bench. "You remember it?" said Oris. "I had it when I arrived to the orphanage, didn't I? Who gave it to me? What did they say about it?"

Fleda slowly shook her head, and her answer came slow as well, infuriatingly slow to Oris' mind. "No, Oreceot. I do not remember any of that." Oris frowned, but Fleda continued. "The mind does not work that way. Or at least mine does not. Some details remain while others fade. And I am sorry to say that often the details that linger longest are the less pleasant ones. Such as the children who had to be penalized most often for causing trouble." She arched a brow at Oris. "That is why I remember your amulet."

Oris had gone stony. "You were never supposed to take the amulet from me," she said, fighting not to growl. "It was mine. My one thing."

"And what *were* we supposed to do, Oreceot?" said Fleda. "Once you got something into your head, you never listened. *Never.* It mattered not what anyone else said, what the rules were that everyone else had to follow. You did not care if we reduced your meals, and of course we would not starve you. We have never been in the habit of throwing children into a constable's cell for disobedience, though mayhap we should have considered it."

Oris could hear the jest in her tone, but she did not smile. Her brow only furrowed deeper. Fleda sighed and shook her head.

"Never mind," she said, all humor fading. "I have no interest in reviving old arguments, and I doubt you do, either." She turned to the attendant, who had been watching the conversation wide-eyed. "Hyla, would you fetch the logbooks from . . . oh, it would have been 1295, would it not? Octis, if I recall correctly, though I might be a month or two off in either direction. I recall it was an unusually warm summer."

"Of course, Matron," said Hyla. Hastily she rose from the table and withdrew from the room. Oris thought she looked grateful just to get away from the awkward situation.

The silence that followed was excruciating, at least for Oris. Flip seemed bored, his gaze wandering about the dining hall, resting on a few dishes that had not been cleared away and the scraps of food upon them. Silvin looked slowly back and forth between Oris and Fleda. But Fleda herself did not seem ill at ease. She merely looked annoyed. She did not exactly avoid looking at Oris, but her sharp gaze spent most of its time elsewhere, focusing on clatters from the kitchen and the shouting children outside. Oris sat there all the while with arms folded, staring solidly down at the table. She could feel the bone-deep weariness in her own body, but gone were all thoughts of sleep, replaced by a smoldering anger.

"How have you been finding your way out in the world?" said Fleda suddenly. "Have you been staying safe?"

A single peal of hysterical laughter burst out of Flip before he could choke it off. Fleda looked somewhat alarmed.

"I've traveled a great deal." Oris did not look up at Fleda as she spoke. "I learned to fight. I've served as a guard and sellsword across most of the nine kingdoms."

"Is that where you picked up that Heddish accent?" said Fleda. "I am grateful, at least, that you did learn to take orders eventually."

"In fact, she's got a bit of a problem with that," said Flip with a grin. "It's a trait we share. It required us to change companies rather often."

Fleda's sharp gaze turned to him, and Flip's face wilted a little. "And who are you, young man? Oreceot's . . . companion?" She gave another glance at Oris, and then at Silvin. "Or I suppose not. A friend, then. You seem like the sort of company she would keep. I shall ask you to speak properly under this roof. *She has* a bit of a problem, not *she's got.*"

"I . . . yes, madam," stammered Flip. "Matron. Thank you." He sat up a bit straighter.

Silvin hid a smile. Matron Fleda turned to her.

"And you?" she said. "Who are you?"

"I am a friend," said Silvin, letting a bit more of her smile show.

Again Fleda's eyes went to Oris, and her brows raised. "Hmm."

They were all rescued as Hyla returned, bearing a few heavy tomes bound in leather. "I brought the logbook for the period you asked, Matron," she said, breathing heavily as she dropped the books on the table with a *thud.* "And I brought the ones before and after, just in case."

Fleda gave her a thin smile. "You are dutiful as ever, Hyla. Thank you." She pulled off her wide spectacles and replaced them with a smaller pair that did not make her eyes look quite so large. With Hyla's help, she pulled out the middle logbook and flipped through it. Though her fingers were wrinkled and crooked, she turned the pages with the sort of ease that only comes with decades of practice, her eyes flitting to the date markings in the corners. Under her breath she muttered to herself, "No, no, no . . . ah, here . . . yes, and then Bridin in Yunis . . . ." Suddenly she stopped, tapping the page with her forefinger. "And there we are. The day you arrived."

Oris could not help herself. She leaned forwards to look at the page. But the ink was somewhat faded with time, and she could not make it out upside down. "That is the log for it?"

"I should say so," said Fleda. "I wrote it in my own hand. It has always fascinated me, the way that words we have scribbled, even if we think nothing of them at the time, can spark such vivid memories. I remember where I was sitting when I wrote this. I remember the smell of the air." She leaned in a bit closer, tracing the lines with her finger.

"Well," she said at last. "I can answer some of your questions, it seems. Your age was reported as five years when you came here, though such reports are not always accurate. It does indeed appear that you were admitted with the amulet already in your possession. It does not say who gave it to you."

"That's all right," said Oris. "I remember who gave it to me. I only want to know if he's the one who brought me here as well."

"Well, we have the name of the man who brought you," said Fleda. "It was . . . hm. A smudge here. Lewis? No. Lowis."

Silvin shot up straight on the bench. "Lowis? Lowis of the family Renkin?"

Fleda looked up, blinking hard in surprise. "That is indeed what it says here. Why? Do you know the man?"

Silvin looked suddenly like a puppet whose handler had dropped her. She sagged, and it was as though the weight of all the long miles behind them, which she had been holding at bay, pressed down on her at once. After a moment, she rose from the table and walked away, out of the dining hall and towards the orphanage entrance.

Oris and Flip shared a troubled look.

"Go after her," said Flip.

Oris nodded and went. When she came to the entryway, she found Silvin standing there. One hand was on her hip, and the other was pinching the bridge of her nose hard. She looked bent, haggard beyond belief or hope.

"What is it, Silvin?" said Oris. "Who is Lowis? Is he a servant of the enemy?"

"He is the opposite," whispered Silvin. "I never met him, but I heard many, many stories about him. He was a Mystic. He taught Jordel." She lifted her face from her hand and looked at Oris. "I have told you that Jordel's master, Kal, is a man I despise. But Lowis came first, and from what I understand, he was Kal's mirror. He bears more responsibility than anyone else for shaping Jordel into the man he became, and who I trusted with my life. He taught Jordel many of the things that Jordel would go on to teach me. Including everything I know about you."

"Was." Oris had not heard Flip approach, and his voice surprised her. She turned to see him leaning against the opposite wall. He looked upon Oris and Silvin with inestimable weariness in his eyes. "You keep saying was."

A pit had been growing in Oris' stomach. It swelled still larger as Silvin's eyes began to shine, and she nodded. But her voice remained steady. "He died. Killed by Elves, a day's ride north of here."

"Elves?" said Oris. "Sky save us."

Silvin's eyes were grim. "It did not save him. He was killed when Jordel was a young man, not yet a knight. I think . . . ." Again she stopped, hanging her head.

"What?" said Oris. "Silvin, you think what?"

Silvin met her gaze. In her eyes was sadness, and fury, and a deep, abiding pain. "I do not know the exact date. I would have to write someone in my order and have them search our records to be sure. But I would wager a purse of gold that he was killed just after he brought you here."

The streets of Cabrus were bleak and cold with more than just winter's chill. As they stumbled back towards the inn, it seemed to Oris that all three of them were in a daze. The cold stung her skin, but she could not summon the effort to pull her cloak tighter about her. Silvin stared straight ahead, while Flip looked only at his feet.

Oris lurched off to an alley nearby. At its mouth was an empty barrel. Oris gave a piercing scream of rage and lifted the barrel, flinging it down the alley, where it shattered to kindling. A few passersby paused and stared at her, but when she met their gazes, they swiftly ducked their heads and carried on.

"We should try not to attract attention," said Silvin. But she could put no heart in the words.

"What does it mean?" said Flip quietly.

"What does what mean?" snarled Oris.

"It has to mean something," said Flip. "It *has* to. This Lowis, he discovers what you are, he brings you here, and he's killed straight away? And he's killed by *Elves?* You can't tell me that's a coincidence."

"We cannot tell you it is anything else," said Silvin. "They are Elves."

"But . . . but they must have *known,* somehow," sputtered Flip. "They must have—"

"They are Elves," said Silvin. "Would *you* like to ask them why they did it?"

Flip shuddered. "Of course not."

"There you have it," said Silvin flatly. "We might as well ask a storm why it sank a boat. We shall get just as much of an answer."

Oris remained silent while they argued. She simply did not have it in her to speak, unless it was to scream. What could they do now? One person knew, had known all along who she was and what to do with her. And he died before she had learned even the first thing about herself. Silvin's master had known, and he was dead, too. Fate had connived to hide any chance of the truth from her.

Flip sighed. "So . . . so what, then? What do we do now?"

Silvin shrugged. "I think we must head back to the Seat."

"Oh, certainly," said Flip with a snort. "'Hello, Your Majesty. We fled against your orders, took a company of your loyal troops into the Birchwood, and got them killed. Then we took a small jaunt to Cabrus and accomplished absolutely nothing. Won't you please take us back into the fold now?"

"She likely will," said Silvin. In her voice was the same lifeless monotone that Oris felt hiding in her own chest. "She needs us. Needs Oris, at least. Of course, my superiors in the order will likely flay me alive. But that is my problem. It is yours no longer."

"I never listened," said Oris quietly.

Flip and Silvin both looked at her in surprise. "What?" said Flip. "Never listened to what?"

"Anything," said Oris. "You heard Fleda. Even as a child, I never listened. I'd never do what they told me, no matter who it was doing the telling. I always thought I knew best. And nothing's changed. Dark take me, I thought I knew better than the High King herself. Those Steth soldiers dying, all the desperate flight here. And now this, with us not knowing anything more than we did on the Seat. Because I always have to know better than everyone else."

Flip came and clasped her around the shoulders, squeezing her tight. "It's not your fault, love."

"In what way?" said Oris, meeting his gaze. "Tell me one thing in all this mess that isn't my fault."

Flip gave her a sad smile. "Darling. You've been saying it since the start. It's not your fault you're here in the first place. It's not your fault you're who you are. You never asked for it, and you never wanted it. Everything you've done since . . . only a dark-damned fool would blame you for it, and I'd roast them if they did."

She felt a hand on her arm. It was Silvin's. The Mystic's grip tightened for just a moment. "You would not let me take all the blame for Idulen's betrayal," she said softly. "You do not get to take all the blame for yourself now."

That brought a small, sad smile to Oris' face. But then her gaze drifted over Silvin's shoulder, and her expression fell. Silvin turned to see what she was looking at.

There, just a little ways off, was the inn where they had left their things. Surrounding the inn was a little crowd, all of them milling about and murmuring. Oris saw the red leather of constables' armor. The lawmen were trying to push the onlookers back.

Flip saw a man heading away from the inn and hailed him. "Friend! What's going on over there?"

The man turned to look at them. He was balding on top, with a fringe of hair that stuck out wildly and a moustache like a broom nailed to his face. "Only just heard of it myself. Say it was a slaughter. Came crashing in and killed everyone there, the guests and everyone just having a drink. Innkeep only lived because she was in the privy. Say there were blue cloaks, but everyone sees blue cloaks these days when something goes wrong." But then he looked at the inn again, and his eyes widened with fear. "Then again, most times a whole inn isn't murdered. You think it could really be those Shades?"

Oris, Flip, and Silvin looked to each other. Flip's eyes were almost as fearful as the old man's. Silvin's jaw was like iron.

"Idulen was in the Lord Prince's counsel," she said. "He heard of your amulet and—"

"—and the orphanage," said Oris.

And then they were all running.

CHAPTER XXIII
THE BEGINNING OF THE END

Oris tried to prepare herself for the worst: the door kicked in, the windows smashed, blood and bodies everywhere. But then they reached the orphanage. The building looked untouched. There were no signs of damage or violence.

Oris threw the front door open and stormed into the entry hall. Flip and Silvin ran in on either side of her, weapons drawn and Flip's eyes aglow.

The place looked empty. But after a moment the attendant, Hyla, came scurrying around the corner, drawn by the noise. Her eyes were wide, and as she saw them, she clutched her skirts tightly.

"I—Miss Oris," she said, her voice a squeak. "I-it is after hours, the children are—"

"Has anything happened?" snapped Oris. "Has anyone come here since we left?"

"W-what?" stammered Hyla.

Oris went to her and gripped her shoulder. "Has anyone else come? Where is Matron Fleda?"

"U-upstairs," said Hyla. "She retired just after you—"

Oris turned from her to the others. "Where would they be? Why wouldn't—"

Flip's eyes shot wide. "Oris."

There was a flash and then a glow as Oris' amulet erupted in light. It outshone the lamps in the hallway, casting all their faces in a stark relief of blue light and black shadow. Hyla's terrified face was ethereal and twisted in the glow.

"Go fetch Matron Fleda," said Oris. "At once."

Hyla hesitated only a moment before nodding and running for the stairs. Silvin slammed the front door shut and threw its bolt in place. She and Oris stood to either side of the door, hands on their blades. Flip ran to a window in the corner of the room. He peeled back the curtain just a hair to watch the street outside.

There they waited in breathless silence for a long moment. Oris kept glancing impatiently at the hallway where Hyla had disappeared, anxious for Fleda to come. But the matron had not made her way down before Flip hissed, "Someone coming. No, more than one."

"Colors?" said Silvin.

"None," said Flip. "Likely hiding them in the city."

Silvin nodded. And then there came a knock.

Oris and Silvin looked at each other. Silvin tossed her head towards the door. Oris shrugged. Silvin sighed and opened her mouth to speak. But Oris forestalled her with a raised finger. *Sound like Hyla,* she mouthed. Silvin nodded.

"Good eve," said Silvin in a higher, thinner voice than her own. "I am afraid the orphanage is closed until morning."

"My apology for troubling you," said a voice through the door. Oris did not recognize it. "I serve a nobleman, the captain of the mayor's own personal guard. His daughter was killed in the war brewing with Dulmun. He wishes to adopt to heal the hole left in his heart, and he sent me here to make arrangements for a visit at first light."

Silvin pointed to Oris' sword. Oris drew it slowly, sending no whisper from its scabbard.

"In the morning is fine," said Silvin. She spoke quietly in her false, mousey voice. Even Oris had trouble making out the words.

"Eh? What is that?" said the voice through the door.

"The morning, fine then, ser," said Silvin, still more quietly.

There came the shifting of feet outside. The man's voice sounded closer. He had pressed his ear to the wood. "Speak up. I cannot hear you."

Shunk

Oris drove her blade straight through the door. When she pulled it back, it was slick with blood. There came the sound of a body falling outside.

Many shouts erupted in the street. Flip looked over at them with a fierce smile. "We've kicked the anthill now."

"Stop grinning and help us bar this door," said Oris. They seized the furniture from the front drawing room and began piling it up.

Oris did a quick run around the orphanage, making sure the side and back doors were locked as well. She took the opportunity to peer through the windows, confirming what she had already feared: Shades surrounded the building in numbers, though most of them seemed to be concentrated towards the front. But there were still too many to the side and rear to break through before they would be converged upon.

By the time she returned to the entryway, Fleda was just arriving. Too, some curious children had begun to emerge from their dormitories, drawn by the shouting outside and the commotion in the halls. Attendants tried to shoo them back to bed, but it was a futile attempt. Oris lost herself for a moment as she looked upon them. Had she ever really been *that* small? That young? She could not believe it, but she supposed it had to be true.

"Oreceot," snapped Fleda. "What in the *dark* below have you brought here?"

Oris felt a lurch in her stomach, just as she had felt so often when she was a child under the matron's gaze. Over Fleda's shoulder, she saw several children look at each other with wide eyes and nervous grins at hearing the matron speak such an oath.

"Shades have come here," said Oris. "They've come for me, but they won't hesitate to harm you and the children as well."

Fleda's eyes went wide, looking even wider through her thick spectacles. "Shades. Like the ones that attacked the Seat?"

"Yes."

"What under the sky do they want with *you?*"

Oris grimaced. "That is an increasingly long story, and an unimportant one right now. The only thing that matters is gathering the children. We are going to get you all out of here, but you have to be ready."

"Lifemage!"

Everyone froze. The booming voice from outside seemed to shake the floor. Oris felt a terrible pit in her gut. That was Barrick's voice. Fleda stared at Oris in fear.

"You are trapped," called Barrick. "We have you surrounded. Come and surrender yourself to us. If you do not, you will have the blood of these innocents on your hands."

The air fell to silence. Oris' mind whirled, trying to think of a way out of this. Silvin was taking deep breaths, her eyes half-closed.

"Oreceot!" hissed Fleda. "Whatever mess you have brought here, take it away at once. The children—"

"I know, all right?" said Oris. "Give me a moment."

She turned and stalked a few paces off, motioning Silvin and Flip to come with her. They drew together to speak quietly, but over their shoulders Oris could see Fleda staring daggers straight into her. She felt a sickness clawing at her stomach, nauseating her. She dragged her gaze away from Fleda to Silvin and Flip.

"I'm not going to let anything happen to the children," she said. "Does anyone have a brilliant idea? Because I'm not seeing a choice other than trying to fight our way through them."

"Mayhap we could try to break through the back?" said Silvin. "There will be fewer of them, and we might be able to create a gap for the children to flee through."

"Oh, come now," said Flip, as though that was the most foolish thing he had ever heard. "He doesn't really mean to let the children leave even if Oris does surrender herself. Not even if she dies willingly without a fight."

"What?" said Oris. "Why not?"

"I wouldn't if I were him," said Flip with a shrug. "I'd not want word of this, or your death, to reach the Seat. Why do you think he slaughtered everyone at the inn where we were staying? The High King has no idea where we are. No one does. I'd want to keep it that way. Let Enalyn stew, thinking you've vanished. Expend more resources trying to find you, after she's already stretched thin with Dulmun to the east."

"You'd kill *children* to achieve that end?" said Oris.

Flip gave her a hard look. "Of course I wouldn't. But they would. They already did, Oris. We were all there on the Seat."

"They did not kill the children." The tone of Silvin's voice sent thin, icy fingers of fear sliding down Oris' spine. She spoke in a hopeless monotone, with none of her fiery anger behind it. She was not looking at either of them. Her eyes were boring into the opposite wall, as though she was looking at some far-off vision invisible to everyone else.

"What do you mean?" said Flip. "I heard they left no one alive."

"They did not kill the children, but they did not leave them, either," said Silvin. "They took them. They dragged them off alive. Just as that woman said in the Birchwood."

At last her eyes seemed to focus, and she looked at Oris. But there was still no animation in them, no spark.

"I may have something," she said.

"What?" said Oris. "It can't be a good idea, the way you're looking."

Silvin ignored that and went to Fleda and the attendants. "Do you have a length of sturdy rope?"

Fleda blinked. But she seemed to know better than to waste time with questions, and she motioned sharply to Hyla, who ran to a nearby closet. She pulled from it a rope about ten feet long.

"That will do," said Silvin. "Flip, over here."

She led Flip down the hallway that led to the dormitory and the stairs. Oris waited only a moment before following a few paces behind.

"What's the plan?" she said. "Something like the river trick in the Birchwood? I hope it's less cold and wet."

She stopped as Silvin leaned in and whispered something in Flip's ear. Oris strained to hear, but she did not reach them before Silvin pulled away.

Flip grinned. "Oh, that's hilarious. She'll hate it."

"You shall have to go first," said Silvin.

"Of course."

Oris scowled, folding her arms. "What in the *dark* below are you two talking about?"

Still grinning, Flip turned to her. He placed a hand on her shoulder.

"My darling, dearest one," he said. "You'll understand one day, and mayhap even forgive us."

Oris' eyes shot wide.

The lightning rocked through her. Every muscle seized, her limbs twitching.

Silvin struck quickly. One punch deep in Oris' gut doubled her over. Then both clenched fists crashed into the back of her head. Oris fell to the stone floor.

"What under the sky are you doing?" cried Fleda. She moved forwards, but Hyla restrained her, fear in her eyes.

Oris was dimly aware of Flip and Silvin dragging her to the base of the stairs. Silvin took the rope she had been given and bound Oris' wrists to the bannister. The knots were tight, tight enough to pierce the veil of confusion and pain that had clouded Oris' mind.

Silvin straightened and turned to Fleda. "I do not have as much time to explain this as I wish I did. But Oris is more important than you can possibly imagine. The survival of Underrealm itself depends upon her. So Flip and I are going to go out there, and we are going to distract the ones pounding at your door. Once that happens, and not an instant before it happens, you will cut Oris free." From her boot she drew a dagger—the same she had once used to carve the tattoo from Enfil's neck—and placed it in Fleda's shaking hand. "Then you will get Oris out of here. We should pull most of them from the back of the building, but there may be one or two left when you run out the back. Oris can deal with them easily."

"No," groaned Oris. "No . . . stop. Please."

Flip and Silvin both looked to her, their eyes wide. "Dark below, she's already coming out of it," said Flip. "What a demon. I suppose I shouldn't be surprised."

Silvin whirled on Fleda, her voice urgent now. "Do you understand me? This is the only way you and the children survive. The Shades will hunt you down otherwise, to keep word of this from reaching the High King's Seat. This is your only chance."

"No!" cried Oris. She thrashed at the rope holding her to the bannister. But her muscles were still weak, and she was too well tied. She thrashed harder, grunting and then screaming. She placed one foot against the wall and gave a mighty pull. The wood creaked.

"We'd better go before she gnaws her own arm off," said Flip.

"Do you understand?" said Silvin.

Fleda's fingers tightened on the dagger. "I do," she said flatly. "I suppose I am grateful."

Flip and Silvin took a step closer to Oris. She stopped thrashing against the rope, her chest heaving with ragged breaths, and stared up at them in fury.

"Listen," said Flip. "Don't stay mad at us forever, will you? You'll understand when you're a bit older."

"Go to the dark below," spat Oris, "and then please yourself once you're there."

Flip's smile only widened. Then Silvin stepped forwards. Oris could see the torment in her eyes, the grief, and under it all, a faint streak of hope.

"We have to," she said, her voice frighteningly small and quiet. "You are the only one of us who truly matters."

Her hand stretched out, reaching for Oris. But Oris kicked up at her, and Silvin drew back her hand as if from a striking serpent.

"Don't *touch* me," snarled Oris. "Don't you *dare* touch me if the next thing you're going to do is walk away." She yanked again at her bindings, and the wood of the bannister squealed in protest.

Tears sprang from Silvin's eyes. Dimly, Oris realized it was the first time she had seen Silvin truly weep. She had not even cried when she found out about Jordel's death. Over her shoulder, Flip was still wearing his splitting grin, but Oris knew him well enough to see the hurt beneath it.

"You'll regret that sooner than later," said Flip. "Honestly, my love, remember what I said. Try not to hate us both forever, won't you? You've been nothing but the highest of delights. Mostly."

He put a hand on Silvin's arm and pulled her gently away. Silvin never stopped looking back over her shoulder at Oris, not even as she vanished around the corner and out of sight.

"Dark take you!" cried Oris, as her tears began to fall. "Dark take you both, you cowards! I hope he does it slow! I hope you're both screaming at the end!"

And then she collapsed, her whole body limp, the ropes digging into her wrists and marrow-deep sobs keeping her from saying anything more.

• ○ • ○ •

Silvin paused just inside the front door, Flip at her side. She could hardly see, the world was so blurry. She realized at last that she was crying, a sensation even more unfamiliar to her than laughter. With the back of her hand she scrubbed furiously at her eyes.

Flip put a hand on her shoulder. She blinked through the tears to meet his gaze. He only smiled at her sadly.

"She'll understand," said Flip. "She already does, though she can't admit it."

"We have more pressing things to attend to," Silvin choked out. "How do we play this?"

Flip sighed. "Well, they have that dark-damned wizard, and she's strong. That means my usefulness will be limited to keeping her magic away from us. If I can get the upper hand on her, I may be able to do more. But even if not, you're decent enough with those swords. The real problem is that once they realize Oris isn't with us, they're going to try to find out why."

"Then we do not give them time to react," said Silvin. "I will keep Barrick busy, and you do your best to keep everyone else from encircling me and cutting me down."

"A fine plan," said Flip brightly. "I believe it may even last a moment or two."

"Let us hope that is enough for Oris to get the children out, as well as herself," said Silvin. Her tears were mostly gone, replaced by a mounting anger. "We shall make it last as long as we can."

Flip laughed suddenly, long and loud. Silvin's brow furrowed as she looked upon him, but he only shook his head.

"I can't believe I'm about to die," he said. "And die fighting beside a Mystic, in the midst of the most important conflict to befall Underrealm in my lifetime—in many lifetimes. This is everything I've never wanted. All my life I've tried to avoid politicking and enjoy myself. It's hard to imagine being further away from that dream than I am now."

That brought a savage grin to Silvin's face. "I never, not once, imagined I would live this long. For a long time I hoped to die, and then I thought death was always around the corner." Her gaze drifted back down the south hallway, in the direction that Oris lay. "It was only recently that I thought there might be another way. A longer road before the end."

Flip's grin faded, becoming something melancholy. "I know you're a good person."

Silvin blinked. "What?"

"I know you're a good person," repeated Flip. "You may walk beside redbacks, but you do it to make the world better. I won't stand with them, but I'm not trying to fix anything, either. Mayhap there are some other folk out there, better folk than either of us, who manage to do both at once. But it was wrong of me to say my way was any better than yours."

That made Silvin smirk. "You may underestimate yourself. For here you stand now, rejecting my order entirely and fighting to save the world at the same time. Mayhap you had the right of it all along."

Now it was Flip who looked back to where Oris' sobs could still faintly be heard down the hallway. "I'm not doing it for anyone but her," he said softly.

Neither am I, thought Silvin. But even now, even at the end, she could not say the words. And then she forgot thc thought entirely as Flip reached out and pulled her into an embrace. For a moment she froze, and then, slowly, her arms encircled him as well, pulling him tight.

Then Flip pushed her back and gently slapped her cheek. "All right. It's time. Are you ready?"

"I have been ready," said Silvin.

Magelight sprang into Flip's eyes, and he grinned at her. "I'll tell you true: if the bards don't sing songs about us, I'll come up from the darkness below and kill them myself."

"I'll be beside you then, too," said Silvin.

She threw open the door, and they ran screaming out into the street.

• ○ • ○ •

Oris heard the front door slam open, heard Flip and Silvin give battle-cries as they rushed outside. She screamed with them, but hers was thin and pained, a cry of anguish that continued as she heard blades clashing in the street.

She curled into a ball and pressed her knees against the wall, then used her legs to try again to wrench the bannister out. It gave ever so slightly, but not nearly enough. Whoever had built this place had not built it to withstand a siege, but they *had* built it to withstand many generations of children, and that was almost the same thing. Oris could break free given time, but she had no time.

"Fleda," she begged. "Fleda, please cut me loose. Please. I have to save them. I can't . . . I can't stay here. Please."

Fleda looked sternly down at her. The blade was still in her hand, but she was hanging back, out of Oris' reach.

"They are giving their lives to save yours, Oreceot. I do not know what any of this is about, but I know that should mean something to you. I will not free you until you promise not to be a fool. I have more than just your life to think of. I need you to protect the children once we get them out of here."

"You don't understand," growled Oris. "That is my family. I lost one family already in this life. I can't lose another. *I can't.* I won't survive it, Fleda, I don't *want* to. Let me go, and then you can take the children. They won't care about you. They won't chase you if they've got me. *Please.*"

The children had finally begun to grasp the danger they were in, and the younger ones were beginning to cry. Some of the older children and the faculty went to hold them and give whatever sparse comfort they could. Beside Fleda, Hyla was looking nervously towards the front entrance of the orphanage. "Matron, should we not—"

"Dark take it, Oreceot," snapped Fleda. "For once in your life, *listen.* Listen to people who know *better* than you. *Stop needing to be right.*"

Something inside Oris broke. It was not the snap of a restraining leash, but the collapse of a pillar holding up a building. She sagged down against the wall, no longer thrashing against the rope.

Fleda was right. Oris had said as much to Silvin and Flip less than an hour ago. She thought of all of the times she *had* to know best. She had to do it her own way, she could never listen to anyone else once she had made up her mind.

When her amulet had been taken, she had gone very nearly feral, breaking every rule and never stopping until she got it back. And the punishments that followed were ten times worse than they would have been otherwise.

Disobeying the High King to chase death itself across Selvan. And then, when she faced it at last? When she confronted Barrick, and saw the sickly energy around him that made her want to retch? There was nothing inside her to answer it. Only that pit in her stomach, that emptiness.

She felt it now, swelling through her, threatening to envelop her. Nothing. Nothing at all.

She gave herself to it. She let go, and she sank into the void.

Or . . . no.

Not a void. Not emptiness. Not a pit or a hole at all.

This was not darkness. This was not absence.

This was an ocean. An endless depth of something cleaner than the purest water, still as winter air. She thought of Barrick again, of the crawling in her skin at the sight of him. And she let the energy swell around her, *into* her, and she calmed. The fear vanished.

She had never been empty at all. It had never been a hole inside of herself, not a space to be filled.

It was *her.* It was what *made* her.

True emptiness was loss. It was the loss of her amulet, seeing it dangle in Fleda's hand. It was Flip and Silvin, saying farewell forever and trying to convince her it was for the best.

Taking the choice away from her. Love in their hearts, but still trying to control her, and still trying to take away that which was hers.

Hers.

It is mine, she had told Fleda when she was a child. *Mine.*

This you shall not take from me.

When had she closed her eyes? She opened them now and looked up at Fleda. The matron flinched and drew back, as did the children and faculty around her.

The room . . . something was wrong with the room. The light was brighter. The colors were sharper. It seemed to be a familiar sensation, but Oris could not place it. Then she remembered the Seat. When Silvin had tested her, and helped her touch magic for the first time.

"Oreceot . . ." stammered Fleda. "Your eyes . . ."

"Cut me loose," said Oris. It was neither a request, nor a demand. It was a certainty. "Then hide the children upstairs."

Hyla looked to Fleda uncertainly. Fleda gave her a shaky nod and handed over the knife. Hyla ran forwards and began to saw at Oris' bonds.

• ○ • ○ •

The Shade brought his axe around in a backhand swing. It was the opening Silvin had been waiting for. One of her pommels came up and drove into his armpit. He wrenched to the side with a cry of pain. Silvin brought the other blade around and hacked halfway through his neck. His body jerked strangely as it tried to remain upright, and then he collapsed to the street.

That makes . . . what? Six? She quickly counted the corpses on the street. *Only five. Pity.*

They had plunged straight into the Shades, who had drawn back in alarm. But once they saw only Flip and Silvin attacking them, they had surged forwards again.

A quick glance told Silvin that any passersby had vanished, leaving the street to the combatants. She had to imagine the King's law had been summoned. But they would not arrive until after this fight was already over.

Flip had sidled into the corner of the building, while Silvin had positioned herself in front of both him and the door. Some Shades tried to fire arrows, but Flip was able to do just enough to block the shots while also keeping the Shade wizard occupied. They could only come for Silvin one or two at a time, and that had gone poorly for them so far.

But one had feinted and landed a solid blow to Flip's head. It was bleeding. Silvin had taken cuts from at least two swords. Or had they been axes? She could not remember, and it did not matter.

Barrick had not even joined the fray yet. He stood there behind more of his battle-kindred, arms folded, glaring at her. That was fine with Silvin.

"We've got to have given Oris enough time, right?" said Flip quietly, as the Shades mustered their courage for another charge.

"We have to hope so," said Silvin.

"You're a wildcat in a fight," said Flip. "I thought I should tell you that before either one of us falls."

"And you are an adequate wizard." Silvin shot him a savage grin over her shoulder, and Flip returned it.

Clang

The crash of Barrick's sword against his shield made everyone on the street freeze. The Shades looked back to their leader. Barrick pushed forwards through them, shouldering them aside. His gaze never left Silvin.

"Very well," he said. "Consider yourself honored. You have earned a swift end to this pathetic farce."

Dark below, cursed Silvin in her mind. The day she had met Flip and Oris, she had been able to surprise Enfil and end him. She did not have surprise on her side now.

The Shades drew back. They formed a sort of half-circle behind Barrick. There was no way to run through them. Nowhere to go but back in the orphanage.

And then Silvin saw still more of the Shades appearing. But these were coming from around the sides of the building. They had been drawn from the perimeter by the fighting at last. She thought she would collapse with relief. There was nothing between the orphanage and escape now.

Go, Oris, she thought. *Go you beautiful, mad fool. Go and survive.*

But she only smiled up at Barrick and moved to meet him.

He came for her hard, trying to end the fight quickly. She had expected that. So she danced. She let her blades meet his when she had to, but for the most part she merely stepped around his blows. To the side, then back, circling him, keeping one wary eye on the Shades surrounding them.

In the crowd she spotted Idulen, looking at her in wide-eyed fear. Her lip curled.

Barrick spun, his sword hissing through the air. Silvin dropped to one knee to duck it and came up swinging. Barrick's head flew back, but not far enough. The tip of Silvin's blade slashed straight up his cheek, leaving a thin line of blood but missing the eye.

They both stepped back from each other, Barrick growling. But then, even as Silvin watched, the wound on his cheek slowly stitched itself shut. In a moment, it was as though he had never taken the wound.

"Your efforts are pointless," said Barrick. "You will not keep me from entering that orphanage. You will only grant me the chance to carve you limb from limb while the Lifemage watches." He looked across the orphanage's front, to the windows along its length, and raised his voice to a shout. "Can you see us? Do you have a good view? I would not want you to miss any details, you coward!"

But he had not noticed his soldiers circling in from around the back of the orphanage. Silvin wanted to grin, but she did not. No need to give him any reason to suspect she had a plan. She was faster than him, but not by much. And he was ever so much stronger. With his master's dark enchantment spurring him on, she could not hope to tire him out and strike him when weakened.

All she could do was buy as much time as possible.

Barrick went for a bull rush. Silvin tried to push off the shield and move around him. But he spun to his right when she had expected left. His sword came around and left a long slash down her arm.

Silvin gritted her teeth and drew back, even as Barrick showed his teeth in a grin. Rage boiled up inside her, white-hot and insistent. Her breath came faster, her nostrils flaring.

"Careful, Silvin," said Flip through gritted teeth. His eyes blazed as he held off a fresh assault from the Shade wizard.

Silvin answered only with a savage growl. *Two deep breaths,* she tried to tell herself. But she could not summon them.

And why resist? a part of her mind asked. *Let it go. Let it rip through you. You could end him, and them, right now.*

No. Who knew how far away the children were? And Oris? They might be far enough away, and they might not. But certainly Flip was too close. Not to mention all the other innocents nearby, simply living their lives in Cabrus.

At least Oris had never had to see that side of her.

Two deep breaths. In, out.

She sprang. It surprised Barrick. His blade and shield came up, his actions more instinct than intent. It gave her a hint of an opening.

The tip of one blade plunged through the chainmail under his breast plate. Barrick grunted with pain.

But then his shield lashed out, slamming into her face. Silvin reeled back, stars exploding in her vision.

Barrick's sword came around. Silvin managed to get her blade in front of it, but it knocked the sword away to skitter across the cobblestones.

Barrick dropped his shield and grabbed her by the throat with his left hand. He lifted her off the ground and plunged his sword through her gut.

In a flash of white-hot agony, Silvin felt one handsbreath of steel erupt out of her back.

She gasped, and fire raced through her lungs. Blood spattered from between her teeth onto Barrick's raised forearm. She could only stare at him without comprehension. Dimly, from the corner of her eye, she saw Flip's look of horror.

The pain . . . the pain was excruciating. She was losing focus.

Cannot lose focus.

Rising to meet the pain came the rage.

Cannot let it control me. Be better. Be good enough to let yourself die.

Be good enough to deserve her.

Barrick dropped her. The street slamming into her body brought a fresh wave of agony. She tried to scream at the hideous sensation of steel sliding back out of her insides, but only a choking groan came out. More blood spattered from her mouth to the stone, joining the pool spreading from her belly.

The door to the orphanage slammed open.

Silvin's gaze was already wandering. The thought of focusing on anything was laughable. Yet her head turned, drawn to the open door. Dimly, as though through a deepening shroud, she saw Oris standing there.

"No," she moaned weakly. *Dark below, no. You were supposed to run. You were supposed to—*

She froze.

Oris' eyes were glowing.

CHAPTER XXIV
THE END OF THE BEGINNING

BARRICK STOOD LOOMING OVER THE MYSTIC WOMAN. BUT HIS ATTENTION belonged only to the Lifemage. Within his grasp at last. He had faced her twice already. He knew she stood no chance against him.

And yet . . . and yet her eyes.

His father's words drifted into his mind. *If she masters herself, you will be in grave danger.*

Barrick shook his head savagely, banishing the thought. Mastering herself? It had taken the Lord years. Whatever paltry scrap of power the Lifemage had uncovered was as nothing in the face of his father's might.

"Finally," growled Barrick. "Done sending your whelps to fight for you?"

Beneath her glowing eyes, the Lifemage's lips twisted in a smirk. "A fine boast, coming from one who's only here because his father's a coward."

White-hot rage filled Barrick in an instant. "Insult him again, and I shall draw a price in blood from those you love." He pointed to Silvin with the tip of his sword. "I have gutted your Mystic sow already. Come and join her in the dark below."

Yet still he did not step forwards. Still he did not launch his attack.

The Lifemage looked down at Silvin. Anguish flickered across her face for a brief moment. But then she returned her gaze to Barrick.

"I can see it, you know," said the Lifemage. "I can sense his presence within you. He's watching right now, isn't he? Or do you even know?"

"My father is always watching over his children," said Barrick, his lip curling.

The Lifemage cocked her head. "Is he? Here, then. Let us see what kind of man you are without him."

She did not move. She did not raise a hand or speak a word of power.

But something . . . happened.

A searing pain burst across the back of Barrick's neck. And his world shattered.

• ○ • ○ •

For an instant, Barrick's eyes erupted in a white glow. He spasmed, reaching up towards the back of his neck, and then he collapsed on the ground. His body writhed and contorted, twisting on the street in agony.

Oris ignored him. She ignored the other Shades standing in the street, all of them looking between her and their commander with a mixture of fascination and horror.

Instead she went to Silvin. The Mystic lay in a pool of her own blood, clutching a wound in her belly. Her eyes were anguished as Oris knelt and cupped the back of her head in one hand.

"You were supposed to leave," croaked Silvin. "They will kill you."

"They won't," said Oris. "And they won't kill you, either. I told you you're not allowed to go. Can't lose you. Either one of you. I won't."

She placed one hand on the wound. Silvin's blood bubbled out fresh and warm, covering her fingers. Oris pressed harder, ignoring Silvin's deep hiss of pain.

There came a blinding flash of light. Oris was vaguely aware that the glow in her eyes grew brighter for a moment. She felt a mild flash of surprise as light erupted from Silvin's eyes as well, quickly hidden as the Mystic closed them and gave a long, lingering scream of agony.

"I'm sorry," muttered Oris. "I wish I were better for you."

Silvin's scream subsided at last. Her face was squeezed tight in a grimace of pain. But then, suddenly, her eyes snapped open. Her expression relaxed, and she stared down at her belly.

There was the wound. Silvin lifted a hand and wiped away the blood that soaked her. No fresh blood came to replace it. And Oris knew—*knew,* somehow—that the pain was gone, despite the open hole that still gaped in her belly.

"I . . . what did you do?" breathed Silvin.

"I remembered what I felt at Wellmont," said Oris. "And every time I've seen the shadeborn since. I thought it was an emptiness, and it frightened me. But it's just . . . me. I still don't know how to fix you. Not really. But I can keep life in you, at least."

A thought struck her, and she looked over her shoulder. There, still tucked in the front corner of the building, was Flip. No glow came from his eyes. He was frozen, staring at her in fascination, as were the Shades in the street.

Oris smiled at him. Flip gave her a weak smile back.

"Doing all right?" said Oris.

"Not by half," said Flip. "Took you long enough to join us."

"Got tied up with other things."

Flip covered his face with a hand as he groaned. "Dark take you. That was bad by *your* standards."

"I'm glad you're not dead."

"I'm glad I'm not dead, too."

Metal crashed into stone, and the smile fled Oris' face. Barrick had slammed one gauntlet into the street. Now he levered himself up heavily onto hands and knees. His eyes were still wild and unfocused. One hand rose to probe at the back of his neck.

The tattoo was gone. In its place was only a burn mark, a circular scar that looked more like an archery target than anything else. Barrick's fingers probed it, and he winced. His gaze darted to Oris.

"You," he growled. "What did you do?"

"I severed your connection to your father," said Oris simply. "I think you've lived too long with that tether. Let's see how you fare without it."

Barrick's limbs had stopped shaking. Like a mountain rising, he climbed to his feet. Oris rose to meet him. Breaking the magic had done nothing to reduce his size or his strength, and he still stood a good two heads above her. But Oris looked up at him unflinching.

“I will crush you,” he hissed. “I shall smear the pulp of your head across half the streets of this putrid city. And then my father shall grant me his boon again. You have accomplished nothing.”

Oris shrugged. “If you say so. Let’s match blades and see.”

Flip snickered.

“Shut it, Flip.”

“Shutting it.”

Barrick leaped for her, and Oris raised her sword to meet him. The Shades in the street surged forwards, coming to help their master. But they drew up short as Silvin shot to her feet, weapons in her hands once more. The Shades had seen her fell many of their number already, and now they wavered as she warded them from Oris and Barrick. Light blazed in Flip’s eyes again, as well as the eyes of the Shade wizard.

But Oris only had a moment to take this in before Barrick was upon her. She parried his first blow, but could not move quickly enough to avoid his shield. It crushed her, slamming into her face, and she fell back with a grunt. She probed her nose with one hand, and it came away bloody.

Barrick gave a savage grin. But Oris only grinned right back up at him, blood dripping down into her teeth. Barrick’s face fell, ever so slightly.

Oris brought her sword around for his head. Barrick blocked it easily with his shield. But Oris had put no strength in the blow. As it bounced off, she brought the sword around for another swing. In light, dancing circles she swung the blade around, halfhearted in strength but with whirling, flashing swiftness. She could see the confusion in Barrick’s eyes as he blocked each weak blow.

Her other hand whipped her dagger out. While Barrick was blocking another high, light swing, she plunged the dagger into his thigh.

Barrick cried out, stepping back. Oris let him. Breath hissed hard between his teeth as he looked down at the dagger, and the blood now seeping out around it.

“Honorless tricks will not save you,” he snarled.

Oris actually laughed, shaking her head. “If you think I care about *your* views on honor, you’re sorely mistaken. The man who murders innocents, who threatened the children of this orphanage.”

Barrick’s grimace turned to a smile, and he yanked the dagger from his flesh. He stepped to the side, circling her—but then he stumbled. His smile faltered, and his eyes darted to the wound again.

"Something wrong?" said Oris, still smiling.

Barrick roared and barreled forwards. But his wounded leg twitched as he stepped on it, throwing off his balance. Oris avoided his blade easily and spun around him, giving him a deep slice on the back of his shield arm. Barrick nearly fell as he took another step on the wounded leg. He turned to her with wild eyes, his hair scraggly as it fell down into his face.

"How long has it been?" said Oris. "How long since a wound meant anything to you in a fight? Do you even remember how to push through the pain?"

"I remember more than you could ever hope to learn!" roared Barrick. "I am my father's favored son! An agent of his just will! Your simpering means nothing to—"

Oris feinted towards him. Barrick flinched, hiding behind his shield. But Oris did not press the attack. She only grinned at him as he lowered the shield again. Fear and shame filled his eyes.

"Your master has banished all your hurts for a long time, and that has made you weak," said Oris. "I bear the scars of every wound life has ever given me. That is strength."

Barrick screamed in hatred and rushed her.

Oris laughed and met him.

● ○ ● ○ ●

The Shades still pushed towards Silvin. Two of them had tried their luck with her, and their corpses had joined their friends' upon the street. Now the rest of them were even more hesitant. Silvin saw how their glances kept sliding past her, to their commander who battled with Oris in front of the orphanage.

"Today is not going to go your way," said Silvin. "You are about to watch your leader die, and then you are all going to join him."

Nervous glances. In their midst, towards the back, Idulen's face was Elf-white, his skin covered in a thin sheen of sweat.

Silvin cocked her head.

"But," she said, straightening slightly, "it does not have to be that way. I will let you flee, if you are wise enough to do so. All of you may leave this place, to crawl back into whatever holes you have slithered from. All but one."

They flinched as she raised a blade. But she only used it to point at Idulen's horrified face.

"Give me that one, and the rest of you may leave."

A long moment of silence stretched. She watched Idulen's face change, from certain to uncertain and then to a different, fatally worse sort of certainty.

He tried to turn and flee, but six of them seized him before he could manage it. They dragged him screaming through the crowd. One of them, a young, tall man with a bald pate, sneered as he threw Idulen to the ground at Silvin's feet.

"Have him, then," said the Shade. "And good riddance."

"A wise choice," said Silvin. "You may flee now."

Most of them did. But the bald one only drew back a few paces, as did one other of his companions. They sheathed their blades and stood, never taking their eyes from Idulen.

Idulen tried to crawl away from Silvin. She flipped out a dagger and threw it. It sank through his wrist, and he screamed as he rolled over on his side, clutching the wound.

"A traitor to your liege lord, and a coward to the end," growled Silvin as she stepped forwards. "Even those you betrayed the High King for have no stomach for you. Look. They are staying just for the satisfaction of watching."

"Wait!" cried Idulen, looking up at her in sheer terror. "Wait. I-I-I have information! I can provide counsel on—"

Shunk

Silvin plunged one sword into his gut, the other through his chest. She gave each of them a little twist for good measure.

"Mayhap they shall listen to your pleas in the darkness below," she growled. "But I doubt it."

A few paces away, the last two Shades watched Idulen twitching on her swords. Then they turned and vanished into the streets of Cabrus.

• ○ • ○ •

One Shade still remained: the wizard, her eyes glowing as she and Flip held each other off in a duel of wills. Hardly could one of them snap off the beginnings of some spell before the other cut off the source of its power. The glow in their eyes rose brighter and brighter as they each sought an advantage. But the Shade was distracted. Her eyes kept going to Barrick, flagging in his duel with Oris, and to Idulen who lay dying.

Flip grinned at her across the street. "Things aren't looking good for you, friend. Might be time to turn tail and run."

Her eyes darted to him, and then back to Barrick.

"Oh, go on," said Flip. "I'm more interested in your master anyway, now he's got no enchantment to protect him."

Her lips twisted. Her shoulders jerked. And then she turned to flee.

"Ha," muttered Flip. "Dark-damned fool."

He sent a lightning bolt rocketing after her. But she whirled and swept a hand through the air. The bolt arced into the ground, crashing harmlessly into the street and cracking a cobblestone. Then the Shade vanished around the corner of a building.

Flip's face fell. "Dark take it," he muttered. "I truly thought that would work. Ah well. There are other pleasures in life."

He turned and fired another lightning bolt into Barrick's back.

• ○ • ○ •

Barrick already reeled from the many wounds Oris had given him. A wide cut on his cheek left blood dripping from his chin. His arms were criss-crossed with lines of red, and both his legs had been pierced. They shook as he tried to remain upright.

When Flip's lightning crashed into him, his body seized up, as Oris' had done inside the orphanage. When at last Flip released the bolt, Barrick went crashing to the ground. Weakly he pushed himself up on one arm and then climbed to his knees.

The point of Oris' sword came to rest at his throat. He froze.

Oris smiled down at him. "And that is the end of that."

Barrick's glare up at her was pure hatred. "You have accomplished nothing here," he said. He tried to force strength into his words, but they only cracked. "Underrealm will fall. All of you will beg for my father's mercy before the end. My death today means nothing."

Oris raised her brows and gave him a little smile. "Your death? Oh no, friend. You don't get to die here. They tell me my power isn't death, but life. No, we'll be taking you back to the Seat. And then the Mystics and other servants of the High King will take their time with you. Before they're done, we'll learn everything you know about your brethren and their future plans."

Barrick's snarl fell away, to be replaced by empty uncertainty. But then the grin came back into his expression. He started to laugh.

Oris frowned down at him. A few paces away, Silvin's eyes shot wide with recognition.

"Oris!" she cried.

But before Oris could respond, Barrick seized her sword. The blade bit into the flesh of his hand. Oris felt it grinding on bone.

Barrick pulled the sword into his own throat. It sank through the flesh to pierce out the other side. Blood spurted out, splattering across Oris' sword hand and legs. Barrick spit at her, and more blood splashed across her tunic. His grip relaxed, and Oris yanked the sword away from him.

As Barrick's shoulders started to sag, Oris gave him a smile of purest ice.

"You're a fool, Barrick," she said. "And you have learned nothing today."

The world around her grew brighter as her eyes started to glow. Barrick's expression became one of fear.

Oris stepped forwards and seized his throat, hard. Barrick gave a gurgling scream of pain. Then the light in Oris' eyes grew brighter, and brighter. Barrick's eyes glowed in tandem with them.

The blinding flash died away.

Barrick lay on the ground, groaning, his breaths ragged and rasping. Across his body, the skin was still laid open, the flesh and tendon visible beneath. But no fresh blood came pouring forth to join the old. Every wound remained, but they were no longer able to kill him.

Oris sniffed. She turned to Flip and Silvin, standing together a few paces away, and looking at her with wide, awestruck eyes.

"You'd better go summon a constable," said Oris. "We've got a lot to clean up."

CHAPTER XXV
FIRST AND NEXT STEPS

The constables arrived before Silvin could reach them. Someone in the pauper's quarter had at last overcome their fear of the King's law to notify them, and they were only a few streets away when the fighting stopped. All of them drew their blades at the sight of the carnage. But Silvin flashed her Mystic's badge at them, and after a moment's conversation they put their blades away.

Barrick was bound in chains and dragged off to a cell. Silvin ensured they would place him under heavy guard.

"He may still have some trickery in him," she told the constables. "Do not remove his chains for an instant. Once he is in the cell, do not let him within arm's reach of you or anyone else. And you had better post a wizard or two on his guard at all times, in case he should find a way out of his chains."

The constable captain, a man of middle years with a heavy scar on his upper lip, glanced uncertainly at Barrick. "If he is one of those shadeborn the tales tell of, a wizard will be of little help."

Oris smiled at Barrick. "He is a shadeborn no longer."

Barrick snarled at her. But only a rasping gargle came from his ruined throat.

While they were still dealing with the King's law, Oris sent Flip into the orphanage to inform them the danger had passed. When the constables left, she entered the orphanage herself.

The faculty had put the children to bed once more. But Matron Fleda remained awake, as did Hyla. They sat upon cushioned chairs in the front room. Hyla looked bleary-eyed and miserable with the late hour, but Fleda's eyes were still sharp, and they appraised Oris keenly as she stepped through the entryway.

"It is done, then?" she said.

Oris nodded. "It is."

Fleda nodded. Then her gaze dropped to Oris' feet. "You are getting blood on my rug."

Oris looked down and saw it was true. She was leaving faint red footprints everywhere she walked, and they had stained the intricate patterns of the rug just inside the door—Idrisian in make, if she guessed right.

"Sorry," said Oris, quickly stepping off the rug.

But Fleda waved a hand. She rose and stepped forwards to stand a pace from Oris. Hyla was only a moment behind her, blinking her eyes hard.

"It is done," said Fleda. "The rug can be replaced, unlike a life. You saved many lives here tonight, Oreceot. All of them, in fact. Of course, you brought the danger with you as well, but you did not know it when you brought it. We are all grateful. I, especially, am grateful."

Oris swallowed hard. "I couldn't have done anything else, Matron."

"Oh, you could have," said Fleda. "But you did not. Accept the gratitude, you silly girl." Briskly she lifted her hands and clapped them together. "Now, sheer hospitality, to say nothing of a life debt, demands that we get some food in your bellies. Hyla, would you tell the cooks to put something together? The best we can manage on short notice."

Hyla's face fell, but she quickly mastered herself. "Of course, Matron."

But beside Oris, Flip gave a thin little groan. Fleda's eyes shot to him.

"You object?" said Fleda. "I cannot imagine you are anything other than starving after your ordeal."

Oris met Flip's gaze, and when she saw the anguish there she smiled.

"We could eat a horse, each of us," said Oris. "But that isn't Flip's objection. Forgive me for saying so, Matron, but we wish to go and eat somewhere else. Somewhere with ale, and wine, and brandy, and anything else they will pour down our throats. We want to drink until we collapse, and then we want to sleep for a week."

Fleda lifted her chin and sniffed disapprovingly. But she said only, "I suppose I understand that. And I suppose you deserve it as well."

But then Fleda took another step closer and laid a hand on Oris' arm. Her face softened suddenly, losing its flintiness and looking suddenly . . . somehow older than Oris had ever seen it before. But also warmer, and happier, and sadder at the same time.

"I am sorry that you did not have an easier time here, Oreceot," said Fleda. "And, it seems, that you are not having it any easier out there. Things can be difficult even between children and parents who love each other very much, and I am not able to be a parent here. But I was always proud that you were one of our children. And I *remembered* you. That is not always the case, though it sounds terrible to say it. I remembered you, and I was proud. I hope you believe that when you leave here, if you did not already."

Oris laid her hand on top of Fleda's. "I believe you. And for my part, I'm sorry I wasn't the sort of child who would have gotten along better with you. It's not because you were evil, any more than it's because I was. I think that now I can be grateful for everything you did, and that's a great deal. I can let the less pleasant memories fall by the wayside. Not to be forgotten, but to be understood."

Fleda arched one eyebrow. "My goodness. So you have found some wisdom out in the wide world after all."

"She hasn't," said Flip. "She's only good at faking it."

"Flip."

"Shutting it."

"I'd ask one thing before we go," said Oris. Fleda gave her a quizzical look. "Could I walk through the place? One more time? I never really got to give it a proper farewell when I left."

"When you ran away, you mean," said Fleda. But not as snippily as she might once have done. She gestured towards the dining hall. "Of course you may. I only ask that you do not enter the dormitories, for I believe they are still trying to wrestle the children into slumber. And I ask that we do not linger too very long, or Hyla will collapse where she stands."

Hyla jerked suddenly upright where she had been slouching with drooping eyelids. "Not at all, Matron. I am happy to be of—"

"Oh, hush, Hyla."

Oris took her time, but not too much of it. Silvin and Flip excused themselves and waited in the front room, while Fleda and Hyla accompanied Oris on her walk. In the dining hall, she ran her fingers along the tabletops, worn smooth by years and years of use by tiny hands. In the courtyard, she sat on the rim of the fountain she had leaped into countless times, ignoring the faculty's outraged cries as she soaked herself and splashed any child within reach. It had once seemed as wide as a little pond, and now she saw that it was only two paces across. The courtyard steps, too, were strange. Had they always been so short? *Of course they were,* she thought. *They were built for children.*

She did as Fleda had asked, and did not enter the dormitories. But she did walk down the hallway, running her fingers along the rough wood of the three doors. And she listened to the hushed whispers of children inside who still dared to defy curfew. She smiled.

Before heading back to the entrance, she looked to Fleda again. "Might I go upstairs?" she said. "If you would permit it, I would like to see the . . . the faculty room."

Fleda's look was very knowing. She nodded. "You are no longer a child," she said. "Upstairs is not off limits to you anymore."

Oris nodded and climbed up. She still remembered every spot that had once creaked underfoot when she was little—but there were new spots now, and despite her care, she made more noise than she wished.

At the top, the long, dark hallway stretched before her, with the thin outline of candlelight rimming the door at the end. There were more doors along the wall to her right. Suddenly she realized that she did not know what lay behind them, and had never known it. She almost asked Fleda. Then she thought better of it. Instead, she walked down the hall to the faculty room. The door opened easily under her hand.

There was the cabinet. Like everything else, it was far smaller than she remembered. The top of it was a few fingers below her chin. She clicked open the latch and swung the wide doors open. There was the shelf where her amulet had once lay, where she had reclaimed it in the dead of the night, only to be caught in the act.

She turned back to Fleda in the doorway. "In a sense, this is where tonight began," she said. "Or at least, it's where the ending began."

Fleda frowned. "I do not quite follow you."

"No," said Oris. "And you don't need to." She sighed and closed the cabinet doors. "There's a question I never thought to ask you, Fleda. Were you an orphan?"

That clearly surprised the matron. She blinked twice, tilting her head. Beside her, Hyla suddenly perked up, and though she tried to hide it, she looked at Fleda with a sudden, keen interest.

"Few of the children ask me that," said Fleda finally. "The answer is both yes and no. But no, not really. Not in the way you mean. My parents died when I was in my twenty-fourth year. Some would say that gave me the title, but I have been here too long to believe it. In fact I came here in the first place because their loss made me think what my life would have been like if it had happened ten years earlier. I wanted to . . . well, *fix* it is the wrong thing to say. But when it happened, I was old enough to understand my own grief. I wanted to make things easier for those who were still too young to understand theirs."

Tears sprang into Oris' eyes, and she wiped them away. "My family were alive when I was taken away and brought here," she said. "They were alive. I only just learned that. I don't know who they were. Or who they might still be, because who knows? And I don't know how to find them. It's why I came here."

Fleda's face softened again, as it had done downstairs. Her fingers tightened on her walking stick. "Oreceot," she said softly. "I did not . . . are you sure?"

"Yes," said Oris. "And you couldn't have known. It's not . . . I'm not telling you because ..." She stopped, sighed, and shook her head.

"Don't take their things, Fleda. Please. Not their one thing. Let them have that."

For just a moment, she thought she saw Fleda's chin quiver. And then it was gone, and the matron only nodded.

The inn where they had left their possessions had been attacked, and they did not wish to deal with the constables and whatever other representatives of the King's law might be watching over it. So they found another, closer inn, and Silvin secured them a bed for the night from a wide-eyed innkeeper who gawked at the sight of them, dirty and blood-stained. They went to the inn's baths and, without disrobing, they scrubbed their skin free of the grime. Then they convened in the common room, claiming a table in the back corner, and tried to ignore the many eyes that stared openly at them.

"I mean to do as Oris said, and drink until I forget who I am and who you both are," said Flip, waving down a server.

"What of you, Silvin?" said Oris. "Do you drink tonight?"

Silvin smiled at her. "Oh yes. I drink tonight. You two will watch out for me?"

Flip put a hand over hers. "Always."

Whiskey was brought for them, and wine, and beer. Drink had never tasted so sweet, nor had food. They did not speak for a while. They only drank and ate, and stared at their hands and at each other. But Flip and Silvin stole glances at Oris more than anything else.

When they had sated themselves and were well into their cups, if not quite silly with drink, Flip spoke at last. "What now, O mighty Lifemage?"

Oris chuckled. "Not mighty. Just a first step."

"Yet you found your magic," said Silvin. "That is no small matter."

"I learned one trick," said Oris. "I know little of magic, but I know that Flip can do a thousand and one spells. I am no wizard yet. And I shall need to be. This first taste has only made me realize how much more there is for me to learn. But this coming war will not wait forever for me to learn it."

"You will do it," said Flip. "The first step is the hardest. It will get easier. And we will be here to help you, and to guard you while you do."

Oris gave the barest of nods. Her gaze was far away, and she hardly seemed to be listening. Then she gave another nod, deeper, firm, and it was as if she was nodding to herself.

"I'm what I am," she said. "It's time to act like it. We'll take Barrick to the Seat. And there, we'll join the High King. Truly, with all our hearts and strength. And we'll fight this war. Until it ends, or we do."

"So says the Lifemage," said Silvin. The words slurred ever so slightly. "And I am honor-bound to obey."

Oris looked at Silvin, but she could not quite allow herself to reach over and take her hand as Flip had. "Thank you. For finding me, and for protecting me, and for allowing me to do what I needed to do, even when it was not what you wanted or thought was right. We would have died a long while ago, alone and ignorant in the woods, if not for you."

Silvin dropped her gaze. "It is only my duty."

Oris' hand twitched. Then it slid across the table, and she laid just the tips of two fingers on Silvin's wrist. Silvin closed her eyes, taking two slow breaths.

“You walk far beyond the bounds of duty,” whispered Oris. “You know it. And so do I. Always am I mindful of it, just as you are.”

Flip’s mouth twitched towards a smirk as he glanced at Oris’ hand, but he withheld himself. “You have my gratitude as well, for what that is worth.”

“It is worth your weight in gold,” said Silvin.

“I’m not very heavy.”

“I know.”

“But before we retire, I need you both to know something,” said Oris. “You are never again to try what you tried to pull tonight. You are not allowed to die for me. You are not allowed to die at all.” She held Flip in a long stare, and then she did the same for Silvin, waiting in a fervid silence until Silvin at last lifted her eyes. “You are mine. Both of you. Whether you like it or not. No heroic sacrifices. No giving your life for mine. We look out for each other, because we need each other.”

Silvin’s jaw tightened and then relaxed. “All right,” she said in a small voice.

“Swear to me.”

Silvin and Flip frowned. “What?” said Flip.

“Swear it to me,” said Oris. “Here and now. Because I promise you, if you ever try anything like that again, and you leave me, I will not be long in joining you in the darkness below.” Her voice grew thick. “You thought you were saving my life, but I could not have survived it. I would have chosen not to. Swear to me you will not do it again.”

A long silence stretched. Then, at last, Flip and Silvin nodded.

“I swear it,” said Silvin.

“I swear,” said Flip.

“Good,” said Oris. She released them from her gaze at last and nodded. “Good. Someone get another bottle.”

KEEP READING

You've seen the war that will shape Underrealm for years to come.

Now learn how that war began.

The Nightblade Epic tells the tale of Loren of the family Nelda, a humble forest girl who finds herself dragged into kingdom-shattering schemes of merchants and nobles.

And in the shadows, she discovers the servants of the Lord for the first time.

In this series you'll learn:

- What led to the battle of Wellmont
- What really happened to Silvin's master, Jordel
- How the High King survived the attack on the Seat

It's all in the pages of the Nightblade Epic, the first series of Underrealm. Get it here:

Underrealm.net/NBE

THANK YOU TO MY PATRONS

A number of you contribute to my Patreon. Your unswerving support means the world to me, and many times it's kept me going when I would otherwise have had to quit. Each and every one of you has my sincere gratitude.

If you'd like to become a supporter, you can find my Patreon at:

Patreon.com/GarrettBRobinson

(Patrons are listed in order of lifetime support).

STUDIO EXECUTIVES

Sybil R. Case, Kris Nieder, A Howard, Mysery, Dakota Heath, Robin Arsenault, London Johnson

PRODUCERS

John Maryn, Harlan Gross, Sara McKenney

ABOVE THE LINE

Sara Scimone, Hank Green, Kelsey Nolen, Jesse S, LupineKing, Predawn, Sarah, Dia Chappell, Renae Brown, Gerald Hornsby, Mike C, Lia Marie, Lauren Brender, Thoth Process, Katy Schneider, CherryFlight, Dorothy Holzman, Dwight Kuhl, Meri, Tammi Labrecque, Spinnerlynne, Aidn White, Jenni Schimmels, John Dickerson, Maria Mejia, Simon Huggins, Corynthia Dorgan, Elizabeth Petroff, Jeff Barrows, Quinn, Mary, Samantha DeShong, Zachary Savn

PATRONS

Kai Chochinov, Luigrein, Kakirtog, the Charr in gold, Rosie Reast, Annabel Heindla, Brenna Gawain, Donovan Scherer, Mr. C, Kyle Hamman, Chad Kukahiko, Maeve Shea, William Johnson, Lady Bee Games, Nicholas Rem, Amber Morant, Cathleen Mitchell, Alicia Garner, Melanie Shukost, Kimberly Grube, Ailysha, Ashton Sanders, David Blaskowich, Edwin Wallum, Eric Cerini, Game Programming

Academy, Jenny Kira Franke, Mary Paulk Powers, Matthew McCray, Nancy Pillot, Paul Tressler, Peter Bromage, Sean Cheasley, Stephanie Glinski, Steven Geyer, Wicketbird, Brett Kane, Michael Bishop, CJ Edmunds, Tim Bee, Summer Wilson, Cameron Dunham, Megamickel, mischievousblade, Jim Wilbourne, Mark Junk, James Wood, Susan N

THE BOOKS OF UNDERREALM

THE NIGHTBLADE EPIC
NIGHTBLADE
MYSTIC
DARKFIRE
SHADEBORN
WEREMAGE
YERRIN

THE ACADEMY JOURNALS
THE ALCHEMIST'S TOUCH
THE MINDMAGE'S WRATH
THE FIREMAGE'S VENGEANCE

THE TALES OF THE WANDERER
BLOOD LUST
STONE HEART
HELL SKIN

THE RESURRECTION CYCLE
LIFEMAGE DAWNING

RISE OF THE NECROMANCER
QUEST

THE TENTH KINGDOM
A CLOAK OF RED

THE CHRONICLES OF UNDERREALM
COLLECTION ONE

THE BOOKS OF UNDERREALM

CHRONOLOGICAL ORDER

NIGHTBLADE
MYSTIC
DARKFIRE
SHADEBORN
BLOOD LUST
THE ALCHEMIST'S TOUCH
WEREMAGE
THE MINDMAGE'S WRATH
STONE HEART
THE FIREMAGE'S VENGEANCE
HELL SKIN
YERRIN
LIFEMAGE DAWNING
QUEST
A CLOAK OF RED
THE CHRONICLES OF UNDERREALM

CONNECT ONLINE

DISCORD

Discord is a free voice and text chat engine for gamers, geeks—and for readers like you.

Legacy Books has a Discord server that we think is pretty awesome. You can chat with Garrett Robinson and ALL the authors of Underrealm, as well as many other readers just like you:

Underrealm.net/Discord

Garrett can also be found on the following social media:
Twitter: @GarrettAuthor
Facebook: GarrettBRobinson
Tumblr: GarrettAuthor

ABOUT THE AUTHOR

Garrett Robinson was born and raised in Los Angeles. The son of an author/painter father and a violinist/singer mother, no one was surprised when he grew up to be an artist.

After blooding himself in the independent film industry, he self-published his first book in 2012 and swiftly followed it with a stream of others, publishing more than two million words by 2014. Within months he topped numerous Amazon bestseller lists. Now he spends his time writing books and directing films.

A passionate fantasy author, his most popular books are the novels of Underrealm, including The Nightblade Epic, The Academy Journals, and The Tales of the Wanderer series.

However, he has delved into many other genres. Some works are for adult audiences only, such as *Non Zombie* and *Hit Girls,* but he has also published popular books for younger readers, including The Realm Keepers series and *The Ninjabread Man*, co-authored with Z.C. Bolger.

Garrett lives in Oregon with his wife Meghan, his children Dawn, Luke, and Desmond, and his dog Chewbacca.

Garrett can be found on:

EMAIL: garrett@garrettbrobinson.com
TWITTER: twitter.com/garrettauthor
FACEBOOK: facebook.com/garrettbrobinson

EPILOGUE

THE LORD HAD WATCHED THROUGH BARRICK'S EYES, AND HE HAD SEEN the sign of Oris' magic. Then he had felt the flash of her power, sensing it through the connection. It had made him wince with pain.

When he was able to focus again, the connection was gone. Severed. He could not find Barrick at all.

He sighed.

The attendant appeared beside him. "Barrick . . ." he said.

The Lord nodded. "Yes. He is gone. She has begun to master her power."

The attendant shook his head. "Father, we must stop her now, at once. We still have troops in the Birchwood. Muster them all, and march upon Cabrus. Wipe her out before she can gain any more power."

The Lord slowly shook his head. "The Birchwood is being watched. I might indeed be able to kill her. But before our forces could return to the Birchwood, or any other point of strength, Selvan's armies would wipe them out. The war would be lost in one stroke."

"The war will be lost regardless, if she comes into her own," said the attendant.

The Lord looked up at him. "Do you have so little faith in me? I have had many long years to learn my power. You have been here for all of them."

"I do not doubt your strength," said the attendant, bowing his head. "I doubt our numbers. If the Mystics and the other kingdoms rally behind her, we cannot withstand them all. We can gather other troops. But who knows if we will ever be granted another opportunity like this one?"

But to the attendant's shock, the Lord only smiled. It was a calm, gentle smile, the warm glow of fatherly affection, but it held the weight of a mighty king's pronouncement.

"No," said the Lord. "This is no fatal omen. It only means that the coming conflict will be a real fight. A true test. As it should be."

The attendant took a long, deep breath. "Father . . . I would rather win than have a fair fight. We owe that to our kindred. We owe it to Underrealm."

"Nothing is set in stone, my son. Nothing but balance. Half the time, life wins. Half the time, death."

The Lord turned back to his desk, bending over it to pore over his map again.

"It is our turn."

But the attendant's eyes filled with fear.

www.ingramcontent.com/pod-product-compliance
Lightning Source LLC
Chambersburg PA
CBHW030429310726
48979CB00009B/1686/J

* 9 7 8 1 9 4 1 0 7 6 8 4 2 *